THE SANGUINE SANDS

BOOK TWO OF THE SHARDED FEW

ALEC HUTSON

For Mihir, thank you for all your support

The Fangs

The Ember

Flaü

Kething's Cross

The Sea
of Salvation

Agrid

Ter Drummon

Karath

The Belt

Qat

Sorn

Zakaria

Derambinal

Khan-Anok

Salah Desert

The Breakers

| Hold | Town | City | Oasis | Ruins |

The Frayed Lands

Gendurdrang
(Ruins)

The Firemounts

The Duskhold

Phane

The Glass Sea

Ashasai

Kezekan Steppes
(The Anvil)

Zeman River

The Tangle

ALBIA

WHAT CAME BEFORE

What's broken will be mended
What's lost will now be found
As the children turn their little faces
Towards the swelling sound

Of a thousand burning hoofbeats
Racing from the West
And the mothers weep with tears of joy
That they could be so blessed

For what's broken will be mended
What's lost will now be found
And at last the line of empty kings
Will once again be crowned

- Geltish children's rhyme, origins unknown

A thousand years ago, the Radiant Emperor was overthrown and the Heart from which he drew his power shattered. Afterwards, it was found that men and women could bear these fragments in their flesh, gaining great strength and power. The Sharded Few, as they came to be called, divided the world between themselves and set to striving against each other for dominance. In the north, great holds arose – the Duskhold of the Shadow, the Windwrack of the Storm, and the Ember of the Flame, while in the south the Sharded Few came to rule over great cities – blood-drenched Ashasai, sand-scoured Derambinal, and the canyon city of Chan-Anok. Their rivalry has lasted centuries, with factions waxing and waning, but none have been able to claim preeminence . . . yet.

Deryn is an orphan, indentured by his mother before her death to a slaver in the foothills of the Fangs and forced to ascend the towering skyspears in search of tree crabs. On one such climb, he encounters a starving girl from the northern Wild who begs him for the crab he has recently caught. Later, the slaver discovers this act of kindness and has his son, Heth, flog him as punishment. While Deryn is recovering from his wounds, a mysterious man arrives at the crabber camp and demands food. When the slaver refuses, the man brutally kills him, revealing himself to be an Unbound, one of the Sharded Few who swears no allegiance to any hold. The Unbound claims lordship over the camp, forcing the slaves to treat him like their new master. Soon after this, the Wild girl emerges from the forest asking for someone to come help her sick father. Fearing that the Unbound will hurt her, Deryn flees with her into the woods at the cost of his friend's life. Before they can get far, though, they encounter two travelers who have been chasing rumors of an Unbound in the area. One of them is Kilian Shen, the nephew of the Duskhold's lord and a powerful shadow-sharded, and the other is a hound, a servant gifted with the ability to sense those who are Imbued – capable of bearing a shard – or Hollow, those who do not sicken or die when near the great shards of the Heart that lie in each of the holds, which makes them valued servants to the Sharded Few.

Kilian arrives at the camp and defeats the Unbound, claiming his shard, and the hound discovers that Deryn and the Wild girl, Alia, are both Imbued. The slaver's son, Heth, is Hollow, and so Kilian intends to return with all three to the Duskhold. On their journey east, he explains to them about the nature of the Sharded Few, the core skills of Channeling and Beckoning, and the talents that the Sharded attain after gaining more fragments. There are four classes of Sharded, named after ancient military ranks of the First Empire – *arzgan*, those who have not yet gained any talents; *sardor*, who have attained only first tier talents; *kenang*, who wield a second-tier talent; and finally *famdhar*, who have reached the pinnacle of strength among the Sharded and boast at least one third-tier talent. Most of the Sharded Few are incapable of moving past the ranks of *arzgan* or *sardor*, and only a very few can ever call themselves *famdhar*.

On the road to the Duskhold they are attacked by an enormous creature called a riftbeast, which has emerged from the Frayed Lands. They are saved by Azil Shen, the adopted son of Cael Shen and one of the most powerful shadow-sharded in the world. Wind-sharded who had been chasing the riftbeast arrive soon after Azil has slain the monster, and they agree to transport Deryn, Heth, and Alia to the Duskhold. There, Heth is placed among the Hollow as a guard, and Deryn and Alia are brought before the fragment at the heart of the hold to determine if they are worthy of becoming shadow-sharded. Deryn is granted a shard, but Alia is refused and she is forced to join Heth as a servant in the Duskhold. Alia chafes at this, as she is used to a life of freedom in the Wild, and Heth quickly becomes disillusioned despite having been raised to respect his ancestors who had once been Hollow in the Ember. Deryn, meanwhile, thrives as a novice, quickly demonstrating his aptitude. Another novice, Kaliss, is charged with educating him about history, the nature of the Sharded Few, and the current state of the world.

Later, Heth realizes that Alia has fled the Duskhold and he knows that when she is caught she will be executed, so he finds Deryn and together they go in pursuit of her. They find her first, but soon after other shadow-sharded arrive, including Rhenna and Nishi, the children of Cael Shen. To save Alia's life, Rhenna offers to take her on as a handmaiden. Heth returns to the Hollow, and Deryn to his training. This continues until it is time for the Delve, a tournament in which novices venture into the tunnels beneath the Duskhold to overcome challenges and claim shards hidden by their instructors. Deryn discovers a shard on the Delve, but he is betrayed by another novice and pushed into a chasm. When he wakes, he finds himself trapped deep underground . . . and that a small shadow-creature has appeared and taken interest in him. The shadow-thing eventually leaves, and Deryn manages to free himself and find a tunnel he hopes will lead him back to the Duskhold. Instead, the way empties into a vast cavern inhabited by a balewyrm, a monster of legend. He hides from the beast, and in its lair discovers the remains of a powerful Sharded and a wind-sharded sword. While the balewyrm searches for him, Cael Shen and his three children, along with powerful storm-sharded who have arrived as part of a delegation from the Windwrack, burst into the cavern and battle the balewyrm. Despite its great strength, the monster is driven off, and Deryn learns that after the shadow-creature left him it went to alert Cael Shen that Deryn was about to stumble into the balewyrm's lair. Deryn learns that this is a shadow elemental – a creature from the shadowrealm – and that it has bonded with him, making him the Duskhold's first elementalist in centuries. Mysteries abound, though, as to why the elemental has chosen him and what its purpose is in this world.

As Deryn recovers from his ordeal, Alia accompanies Rhenna to a feast celebrating the arrival of the storm-sharded delegation, where she meets the famed Mother of Storms, as well as the heir to the Windwrack, Prince Lessian, and the fearsome Warden Harath. In an attempt to mend relations between the Storm and the Shadow, the visiting warriors are invited to a friendly sparring session, which ends in a duel between Rhenna Shen and Lessian Khaliva. The Windwrack delegation leaves soon after, and when called to an audience with Cael Shen, Deryn happens to witness the lord of the Ember's Fire Sending. Lord Char is enraged that the Storm and Shadow have become closer, fearing that this new alliance – represented by the betrothal of Rhenna Shen to Lessian Khaliva – might be a threat to the Flame. Rhenna wants no part of this arrangement, but she cannot refuse her father, and a procession sets forth from the Duskhold to deliver her to the Windwrack. Heth is chosen as a guard, and Deryn as one of the shadow-sharded tasked with escorting Rhenna to her new home. Unbeknownst to anyone else, Alia and Rhenna have secretly made plans to flee into the Wild once they are near the Fangs.

The procession is ambushed on the edge of the Frayed Lands by flame-sharded, and Deryn, Heth, Alia, Rhenna and another shadow-sharded, Yvrin, flee into those cursed plains. They seek refuge in a First Empire ruin atop a mesa, the Winter Palace of the Radiant Emperor, and there they make their stand. Leading the flame-sharded assassins is a blood-sharded of great power, who mocks Rhenna that her own father was the one who ordered her death in order to foment war in the north. He claims that the flame-sharded are not warriors of the Ember and Lord Char, but servants of the Unbound King, who commands a host of Unbound from his seat of power in the city of Karath.

While the shadow-sharded battle the flame-sharded, Heth and Alia take refuge in the ruins, where Heth discovers a lost fragment of the Heart of the World, the Light. He is granted a shard, making him the first light-sharded, and returns to the battle in time to help Deryn defeat another mysterious Sharded, a man who had changed his face to look like the shadow-sharded Vertus Balenchas, who had led the wedding procession. Yvrin is killed during this fight, but Heth and Deryn have no time to mourn, as Rhenna is still dueling the blood-sharded elsewhere in the ruins.

His great power is too much for Rhenna, but with the help of Deryn's elemental – now named Shade – Deryn manages to open a portal to the shadowrealm and the blood-sharded is dragged away by the denizens of that realm. Heth is mortally wounded during this battle, but an old woman appears, someone Alia and Rhenna have met before in the Duskhold. She is one of the Elowyn, mysterious and mad immortals who forever wander the world. The Elowyn heals Heth, gives Alia a seed-shard that immediately merges with her, and tells them that the answers they need are to be found in Karath, the famed City of the Dead, in the House of Last Light.

PROLOGUE

The floor moved beneath Brother Piety's slippered feet, intricately knotted tendrils writhing as he hurried down the corridor. Once he might have stumbled, but many years of seeking out the Hallowed Sanctum had imparted in him a certain familiarity with the presence inhabiting this place. The fleshy substance seemed to mold itself around every step he took, keeping him upright even as the ground shifted. To his left, the wall suddenly bulged, as if something massive was sliding beneath its surface. Brother Piety frowned, wondering if the monastery's heightened agitation was related to the news he was coming to deliver.

A red door riven by an uneven seam appeared in front of him. Tangled black strands framed this glistening portal, inset with huge lidless eyes that rolled idiotically as he approached.

Brother Piety couldn't remember ever arriving at the sanctum so quickly, and he found that noteworthy. The presence in these walls was impatient for him to reach the abbot.

With a wet sucking sound the door opened, revealing jagged fang-like protrusions where the two halves had been joined together. In one of his recurring nightmares, this maw snapped shut as he passed the sanctum's threshold, its teeth plunging into his flesh. He never died immediately in those dreams – as he hung there, gasping for life, he could feel the edges of the door grinding into his body, the monastery trying to masticate him into something that could be absorbed into the living substance of its walls.

It took an effort of will not to flinch as he stepped through the door.

Abbot Grace did not turn around when he entered, continuing to stare out the membrane-window taking up most of the far wall with his hands clasped behind his back. Pustules throbbed on the high ceiling, seemingly in time with Brother Piety's quickened pulse. Strangely warped bits of furniture were scattered about, formed of the same fibrous tendrils as the rest of the monastery, and in the center of the chamber a sheet of black ice was sunk into the floor.

"Brother Piety," said Abbot Grace softly, raising his hand and pressing it against the window. The transparent film trembled but did not break. It looked to Brother Piety like the abbot was straining towards the wall of ice looming over the monastery . . . and the great shadow recessed in its frozen depths.

"Father," Brother Piety said, reflexively ducking his head even though the abbot still had not yet turned around. "You must have heard, then."

"I did," the old man replied, his finger drifting along the surface of the window. A rippling shimmer followed in its wake, as if the window were a soap bubble on the verge of bursting. Which it would not, Brother Piety knew. Every aspect of the monastery was stronger than stone. It had to be, given where it had come from.

Abbot Grace finally turned away from the glacier outside and faced Brother Piety. He was small and craggy, and so emaciated that with his teak-brown complexion he looked to have been crudely whittled from a piece of driftwood. His lips were set in a thin line, his black eyes hooded, but Brother Piety could still sense something unusual in him. A barely restrained excitement, almost a giddiness.

"Tell me what happened. Leave nothing out."

Brother Piety swallowed, wishing he'd rehearsed what to say in this moment. If he forgot an important detail and Abbot Grace realized that later, he'd most certainly have to serve penance for such a failure.

"We were up on the northwest scaffolding, doing our ablutions in the water we'd gathered that day from below the clavicle. It's been unseasonably warm this summer, as you know, and there's far more runoff than usual. Some years we can only perform the ceremony once a fortnight, but recently there has been enough of the holy water that we can do it every other day. Brother Temperance thought we should store some for the winter months, and while I did agree with his arguments, I decided . . . I decided . . ." His explanation withered under the abbot's gaze, and he took a steadying breath.

"Describe what happened, Brother Piety."

"He shivered."

Abbot Grace's expression did not change, but something sparked in his eyes.

"At first we thought there must have been an earthquake," Brother Piety continued quickly, his words threatening to run away from him. "But although we heard the ice cracking, the scaffolding wasn't swaying like if the ground had shifted below us. And when we shouted down, none of the brothers in observance today had felt a trembling. Some of the others had seen the shiver, though. And one of our brothers – Brother Charity – he swore . . ." Brother Piety's words faded again, as if he hesitated giving voice to the impossible.

"He swore what?" Abbot Grace said mildly after the silence had stretched on for a few moments.

"He swore he saw the Eye flutter."

For the first time, surprise leaked through the abbot's serene mask. "Did anyone else see this?"

"No," Brother Piety replied. "And Brother Charity is prone to visions, so I can't promise that it truly happened . . . but I'm certain he *thinks* it did. There is not a false bone in his body."

Abbot Grace looked thoughtful, tapping his chin with a finger. "Do you have any explanation for the . . . the shiver?"

"I thought it might be because of the additional ablutions—"

"*No.*"

This new voice was achingly beautiful, yet still it felt like a sliver of ice had been jabbed into Brother Piety's spine. His hands clutched reflexively at the hem of his robe as he turned towards what he was certain had been an empty corner of the sanctum just moments ago.

The figure in tattered robes was half again as tall as a man, gaunt and angular, with a misshapen hump rising behind its hooded head. Spidery, strangely jointed gray fingers emerged from dagged sleeves, and from the way the folds of its robes fell about its lower body it looked like its legs were back-bent, though – and thank their Lord for this – Brother Piety had never seen one of the Adored fully unclothed. Its face was also hidden, recessed deep within its cowl.

Brother Piety *had* gazed upon the visage of another Adored before ... And he never wanted to do that again.

"Brother Mercy," Abbot Grace said, sketching the Sun of their Lord in the air as the creature glided away from where it had emerged, the wall re-knitting behind it.

"*Abbot,*" the Adored whispered in its crystalline speech. "*Brother. We greet you on this blessed day.*"

Brother Piety could only duck his head slightly – he always found himself tongue-tied in the presence of the Adored.

An uncomfortable silence descended, until after a long moment the Abbot cleared his throat and addressed the shrouded figure looming over them.

"You claim to have knowledge that it was not our prayers that touched the Body?"

The Adored raised its hands, strangely elongated fingers contorting into a mudra that Brother Piety could not interpret.

"*Yes. We are certain. Something happened far to the south, in the unraveled place. Now the aether trembles in febrile excitement.*"

"Far to the south . . ." the abbot murmured, glancing at Brother Piety. "Do you think the Heart has been found?"

"The Heart?" he stammered. "But it was destroyed with the emperor."

The abbot shook his head. "I forget you have not yet been inducted into the deeper mysteries. This is a higher gnosis, Brother

Piety, so do not speak of what I say outside this chamber, but it has always been known that the Heart of the Heart survived. We allow the story that it was destroyed during the Sundering to persist because we do not want our younger and more impassioned brothers to throw away their lives searching for it. But it has long been accepted doctrine that when the awakening is imminent, it would reveal itself."

"When the awakening is imminent," Brother Piety repeated in an awed whisper. Could it be? Was it truly possible that their vigil was ending?

"If it has been found, then this news cannot stay hidden for long," Abbot Grace said, and from his tone Brother Piety knew he had settled on a course of action. "I want the word spread to every temple. Not just the hierophants of Flail and Karath and Ashasai – every cleric should be informed, no matter how small their congregation. And if they do not have an altar of black ice, send messengers. Someone somewhere will eventually hear of its discovery . . . if this has truly happened."

"I will tell the Senders at once," Brother Piety murmured, hoping that there was nothing else and he would be allowed to leave this chamber before . . . before . . .

But as he began to turn away a raspy command stilled him.

"*Wait,*" the Adored breathed, unknotting its hands as it slid closer to him. "*We would have a taste, Brother.*"

Brother Piety schooled his face, but he couldn't keep himself from flinching. Abbot Grace noticed this, of course, and he clucked his tongue in reprimand.

"Brother, it is a great honor."

"I know," Brother Piety murmured, with effort keeping himself from leaning away from the Adored. "I am sorry, Father."

With fumbling fingers he undid the front of his robes, trying to ignore the quickening of the Adored's breathing. There was a smell coming off the creature, overly sweet, like flowers on the verge of wilting. Then he pulled the cloth aside, revealing the pale blue shard sunk into his chest. He shivered, but not from the cold air licking his bare flesh – after all, he had not felt the chill of these lands since he had been granted his fragment decades ago. No, he shivered in antici-pation, and he hated himself for that.

The head of the Adored ducked lower, something like a rapturous sigh issuing from the depths of its cowl. A memory of crab-like mouth parts fluttering wide came to Brother Piety, but he banished it quickly, trying to empty his mind.

A serpentine tongue emerged, slithering forth. It flickered down to lightly touch his shard, and Brother Piety gasped as some of the *ka* he had spent the last few days gathering was drawn out, sucked forth like the Adored was an insect drinking blood. Another lick, and a wave of dizziness washed over him. He might have stumbled, but the unnaturally long gray fingers of the Adored were clamped on his shoulder, keeping him upright.

A final, long lap at his *ka*, and then the tongue retreated back into the shadowed recesses of its hood. As always when an Adored fed on him, Brother Piety felt sullied . . . almost violated.

But the worst part was the pleasure.

The Adored drew away, its movements far more sluggish than a moment ago, as if it had indulged past the point of satiety. It took Brother Piety several tries to retie his robes, the knot slipping from his numb fingers.

"You are dismissed, Brother," Abbot Grace intoned without emotion. "Go tell the Senders our message. Someone has found the Heart of the Heart, and we must know who . . . so what is dead will finally rise again."

"What is dead will rise again," Brother Piety slurred, repeating the mantra as he turned away from the abbot and the angel of their Lord.

1

DERYN

A chill wind slithered across the plains and the tall grass bent and rippled.

Ash's ears perked up, as if she could understand whatever secrets the Frayed Lands were whispering. The pony's head turned to the north, staring out across the grasslands at the colors seeping out from beneath the distant horizon.

"Calm," Deryn murmured, reaching around Alia to pat the side of the pony's neck. The girl slumped in front of him stirred as he brushed her shoulder, sitting up a little straighter in the saddle.

"She senses the wrongness," Alia said sleepily. "As can I."

"It's your shard," Deryn told her, picking a stray piece of grass from Ash's mane. "Everything seems strange after it first enters you. On the morrow, you'll feel much better." Deryn remembered waking for the first time after being granted his piece of the Shadow – all the various aches and pains that had accumulated during their journey to the Duskhold had vanished without the slightest trace. Before that, though, the exhaustion had been debilitating, like something vast and heavy pressing down on his soul.

Alia's hand slipped from where it had been lightly resting on the reins. She spread wide her fingers, studying the glowing green fragment embedded in her palm. It looked to Deryn like the skein of dark lines radiating out from the shard had grown more dense since this morning, like roots spreading beneath soil.

"It's not the Seed inside me that I feel," she said softly, then raised her gaze to the colors pulsing above them. For a brief moment, the dominant hue had been a deep, bloody red, as if a wound had been cut into the sky. "It's this place. There is a poison flowing from the north."

Gendurdrang. Deryn shifted uncomfortably in his saddle at the thought of the dead city. A thousand years ago it had been the capital of the First Empire, the seat from where the Radiant Emperor had ruled all that was known. But after the Heart that had been the fount of his power had been shattered, the very fabric of reality had been torn, allowing strange creatures from elsewhere to enter the grass- lands. Deryn remembered the vast insectile monster looming over him in the lashing rain, legs as huge as skyspear trunks stabbing the ground. And more than just riftbeasts might be leaking into these plains. Alia, with her newfound connection to the land through her seed shard, must be able to sense something.

"Every step we take we're getting farther from the source of that taint," Deryn said, trying to comfort her. "And once we leave the grasslands you should feel much better. Rhenna thinks it will only be a few more days of riding."

"What do I think?"

Rhenna had twisted about to stare at them from where she sat with Heth on the back of the great bay stallion that had once belonged to Yvrin. Deryn flinched when his gaze fell on the steppe horse, feeling a pang of sadness. This time yesterday, they had all been ascending the steep slope to the top of the mesa and the ruins of the Winter Palace, still hopeful that they could escape their pursuers without suffering any more tragedies.

But that had not happened, and in a single blood-soaked morning everything had changed. Yvrin now rested beneath a cairn of stones, surrounded by the unburied bodies of the flame-sharded. Heth and Alia had somehow become members of the Sharded Few, even though he was Hollow and she had previously been rejected by the Shadow under the Duskhold. And Rhenna . . . if what the blood-sharded had claimed was true, she had been betrayed by her own father in an attempt to foment a war between the Flame and the Shadow. He couldn't imagine what she was feeling.

Rhenna spoke again, sounding slightly annoyed that he had not yet answered her. "Are you deaf? *What* do I think, Deryn?"

"Apologies, Lady Shen," he hurriedly replied. "My thoughts are wandering. I was telling Alia that we would leave the Lands in a few more days if we continue our current course." Deryn glanced away, trying not to stare at the dark circles under Rhenna's eyes. She looked as exhausted as he felt.

"You shouldn't call me Lady Shen," Rhenna admonished him, swiveling around to look again in the direction they were riding. "Rhenna is fine, though when we reach Ter Drummond, perhaps another name entirely would be best. There might be a few in the city who know me." She squinted into the distance, her mouth tightening. "I traveled along the edge of the Frayed Lands once when my father led a delegation to our western holdings. We skirted this cursed place for six or seven days, though I would guess this time we will reach the border in less than three days. Our route is much more direct than the one I took before."

"Will we ride during the night?" Deryn asked, unable to keep the anxiety from his voice.

"No," Rhenna said with a shake of her head. "The horses need rest . . . as do these two." She gestured at the boy slumped in front of her – Heth was listing dangerously to one side, though Deryn knew Rhenna had the strength and reflexes to haul him back in the saddle if he did indeed start to slip from the horse.

"But where will we camp?" Deryn asked, staring out at the endless sweep of the plains with some trepidation. The thought of what might be lurking in the waist-high grass made his palms grow sweaty – this place was not natural, nor were its inhabitants.

"We are all Sharded," Rhenna said curtly, her tone withering. "No snake or lion can threaten us, and if a riftbeast comes stomping in this direction, we'll see it approaching from afar."

What about other Sharded? Deryn wanted to say, but he bit back this question. Several times he'd thought he'd glimpsed something moving behind them. It might have been his imagination, or simply a long-horned deer that had become separated from the great herds that roamed these lands . . . But what if it was the People of the Wind? They'd come upon a dozen dead Crow tribesmen scattered about the base of the mesa after they'd descended, most of them burned beyond recognition, the result of the battle they'd witnessed between the Wind and the Flame while standing on the plateau above. More would come to learn why so many of their warriors had not returned, and they would have little trouble tracking them across the grasslands.

It was not a matter of *if* they would be caught, but *when*. Rhenna was strong, but surely the Crow would come in numbers, and with champions who could rival her in power.

"Look," Rhenna said, and Deryn followed where she was pointing. Something strange hunched in the hazy distance, rising up from the monotony of the plains. Not since they'd left the mesa had they seen anything like this. He shielded his eyes, trying to figure out what it was. It almost looked like a series of sundered arches – perhaps it was the bones of a city long abandoned, a remnant of the First Empire. Deryn's mood brightened at the sight, for he would gladly brave ghosts if it meant they didn't have to sleep out in the open, vulnerable to whatever creatures lurked in the long grass.

"We'll camp there tonight," Rhenna stated, spurring the stallion into a canter.

IT WAS NOT the bones of a dead city, but bones in truth. Vast ribs curved into the sky, yellowed and pitted, some shattered while others yet remained unbroken. Their size staggered Deryn, and a tingling numbness spread through him as they approached. By the time they reached the great bones sunk into the grass, night was falling, the first faint stars speckling the sky. To the north, the spectral lights of Gendurdrang still blazed, but now the colors bleeding from the ruins evoked twilight – deep blues and purples instead of the red and orange bonfire that had earlier danced on the horizon.

Alia was the first to break the awed silence. "What is this?"

"The remains of a riftbeast," Deryn answered, unable to look away from the bones. "Probably slain by the People of the Wind."

"But it looks nothing like the one that attacked us," Heth said softly, the first words he had spoken since this morning. "That rift-beast was like an insect. This . . . this looks like the skeleton of an enormous animal."

"There are many kinds of riftbeasts," Rhenna murmured, and from her tone she was as unnerved as the rest of them by the sheer size of the bones. Deryn's unease deepened further to hear this, as he'd once watched Rhenna throw herself at a monstrous balewyrm without hesitation. Yet even that creature could have coiled its massive bulk within this ribcage without coming close to brushing its scales against bone. This riftbeast – if it indeed had been a riftbeast – would have been far larger in life than the monster Azil had saved them from on the road to the Duskhold.

"Look at the ground," Alia said, and the edge to her words pulled Deryn's gaze from the ribs.

A fist of ice clenched in his gut when he saw what had drawn her attention. The high grass had mostly disappeared in the area bounded by the ribs, just a few desiccated tufts emerging from the cracked and broken soil. Beyond the bones it still flourished, but within it was as if the vitality of the grass had been leached away by whatever was buried beneath.

Ash stopped just before passing between two of the ribs and tossed her shaggy head, refusing to enter the patch of blasted earth. The steppe stallion also hesitated, but Rhenna gave a sharp command and kicked her heels into his flank and with some reluc-tance the horse trotted forward. Deryn spurred Ash on by doing the same, joining the stallion where it had stopped in the center of the cleared area. The few unbroken ribs curved high above them, etched against the shifting colors of the sky. Ash *whuffed* and pawed at the bare earth, clearly expressing her displeasure.

"Are you sure this is where you want to spend the night?" Heth asked, gazing up at the bones dubiously.

"Yes," Rhenna said, sliding from the stallion's back. Little puffs of dirt rose from where her boots touched the ground. "Here, nothing will be able to sneak up on us."

"Perhaps we can just ride on through the night," Deryn offered, though merely uttering this suggestion made him dizzy with exhaustion. It had been days since he'd last laid down in his bedroll, and while he'd found that after gaining his shard he required less rest, he knew he was still rapidly approaching the limits of his endurance. And Heth and Alia clearly needed to sleep and allow their bodies to finish absorbing their newly gained fragments.

Rhenna shook her head. "No. We have to rest, and we won't find a better spot than this." Something flickered in her face, and she smiled sourly. "Though . . . I suppose we should all agree. I am not Lady Shen to you anymore."

Deryn shared a quick glance with Heth. In the Duskhold, Rhenna had occupied a position far above them, and disobeying or even disagreeing with her would have been unthinkable. But it was true that their situation had changed dramatically.

"I think you're right," Deryn said slowly. "We stay here and leave at first light. With rest, we'll be far more ready for anything that might find us."

Rhenna nodded at this, relief softening her features. Whether that was because they wouldn't be riding on during the night or because they had deferred to her judgement, Deryn wasn't certain, but he felt like some questions about the group's new dynamic had been answered. She might not be a lady anymore, but she was still their captain.

And Deryn took comfort in that, as he couldn't imagine having to shoulder the burden of leadership right now. He swung down from Ash, then reached up to help Alia dismount. The girl pursed her lips, her own apprehension obvious as she stared at the jagged shadow cast by one of the ribs, and then she sighed in dismay and slid into his waiting arms.

THE COLD BARELY TOUCHED HIS Sharded body, but still Deryn wished that Rhenna had allowed Alia to start a fire. He understood why she had refused – after all, who knew what might be drawn to the flames – but it would have been a great comfort to push back the dark and feel a little warmth. Instead, they huddled in the barren patch within the bones and chewed on food they had scavenged from those dead Crow warriors. Mostly this was salted and dried meat, though Heth had also found a bag of fist-sized green fruit that tasted deliciously sweet.

After the meal was finished, Alia and Heth curled up and quickly fell asleep. Deryn and Rhenna stayed awake despite their own exhaustion, sitting across from each other without speaking, lost in thought.

The food was all they had managed to scavenge from the bodies of the wind-sharded. Whatever fragments they had once possessed had already been removed by the flame-sharded, though none had been foolish enough to try to merge those shards before their ascent to the Winter Palace. They had known a battle was waiting for them and had not wanted to be debilitated from the ordeal of merging another fragment. Instead, white-glowing wind shards had been found in the pockets and pouches of those slain by Yvrin and Deryn, though the number of fragments were far too few for the number of Crow warriors who had perished. Deryn could only assume that the blood-sharded Ashasai who had led the assassins had taken quite a few shards with him when the creatures from the shadowrealm had dragged him into the rift opened by Shade.

Still, the number of fragments they had gained after the battle was staggering. Rhenna had insisted Deryn claim the shards of those he had personally killed, and after apportioning out the remainder from the flame-sharded that had been slain by Yvrin – along with the six that had once been borne by the steppe-girl herself – Deryn found himself in possession of seven more shards. It had felt strange, accepting fragments that had once been part of Yvrin, but Rhenna had insisted that she would have wanted them to take her shards. Deryn wondered if some slivers of Yvrin's past were locked inside her shards, and if he would witness those moments when he finally merged the fragments. The memories that he'd experienced when he had absorbed the shards he'd discovered in the lair of the balewyrm were still searingly vivid. He remembered colors pulsing in the sky above rippling grasslands . . . and Deryn was now certain that the dead warrior had once journeyed through these same cursed lands. The most disturbing image in that tumbling rush had been a skeletal king clad in ragged finery sitting on an amber throne . . . had that also been glimpsed somewhere in the Frayed Lands?

Deryn surfaced from his thoughts as a glimmer of pale light drew his gaze. Rhenna had pulled forth one of the shards and was examining it with an expression of intense curiosity. Wan light played across her face, throwing her features in stark relief.

He knew which fragment this was. It had been pulled from the body of that mysterious Sharded who had somehow changed his appearance to look like Vertus . . . the man who had stabbed Yvrin in the back after she had broken his shackles.

"What is it?" he asked, speaking softly so as not to wake their companions.

Rhenna held up the shard, as if comparing it to the stars glimmering between the dark ribs arching above them.

"There is only one possibility I can think of," she murmured, then clenched her hand around the shard. Darkness rushed in, and Deryn blinked as his shadow-granted vision adjusted. "But I believed those Sharded to be just a story. A legend."

Deryn thought back to his lessons with Kaliss at the underground lake, the ghostly radiance of the gazebo seeping across the black waters. During the long ride today, he had turned over what had happened atop the mesa again and again and had come to what sounded like the same conclusion as Rhenna. "A soul shard," he finally said.

Her silhouette nodded. "It must be. The only other possibility is that this is an ice shard, for no one has encountered those fragments since contact was lost with the monastery of Kara Dum centuries ago. But the histories describe the light of an ice shard as a cold blue, like the water beneath a frozen lake. And the talents you said this Sharded demonstrated were powers that should have been unique to the blood and wind-sharded . . ." She shook her head, sighing. "I remember Saelus speaking of the soul-sharded during one of our lessons. He mentioned them in passing, almost dismissively, as if he did not truly believe in their existence. But for some reason, what he said still lodged in my memory – he told us they were known to be thieves. At the time, I thought he meant that they stole artifacts or other treasures. But now I think they steal something else."

"Shards," Deryn said, remembering the different colors of the fragments that had been pulled from the dead man's body.

Rhenna shook her head. "No. We all steal shards – it is the nature of the Sharded Few. But when those shards enter our bodies they are absorbed by our own. Changed. If I were to merge this shard I'm holding, it would become a piece of the Shadow." She paused for a moment, as if reconsidering what she'd just said. "Or it should. Saelus called the soul-sharded thieves, and I now believe they earned this title because the shards they absorb do *not* change but remain what they had been before . . . and with the powers they had once granted now transferred to the new bearer." Another brief hesitation, and Deryn sensed that she had turned and was staring into the deeper blackness beyond the ribs. "If I am right, this revelation would shake the very foundations of our world. The soul-sharded are not a myth, but are hiding amongst us, stealing our bodies and our powers . . ." Rhenna's voice trailed away, as if awed by the implications of what she had just said.

"But why was the soul-sharded even there?" Deryn asked, trying to recall what the man had said after murdering Yvrin. He had wanted to steal Shade away from him, that Deryn remembered clearly.

"I don't know," Rhenna admitted. "But with this strange Sharded among the attackers – let us assume he was soul-sharded – and with their leader being such a powerful blood-sharded, I do indeed believe that they were not sent from the Ember. Someone else wanted us dead. Wanted *me* dead."

Deryn swallowed, shifting uncomfortably. He hoped the darkness hid his expression.

"You believe my father sent them," Rhenna muttered tiredly.

Deryn felt jealous of the others, sleeping so innocently. "I . . . I don't know, Lady. Rhenna. Your father . . . he is frightening. I saw him cut the head off another novice without the slightest remorse or hesitation. But to send assassins after his own daughter . . . how could anyone do that?"

Deryn was expecting an immediate outburst, some vehement denial, but it was a moment before Rhenna replied. When she did speak, she sounded even more exhausted. "It seems impossible. But it's true that if the Ember was believed to have been responsible for my death that war would be justified in the eyes of every other hold. No one would blame my father for whatever vengeance he inflicted upon the Flame. And he and I are not close, that is also true. I have tried to be the dutiful daughter, but he has always favored Nishi, and in the history of the Duskhold siblings have fought to the death before to sit beneath the balewyrm's jaws. I do not want to believe it, but there is some small voice inside me whispering that arranging my death on the road would be as much about securing my brother's place as lord of the Duskhold as it would be an opportunity to assure our hold's ascendency in the north." Rhenna's grip on the white-glowing shard must have loosened, as pale light had begun to trickle out from between her fingers. "And yet . . . I am certain that not everyone in the Duskhold would meekly bow their head if this was all revealed to be my father's doing. Azil would never countenance such treachery. He would stand with me if the truth was known."

"Then we could return to the Duskhold," Deryn suggested.

"And do what?" Rhenna replied sharply. "Level accusations against my father? It would tear the hold apart, and in the end, those who supported me would lose. My father's position is unassailable. And if I instead said nothing, agreeing with the belief that the flame-sharded were behind the attack, then there would be a war anyway. One that engulfed the entirety of the north and not just our hold."

"An unjust war," Deryn said. "Sparked by a lie."

"Would it be? *I do not know what to believe.* That blood-sharded Ashasai claimed he was sent by the Unbound King, who had in turn been hired by my father to give the appearance that the Ember was behind the attack. We *must* go to Karath and find out the truth. If this indeed was my father's ploy, we shall reveal it to the world. But if Lord Char was truly responsible, and the Ashasai was simply trying to bait me into revealing myself back in the ruins . . . then I shall tear down the Ember with my own hands."

"You should tell them everything," a voice said softly.

Surprised, Deryn turned his attention to where Alia huddled. He had thought she'd fallen asleep some time ago.

"Tell them what?" Rhenna asked, but from her tone it sounded to Deryn like she already knew what her former handmaiden was referring to.

Alia's vague shape moved as she sat up. "The other reason you don't want to go back to the Duskhold."

Rhenna grunted in annoyance. "I don't think that's necessary."

"They should know," Alia insisted. "Especially if they are going to follow you to Karath."

The daughter of the Shadow sighed. "Very well – I suppose that is only fair." She shifted, turning towards him again. "Deryn, this wedding procession was a farce. I was never going to allow myself to be married."

"What?"

The darkness around Rhenna writhed in agitation. "I would have refused to be used as a gift to seal an alliance. An object to be given away. The women in the Windwrack are not allowed to be warriors – I would be expected to do nothing but bear children and run the household, and I cannot imagine a more terrible fate. My plan was to sneak away from the procession when we were beyond the Frayed Lands and flee into the Wild."

"And I would go with her," Alia added. "We'd leave these rotten holds with their Hollow slaves far behind. There is freedom to be found in the north, beyond the mountains."

"So that is the other reason you do not want to return," Deryn said slowly, realization dawning. "If what the Ashasai said was a lie, your father would surely insist you follow through with your betrothal."

"Yes," Rhenna said bitterly, scowling. "I am no longer a lady of the Duskhold, no matter who was responsible for the attempt on our lives. I promise you, I will die before being bound by vow to Prince Lessian Khaliva."

One of the horses whinnied, as if to punctuate this statement. Then a moment later Ash blundered closer to where they were sitting, nearly trampling the sleeping Heth, who came awake spluttering as the hooves churned the ground near his head.

"Silver Shrike!" he cried, rolling away from the pony. Deryn surged to his feet to try to take hold of Ash's reins, but failed to grab them.

There was more commotion elsewhere, and he sensed Rhenna had also risen and was trying to keep the steppe stallion from bolting into the long grass.

"What has upset them?" Alia cried as Deryn's fingers finally closed around a strip of leather. Ash tossed her head, but he was one of the Sharded Few and easily kept her from breaking free again.

"I don't know!" he shouted back, trying to restrain the pony without hurting her. A shadow flickered in the corner of his eye, and then Shade was among the pony's stamping hooves. For a moment, he thought his elemental had caused this chaos, but despite the shadow-dog's sudden appearance, the pony's agitation began to subside. Both horses had stopped their whinnying and were now mostly still, though the quivering in their flanks suggested that they still wanted to flee this place.

Into this sudden silence Alia spoke, her voice heavy with dread.

"Out there. There's something in the grass."

Deryn peered between the ribs, but he couldn't see what the Wild girl had glimpsed.

"Come to me," Rhenna commanded, and with his eyes still on the darkness, Deryn pulled Ash closer to her as Heth and Alia joined them in the center of the barren patch. Heth was brandishing the Sharded spear they'd taken from the Crow; the red metal of its tip was black as blood in the spectral green light spilling from the Wild girl's fragment.

"What did you see?" Deryn asked, quickly switching the hand holding Ash's reins so that he could grip the hilt of his wind-sharded sword.

"There!" Alia hissed, pointing out into the sea of black grass.

Points of cold blue light floated in the darkness. Deryn allowed himself to hope for a moment that these were insects like the wraith bugs that had swarmed among the skyspears at night, but that hope was dashed when he realized these lights were not moving . . . and they were also paired so closely together that it was not hard to imagine what they must be.

Eyes.

"Over there," Heth said hoarsely. Deryn tore his gaze from the unblinking lights to follow where the boy was indicating with his spear and sucked in his breath in dismay – a half dozen more points of cold light hovered out beyond the bones. And as he watched, more were emerging from the black, like stars in a darkening sky.

"It's freezing," Alia said, and she was right. It felt like winter in the depths of the Fangs, far colder than it had been earlier. Gooseflesh pimpled Deryn's arms, and in the green light of the seed-shard he could faintly see his breath misting the air.

"Prepare yourselves," Rhenna said tightly. "But do not attack until we know what is out there." The darkness spasmed as a javelin of shadow materialized in her hand. No doubt she had already formed her Ghost Chitin armor, and with a flicker of will, Deryn did the same. He glanced worriedly at Heth and Alia, wondering how he could protect them if all those things out there attacked at once.

For it was as if the constellations had fallen from the sky. Deryn tried to see if there was a path through the grass empty of those blue-glowing motes, but they seemed to be surrounded on all sides. And as these lights drew closer he could make out vague shapes, shadows of deeper black hunched in the darkness.

Shade was standing rigid, the elemental's attention focused between two particular ribs.

"What is it?" Deryn hissed, just as a sound he had never heard before began emanating from the shadow-dog, a hollow whining. It almost sounded like he was scared.

"Something is coming," Rhenna warned, drawing back her javelin, its point aimed at the spot Shade was fixated upon.

The darkness shivered as something large pushed its way through the grass. Ash reared back in a panic, nearly tearing herself free from Deryn's grip before he managed to control her.

Something emerged from between the bones, the faint radiance cast by Alia's shard sliding across a nightmare given substance. In life, it had been a great wolf, but death had come for the creature long ago. Patches of ragged gray fur covered the withered hide stretched taut across the beast's body, though bone was still visible in places. Half of the flesh on its face had sloughed away, revealing fangs as long as a man's forearm. The monster was nearly as large as the steppe stallion, and the cold fires blazing in its eye-sockets were level with Deryn's gaze. Hanging from its jaws by a topknot of hair was the severed head of a man.

"Hold," Rhenna said, her voice strained.

Deryn understood why she had not given the word to attack, for the creature had settled back on its haunches like it was waiting for something. Still, Deryn reached down inside himself and grasped his *ka*, shaping it so that with a thought he could summon forth the Breath of the Mother. Though only the Broken God knew if the frozen winds of the shadowrealm would even bother something that was already dead.

The severed head was much fresher than the wolf-thing. There was no rot – its skin was pale, save for the dark twisting tattoos showing that this man had once belonged to the People of the Wind. There was even still some blood dripping from the stump of its neck, and a bit of spine dangling down glistened wetly. Deryn couldn't be sure which of the tribes this man had come from, but the few black feathers still threaded in his topknot suggested he had once been a Crow warrior.

The other creatures thronging the long grass made no move to join the wolf inside the space bounded by the ribs. They seemed to be waiting, but for what Deryn could not guess.

And then the eyes of the dead man slid open.

Alia gasped, clutching at Deryn's arm. The reins fell from his numb fingers, though Ash thankfully did not seize this chance to bolt, perhaps also paralyzed by fear.

The dead man's eyes were pits of blue flame. Bloodied lips writhed as it spoke, even though the rest of the face remained slack.

"*Children,*" it murmured, the words reverberating strangely, as if echoing up from a great depth. "*Beautiful, broken children.*"

Rhenna stepped forward, interposing herself between the rest of them and the rotting wolf.

"What are you?" she asked, and the lack of any tremor in her voice awed Deryn. "A ghost?"

"*You have found the Light,*" it continued, ignoring her question. "*Once more, Algeroth's essence spills into this world. So sweet the taste. So sweet.*" Its eyes closed and its lips curved into a pleased smile, as if it could truly taste something.

"Are you friend or foe?" Heth called out, his knuckles white around the haft of the Sharded spear.

"*Light-bearer,*" the thing said, the wolf moving its head so that the dead Crow warrior now faced Heth. "*Vessel of the Radiance. You must bring others to drink deep, as you have, then embark on a pilgrimage to my Eternal City. On my throne I wait for you with joy undimmed by the turning of these long years.*"

"You want his shard?" Rhenna asked.

"*I do not want it,*" said the head. "*I need it.*"

"Then why don't you just take it yourself from the palace?" she continued, and Deryn noticed that she had subtly shifted her stance, as if readying herself to hurl the shadow javelin.

The head grimaced. "*I could not. You must bring it to me.*"

"And why should we do this?" Deryn asked, drawing the attention of the cold eyes to him.

"*Because I have given you a gift, dark-bearer. The ones who hunted you are dead. A war band followed your trail with red and bloody thoughts. Now they have joined my legion and will not trouble you. I will provide safe passage for you through these lands . . . through my realm. So you may go and find others to claim the Light—*"

A shiver passed through the head, the dead muscles under its skin rippling unnaturally. "*What is this?*" it suddenly shrieked, and Deryn jumped in surprise. "*I smell her! Her scent clings to you!*" It gnashed bloody teeth in agitation. "*You have been in her presence! Are you a trap to draw me out?*"

"We don't know what you're talking about," Rhenna replied, glancing at Deryn uneasily.

"Do you mean the old woman?" Deryn asked, then hesitated as he tried to remember what Rhenna had called her back in the Winter Palace. "The . . . the Elowyn?"

The head fairly snarled in reply. "*Those relics? No, I speak of the betrayer. You have been in her presence. But how? What does this mean?*" The head sounded uncertain, almost confused.

Silence descended, and then the dead wolf turned away. It seemed to have fallen into its own thoughts, not caring any more about them.

"Who are you?" Rhenna cried after it, and Heth made a hissing sound like he would have been happy to let it just disappear once more into the night.

Deryn did not think the creature would answer her, but it paused, half-sunk in the shadows beyond the ribs.

"*I have been known by many names, but the first given to me was Arenkinas.*"

Then it was gone, slipping into a dark now empty of those blue floating lights. Deryn swayed, finally unclenching the *ka* he had been ready to unleash and letting it diffuse once more throughout his body.

"What's the matter?" Alia asked, and Deryn saw that she was staring at Rhenna. The shadow-sharded woman now looked even more stricken than when she had been facing down that horrific wolf.

"I know that name. I remember it from one of the history books Saelus forced us to read. It was *his* name before he ascended to the throne." Rhenna swayed, laying her hand on Alia's shoulder to steady herself. She had the look of someone whose world had just been completely upended. "Segulah Tain. Arenkinas was what he had been called before he was crowned a thousand years ago . . . That wolf-thing just claimed to be the Radiant Emperor."

2

HETH

Sharpened.

That was the only way Heth could describe the world he had awoken to: the colors were brighter, the smells stronger, the sounds louder. Sunlight drenched the grasslands in shades of gold and green he was certain he'd never seen before. Even the etiolated white of the ribs they'd camped beneath had a stark beauty. When Deryn had found him staring in wonder at the pitted and cracked surface of the bones, the shadow-sharded had clearly understood what he was experiencing, clapping him on the shoulder.

He knew. He knew what it was like to peel away the gray membrane covering everything and see the true beauty hidden beneath.

The rest of that first day passed in a haze. He'd found himself tumbling into sights and noises he likely would not have even noticed before: the hiss of the tall grass scraping against the belly of the steppe-stallion . . . the patterns woven by a flock of birds agitated by their passage . . . the smell of Rhenna seated behind him in the saddle, sweat and sweetness and something slightly bitter. This desire to intensely focus on one thing even as the rest of the world faded into the background was not dissimilar to how he'd sometimes felt after a few too many cups of wine. Except this time he was drunk on reality itself.

He wasn't sure how he'd managed to sleep after the visitation by that nightmarish wolf. To see something that had clearly died long ago moving and inhabited by a power or spirit from beyond the veil, withered flesh clinging to ancient bones, had been horrifying. And every time he thought of that head he couldn't help but shudder. The next day they'd found what must have been the Crow war party where it had come from. It was impossible to tell how many they had been in life, since among the jumble of limbs and savaged torsos there had not been a single head. Most had not been members of the Sharded Few, as their torsos lacked the telltale scarring that resulted when a fragment was removed. Still, the danger posed by the dead creatures that had visited the night before was evident. After this gristly discovery, Rhenna and Deryn had pushed the horses harder, and they all were constantly twisting around to watch the plains behind them for any signs of pursuers.

That night, they were forced to sleep out in the open. Heth had been worrying about bedding down in the long grass and what might creep up on them in the darkness, but Rhenna had summoned a great black hand formed of shadow and used it to flatten an area large enough for all of them to sleep comfortably. The last time he'd seen this talent she'd seized the blood-sharded Ashasai back at the Winter Palace. He'd always assumed that the abilities of the Sharded Few would be suited only for combat . . . but of course, there were all sorts of uses for a giant floating hand.

"You must be wondering what your talents will be," Rhenna said when she saw him staring at the dissipating wisps of shadow.

"I . . . haven't even thought about it," Heth admitted. "The idea that I could do something like that seems impossible."

Rhenna took the horses by the reins and led them into the clearing she had created. Deryn had already dismounted, leaving Alia still astride Ash. The Wild girl looked dazed and bewildered, and Heth suspected she was also trying to come to grips with her heightened senses.

"When your first talent manifests it will be like remembering something you'd forgotten," Rhenna told him. "As if it had always been there, just slightly out of reach." She gently put her hand on Alia's leg and the Wild girl flinched. "Alia. You should get down. We're staying here tonight."

Alia looked around like she had just noticed that they'd stopped. She must have been deep inside herself, drifting on the same strange currents as Heth.

"Yes . . . of course," Alia murmured, sliding awkwardly from the pony's back.

Rhenna frowned at the swaying girl, then raised her face to the darkening sky. "It will be night soon. I know you'd both probably like to rest, but we should have our first lesson before evening falls."

"Lesson?" Heth asked, his stomach twisting with hunger when he saw Deryn untying the saddlebag filled with food.

"Come, you can eat at the same time," Rhenna said, motioning for them to follow her into the middle of the clearing. She settled herself cross-legged on the flattened grass and patted the spot beside her. "It is customary for novices to have a few days to recuperate before their introduction to the most important aspects of their shards, but we need to start you both on your journey as soon as possible. Right now you are both *arzgan* – single-sharded, and far too weak. We must raise you to *sardor* quickly, because once you each gain a talent, you will be far more formidable."

Alia sank down beside Rhenna, and Heth found a spot across from her. Deryn joined them a moment later, pressing a strip of dried meat into Heth's hands before reaching across to offer the same to Rhenna and one of the sweet green fruits to Alia.

"First, I should make something very clear," Rhenna said after taking a moment to chew and swallow a mouthful of the leathery meat. "I have only my own experience to draw upon as one of the shadow-sharded. We must assume the basic principles are the same no matter which type of shard one bears, but I do not know this for certain." Rhenna adjusted her posture, sitting up straighter and throwing her head back so that her glistening black hair fell over her shoulders. "Now, there are two skills that every member of the Sharded Few must master: beckoning and channeling. Let us begin with the latter. I know you feel different since gaining your shards. Your body is stronger, your senses heightened. And inside you, something is unsettled. A churning. That is your *ka*, the energy flowing from the fragment lodged in your flesh. Before you can merge more shards and increase your power, you must master this tempest. Reach down. Feel the *ka* pushing through your pathways. You must calm it, transform it from a raging, flood-swollen river into a gentle stream. Once you have done this, you will be ready for more shards."

Heth concentrated, turning inward. There was his heartbeat, unnoticeable unless he made an effort to sense it. And it was the same with his breathing. But Rhenna was right – beneath the usual working of his body something new throbbed, almost perfectly matching his pulse. He stretched mental fingers towards this, but it remained stubbornly just out of reach.

"Can you grasp it?" Rhenna asked.

Heth shook his head, grimacing as the energy seemed to contort itself to avoid his touch. From Alia's look of frustration, she had also been unsuccessful.

"Do not worry overmuch," Rhenna said. "Very few can begin taming their *ka* so soon after gaining their shard. Continue practicing and it will come soon enough, I promise."

Heth sighed, abandoning his fumbling attempts. As if to mock him, he felt a strong surge of energy push outward from his shard. "You said there were two skills we must master?" he asked, trying to mask his disappointment at his failure.

"Indeed. The other is known as beckoning." Tendrils of darkness emerged from the lengthening shadows to wrap themselves around Rhenna's upraised arm.

"Yes," Alia said softly. "Lord Kilian spoke of this on the journey to the Duskhold."

Heth remembered the black serpents slithering from the shadow of the old mill to restrain the Unbound Sharded who had killed his father. At the time, it had seemed so unnatural, a violation of nature .

.. and yet less than a year later here he was being told that this was an ability he would have to master. He shook his head at the impossibility of it all.

"That will take even longer to learn than channeling," Rhenna assured them. "And it will be more difficult. In the Duskhold, we practice using the wraithling flame, which creates a shadow that is particularly susceptible to beckoning."

"I remember the darkness felt different after I got my shard," Deryn said. "It had a substance, almost a weight to it. Grabbing the shadows was like trying to hold a handful of wet eels, but even in the beginning I could at least sense its new solidity."

"And so I must do the same with the light?" Heth asked dubiously. Though it was true that the light *had* seemed different since he'd gained his shard. Heth focused on the crushed grass around them, burnished a deep bronze by the fading day. The idea that he could shape and control light itself seemed ridiculous, yet when he concentrated he found he *could* see the rays slanting down from above, and they *did* have a sort of texture that he almost thought he might be able to reach out and touch . . .

"Oh!"

Rhenna's startled exclamation dragged Heth from his attempt. Blinking, he glanced about in annoyance.

And sucked in his breath. A patch of the flattened grass near them had started to tremble. As he watched, the blades slowly began to stand once more, the folds and creases caused by the force of the shadow-hand pressing down disappearing. Alia's hand was extended towards the trembling grass, and the seed-shard set in her palm pulsed in the center of its nest of tangled black lines. Her face was flushed, a sheen of sweat having broken out on her brow. Then with a grunt, she reached her limits, and her face went slack as she sagged backwards. Immediately, the grass began to collapse again.

Rhenna brought her hands together sharply, her eyes wide with excitement. "Impressive," she breathed, offering one of her rare smiles.

"I felt it," Alia murmured, brushing back a sweaty lock of hair.

"The grass, yes, but also below the ground where there is this vast web of roots all knotted together, humming with life . . . I reached out, and it answered." She sounded awed, as if she had touched something almost transcendent.

Both shadow-sharded looked just as surprised.

"Beckoning on your first attempt is remarkable," Rhenna said. "That old woman was right – you were born to bear the Seed."

"Kaliss was a prodigy among the novices," Deryn added excitedly, "and still it took her months before she could grasp the darkness."

Heth's frustration at his own failure deepened, and he tried once more to beckon the light that still lingered. This time he did not even come close, the last red rays of the day refusing his strained entreaties.

"Congratulations," he muttered grudgingly, not bothering to try to hide his dejection.

Deryn grinned and reached over to put a hand on his knee. "Don't feel bad. It might be that beckoning is different with a seed-shard. After all, grass must be easier to touch than darkness or light."

"I suppose," Heth replied, taking a bite of the dried meat.

It tasted terrible.

THEY REACHED the western fringe of the Frayed Lands three days later, where the sea of grass lapped against a line of stunted trees like they were breakers along the coast. The days had already begun to blend together for Heth – from dawn to dusk they rode, stopping only when the horses needed to rest or they happened upon a source of water. The way had been free of dangers, although he suspected this was not simply good fortune, as at least once they had glimpsed a dark shape prowling the horizon behind them, something that could very well have been a monstrous wolf. The steppe stallion had panicked once when it nearly trod upon the flensed corpse of a great serpent hidden by the long grass – the snake had been savaged by fang and claw, its head removed. It felt to Heth like they were being shepherded across the plains, protected by invisible forces.

Heth had distracted himself by practicing the techniques Rhenna had introduced. Channeling came quickly – by the second day he had managed to successfully smooth the *ka* pulsing from his shard and guide it through his body. Before when he'd done this, it had dissipated in a tingling rush, but now he could push the energy into his limbs and fingers . . . and it might have been his imagination, but he thought he might actually feel his flesh hardening and muscles growing stronger. It was intoxicating. Beckoning still eluded him, though he found that he could come closest when the midday sun was at its highest point, blazing in the cloudless sky. He was certain now that the light pouring down had a substance that had been lacking before he'd gotten his shard, yet it was smooth, so smooth, and his mental touch slid away when he tried to grasp it. Still, he was making progress.

A weight had lifted from his shoulders after they finally ascended the slope climbing out of the grasslands, and both horses halted as they reached the line of trees. Rhenna had twisted around in the saddle to stare out over the shimmering plains. Colors played upon the distant horizon, thrumming in the sky like plucked strings. No other movement had drawn his eye, but Heth suspected that somewhere out there monstrous things were slinking through the grass, coldly burning blue eyes fixed on the ridge where they had stopped.

"Come on," Rhenna said, kicking the stallion's flank to spur it into the scrubby forest. "There should be a good place to camp somewhere ahead."

As they clopped forward, Heth kept himself turned with his gaze fixed on the shifting colors of the grasslands, until the branches grew too thick to see anything. When that finally happened, he let out a deep breath that had been trapped in his throat. He hoped he would never set foot in the Frayed Lands again . . . but he had a sinking feeling that the road he traveled would lead him back here once more. After all, the shard his fragment had come from was still there, hidden beneath the Winter Palace of the Radiant Emperor. Would he someday return, bringing others to claim fragments? He had been thinking about that during the last few long days in the saddle. The Windwrack, the Ember, the Duskhold . . . at the heart of all the great northern holds was a shard. Could what he'd found become the foundation of a new hold? The thought was dizzying, far too impossible to even be entertained. Before he even considered such a future, he needed to find others who could also bear the Light.

THEY RODE for the remainder of the day and then camped in the tumbled ruins of what might once have been a watchtower in the days of the First Empire. Heth slept like the dead, and for the first time since their encounter with the unnatural wolf his dreams were untroubled by eyes like blue ice staring out from shifting black grass. They breakfasted on the last of the Crow warrior rations as Rhenna described the way to the distant port of Karath, sketching their route in the loose soil with a stick.

"Here are the Frayed Lands," she explained, indicating an expanse of moss. "And here we are." She ground the point of her stick into the dirt next to it. "I don't know where exactly we've exited the plains, but we've been traveling west, so we must be in the territory my family wrested from the Ember in the old wars between Shadow and Flame. I expect the Fangs will be visible soon."

Heth shared a quick glance with Deryn. They had both grown up in the shadows of those mountains.

Rhenna caught this look and nodded. "Yes. If we were to turn north and west, we would eventually come to your twelve towns. To be honest, that was the way I would have traveled if things had not gone so spectacularly awry. After abandoning the wedding procession, Alia and I were going to pass through your villages and into the Wild beyond."

"We could still do that," Alia offered quietly.

"I can't," Rhenna said with a grimace, then hesitated before she spoke again. "But this is your best chance to leave, if you wish. All of you. You could return to your homelands, find someplace to hide and try to weather the storm that is most certainly coming." Her gaze slid to each of them in turn. Heth knew she was trying to show a flinty determination, but she could not completely hide her nervousness. Rhenna was offering them an escape, a last chance to turn away. Heth saw Deryn shake his head slightly, and so he did the same. Alia didn't even bother.

"Very well," Rhenna said, her tone gruff but unable to entirely hide her emotions. "Then we'll continue pushing west until we reach a settlement. All roads in these lands lead to Ter Drummond, and that's where we're headed." She stabbed her stick in the ground to indicate where she guessed the city to be.

"Ter Drummond," Heth said. "I always wanted to go. My father claimed he was going to take me there next summer."

Rhenna drew an undulating line in the soil that passed through the mark she'd made for the city. "This is the river Havilas. In the south it merges with the Belt that girdles the world, and Karath is at the mouth of that river on the Sea of Salvation. In Ter Drummond, we'll find a boat to take us down the Havilas and then go west. There should be plenty of river-traders that ply that route."

"Doesn't Ter Drummond fall under the Shadow?" Deryn asked, staring at the crude map she'd drawn. "Won't it be dangerous for us to go there?"

Rhenna shook her head. "Ter Drummond was declared an independent city in the treaties that ended the old wars. Both the Ember and the Duskhold are allowed to keep an embassy within its walls, but each is strictly limited to no more than five Sharded at any time in the city. It is a neutral ground between our realms."

"Let us hope that's still true," Heth murmured.

"Word might not have even reached my father about what transpired on the road," Rhenna said, brushing her legs clean as she stood. "And he is not rash. I doubt that war has already started, and the agreements governing Ter Drummond were meant to keep it from becoming a battlefield." She glanced up at the ascending sun, her lips pursed. "Still, we should move quickly."

THEY MOVED through sparse forests and meadows spattered with red flowers, riding the horses when possible and walking them when the way grew too tangled by roots and branches. This land must have once been thickly settled, as monuments to the First Empire were scattered about, though now these were mostly swallowed by the wilderness. A great stone face lay on its cheek half-buried in leaves and earth with a strange symbol Heth had never seen incised into its forehead. Elsewhere, crumbling walls suggested the borders of long-lost towns, and more than once Heth realized they were following the remnants of an old road. He supposed that this area had been abandoned after the cataclysm that formed the Frayed Lands, and after spending days out on the grasslands he could understand why no one wanted to live so close to that unnatural place.

In the late afternoon they encountered a grizzled old trapper and his son checking their snares. The man could have hidden when he'd first heard the clopping of hooves, but instead he held his ground with his hand resting lightly on the hatchet at his belt. Heth guessed that robbers and brigands must not be very common in these lands, as he displayed wariness but very little fear, and the trapper had informed them that they could reach his village before dark. There were no inns, he'd said, but someone would certainly let them stay in a spare room or hayloft for a valanii or three. And if they continued west, they'd make Ter Drummond by the next day. Rhenna thanked the trapper for his kindness, but after leaving him behind, she turned from the rough directions he'd given, making sure to skirt his village.

The thought of sleeping on something softer than the ground had excited Heth, but Rhenna shook her head firmly when he asked her about this.

"The fewer that know we came this way, the better," she explained. "It's easy for the newly Sharded to lose control for a moment and reveal their true nature. If that happens in a small village, word will spread like wildfire, and soon it will be common knowledge that a group of Sharded came from the direction of the

Frayed Lands. Any hunters from the holds would recognize us imme-diately from our description, and I'd prefer we keep our movements secret, at least until we're safely traveling down the river."

"Then why are we going to the largest city in these lands?" Heth asked, still annoyed he was missing out on a good night's rest.

"Because that is where we'll find a boat going to Karath," Rhenna replied. "It is a chance we must take."

3

HETH

Two mornings later, they crested a knoll and beheld Ter Drummond. It was easily the largest city Heth had ever seen, a jumble of stone buildings and slate gray roofs brooding on both banks of the Havilas. It had rained for much of the past two days, and the dark limestone glistened wetly above the swollen river, shreds of mist like tattered banners clinging to the squat towers of the fortress rising at the city's heart. A curving ribbon of white stone spanned the water, linking the two halves of the city. It looked decidedly out of place beside the rest of the buildings, far too graceful. This must be Ter Drummond's fabled bridge, the crossing that the city had grown around.

"How can men build such things?" Alia breathed, her eyes round with wonder.

"It is a remnant of the First Empire," Rhenna answered as she began to lead the stallion down the grassy slope to where a muddy road wended towards the city. "The ancients were capable of feats that are but dreams today."

"Something is burning in the city," Deryn said, pointing at the gates on the eastern side of the river.

Heth squinted into the morning haze. He was right – threads of smoke were trickling from just within the walls to join a dark pall, as if a larger fire had been burning earlier.

Deryn shared an uneasy glance with Heth, then tugged on Ash's reins to get her to follow Rhenna.

They started on the road below, falling in behind a string of wagons overflowing with goods and produce. Heth's stomach grumbled at the sight of so much mounded corn – days of chewing on dried meat had given him a new appreciation for vegetables – and he sank into memories of festival days in Kething's Cross when he'd gorged on roast sweet corn dripping with butter and spices.

As the city swelled larger, he began to grow more and more excited about the inns and taverns that awaited within. He hadn't eaten a truly delicious meal since the journey to the Duskhold, when Kilian Shen had treated them to feasts at every stop. Rhenna had spoken of staying out of sight as much as possible, but surely they could indulge at least once before they departed the city.

Deryn's elbow jolted him from his thoughts. "Strange there are no guards," he murmured, nodding towards the looming gates.

Heth frowned when he saw that Deryn spoke true. The great doors were flung wide, and the wagons in front of them were passing through without being inspected. He couldn't even see anyone standing on the parapets above – it appeared that the entrance to the city was unguarded. Heth glanced at the murder holes set in the walls as they progressed into the shadows of the gatehouse, wondering if anyone was standing on the other side of the stone with arrows nocked. Surely they would not leave the city undefended, even if the surrounding lands were safe . . .

"Silver Shrike," Deryn whispered as they passed out of the gatehouse tunnel.

It looked to Heth like this area had once been a market area for the goods coming in from the surrounding farms, as there were still a few wooden stalls and small buildings intact in the sprawling space. But the rest was a smoking ruin, just mounds of blackened timber and scattered ashes. A fire had raged here, though it seemed not to have touched the surrounding stone buildings or spread to the great oak in the very center of the square. Nothing moved amongst the wreckage, even though there must be plenty to scavenge. The people of Ter Drummond were keeping well away from this place.

One of the ruddy-faced farmers who had preceded them into the city pointed at the tree, and when he spoke, his voice quavered. "Whas that, eh? Those are men, ain't they?"

"They are men now," Rhenna replied quietly. "Once they were the Sharded Few."

Five bodies encircled the gnarled trunk like a gristly necklace, arms spread wide, spikes of black iron driven through their wrists. They were all naked save for their smallclothes, rivulets of blood veining their bodies. None had any visible cuts, but patches of their flesh had turned a putrescent, rotting black, as if afflicted by extreme frostbite. Heth noticed that they all shared one identical wound – in the center of their brows were ragged indentations, like something had been gouged out. Heth had seen the same marks after Rhenna had ripped the fragments from the heads of the flame-sharded after the battle atop the mesa.

These men had been Sharded from the Ember.

"How many did you say each hold was allowed to keep in the city?" Deryn murmured.

"Five," Rhenna answered, her gaze moving rapidly over the devastation. "This should be all of the Flame's servants in Ter Drummond."

"These here were the Sharded Few? Old Lord Char's men?" The farmer sounded worried and incredulous, and he'd taken off his hat to knead its straw brim with his hands. "Surely cannot be. Who could do this?"

"The shadow-sharded," Rhenna replied, then abruptly began leading the stallion away from the city gates. Heth hurried to catch up with her as she skirted the edge of the ruined market.

"What happened here?" he hissed, unable to tear his gaze from the hanging men.

"That should be obvious," Rhenna replied quietly. "The war has begun."

"But that's not possible. The ambush was only a few days ago. There's no reason why anyone should know we were even attacked."

The corner of Rhenna's mouth lifted in a cold smile. "Well, they apparently do. Take that for what you will. My father has declared war and the shadowspeakers have informed the realm. I imagine that if we'd arrived late yesterday, we would have witnessed quite the show."

Hooves clattered as Deryn joined them. His face was pale, his hand on the hilt of his Sharded sword. "There are crows in the branches, a whole flock. But they're just watching. It's like they don't dare feast on what's right in front of them."

"It takes time for the power of the shards to fade," Rhenna explained, guiding her horse towards the entrance of one of the wide cobbled streets spilling into the market square. "They would break their beaks trying to peck out those eyes. In a few days, if they have the patience to wait, the bodies will be as soft as any other corpse."

Rhenna glanced back in alarm to where Alia was trailing behind them. She relaxed visibly when she saw that the Wild girl was keeping her seed-shard well hidden in her clenched fist. "Don't allow anyone even the slightest glimpse of what you have there," Rhenna warned. "Before we do anything else, we'll find some way to hide it. If the wrong person sees what you have there, we might also find ourselves hanging on that tree."

Alia swallowed, covering her closed right hand with her left.

"Can other Sharded sense us?" Heth asked as they turned onto the street and left the smoldering ruins of the market behind. The buildings rising up here were solidly built of stone and wood and had been untouched by the flames summoned near the gate. Still, most of the residents of Ter Drummond must be in hiding, as only a few folks could be seen, peeking out from behind closed shutters or hurrying along with their heads down and shoulders hunched.

"If Sharded are close enough and decide to investigate, they will know what we are," Rhenna replied, scanning the painted signs hanging above a line of shopfronts. "So we should not give them any reason to investigate. Stare at the ground if we encounter any shadow-sharded and pretend to be over-awed. They like that." She grunted in satisfaction as she caught sight of what she sought. "Ah, here we are. Deryn, stay with the horses while we're inside. We'll only be a moment." She handed the reins to him and then pushed through a door below a wooden board showing a varied collection of objects: a needle, a cleaver, and a cup. Heth recognized these symbols, for almost the exact same series of images had been used to represent the general goods store in Kething's Cross.

A bell chimed as they entered the shop and a thin-faced man with an impressive white mustache looked up from the lengths of fabric he'd been measuring.

"Close the door," he grumbled, pushing the bindles of cloth to one side of the table he stood behind. The rest of the establishment was filled with rickety shelves crammed with every manner of household goods, from buckets to shears to piles of folded clothing.

Rhenna strode across the room and tossed a pouch in front of the store keep. Heth just kept himself from gasping, for he knew what was inside. "I want to change these into valanii, and we need a few things as well," she said, her voice sharpened to reflect the casual arrogance of the rich.

The change in the old man's demeanor was immediate, and he ducked his head. "Yes, mistress," he mumbled, gently pouring the contents of the pouch out onto the table. His bristly eyebrows lifted as gold and silver rings clattered upon the wood. Heth knew Rhenna had pulled them from the fingers of the dead flame-sharded, and it was probably more wealth than this shop typically saw in a month. So much for being circumspect.

The shopkeeper plucked one of the rings from the table and carefully dragged it against a chunk of flat black rock – a touchstone, for testing the purity of a metal. His father had kept one that looked almost the same on his desk back in Kething's Cross. The shopkeeper stared at the mark he had made on the touchstone, chewing on his lip.

"Aye, it's gold," he said, setting the ring back down carefully beside the others. "But where did you youngins get your hands on these?"

"They were my mother's," Rhenna said crisply. "She died and we must leave this city. We are also pressed for time, so this is a rare opportunity for you."

The shopkeeper gave her a long, measuring look as he brushed his fingers through his mustache. He didn't believe her, but Heth suspected the shopkeeper's greed would soon win out.

And he was right. Finally, the old man sighed, stepping back from behind the table. "What do you need? I warn you, I might not be able to change these with what I have in my strongbox."

Rhenna rattled off a list of goods, and the old man began to wander about the store pulling things from shelves, including a pair of black-leather riding gloves that reached nearly to Alia's elbows when she tried them on, along with four hooded cloaks that would suitably attire a gang of brigands, and bedrolls, ropes and torches in such quantity that it appeared they were about to mount an expedition into the Wild. Heth was a little concerned about this – Rhenna had claimed they would travel the river all the way to Karath, but it certainly seemed like she was preparing for a different journey.

"What happened near the gate?" Rhenna asked offhandedly as the shopkeeper puttered about collecting what she'd requested. "How did the market burn down?"

The old man scowled, throwing a sharp glance at the door. "You must've seen those poor souls strung up? They were Sharded."

"Truly?" Rhenna exclaimed in mock surprise. Not very convincingly, Heth thought, but the shopkeeper wasn't paying much attention.

"Aye," he said, tugging on the ends of his long mustache in agitation. "Nobody knows what started it all. Usually the Shadow and the Flame stay far away from each other, don't even drink or eat in the same taverns, one on the east side of the river an' the other on the west. But something happened. Word is there were two boys from the Ember down in the market and every shadow-sharded in the city suddenly attacked. But Char's men must have got some kind of warning off because the rest of the fireboys appeared soon after. Fella who came in earlier said at least two dozen died, maybe more. I could see the pillars of flame from my window rising over the buildings, even smell the burning flesh an' hear the screams. Lucky most of the city is stone or the whole place might have gone up." His face twisted in distaste. "Damn the Sharded."

"And the shadow-sharded?" Rhenna asked. "Where are they now?"

The old man shrugged. "Slunk back to their manse to lick their wounds, I reckon. At least a few of 'em looked to be in pretty bad shape from what I heard. Serves 'em right; they broke the treaty. I don't know why, an' I don't care. But this will mean war, mark my words, unless that Lord Shen goes groveling to Old Man Char and begs forgiveness."

Rhenna snorted at this. "That won't happen," she said, and the shopkeeper sighed again.

"You're probably right. Bloody mess this will be, and us low folk will have to suffer for it. You know, my brother was dragged off to fight in the south against those desert bastards and he never came back." The shopkeeper grunted as he returned with a final armload and dumped it on the table. "Aye, that should do it," he said, slightly out of breath. "Now, let's get down to hagglin'."

RHENNA HAD DRIVEN A HARDER bargain than Heth had expected – given her privileged position in the Duskhold, he had assumed that she would have little sense of how much things were really worth, but from the number of coins the old shopkeeper handed over after changing the rings – along with his disgruntled expression – she must acquitted herself well. He doubted he could have done a better job, as his father had always lamented that coins slipped through Heth's fingers like water. They would certainly be able to book passage to Karath and live like nobles for a few months without having to worry about money.

Deryn hurried to help as they emerged from the shop carrying the bedrolls and four bulging traveler's packs. A few more folks were out in the streets by this time, the traumatized city slowly starting to recover. Still, they were strangers here and would certainly attract some unwanted attention, so Rhenna donned her new cloak almost at once, pulling the hood up to hide her face.

"It's unlikely they'd recognize me," she said as she swung back up into the stallion's saddle, "but not impossible. Almost certainly some saw me when I accompanied my father on his western tour of the realm. Though of course they'd never expect to see me here again without an entourage of Sharded."

"Especially if word has gotten out that you're dead," Heth added, taking up the reins like he was a servant leading his mistress's horse.

Deryn glanced at Rhenna as he helped Alia up onto Ash. "You're sure they know?"

"Someone does," Heth replied, keeping his voice low. "The shadow-sharded ambushed the flame-sharded this morning. They must have attacked as soon as they heard about what had happened to the wedding procession."

"But they wouldn't have found our bodies," Deryn pointed out.

Heth snorted. "No, just a bunch of charred corpses."

"My father will know I am alive," Rhenna said with an edge that brooked no argument. "If they have been told that I am dead, it is because he wants this war."

Silence followed this pronouncement. Rhenna's face was shadowed under her cowl, but Heth could see her clenched jaw. To even think it possible that her father had planned her murder . . . he couldn't imagine what she must be feeling. His father had been hard, even cruel at times, but Heth had known that in his own way, he had cared deeply about him.

The streets grew more lively the deeper they pushed into the city. Matrons wearing bonnets similar to what the older women sported in Kething's Cross passed them carrying baskets filled with the day's purchases, children clutching at their long shawls, and groups of men loitered outside doorways arguing in loud voices with the emphatic hand gestures common to the north. Heth saw his first guardsmen, gawky boys in ill-fitting chainmail and poleaxes that looked more ornamental than practical, a red horse prancing beneath a white arch emblazoned upon their gray tabards. Many of the barrels and crates that came up the Havilas to Kething's Cross had been stamped with the same design.

The pale arch suddenly materialized as the street they were traveling ended at the edge of the river cleaving the city. From a distance, the ancient bridge had looked flawless as a pearl, but now standing only a few hundred paces away Heth could see that the white rock was riven with cracks, and chunks had sloughed off to fall into the water flowing below. Still, this decay was not deterring the stream of travelers crossing from one side of the city to the other, and given that the bridge had stood for a thousand years, Heth couldn't blame them for their confidence.

Broad wooden piers lined with boats jutted into the river in the shadow of the great arch. There were tiny skiffs that looked barely large enough for a pair of fishermen, and a few hulking galleys bristling with oars moored a little way out in the river proper. The Havilas ran swift and true down from the northern mountains, and any who wanted to trade with the twelve towns upstream would have to fight hard against the current to reach them. The brawny rivermen who pulled those oars had been some of the rowdiest visitors to the inns Heth had frequented in the Cross.

This was not the only dock in the city – Heth could see several on either bank as he gazed up and down the river, some much larger. But this was the closest, so at Rhenna's direction he led her stallion over to where the rotting planks joined with the land.

A few weathered dockworkers who had been busy unloading cargo from a flat-bottomed barge stopped to stare as Rhenna and Alia slid from the horses. They shared leering glances, snickering as they muttered between themselves. Heth would have wagered that very few young women paid a visit to these particular docks.

"You there," Rhenna said imperiously to one of the men, and his snide grin abruptly vanished. "I need passage to Karath. Where can I find a boat that will leave soon?"

The dockhand blinked at her like she was speaking Kezekani, then glanced uncertainly at his friends. "Uh, Karath, ye say? Not many go all the way to the sea. Mayhap ye need to change boats when ye reach the Belt."

"I would prefer not to," Rhenna replied sharply, crossing her arms. "Are you saying all these boats I can see only ply the Havilas?"

The dockhand rubbed at his neck like he was ashamed for disappointing her. "Well, ye see mistress, rivers are tricky beasts and captains prefer to stay with the ones they know best. But don't ye worry, get down to where the rivers join together at Ter Vhalin and ye'll find something going west—"

"What about the Kin boat that came in last night?" interjected another dockhand, a freckled boy with a shock of wild red hair.

The one who Rhenna had addressed scowled at the interruption. "You think this here lady wants to float down the river with the mudders?" he snapped, but his workmate just shrugged before leaning over to spit into the water.

"She looks like she's in a rush, is all," the boy said after wiping his mouth.

"And I am," Rhenna agreed. "Now, what did you mean by 'the mudders?'"

"That's just what some call 'em," replied the red-haired boy. A little evasively, Heth thought. "The Kin are river folk from the Belt. Live on their boats, hardly spend any time on land. Queer folk. These ones brought barrels of pepper and dried spices from the isles, is what I heard. Might be willing to take a few passengers back to Karath if the coin is good."

"Are they here?" Rhenna asked, looking out over the dilapidated boats slouching against the docks with a critical eye.

"That's them," the boy replied, nodding at a large, squat galley moored out in the river. It hunkered lower in the water than the other boats of similar size, though a much larger foredeck made it look like a tower was rising from the back of the vessel. Eyes had been painted on a prow which tapered to a sharp point like the nose-horn of a great beast.

Rhenna pursed her lips as if considering what the boy had just said and then nodded to herself. "A copper valanii to whomever will row us out there."

"Soiled wanting ta come aboard!"

The face of the sailor peering over the balustrade was seamed by the sun, a livid scar curling from his brow down to his cheek. Something glittered in his ear, catching the light as he turned away from them.

The red-haired boy who had rowed them out to the Kin boat in his skiff set down the oars with a scowl. "Soiled?" he muttered quietly. "My father worked the river, and his father before him. Got as much water in my veins as they do."

"Are they saying we're dirty?" Deryn asked, shifting in his position at the front of the little boat to look back at the dockhand. As he did this, his shadow rippled, but luckily the dockhand was busy staring daggers up at the sailor and failed to notice Shade's movements.

"I think by 'soil' they mean the earth," Alia murmured, her knuckles white from clutching the wooden plank she was sitting on. Being from the Wild, she must not have spent much time on the open water because she was obviously discomfited by the bobbing of the boat in the river's current.

"Aye, they do," the boy agreed sullenly. "The Kin live on their boats, almost never set foot on land. Believe they're above the rest o' us who work the river, one of the reasons no-one likes 'em." Something disturbed the water nearby, and the boy jerked his head around to stare at the widening ripples. He was afraid, Heth realized, though of what he couldn't imagine. Surely anyone who claimed such familiarity with the river wouldn't be scared by a few fish. He was just about to ask what had alarmed him when the sailor on the deck returned his attention to their rowboat.

"Nek Tov says you can come up," he said, then flashed a gap-toothed smile before heaving something over the side, a wood-and-rope ladder that clattered against the hull near where they floated. "Welcome to *The Morning Dream*, Soiled."

"I'll stay down here," the dock boy muttered, his gaze still fixed on the river's surface. "We don't mix well with mudders. Do your business quick – once the sky starts to get dark, I'm headed back to land with or without you."

"I understand," Rhenna said as she took hold of one of the wooden rungs and started to climb. Alia followed just behind her, and then Deryn motioned for Heth to go next. Once more he was caught off guard by the new strength in his arms – hauling himself up took almost no effort at all, as if he was as light as a feather. The feeling was intoxicating.

He found Rhenna and Alia surrounded by a motley crowd of sailors after he swung himself over the balustrade and onto the weathered deck. At first Heth thought they were all men, but then he realized that there were women as well, though they wore the same garish, brightly colored rags and their hair was also hacked short in a ragged style. Swirling black lines were inked on several faces, and chunks of gleaming opalescent stone dangled around wrists and necks. Their skin had an odd pallor Heth had never seen before, gray as river mud.

The crowd of sailors parted as a huge man bedecked in a red-tasseled jacket and tri-corner hat made a stomping approach. He peered at them with bulging dark eyes, fleshy lips twisted into what suggested mild distaste.

"Drowned saints," he bellowed, addressing the crowd of sailors. "What do we have here?" His gaze settled on Deryn, but Rhenna stepped smoothly in front of him to draw his attention away.

"You must be the captain," she said, drawing herself up.

"Aye," he replied, narrowing his eyes suspiciously. "I'm Nek Tov of *The Morning Dream*. Who might you be, and what are you doing on my boat?"

"My name is Gilia, and my associates and I require passage to Karath."

"Greetings, Gilia," Nek Tov said, thrusting out his hand. Rhenna stared at it for a moment before clasping it, and then a shiver of surprise passed across Nek Tov's face, along with a wince of discomfort. When she released his hand he subtly flexed his fingers, as if making sure they still worked properly. "Why would we take you to the City o' the Dead, lassie?" he asked, a new tone to his voice.

Rhenna drew forth her bulging purse, and though the man's wry smirk did not waver, something sparked in the depths of his dark eyes. Around him the crew began to mutter and shift, and if Heth hadn't known Rhenna was Sharded he might have felt nervous about their covetous glances.

"A bag full of copper bits, no doubt," Nek Tov grumbled, but he waved for Rhenna to follow him towards the raised foredeck. When they'd ascended to the higher level, he turned back to them and sighed.

"You must be some spoiled little things to flash such coin in front of my crew," he said, his tone reprimanding. "On any other boat on this river, you'd get your purse slit if you were lucky, and your neck if your weren't."

"But not this one?" Deryn asked, somewhat hopefully.

Nek Tov shook his head. "Nay, of course not. We're the Kin, and our boats are our home. If we take you on, you'll have the same hearth-rites a guest would have among the Soiled." His shrewd gaze studied them carefully. "The question is why you're in such a hurry. Surely those boys back on the docks tried to warn you about us."

Rhenna shrugged. "I do not care about the petty rivalry between your peoples."

Nek Tov grunted at this. "I ain't going to grant guest rites to a bunch of thieves," he said, scratching where a chunk of flesh was missing from his chin. "Is that it? Did you all find some poor fool's strongbox in the ashes of the market and want to get out before someone comes looking?"

"Nothing like that," Rhenna replied curtly. "My family has pressing business in Karath and is sending me as an envoy."

Nek Tov wrinkled his nose like he'd caught a whiff of something bad. "*Hm*. You're not a very good liar, girl . . ." His eyes drifted back to the bag Rhenna held, and in that moment Heth knew they had him. ". . . But your business is your own. Behave yourself and stay out o' the way and we can bring you to the Dead City. We only have a single spare cabin, though, so you'll all have to bunk together."

"My men can find a place somewhere," Rhenna immediately replied, having caught Alia's sudden look of horror.

"Two hundred valanii for the lot of you," Nek Tov said, and from his tone he must have been expecting this to be the opening salvo for a long and vicious bout of haggling.

"Done," Rhenna replied quickly, and for the first time the old sailor looked surprised. "It will have to be the equivalent in gold, but I expect you have a way to measure purity."

"Aye," Nek Tov said, eyeing her warily like she was more dangerous than he had initially thought. "Gold is good. Easier to change when we get to Karath."

Heth, for his part, had just stopped himself from gasping when the old sailor had thrown out his first and obviously ridiculous proposal. Two hundred valanii could go a long way towards buying a boat *and* the wages of a crew to take them down the river. Deryn must have been thinking the same thing, because his eyes were bulging and his mouth was hanging open.

"We wish to leave as soon as possible," Rhenna said, reaching into the pouch and drawing forth a glittering handful of jewelry. "Here is a deposit for our place aboard." She picked up an intricately knotted golden bracelet inset with green stones and held it out for Nek Tov. He extended a calloused hand, then stayed staring at the bracelet for a long moment after she'd dropped it into his palm.

"We leave tomorrow morning," he finally said with a shake of his head.

Rhenna frowned. "Tonight would be better."

The old sailor chuckled. "That may be, but I have a few of my people out in the city. They won't be back until late, if not tomorrow, though they'll return by the dawn because that's when they know we're pulling anchor. You and your friends should be on the docks when the sky first starts to lighten, because I'll have a boat there waiting for you."

Rhenna did not look pleased, but nodded tightly. "Very well. We'll be there. And if we arrive and you've already left . . . I promise that I'll find you. I can be very tenacious when I've been wronged."

Nek Tov looked affronted. "Girl, we've struck a deal an' the Kin never go back on their word." He slipped the bracelet into one of his long coat's many pockets, then spat lightly in his hand and held it out towards her. She looked at it with something like bemusement for a long moment, and then to Heth's great surprise, she also spat in her hand. Heth wasn't sure if her surprise stemmed from this odd – and disgusting – manner of sealing their pact, or if she was simply amazed that he would dare to clasp hands with her again. This time she did not squeeze too hard, though, and Heth thought he saw some small relief in the captain's face.

"Tomorrow at dawn, then," Rhenna said, releasing Nek Tov's hand. "Do not forget about us."

4

DERYN

The *Cat's Rest* was an apt name for this tavern. It was low-ceilinged and windowless, filled with comfortable furniture carved from black wood, with the only illumination the candles scattered on the tables and the glowing coals in the hearth. It wasn't like the eating houses Deryn was familiar with back in Kething's Cross – there was no minstrel strumming his strings by the fire, or loud conversations as patrons tried to be heard over the din. This place was quiet and dark, and only a few folks huddled around tables, some speaking softly while others ate in silence. It was, Deryn decided, the perfect place for them to enjoy a real meal, but Rhenna had still chosen a table in the corner as far from the fire as possible, and she had kept her hood drawn up even after they'd sat down. Deryn thought this made them look *more* suspicious, but he wasn't about to suggest this to Rhenna. *The Cat's Rest* was clearly well-suited for shadowy doings, and he suspected that the slim, sharp-faced man behind the bar was known for his discretion.

"What will we do when we reach Karath?" Heth asked, hands clutched protectively around a foamy tankard of black ale. His fourth, by Deryn's count.

Rhenna poked at the lamb bone on her plate with her knife,

searching for any remaining scraps of meat. They had fallen upon the food like a pack of starving wolves, and while a second round had quickly been ordered, it was yet to arrive. "I don't know," Rhenna replied, finally setting down her knife with a disappointed sigh. "I must learn if it was my father who hired the servants of the Unbound King, though of course I can't simply walk up to Xend an-Azith and ask him."

"Because if he was involved, he'd try to finish the job there and then," Heth agreed, stirring the head of foam on his drink with his finger.

Rhenna nodded. "Yes. So we'll have to find another way. Perhaps we can find one of his followers and . . . convince them to tell us."

Deryn grimaced. "Just remember that everything will be very different in the City of the Dead. Our Sharded strength will go away."

"I know," Rhenna said, frowning. "But we won't be entirely help-less. Heth is an accomplished swordsman, yes? He was teaching you how to fight, if I remember correctly. And I've trained my whole life as a warrior."

A flush darkened Heth's cheeks. "I was the best in my sword-hall," he admitted, drawing himself up a little higher in his chair.

"But what if that servant of the Unbound King we *convince* to talk knows nothing? We *kill* him and kidnap another, work our way up the ranks until we find someone high enough to be privy to such plans?" Deryn hoped his tone made it clear how ridiculous he thought this stratagem to be.

"Then we infiltrate his ranks," Rhenna said, somewhat testily. "We are all Sharded here and so can claim to be Unbound fleeing our holds." She drummed her fingers on the table. "Well, in truth, they might recognize me. And Heth . . . if they see his shard, they'll know he's something new, something different. We don't want that happen-ing, either, because Xend would certainly want to go claim that shard under the Winter Palace. It will have to be Deryn."

"I'm not sure that's such a good idea, either," Deryn said, distracted by what Shade was doing. Despite his whispered entreaties to stay curled up by his feet, the elemental was at that moment slipping through the maze of chairs and table legs, seemingly intent on something near the hearth.

"I assume you're talking about your . . . companion," Rhenna said flatly, noticing where Deryn's attention had been drawn.

"Yes," he murmured as Shade finally reached the crackling flames. The elemental's black shape was picked out against the glow, but luckily all the other patrons in the tavern were oblivious. "I can't control him. Almost certainly Shade would show himself to the Unbound King's followers."

"And you're almost as interesting as Heth," Rhenna said, sounding frustrated. "Elementalists are exceedingly rare. There's the water witch in the Sea of Salvation, and the bloodlord in Ashasai, and those were all we in the Duskhold knew about before you gained your elemental. No, you're right, there's too much risk of unwanted scrutiny. But if none of *us* can . . ."

Her gaze slid to Alia, who had clearly not been paying attention to the conversation while staring hungrily at the door that led to the kitchen. She'd devoured the bowl of buttered mushrooms and leaks that had been set before her and was clearly anticipating the arrival of a second helping. But she must have felt the weight of their gazes, because she shifted her focus back to the table.

"What?" she asked. "Don't worry, I'll share my mushrooms."

"No," Heth said forcefully, startling Alia as he brought his tankard down hard, several patrons turning towards them at the sound.

"Who else, then?" Rhenna hissed, lowering her voice.

Heth scowled, gesturing sharply towards Deryn. "He can learn how to bring his dog to heel. Or I can tell them I found this shard in a barrow in the Fangs."

"You are most definitely not an option. And do you really think Deryn can control that thing?" Rhenna snorted, indicating with a lift of her chin the elemental hovering beside the flames. Deryn suddenly realized what had drawn Shade's interest – an almost comically fat cat was curled on the hearth, basking in the heat. He swallowed nervously as the elemental flowed closer until Shade was poised above the blissfully unaware cat. Was he going to scare it? Eat it? Surely whatever was about to happen would create enough of a commotion that everyone in the common room would turn and look . . .

Shade vanished into the cat's shadow. Deryn blinked, sharing an uncertain glance with Rhenna and Heth.

And then the cat's shadow stood up and walked away.

"You must be jesting," muttered Heth.

They watched as a now decidedly more feline Shade retraced his path through the common room and settled once more under their table. Somehow, no one else had noticed, not even the still-sleeping and now shadow-bereft cat.

"I suppose that might raise some eyebrows," Heth admitted with a sigh. "But I still don't agree that Alia should be the one."

"The one who what?" the Wild girl asked innocently, placing her chin on her fist.

Heth rubbed at his face angrily instead of answering her. "I'm going upstairs," he said, pushing back his chair and rising unsteadily to his feet. Before he departed, he set his hands on the table and leaned towards Rhenna. "But this conversation isn't finished. It's too dangerous for her."

Rhenna regarded him with raised eyebrows from over steepled fingers. "Get some sleep," she said mildly. "We'll discuss this again on the boat to Karath."

Heth nodded jerkily, then made his way with a slight unsteadiness to the doorway. Deryn watched him go, then turned to Rhenna. He noticed that Alia had vanished from her seat as well, making her way to the bar to investigate a steaming platter that had just come from the kitchen, too impatient to wait for a server to bring it to their table.

"Thank you for not rising to his bait. He shouldn't challenge you like that."

Rhenna shrugged. "He cares for her. I can respect that . . . and I also would prefer to keep her from harm's way. But there's more strength in her than he realizes. I would trust her with my life."

Deryn was just about to ask if Alia had ever spoken to her about her upbringing in the Wild, but the question died in his throat when Rhenna suddenly sucked in her breath and pulled her cowl down to hide her face.

"What is it?" he asked just before he felt it himself – a febrile trembling in the air, like something vast and huge had suddenly exhaled.

Every candle flickered as a man entered the common room. He was short, but broad-shouldered and barrel-chested, with a streak of white in his cropped hair. His silver-trimmed black doublet was of fine make, though one sleeve was nothing but tatters and the rest of the shirt was pockmarked by charred holes. Deryn swallowed when he noticed the man's face. A mottled burn crept up from beneath his collar to cover much of his neck and half his jaw, the flesh pink and glistening.

"Stay quiet. Do nothing," Rhenna whispered, hunching lower in her seat. Deryn realized he was staring, but the man didn't glance their way as he approached the long bar. Farther down the length of polished wood, Alia had gone perfectly still, her eyes wide and lips parted in shock. She could feel it as well, then.

This man was shadow-sharded, and powerful.

"Barkeep!" the newcomer shouted at the man who had been polishing glasses behind the bar, but now had frozen. "Do you have any bottles of melikanis?"

"My . . . my lord?" the balding barkeep murmured, his voice little more than a whisper. He had the look of a drowning man who hadn't expected to find himself in such deep water.

The man growled and slapped his palm on the bar top, sending up a spray of wood slivers. "Numbwine! Do you have any bottles?"

The crack of the splintering bar had made the barkeep jump. "Numbwine," he said quickly. "Yes, we have some, my lord. It's down in the cellar."

This seemed to mollify the shadow-sharded somewhat. "Good. Excellent. You wouldn't believe how many taverns in this city do not carry any." He attempted to smile, but then winced, his hand going to his ravaged jaw. "*Ah*. I need you to collect every drop you have in your stores."

"Yes, my lord," the barkeep replied immediately, then snapped his fingers in the direction of the serving girl. She was gaping at the shadow-sharded, her hands frantically kneading the hem of her dress. "Heran, you heard the lord. Go put every bottle of numbwine we have in a sack."

The Sharded grunted in satisfaction after the girl nodded shakily, then spun on his heel and without another word strode back the way he had come.

Deryn risked a sigh of relief, for if the Sharded had not been so focused on his task, he certainly would have noticed—

The man stopped abruptly, turning to face Alia. She swallowed, ducking her head like she was not worthy of meeting his gaze, her long golden hair veiling her face. Deryn tensed. What was it? Had he sensed her shard? Or was it because she clearly hailed from the northern Wilds, an uncommon sight this far south?

"Oh, by the Mother," Rhenna murmured.

Right beside where Alia's gloved hand rested on the bar a delicate sprig had risen, tiny green leaves in the process of unfurling. Deryn remembered that Rhenna had said some newly Sharded struggled to control their beckoning – it was the reason why they had avoided staying at the village near Ter Drummond. Alia still hadn't yet realized what she'd done . . . but the shadow-sharded was staring with wide eyes at that trembling little shoot.

He moved almost too fast to see, and Alia gave a strangled yelp as he clamped down on her glove, pinning it to the bar top, while in his other hand a glistening black scimitar formed.

"Who are you?" he snarled, motes of blackness swirling around him like a swarm of angry insects.

"No one!" she cried, looking stricken. "Just a traveler!"

"Unbound scum," the shadow-sharded said, his arm drawing back as he prepared to sever her hand at the wrist with his Umbral Blade.

Deryn exploded from his chair, summoning his Ghost Chitin as he vaulted over the tables. The shadow-sharded had his back to him and was so focused on Alia that he did not realize someone was charging across the room until a moment too late, starting to turn just as Deryn's fist slammed into the side of his face.

It was like punching stone.

Still, Deryn's blow had landed on the burned patch of skin, and the shadow-sharded shrieked, reeling away, the hand that had been holding Alia immobile flying to where he had been struck. Ignoring the pain that had lanced from his knuckles all the way up his arm, Deryn seized Alia and threw her behind him, bracing himself for what he knew was coming.

A cold so deep it burned blasted Deryn in the stomach as the shadow-sharded stabbed him with his Umbral Blade. For a moment he thought the shadow-sword was going to pierce his Ghost Chitin and bury itself deep in his gut, but his invisible armor somehow held, though he felt cracks spiderwebbing its unseen surface. Even though the edge had not cut him, the blade's unnatural coldness still seeped through his Chitin, numbing his flesh. Deryn gasped – another blow and he would be chopped in twain. He poured his *ka* into his Ghost Chitin, desperately trying to knit it back together before the shadow-sharded's next swing.

A tendril of blackness wrapped around his body, and then he was tumbling through the air to smash into something wooden, which crumpled under the impact. Screams erupted as he lurched to his feet among the wreckage of a table, the patrons who had been seated there a moment ago now sprawled on their backs. He swayed as he set himself into a defensive stance, expecting the shadow-sharded to crash into him like an avalanche sweeping over a cliff.

But the burned man wasn't focused on him any longer – he was facing the cloaked and cowled Rhenna, who had risen from her chair. A nest of shadowy serpents writhed around her, and Deryn realized it was one of these beckonings that had pulled him from harm's way.

"You are shadow-sharded," the man said as the buzzing motes of darkness around him intensified again.

"I am," Rhenna said simply.

"Are you Unbound?"

"No."

The man growled in frustration. "You are from the Duskhold? Why were you skulking about in here, then? You should have come directly to us. We could use your help!"

"I saw what you did by the gates," Rhenna said, moving out from behind their table. The black tendrils of her beckoning slithered around her, and the man stiffened as he realized that she was preparing to continue the fight.

"We had to," spat the shadow-sharded. "You don't understand – war has broken out between the Shadow and the Flame. And ours was not the first blow! That cowardly Lord Char *murdered* Cael Shen's daughter during her wedding procession to Flail!"

"Are you so sure of that, Kalest?" Rhenna replied, reaching up to draw back her cowl.

The shadow-sharded's face collapsed into shock. "What sorcery is this?" he murmured hoarsely, steadying himself on the bar.

"Someone tried to assassinate me, but it was not the Flame."

The man she'd called Kalest narrowed his eyes. "You're some sort of illusion; I know the Flame have such a talent." His gaze went to the hearth. "Fire Shaping. I had no idea it could be so convincing."

"I'm no illusion. I am truly Rhenna Shen, daughter of the Duskhold. We were students together under Saelus."

The shadow-sharded did not look entirely convinced, but he at least seemed to accept that she was not the creation of a Flame talent. "Then you must come with me to see Scalva. He was injured during the fight in the market, but he's well enough to judge the merit of your claims. And if you truly are Rhenna, then we must send word to your father at once."

"I can't allow that," Rhenna said as she summoned a half-dozen identical Mirror Wraiths, each one holding a javelin of gleaming darkness.

The shadow-sharded grimaced and made a sharp gesture with his arm. Alia shrieked as she was lifted into the air by a swarm of shadowy motes and carried kicking and flailing back to where Kalest waited. The Rhenna wraiths snarled and took a threatening step forward, but the shadow-sharded's Umbral Blade flared into existence again.

"I must insist," Kalest said, pressing the shadow scimitar to her neck. "You seem to care about this Sharded. Come with me and I will not hurt the girl."

The Mirror Wraiths growled and bared their teeth, but they stopped their advance.

"Good," Kalest said, and Deryn thought he sounded slightly relieved. "Good. Now, follow me, and don't try anything or I'll slit this one's throat like she's a Husking Day sow." He began to walk backwards, keeping Alia between himself and Rhenna's Wraiths. In the entranceway to the room, he paused, shaking his head slightly. "Whatever game you're playing, Rhenna, I can assure you that—"

Kalest suddenly stiffened, his eyes widening. Alia whimpered as the black blade evaporated into wisps of shadow and the motes of darkness that had been swirling around her melted away. The shadow-sharded blinked rapidly, and then a trickle of blood spilled from the corner of his mouth.

"What?" he managed to croak before crumpling to the floor. Behind him stood Heth, light rippling along the blade of the Sharded dagger where it was not streaked with blood.

5

HETH

They were huddled in the shadow of the great white bridge when dawn finally seeped into the sky. It had been a stressful night. Rhenna had kept them on the move, refusing to linger anywhere for long no matter how safe it seemed. They had crouched in darkened alleys, slipped through unlit streets, and laid low in abandoned buildings in the poorest quarter of Ter Drummond. Heth had seen no sign of any pursuit, but invariably Rhenna would grimace or sigh and tilt her head to one side, as if listening hard for something only she could hear. Then she would usher them out again into the night and lead them somewhere else.

"They are looking for us," Rhenna had replied curtly when Heth suggested they stay in the ruin of a collapsing manse that was far more comfortable than the other places they'd squatted. "Scalva Balenchas is my father's representative here, and like many powerful Sharded he can use his beckoning to search for what he seeks. Which, right now, is us. Streams of shadows are flowing through the city, and it is all I can do to stay one step ahead of them."

Heth finally realized the strategy behind Rhenna's seemingly random movements around the city when they reached the great curving bridge over the Havilas just as the sky was beginning to lighten. She had intentionally avoided the river until the time approached when the captain had said he would send a boat to pick them up at the docks. If they had come here directly after the incident in the tavern, the shadow-sharded would have been more likely to find them during their long wait for the dawn to break.

And so they waited, tired and bedraggled, at the end of the pier the captain had pointed out the day before, hoping for some sign that the painted galley wallowing in the middle of the river was beginning to stir. Heth wasn't sure what they would do if the captain decided to forsake the deal they had struck. He had a vision of the oars bristling along the length of the ship suddenly descending to dip into the water, and the predicament they would be in if that happened – the shadow-sharded who had survived the battle with the Flame yesterday might be wounded, but Rhenna clearly thought they were still overwhelmingly outmatched.

The morning's rosy fingers slowly began to stretch across the water, and Heth had just about convinced himself that the captain had betrayed them when he saw a shiver of movement on the galley's deck. His was not the only sigh of relief at the sight . . . but that was strange, since it hadn't come from any of his companions.

They all turned to find a scrawny young man wearing the same colorful garb as the sailors on the galley. His clothes were covered in dark stains that might have been blood but Heth suspected to be wine, and he was swaying so unsteadily that it seemed a small miracle that he was not already sprawled on the pier snoring. He blinked blearily at them with bloodshot eyes when he noticed their attention, then smiled broadly.

"Thought old Nekkie might have decided to leave me behind this time," he said, and then his brow furrowed as he fought to focus on them. "Drowned saints, you lot look awful. Had a rough night?"

"Something like that," Rhenna answered dryly.

"And watcha doin' here? Bit of fishing?"

Rhenna tilted her head in the direction of the Kin rowboat that was slowly approaching the pier. "We're passengers on your ship, headed to Karath."

The man guffawed loudly at this, but his hiccupping laughter died when he realized Rhenna was not joking. "You're serious? Wait, are you all really here or am I having a smoke-see?"

Rhenna sighed, turning away as the rowboat bumped against the piling and an older sailor with a scowling face covered in intricate whorled tattoos leaped onto the dock.

"Come on Cal Canna, you blasted fool," he muttered sourly, grabbing the younger man's arm and almost throwing him into the boat.

"Gev Rin!" the drunken sailor exclaimed, just catching himself from toppling over the far side and into the river. He collapsed in the bottom of the boat between two of the seating planks, his arms and legs flailing weakly. "So good to see you!"

The older man did not bother to dignify this with a response, instead shifting his attention to the rest of them. "This here's the only chance to go aboard, so if ye be wanting to sail on the *Dream*, get in." From the gruffness of his tone, it didn't sound to Heth like he cared one way or another . . . and maybe even would have preferred if they stayed on the dock.

Rhenna ignored his surliness, stepping gracefully into the rowboat and settling herself on a plank. Alia followed and found a seat beside her, and then Heth helped Deryn wrestle the bulging travel bags they'd bought the day before into the boat. The old sailor did not say anything else as he pushed them away from the pier before leaping into the rowboat with surprising agility. He took a moment to clear his throat and spit over the side, then sat heavily and took up the oars again.

"I'm afraid I forgot to introduce myself," the young man said from where he lay, looking up at Rhenna and Alia. "Greetings, maidens, my name is—"

"Cal Canna," Alia finished for him.

"You've heard of me!"

"Your friend said your name," Alia explained, nodding towards where the other sailor was now straining at the oars.

"Not his friend," grumbled the old man.

The drunken sailor seemed not to have heard this muttered aside. "Well, did he say anything else about me?"

"He said you were a blasted fool," Alia informed him.

The young man looked aggrieved. "*Hm*," he sniffed, putting his arms behind his head and closing his eyes. "How rude." The next sound he made was a rattling snore, so with a bewildered shake of his head Heth turned away from him and to the galley they were approaching. It was still a dark shadow etched against the ghostly morning light, but there was more activity on board than when they had been standing on the dock, and then with an audible crack the main sail suddenly unfurled to reveal a trio of golden sunbursts.

When they reached the galley, the old sailor quickly slipped hooks that were dangling down from above through the iron rings driven into the rowboat's side and then shouted up that they were ready. Heth clutched at the railing of the small boat as it was lifted from the water, half-expecting it to fall apart, but soon they were deposited on the galley's deck beside another little boat of the same make. The galley was a hive of activity, sailors rushing about securing ropes, adjusting the smaller sails and scrambling through the rigging. The Havilas flowed south, in the same direction they were going, so on this journey they would rely on wind and current instead of oars.

"Welcome aboard again, Soiled," bellowed Nek Tov as he clattered down the stairs to the sterncastle. He was grinning fiercely, though Heth thought his good mood was more likely to be a product of their imminent departure rather than of seeing them again.

"We are about to get underway?" Rhenna asked, stepping from the rowboat onto the deck.

"At once," Nek Tov replied as a strong gust made the galley's recently unfurled sails belly. "We've got an excellent wind that'll push us down the river like we're a snake sliding down a waterspout. By this time tomorrow, we could be halfway to Ter Vhalin and the blessed Belt. My crew will be happy to see those waters again – the Havilas is a bit too narrow and choppy for our liking." He sauntered closer to the rowboat and peered inside. Heth had already joined Rhenna on the deck and couldn't see the drunken sailor anymore, but he knew the captain was staring down at the young man. Who was apparently still asleep, as a loud snoring was emanating from within.

"Want me to dump him out, set him to work cleaning the bilge?" asked the older sailor who had rowed them over to the galley.

"Let him sleep," Nek Tov replied, twisting one of his jacket's tassels around a finger. "I'll keep him on board until we reach Karath – that'll be punishment enough." He did not turn towards where Heth and his companions stood, but his next words seemed to be for them. "We Kin live our lives on these boats and rivers. Most of us, it's enough. But there's always a few who yearn for the freedom of the Soiled. Cal Canna here . . . most likely he'll be one who leaves us, eventually. But until he does I've promised his ma I won't come down too hard on him for his wastrelly ways. I think she hopes it'll make him appreciate his life here on the water more."

From his tone, Heth knew what the captain thought about the likelihood of that.

"But enough!" Nek Tov said, turning away from the rowboat and its sleeping occupant. "Time to pull anchor. I've got things to do"—he pointed at a red-painted door next to the stairs ascending to the upper deck—"and I don't want to be bothered. Your cabin is through there, first on the right. Don't go poking into any other rooms unless you want to be tossed overboard. Understood?"

Rhenna cocked an eyebrow at this. "I can assure you, Captain, we will respect you and your ship."

"Good," Nek Tov said as he turned away sharply, and Heth sensed he was dismissing them. The captain pointed at the prow of the bow where a few sailors were clustered around a black-iron device looped with coils of thick rope. "Raise the anchor!" he shouted, and the sailors hurried to oblige. Apparently satisfied at the alacrity of their response, he stomped up the stairs to where the ship's wheel was just visible on the sterncastle.

Heth jumped out of the way as a sailor hurried past and then followed Rhenna and the others over to the side of the boat. Their frantic flight through the city seemed almost like a dream now . . .

though the consequences of staying up all night were now evident, as Alia looked ready to collapse and Deryn was leaning heavily on the balustrade like it was all that was keeping him upright.

"We made it," Heth remarked as he came along beside them, resting his arms on the railing.

"We'll have made it when we can't see Ter Drummond anymore," Rhenna replied, staring at the gray-stone buildings clustered along the river's edge like she expected a Black Disc to come soaring over their roofs at any moment. Her gaze flicked to Alia, who was swaying on her feet, her eyes half closed. "Some of us should get some rest. Heth and I will keep watch first – Deryn, help Alia to our cabin."

Deryn raised his head from where he'd laid it on the railing and looked at Rhenna in surprise. "I thought you said Heth and I would be sleeping elsewhere?"

Rhenna waved her hand at the chaos going on around them. "Someone will trip over you. For now, just find a spot on the floor of our cabin."

Deryn ducked his head in thanks and gently took Alia's arm, then led her towards the red door the captain had indicated earlier. Rhenna watched until they disappeared inside, then turned back to Ter Drummond, drawing in a deep breath. A few strands of her long black hair had escaped from the depths of her hood, dancing in the wind. Her mouth was set in a thin line, her eyes slightly narrowed. She looked fearless and resolved, and he wondered if she was truly as strong as she appeared, or if beneath it all her heart was beating as fast as his own.

"I knew him," she said suddenly, startling Heth.

"Who?"

Across from them, the city was sliding away as the galley started to move. Rhenna grimaced, her hands tightening on the wood of the railing. Heth thought he heard a creaking and hoped it didn't shatter under her grip. "The Sharded back at the inn. Kalest. We were adepts together."

Heth swallowed, trying to determine if she was upset with him. Last night had been so stressful that he'd barely had time to reflect on what had happened back at *The Cat's Rest*. "I heard crashing and knew someone had found us, so I grabbed the Sharded dagger and ran downstairs. Alia had a shadow blade to her throat . . . I just acted on instinct."

Rhenna hung her head slightly, allowing a few more dark strands to escape. "You were right to do what you did. Kalest made his choice – he was going to insist we go to the other shadow-sharded, and they would have told my father. And likely they would have also killed you and Alia for being Unbound." She pursed her lips. "But he was not a bad person. He was just doing what he thought was best for the Duskhold. He had been poor, you see. A street rat of Phane. The Shadow had cared for him, given him everything."

"I'm sorry," Heth said quietly, trying not to remember the feeling of the dagger entering flesh, the surprised intake of breath from the shadow-sharded as his heart had been pierced.

"Don't apologize," Rhenna said, and this time she did sound a little angry. "I wanted to speak with you about this without Deryn or Alia here. It's important that you realize that they are different from us. We can do the hard things that need doing . . . but them? I don't think so. Maybe if Deryn is backed into a corner, like we were in the Winter Palace with the Flame trying to kill us . . . but could he stab an enemy while standing behind them? Or would he have instead put his sword point to Kalest's back and demanded he free Alia? Kalest would have Shadow-Stepped behind him and lopped off his head with his Umbral Blade. You and I must be ruthless if we are going to survive being hunted by the Shadow and the Unbound King and whoever else wants us dead."

"Oh," Heth murmured, slightly taken aback. "I suppose I . . ." His words trailed away as something in the water caught his eye. Then it was gone, leaving a slowly widening ring of ripples.

"Did you see that?" he asked, wondering if his exhaustion had finally caught up with him. "It looked like—"

"A head," Rhenna said grimly, then whirled and began striding towards the stairs up to the sterncastle. Heth hurried to catch up to her, trying to recall what he'd seen in that brief glimpse. It had been smooth and hairless, mottled green and brown, with huge, pupilless black eyes and a face that tapered into curving beak. It had looked like . . . like the head of an enormous turtle.

"Captain," Rhenna said as she came to where the man was conferring with the brawny sailor gripping the galley's huge ship's wheel. "We must talk. There is something in the water."

Nek Tov shared a glance with the steersman that looked entirely too untroubled for the importance of this announcement and then motioned for Rhenna and Heth to join him overlooking the deck below.

"Did you hear me, Captain?" Rhenna said, sounding frustrated. "Some kind of river beast. Even if it is not dangerous, you should take care not to collide with it. It looked large enough to damage your boat."

Nek Tov gave a low chuckle, shaking his head. "There's no way we hit her. Only real danger might be if some fool on the shore sees Bassa and sends word we've got an Old Shell with us. There are folk who would pay quite a bit for a piece of her. Shouldn't be surfacing with the city still in sight."

Rhenna frowned. "Then the stories are true."

The captain's expression remained placid. "Some might be. I'd have to hear 'em."

"That a few of the great turtles still live. That there are river folk who keep them hidden, care for them."

"Aye, then, that's true," Nek Tov said, drumming his fingers on the balustrade's wood as he squinted at the sunlight reflecting off the river. "It's my Kin's secret. And I hope you'll keep it tight to your chest as well when you leave the boat." He paused, then slid a glance sidelong at her. "After all, you have secrets you wouldn't want getting around."

Rhenna narrowed her eyes. "What do you mean?"

The captain spread his arms wide, as if to show he was not trying to threaten her. "Just that I've shaken many hands over the years, and never have I felt my bones creak like that. No girl has such a grip . . . unless she's also something else."

"You knew," Rhenna said, her jaw tightening.

The captain doffed his tri-corner hat and ran his fingers through his stringy hair. "Aye. And it doesn't take a brilliant man to draw a connection between a Sharded girl who wants to flee the city as soon as possible and a battle that just broke out between the two great holds claiming these lands. You're Unbound, hoping to find sanctuary in Karath before the Shadow or the Flame finds you and thinks you must be the enemy."

"And yet you agreed to take us on," Rhenna said.

Nek Tov sighed. "I've led my Kin for many years, and it's given me a certain sense about people."

"If what you're saying is true," Heth said, hoping Rhenna wouldn't mind him interjecting. "Allowing us to come on board would be a risk you don't have to take. Why do it?"

The captain turned to him and Heth thought he saw a flicker of respect in his dark eyes. "Because, truth be told, you lot might be useful. You see, about two months past one of the Kin's galleys went missing on the Belt, somewhere between Ter Vhalin and Ferelin. Ain't much between those two towns – way is a little treacherous, that's true, but the Kin would never run aground with an Old Shell feeling out the bottom. Then I got word my cousin's boat also didn't turn up in Ferelin after filling her hold with good Vhalish wine. One boat lost could be terrible luck. Two? Something's hunting on that stretch of river. Pirates, I'm guessing. Or maybe an Unbound is leading an attack from the shore, though why one would want to kill my Kin, I don't know."

"And so you brought us aboard as guards," Rhenna said with a rueful shake of her head. "*You* should be paying *us*."

"Be honored," the captain said, smiling broadly. "The Kin almost never take on passengers. And we'll treat you like family until we see you safe in Karath. This I promise, by the beak of old Bassa herself."

6

DERYN

The cold, hard knot of anxiety that Deryn had been carrying around ever since awakening in the Frayed Lands loosened almost immediately after their departure from Ter Drummond, and by their third day on the river it had unraveled completely. It felt liberating, like he could finally breathe easily again. First they had been hunted by the flame-sharded, then the Crow, and finally the Shadow, but there was no reason for them to fear any pursuit now – Nek Tov had confidently informed Deryn that no boat in Ter Drummond could catch *The Morning Dream,* even if the shadow-sharded realized how they had escaped the city.

And so they could relax. Rhenna spent a good portion of every day in their cabin helping Heth and Alia improve their most basic Sharded skills. Channeling came easily to both, and she often had them sit quietly for half the day or more pushing the *ka* spilling from their shards through their pathways, strengthening their bodies and bringing order to the raw power seething inside them. It was grueling to channel for so long without rest, but Deryn realized that they were in a race against time. Heth and Alia were both *arzgan,* Sharded with only a single fragment. Their strength would increase greatly when they had channeled enough *ka* to merge a second shard, and when they finally gained their first talent – which usually happened no later than their third fragment – they would be far more dangerous. Then they would be *sardor*, the rank that most Sharded found themselves unable to advance beyond. Deryn had somehow already attained the rank of *kenang*, because he had very unexpectedly gained a second-tier talent after merging his third shard. Rhenna was also *kenang*, although she was eight-sharded and thus much stronger than him, and with several more talents to draw upon – including two second-tier talents, the Hand of Night and Mirror Wraiths. He'd seen her use both of these abilities several times, and Deryn had decided that he would be pleased if he eventually gained either talent. Being able to summon multiple illusions of himself to confuse his enemies would give him the time to unleash his Breath of the Mother, an attacking talent that had proven devastating in the battle atop the mesa. Though it had been difficult to control, as he was in truth opening a rift into the wild and unpredictable shadowrealm and allowing its frozen winds to enter this world. He wished he could find a time and place to practice wielding the Breath, because right now it was simply too . . . indiscriminate. But that would have to wait until they were not on a boat full of people in the middle of a river.

Rhenna also devoted time every day to teaching Alia and Heth how to successfully beckon. Alia showed great promise here, coaxing living plants from the ship's wood with apparent ease, though – as had happened back at the tavern in Ter Drummond – she sometimes had difficulty controlling this ability. Deryn had even once found that vines spotted with blooming roses had grown up to wrap the bed Rhenna and Alia shared during the night. Deryn had wanted to ask her what sort of dream had caused this, but he'd bitten his lip and let Heth make a smirking comment that had resulted in Rhenna throwing a boot at him. Truly, it wasn't really Heth's place to say anything, since he was still incapable of beckoning at all. This was no surprise, in truth, since for shadow-sharded it usually took months before they could successfully control the darkness. Heth – being light-sharded – was apparently the same , and it clearly annoyed him that for Alia, beckoning had come immediately and naturally.

While the others labored in the cabin, Deryn spent the days outside on the deck, watching the scenery flow past and the sailors scurry about at their tasks. For a while after they left Ter Drummond, the forests and marshes along the riverbank were regularly broken up by small villages and even a few sizable towns, though none boasted First Empire structures or the tall stone buildings of Ter Drummond. Deryn also tried to catch glimpses of the great turtle that was always keeping pace with the galley – at first he hadn't believed Rhenna and Heth when they'd told him, but then Bassa had made an appearance on an empty stretch of the Havilas, surfacing to help guide their ship around a wreck hidden beneath the surface. Her shell was beautiful, intricate whorls of black and red, though Deryn had noticed several long scratches that looked like claw marks, which made him wonder what other creatures dwelled in the river depths. The length of her neck had also surprised him, as the turtle was capable of lifting her head high out of the water while keeping her shell submerged, and he had seen her do exactly this while nibbling from the branches of a willow that extended out over the river. Her fathomless black eyes had contained an intelligence that had shaken him – not because he hadn't expected to see such aware-ness in the gaze of something that was not human, but because he had actually glimpsed it before in the eyes of another great reptile. Both the Old Shell and the balewyrm he'd encountered under the Duskhold had possessed this intelligence, and coupled with their great age, it had created an almost palpable heaviness radiating from their presences.

Deryn made sure not to while away the entirety of every day. After Heth had finished with Rhenna, he would emerge from the cabin – often more than a little frustrated with his progress – and together he and Deryn would find an empty spot somewhere on the galley's deck to practice sword fighting forms. Of course they couldn't duel each other or work through the progressions at any real speed, but Deryn still found it useful to slowly drill the various movements, ingraining them in his muscle-memory. He also took this opportunity to improve his abilities with his Sharded sword, pushing his *ka* through the blade as he swept it back and forth to summon winds of varying strengths. A few times he'd caused the galley's sails to belly with an unexpected gust, fomenting a mild panic among the sailors, who had frantically looked for evidence in the sky of an imminent storm.

Deryn also spent quite a bit of time channeling his *ka*. He knew he was close – so close – to being able to merge his fourth shard. To come so far so fast was dizzying, but Rhenna had told him that the truly gifted Sharded could keep adding fragments fairly regularly until they finally reached a barrier that was more difficult to break. For her and her brother Nishi that had been after their eighth shard. Other powerful Sharded he'd met – like Jaliska, the weapon master of the Duskhold, or poor, doomed Vertus Balenchas – had seemed to plateau at around the same number. Though then there were the true outliers, such as Rhenna's adopted Salahi brother Azil and Cael Shen himself. Kilian had once told Deryn that no one knew how many shards these greatest of the Sharded Few had merged, but there was no doubt that they were as far above the average *sardor* or *kenang* as those lesser Sharded were to an ordinary man. Given the ease and speed with which he had merged his first few shards, it seemed likely to Deryn that he at least had a potential similar to Rhenna. But could it be possible he was more like Azil? The thought was exhilarating and a little frightening.

Deryn's third and final attempt to better himself during these long and languorous days on the Havilas River was to further investigate his relationship with Shade. The elemental was being surprisingly well-behaved on the galley, keeping mostly out of sight when the sun was shining, although whispers of a black ghost-cat haunting the ship quickly started to circulate among the crew. Those mutterings eventually grew so loud that Nek Tov had to address the ship during the evening meal time, chastising the sailors who'd claimed to have caught glimpses of this ghost-cat for allowing their imaginations to run riot. Luckily, Shade decided to stay curled up in the shadows for a while after this, and the excitement over the apparition quickly subsided.

It was at night, when the galley had found a safe spot to drop anchor and most of the sailors had retired to their bunks below deck, that Deryn tried to deepen his understanding of Shade. Some things had changed over the months they'd been together – he could now feel the elemental's presence, as if whatever formerly tenuous bond connecting them was gradually strengthening. He tried to encourage Shade to communicate with him again, but the moth-wing whisper of the elemental's voice remained just a frustrating memory. Most of the time Shade's behavior was like a pet, brushing against his legs and leaping into his lap as he sat in the evenings trying to push his *ka* through his pathways. Deryn sometimes even felt a low rumbling within the elemental when Shade found a comfortable spot to rest on him, as if when he had stolen the shadow of the cat in the tavern he had also gained some other feline characteristics. He knew the elemental was intelligent, and that it could speak to him when it needed to. Why it remained so stubbornly quiet most of the time, silent about its purpose in this world and why it had chosen him, were mysteries that gnawed at Deryn. He still had that ancient diary of the Duskhold elementalist given to him by the Archivist, but no matter how many times he tried to decipher the code it was written in, it remained stubbornly impenetrable. He'd been surprised when Heth had told him he'd taken the book from Deryn's tent on the same night the flame-sharded had attacked their wedding procession, and even more surprised when he'd learned that it had been Shade – while inhabiting Deryn's drugged body – who had told him not to leave it behind. That must mean that there was something important hidden in its pages . . . but he would need to find someone to help him unravel its puzzling contents.

Unless Shade suddenly decided to speak to him again and share whatever revelations were rattling around inside his little head, although that didn't seem like it would happen anytime soon.

"A BEAUTIFUL NIGHT."

Rhenna's voice came from behind Deryn, startling him. He'd been half asleep, sitting on the deck with his back against a bulkhead looking out over the river, Shade curled up beside him. The Havilas was a great swath of darkness except for where the moon's spectral reflection shimmered on the water. The clouds that had threatened them with rain earlier had evaporated, and the endless sky arching above overflowed with stars.

"I was a rarity among the Sharded in the Duskhold because I enjoyed being outside," Rhenna said, coming to lean against the galley's railing. "My rooms were in one of the towers. I used to love standing on my balcony and breathing the fresh air after being sequestered underground all day. It always surprised me how many of the other shadow-sharded could just stay deep in the hold for days on end, even months."

"The Firemounts weren't much to look at," Deryn replied, stretching out a leg that had been in an awkward position while he'd been drowsing. "Mostly just black rocks and ugly little trees."

"The mountains had a certain stark beauty," Rhenna said, running her fingers along the age-polished wood.

Deryn pushed himself to his feet and joined her at the railing. A splashing came from somewhere in the water, and he wondered if the great turtle had briefly surfaced, or if something else was swimming down there in the dark.

"Is it here now?" Rhenna asked.

"What?"

"The elemental. That thing from the shadowrealm."

It surprised Deryn how much he disliked hearing Shade referred to as a 'thing', but he refrained himself from correcting Rhenna. "He is. He's over there, next to where I was sitting."

"Is it sleeping?"

"I doubt it. I don't think he sleeps."

Rhenna shifted, peering where Deryn had indicated. "Ah, I see it now. A little puddle of shadow shaped like a cat. It must be listening to us."

"I suppose so."

"And it understands what we are saying?"

Deryn frowned. "I . . . don't know. But I think so."

Rhenna grunted something unintelligible and turned once more to the river. "Its presence worries me, I have to admit. We have no idea what it wants."

"He saved us," Deryn pointed out, a little defensively. "If he hadn't opened that . . . that doorway to the shadowrealm, the blood-sharded would have killed us all."

Rhenna's darkened head nodded. "Yes, and I wanted to talk to you about that. I've never heard of such a thing happening before. The Others . . . I don't think anyone in the Duskhold knows they can enter this world. They've always been just these vague entities dancing at the very edges of our perception when we Shadow Walk through their realm." Rhenna shifted, and Deryn sensed something in her posture that suggested to him that she was uncomfortable discussing these creatures. "My mother was obsessed with them. She . . . she went mad. She thought they were stalking her in this world, watching her, always just out of everyone else's sight." Rhenna paused, as if reliving some memory, and when she spoke again a moment later, her voice sounded raw. "Tell me what you saw when you opened that doorway."

Deryn shrugged. "I saw the shadowrealm. You know what it looks like. But this time, those creatures were right on the other side, as if they had been waiting. And there was something else as well . . ."

His words trailed away. Perhaps he shouldn't mention what he had glimpsed beyond that portal, recessed among the flickering barbed limbs of the Others. It was impossible; it must have been a hallucination brought on by stress and exhaustion.

"What was it?" Rhenna turned towards him, and even in the dark he could feel the intensity of her attention.

"I thought it was a face. A human face."

Rhenna was very still now. "What did it look like?"

"I don't know, everything happened too fast. I thought I saw pale skin, silvery hair . . ."

Rhenna's hand shot out and grabbed Deryn's arm and he couldn't hold back a little whimper of pain. Her grip was crushingly strong. "Silver hair? You're sure?"

"I . . . I don't know," he replied, trying to ignore the pain. Rhenna seemed to realize what she was doing and she let go of him. "It might have been gray or white. As I said, it was there and then it was gone."

"Man or woman?"

"If it was a man, he had long hair. Like your father."

Rhenna was silent. Her hands had gone back to the railing, and Deryn could actually hear the creak of the wood as she tightened her hold. If she squeezed much harder, the balustrade might buckle and burst, and *that* would be difficult to explain. The galley's crew would probably guess what they were if that happened, and Nek Tov had implied that he would strongly prefer if their true natures remained hidden.

Suddenly, Rhenna stepped back from the railing. From the violence of her movements, it almost seemed to Deryn like she was angry about something. "Tell me if the elemental does anything unusual," she said sharply, and then strode away back in the direction of her cabin, the crack of her boots striking the deck's wood jarringly out of place in the night's stillness.

THREE DAYS later they reached Ter Vhalin, which was crouched at the confluence of the Belt and the Havilas. It was a somber city of dark green stone, the only splash of color the bright red dome and sunrise-orange minarets of a temple to the Broken God. Deryn's mother had been an adherent to that faith, and when he was younger, she had regularly brought him inside the temple at Kething's Cross to light votive candles and pray for the aid of the divine. He had never quite understood the reason behind this worship, because even the Awakened priests of the Broken God readily admitted that their lord had perished long ago . . . though his mother had held fast to the belief that one day He would be resurrected to rule over the world once more. Whether the Broken God would care or even be aware that His followers had prayed and sacrificed and burned incense in His name during His long absence, Deryn wasn't sure. And since none of his mother's efforts on the Broken God's behalf had done the slightest to alleviate their suffering in the here and now, he had absolutely no desire to ever stand beneath one of those soaring red domes ever again.

And he did not have the opportunity this time, as the galley only moored overnight along Ter Vhalin's massive greenstone docks and then the next morning followed the curve of the Havilas until it joined with the Belt. The difference between the two rivers was immediately apparent. The Belt was much wider and more placid, lacking the snowmelt that came sweeping down from the Fangs to swell the Havilas with cold, fast-rushing water. Despite its greater width it seemed more crowded, as a variety of ships always seemed to be visible: square-sailed carracks with hulls of black wood, oared river galleys, sleek ocean-going ships with upswept prows, and a menagerie of smaller fishing and trading vessels. The Belt was the world's road, linking Karath and the islands of the Sea of Salvation with Ashasai on the shores of Lake Gavras, the largest and richest city since Gendurdrang had fallen a thousand years ago.

"That's quite the sword."

Deryn blinked, surfacing from his thoughts. He'd been resting where the galley's bowsprit joined with the hull, his wind-sharded blade across his knees. Heth had been guiding him through some of the more advanced forms, but he'd gone back to their cabin after the sun had dipped below the water and it had become too dark to train safely.

Deryn glanced up to find the young sailor they'd met on the docks standing over him, and there was just enough light shed by the hanging lanterns to see that he was smiling.

"Ah, that it is," Deryn said, climbing to his feet stiffly. Heth had insisted he hold a rather uncomfortable pose for an unreasonable amount of time – even for one of the Sharded Few – and if the ache Deryn felt right now was any indication, tomorrow morning would be terrible.

"Cal Canna," the sailor said, sticking out his hand. Deryn grasped it, careful not to squeeze too hard.

"I know. We met on the docks."

The young man's face brightened. "Oh! I introduced myself already? I'd completely forgotten."

"Not surprising, I suppose," Deryn said, brushing back his sweaty hair. He'd have to find a barber soon after they finally arrived in Karath, or start wearing his hair tied in a topknot, as having it flop over his eyes during a fight could be disastrous.

The sailor did not look the least bit embarrassed to be reminded of the condition he'd been in on the morning of their departure from Ter Drummond. Instead, he crouched lower to peer more closely at Deryn's sword. "What a beauty," he said, then whistled. "Haven't seen one like it for quite a while."

That made Deryn's head jerk up in surprise. "You've seen a sword like this before?"

"Indeed I have, indeed I have," murmured Cal Canna, displaying a fair bit of brazenness by running his finger down the length of the white-metal blade.

"Where?" Deryn asked in bewilderment. No one in the Duskhold – including the ancient teacher of the adepts, Saelus, and the Archivist in the library – had known the substance the wind-sharded sword had been fashioned from.

"In the Erudinium," Cal Canna said, straightening again and looking him in the eye.

That name resonated in Deryn's memory. The physicker who had cared for him after his bout with Pand En'ok atop the drum tower had claimed to have been trained there. "That's in Karath?"

"Yes," Cal Canna said, climbing with enviable agility a little ways up the bowsprit before finding a seat, his legs straddling the wooden beam. "Though I suppose it wasn't in the Erudinium proper – only the scholars and their guests can go inside. But there's a museum right beside it that's open to the public on certain days." He jerked his chin in the direction of Deryn's sword. "Quite a few things made of palesteel there."

"Palesteel," Deryn said slowly, as if trying out the word for the first time.

Cal Canna's eyebrows lifted. "You didn't know that's what it's called?"

"I didn't. I found this sword in a very old place, and no one knew anything about it."

"Ah, well, it's palesteel," Cal Canna said confidently, lying back on the bowsprit and putting his hands behind his head. "I've always liked learning about what happened long ago. In Ter Drummond I'd been out all night buying drinks for old folks to hear their stories about the Ifashan Jihad—"

"Wait," Deryn said, interrupting the sailor before he could wander too far down this path. "Palesteel. What is it?"

Splashing came from the darkened river below them, and Cal Canna turned his head to look for the source of the sound. "The First Empire forged their greatest weapons from it," the sailor said, clearly distracted. "It was said the Emperor ... the Emperor ... I'm sorry, can you hear that?"

Deryn frowned. He could – it was a scrabbling, like something scraping against wood. Many things. And it was getting louder. As if . . . as if a horde of sharp-clawed creatures were climbing up the outside of the hull—

"Ah!" Cal Canna screamed as a tide of scales and spines welled up from below, surging over the boat's railing and onto the deck.

7

HETH

Heth groaned, rolling onto his side on the floor of the cabin and covering his head with the tangled ball of rags he was using as a pillow. He'd almost been fully asleep, and then whatever commotion was going on outside had dragged him back awake. There were raised voices, shouting . . . what was it? Some kind of celebration? Or an argument among the crew?

"Can you hear that?" Alia murmured groggily atop the wide bunk she shared with Rhenna. "It sounds like a fight."

"It sounds like foolishness," Rhenna snapped, her annoyance obvious. "If I have to go out there—"

The door banged open, crashing against the wall. Heth sat bolt upright and saw a shadow framed in the entranceway brandishing a pale white blade.

"Get up!" Deryn cried, grabbing Heth's sword from where it had been leaning up against the wall and tossing it to him. "We're under attack!"

Rhenna was the first to her feet, throwing back the blanket and leaping from the bunk. "Who?" she asked, pulling on the split-skirt and blouse she'd been wearing the day before. Heth averted his eyes at the brief sight of her undergarments as he also scrambled to stand, then realized there were far more important things to be concerned about right now.

"Zemani," Deryn said grimly, stepping out into the corridor again and glancing back the way he'd come. In the muted light of the hanging ship's lantern, Heth saw that half his face was spattered with black blood.

"Zemani?" Heth repeated incredulously as he joined Deryn outside the cabin. The door at the end of the passageway was half-off its hinges, and things moved in the darkness beyond. Lizard men were attacking the galley? But that was impossible. Zemani dwelled far to the south, deep in the great jungle called the Tangle. They never ventured farther north than the trading outposts that had been established at the very edge of their vast queendom. His father had purchased a pair of eggs from one of these places, warrior-caste eggs that had hatched into his intensely loyal bodyguards, k'Tel and k'Pan. Heth had always been more than a little frightened of their wickedly hooked talons perfect for eviscerating prey and their dead black eyes that only seemed to spark with life when inflicting pain.

"We have to stop them from damaging the boat," Rhenna said, pushing past as she strode towards the broken hatch. "Unless you want to swim the rest of the way to Karath."

Heth followed her out onto the deck, then skidded to a halt, hissing in surprise. Shapes with scales so black they seemed to merge seamlessly with the night were everywhere, flowing up from over the sides of the galley. There were a few flickering lanterns that had not yet been smashed, and in their puddles of wan radiance Heth could see that these were indeed zemani, though they seemed more . . . primitive than the ones his father had retained. K'Tel and k'Pan had dressed in loincloths and tasseled vests and had carried swords at their sides like human warriors . . . but from what Heth glimpsed in those stuttering moments when the lizard men entered the light, he saw necklaces of yellowing talons and that nothing covered their scales except jagged daubs of red paint. They did not wield steel or iron, but instead slashed at cowering sailors with their claws.

Rhenna hesitated for a heartbeat, as if coming to grips with the chaos that had consumed the galley, and then she lunged towards where a knot of zemani had backed an oar-brandishing sailor up against a railing. She arrived like an avalanche, striking one lizard so hard that it went flying overboard with a shriek, then backhanded another with enough force that its head turned all the way around. The last zemani lunged at her with claws flashing, but she caught its wrists and then slammed its body down on her upraised knee, its chest caving under the blow. She let the corpse slide to the deck before she turned back towards where Deryn and Heth were watching her in stunned disbelief.

"Save them, you idiots!" she shouted, and then she was gone, vanishing into the dark to find more enemies.

Deryn and Heth shared a glance, then dashed in opposite directions.

Heth didn't get far, as he stumbled over something in the dark and went sprawling on the deck. While scrambling to stand again his hands found soft flesh, sticky with blood. Had he known this sailor? Who was it? Then something slammed into his side, claws scrabbling at his Sharded skin. If he had still been just a man, great gouges would have been carved into his flesh, blood would have poured forth, his insides might even have spilled out . . . but this just felt like a cat had scratched him. He doubted if his skin had even been broken. Heth put all his strength behind his sword-arm and swung at the shadow that had ambushed him. The steel of his family sword passed through scales and bone with barely a hitch, and the zemani toppled into two pieces, a flood of cold blood or ichor or whatever filled these things cascading down to soak his feet.

Silver Shrike.

"Come on then, you scaly bastards," Heth muttered to himself, grinning as he turned to where the sailors he'd been rushing to save had been a moment ago.

But they were gone. Something else loomed there now, a massive, hunched shape. It looked like it might be a zemani, but it was far too large, almost twice his own height. Heth gritted his teeth in frustration. This flailing around in the dark was maddening – how could he find the sailors or fight these creatures when all he could see were shadows moving in the blackness? If only those few night-lanterns scattered about the ship shed more illumination . . . without even thinking about it, Heth reached out to where they hung and commanded them to brighten.

Light flooded the deck.

Shrieks and hisses erupted from the horde of zemani swarming the galley. There were more than Heth had feared, dozens of them crouched over splayed corpses or perched on the railing or clambering up the masts. But they had all frozen, shielding their eyes and cowering before this sudden blinding radiance.

All except the huge zemani in front of Heth. That lizard man had been intent on ripping the flesh from an arm he'd pulled from one of the bodies at his feet, but as the light washed over the deck he turned towards Heth as if he knew he was responsible for what had just happened.

"Greetings," Heth said, raising his blade. His pulse was pounding at the sight of this monster, but the strength flowing from the shard in his chest was intoxicating. This zemani gleamed in the light like it had been carved from obsidian; it was not only much larger than its brethren but also more thickset, muscles bulging under its scales. Hung on a cord around its neck was the skull of some three-eyed creature Heth had never seen before, glittering green jewels set into the empty sockets. The crest of curving spines rising from its back shivered as the zemani lifted gore-streaked arms and roared a challenge at him.

Heth loosed his own primal scream, surging forward. He slashed with his blade, expecting to feel scales part under the steel.

His family's ancestral sword shattered.

Heth gasped as the glittering fragments spun away. Then a blow struck him on the side of his head and it was like someone had hit him with a hammer. He collapsed to his knees, blood pouring down his face, burning lines carved into his flesh . . . his vision had gone partially dark, like one of his eyes had been torn from his head. Heth struggled weakly as he felt himself being lifted, piercingly sharp claws curling into his stomach and shoulder, and for a moment he was certain he was going to be ripped in half.

Then he was tumbling through the air, limbs flailing, until he struck the river and a cold darkness rushed up to swallow him.

8

DERYN

Brilliance consumed Deryn's darkvision, and he reeled back from the zemani he'd been keeping at bay with wide sweeps of his sword. The sailors crouched behind him moaned in surprise and fear at the unexpected radiance, while Deryn hastily reinforced his Ghost Chitin with more *ka* from his reserves. He had been fully expecting a flood of lizard men to wash over him while he could not see, but no claws scraped against his invisible armor, and when he managed to blink away the worst of the whiteness he found that many of the zemani had found the light even more debilitating – some were slashing at nothing, clearly blinded, while others had curled up on the wood and were making raspy crooning noises. The few that had already recovered were glancing around in bewilderment, as if trying to understand what had just happened.

It had been the lanterns that were hung around the galley at night so that other ships on the river could see them. They had all flared brightly, as if a half-dozen small suns had suddenly risen at once, scouring the shadows from the deck and turning the river into a sheet of beaten gold.

It must have been Heth. It seemed like he had finally broken through whatever barrier was keeping him from beckoning the light.

And all it had taken was to be plunged into near-total darkness while surrounded by a host of ravenous lizard men.

Deryn turned, briefly ignoring the zemani around him to figure out what was happening elsewhere on the deck. Rhenna he couldn't see, but he quickly found Heth, who was confronting an absolutely enormous lizard man sheathed in ebony scales. If he hadn't now been a member of the Sharded Few, Deryn would have been absolutely terrified that this monster was going to rend him limb from limb, but of course he had little to fear with—

"Broken God," Deryn whispered. It had all happened in a heartbeat – Heth's sword shattered, the zemani had struck him on the head, and instead of sliding harmlessly away the blow had smashed him into the deck.

The light abruptly vanished. Deryn's darkvision struggled to adjust, but he managed to make out the silhouette of the monstrous zemani as it lifted Heth's limp body over its head and then heaved him off the galley.

"Get below deck!" Deryn screamed at the sailors he had been protecting as he took off running. *Oh no, oh no, oh no.* Heth hadn't been moving – hopefully the blow had only knocked him unconscious, and when he hit the water he would wake up, but for all Deryn knew, Heth had never learned how to swim. Even a Sharded body would not save someone whose lungs were filled with water. Deryn reached the railing and peered down at the river, his heart in his throat – he'd been praying that ripples would indicate where Heth had struck the surface, but he couldn't see anything. The water below looked black and seamless, like it had simply opened up and swallowed Heth.

He must at that moment be sinking into the cold depths . . . Deryn was just about to toss aside his wind-sharded sword and jump into the river when he noticed something strange. The water seemed to be darkening further, as if . . . as if something massive was rising up from below.

Deryn had held only a vague sense of the turtle's size, and his breath caught in his throat when its great shell breached the surface, water streaming away from its sloping sides. And sprawled in the middle was an unmoving body.

"Heth!" Deryn cried, and then leaped from the top of the ship's railing. For a moment as his arms and legs flailed wildly he thought he might have misjudged the capabilities of his Sharded body, but then he landed hard on the very edge of the shell, the force of the impact traveling up through his bones. Deryn climbed to his feet on the slick surface, grateful that he had somehow succeeded in holding onto his sword, and staggered towards where his friend lay unmoving.

"Heth!" Deryn cried, fearing the worst as he went to his knees. For all he knew, the zemani's blow had snapped Heth's neck or he'd already swallowed too much water. In his Shadow-aided sight Heth's face was a tattered mess, streaks of deeper black that must have been blood leaking from between ragged strips of skin.

"How?" Deryn murmured bleakly, cradling Heth's head. He was dead, his face had been torn away—

Heth's chest heaved as he coughed up a large amount of liquid – whether it was blood or water, Deryn wasn't sure.

"You're alive!" He was hoping for some sort of reply, anything to suggest that the injuries weren't as bad as they looked, but only a guttural moan escaped Heth's lips. Still, he wasn't dead. Deryn wondered if he should tear a strip of cloth from his tunic to try to staunch the bleeding, or perhaps help him sit up to get the rest of the water out of—

He gasped in surprise. Something huge had lifted from the water and now loomed over them – Deryn scrabbled for his *ka*, but then his darkvision sharpened and he could suddenly discern the craggy folds of the great turtle's head and its massive eyes like pools of black water. It was staring down at them with a solemn inscrutability – Deryn couldn't imagine what it was thinking, but at the very least, it didn't seem upset. After all, it had surfaced to save Heth, hadn't it?

A chorus of croaking ululations came from the galley. Deryn turned to see the zemani streaming from the ship, scrambling down the hull or simply hurling themselves off the side to splash into the river below. He briefly thought they must be fleeing something – perhaps an enraged Rhenna – but then he realized that they were intent on reaching something else.

The turtle.

"Fire and ashes," Deryn muttered as he stood and set himself into the Mountain form. He thanked the Broken God that he hadn't tossed aside his blade before leaping from the galley, and the wind-sharded sword almost seemed to agree as it thrummed in his grip. Or perhaps it was anticipating what was coming.

The first of the swimming zemani had already reached the edge of the turtle's shell and were charging across the carapace. Deryn swung the Sharded sword, pushing a thread of his *ka* through the pale blade, and a gust of wind arose that knocked some of the lizard men over and sent a few more staggering back. Others managed to push on, but Deryn had thinned their ranks enough that he thought they couldn't simply overwhelm him with sheer numbers.

The first wave arrived, a maelstrom of claws and fangs. Deryn chopped down, cleaving an arm from its shoulder, then slashed to disembowel a pair of zemani who had been leading the vanguard. He felt his tunic being ripped to shreds, but the talons of the lizard men scraped against his skin without drawing blood. Jaws closed around his wrist, but he shook off this zemani and skewered it on his blade, cold blood soaking his sword hand. More and more of the zemani were throwing themselves at him, trying to suffocate him beneath the press of their scaly bodies. Deryn gave a guttural roar, channeling all his rage into freeing himself before he was buried, and a tangle of limbs and tails went tumbling through the air. He swayed, bracing himself for the next attack, but after the zemani had scrambled back to their clawed feet they hesitated, as if waiting for something.

And then it arrived. A huge shadow had reached the turtle and was now pulling itself up onto the shell. Deryn hissed in dismay and returned his sword to a guard position as the massive zemani that had brutally beaten Heth rose to its full towering height and roared another challenge that made Deryn's insides loosen. The smaller zemani croaked and gibbered in excitement as their black-scaled champion strode towards Deryn, who was having trouble looking away from those flensing claws, each as long as his forearm. They had cut Heth open, but maybe being three-sharded his flesh would prove strong enough to resist.

He swallowed and braced himself.

The zemani's forked tongue flickered in what might have been anticipation. Then it was charging towards him, moving so fast that Deryn gave a little cry of surprise and raised his sword in what felt like a futile gesture given the monster's size and strength . . .

A dark blur slammed into the zemani. The sound was like a crack of thunder, and the lizard man went tumbling – Deryn was sure it wouldn't be able to rise again after such a blow, but almost immediately it surged to its feet. Rhenna stood in front of Deryn in one of the defensive stances he had once learned from Jaliska back in the Duskhold, her chest heaving. Her hair fell in a wild tangle down her back, the cloth she usually used to bind it with having been torn away, and her bare forearms up to her elbows were stained black. She looked terrifying, like a spirit of bloody vengeance given form.

The black-scaled zemani did not seem intimidated. It flexed its terrible claws, the crest of spines rising from its head stiffening, and then it was charging at Rhenna . . . who, rather than waiting for it to reach her, leaped to meet it. They came together in a rending crash – Rhenna caught the first blow on her forearm, and though she staggered she did not fall, then drove her fist into the zemani's midsection with such force that it sounded like a hammer striking an anvil. The lizard man gave a surprised grunt and stumbled back a step, but quickly gathered itself and lunged again, its claws flashing so fast that Deryn could barely tell where one attack ended and another began. Rhenna blocked the first few strikes, but one slipped past her defenses and her Ghost Chitin shimmered as the zemani carved a chunk away that dissipated like the morning mist.

Deryn adjusted his grip on his sword anxiously, unsure what he should do. Even though Rhenna was far beyond him in strength, he certainly could be of *some* help if he went to her aid . . . but did he dare leave Heth's side? What if the zemani swarmed his friend while he was helpless, or the turtle decided it had had enough of what was happening and dove back under the surface? He couldn't unleash the Breath of the Mother, because Rhenna would certainly be struck by the abyssal wind, and if anything convinced the Old Shell to vanish again into the depths it would be a doorway to the shadowrealm opening on its back.

At least the lesser zemani were not joining the battle. They crouched motionless on the edge of the shell with their attention fixed completely on the fight. Deryn was tempted to slash the air with his wind-sharded sword and send a bunch of them tumbling into the river, but then decided he should carefully husband his remaining *ka* – he would need it if Rhenna was defeated.

Which – impossibly – might just happen. How a lizard man could trade blows with an eight-sharded warrior, Deryn had no idea, as she should have been able to easily rip this zemani limb from limb. But it moved just as quickly as she did, its strength appeared to be even greater, and its wickedly curving claws were dangerous even for her. She hadn't been flensed open like Heth, but through her tattered clothes Deryn could see a host of shallow cuts, and blood smeared the zemani's talons.

Rhenna leaped backwards, putting some room between herself and the monster. She had almost reached the front section of the shell, where the turtle's head was still twisted around on its long neck to regard what was happening with a calmness that bewildered Deryn. A half-dozen more Rhennas suddenly flared into existence as she summoned her Mirror Wraiths, and when the lizard man stalked closer, brandishing his claws, she hurled a volley of shadow javelins. Only one was real, and the zemani barely flinched as the length of glistening darkness sank into its shoulder.

"Get back to the ship!" Rhenna shouted at Deryn as the Mirror Wraiths set themselves in a defensive posture. "Protect Alia!"

"How can I help?" Deryn cried, strongly considering just abandoning Heth and rushing at the zemani – after all, if Rhenna fell they were assuredly doomed.

"Leave!" Rhenna snarled just before her illusions swarmed the lizard man, each one snapping off a quick combination of strikes. The zemani grunted, and Deryn thought it must be confused about which had landed the blows, but rather than taking a chance and slashing at one it whirled around, sweeping its tail in a wide circle. Six Rhennas vanished as the legs were swept out from under the original, and she landed flat on her back.

"No!" Deryn cried, lunging desperately towards Rhenna as the zemani champion loomed over her, claws upraised for a killing strike. But he was too far away, too slow. His heart sank as the lizard man shrieked in triumph.

A great shadow swelled above the zemani and then that shriek became a surprised gurgling. Deryn skidded to a halt in shock. The Old Shell pulled back its head, and for a moment it seemed like the lizard man's hand would remain stubbornly attached to its wrist, but then there was a wet tearing sound and blood was spurting from the stump at the end of the zemani's arm. The creature swayed, clutching at its mutilated limb, before taking two stumbling steps and flinging itself into the river. A splash, and the screeching abruptly ended.

Rhenna struggled to her feet – her clothes had been reduced to bloody rags, but she had a look of grim determination as she swiveled to face the remaining zemani. They stared back at her, stunned, and then as if by some unspoken agreement they turned together and leaped into the water.

In a heartbeat, only Deryn, Rhenna and Heth remained on the shell. The quiet was eerie – Deryn couldn't even hear any splashing, as if the horde of zemani had simply vanished when they struck the river's surface. Swimming away under the water as fast as they could, Deryn guessed. The turtle continued watching them for a moment more, and then it twisted its neck around and let its head sink down into the water again.

"Are you all right?" Deryn asked as Rhenna rushed over to them.

"I'm fine," she answered curtly, kneeling to better examine Heth's ravaged face.

She didn't look fine.

"We need to get him to the ship's doctor," Rhenna said as she stood. She raised her arm palm-up, and a huge hand of swirling dark-ness bore Heth into the air.

RELIEF WASHED over Deryn when they burst through the door to their cabin and found Alia huddled against the headboard of the bed. She gasped in surprise and leaped to her feet, eyes wide, as Heth's limp body entered the room floating on Rhenna's Hand of Night.

"Is he ... is he dead?" she cried, rushing to his side with a sob.

"No," Rhenna answered, compelling the hand to drift over the bunk before letting it slowly evaporate so that Heth settled down gently. "But he's hurt. The ship's healer should be here soon. Until then ..." Rhenna's words trailed away as she stared down at Heth, her lips pursed. "Until then, we have to wait. Unless one of you knows something about healing."

"My mother taught me a little," Alia said, coming closer to examine Heth. A few bloody bubbles had emerged from between his lips, but his eyes remained shut. Deryn had feared that at least one had been lost, but by Fortune's sweet mercy they both looked intact. "We need clean water to wash those slashes on his face," Alia contin-ued. "In the Wild there are many herbs that might help, but I don't know what there is on the ship."

"The doctor will bring ..." Rhenna began, but then she paused, blinking in surprise at something that had been hidden behind the door until they'd moved farther into the room. "Mother Dark," she whispered, and Deryn turned to see what had drawn her attention, half expecting to see a zemani crouched in the shadows.

His instincts proved to be right. The wall bulged strangely, a large swath of the wood having been badly warped, and it took him a moment to realize that many root-like growths had erupted from the wall to almost completely cover something – save for a single yellow eye with a dark vertical slit for an iris. It darted back and forth, clearly panicked.

Deryn couldn't blame the zemani, given its predicament.

"That thing rushed in here after you all left," Alia said. "It was hissing, and it had claws . . . I don't know what I did, but the wall came alive and swallowed it."

Rhenna approached the trapped zemani, her lip curled in distaste. "These things attacked us. We call them zemani. I've never heard of them coming this far north or ambushing travelers."

"We'll get answers, don't you worry," rumbled a new voice. Nek Tov entered their cabin trailed by a very nervous-looking Cal Canna, who was carrying a large satchel, as well as another young sailor Deryn didn't recognize. The cutlass the captain was brandishing was stained with black blood, and his tri-corner hat had gone missing, revealing a tangle of stringy gray hair. "Though I have to admit, it's tempting to shove my blade into this thing's guts right now," he added, thrusting his cutlass in the direction of the immobilized lizard man.

"Then you don't know why they attacked us," Rhenna asked as Cal Canna slipped past Nek Tov to crouch beside Heth.

"No, but they must be the reason those other Kin galleys went missing." Nek Tov ran thick fingers through his hair. "As we would have, if it wasn't for you." He motioned to the sailor standing at his side. "Go find some iron chains, heavy ones. The spare anchor, perhaps. I want this thing securely locked away somewhere dark and wet." He jerked his chin towards the door, and the sailor scurried away.

"Your gamble to bring us on board paid off," Rhenna said, turning away from the bound zemani with a final grimace. "Though it was a damn bit closer than I ever would have expected."

They all watched as Cal Canna withdrew a metal flask from his satchel and tipped a small amount of liquid between Heth's parted lips.

"Numbwine. But I can't give him too much. There are a dozen others on board who need a swallow right now."

"He'll heal faster than them," Rhenna said. "Just do everything you can."

Cal Canna nodded and returned the flask to his bag, then pulled out a wash basin, a jar of what looked like honey, a small box filled with needles, and a spool of some glistening thread. "I'm no expert at this," he admitted apologetically. "But unfortunately, Fren Kas is still missing and he's the best healer on board." He hesitated, his gaze lingering on the cuts visible beneath Rhenna's tattered clothes, before he realized what he was doing and looked away with a guilty expression. "Are you all right?" he asked her.

Rhenna grimaced. "I'm fine. Most of them are shallow."

"But it shouldn't have been able to cut you at *all*," Deryn blurted, unable to hold back the questions that had been churning inside him ever since the battle ended. "How could it hurt Heth? Or do that to you? I saw Jaliska catch a sword with her bare hand and her skin remained unbroken."

"The zemani are not animals," Rhenna replied, flexing her fingers like they were bothering her. "You should know that – Archivist Devenal always gives the adepts a long lecture about them, and for you that was only a few months ago."

"I might not have been paying very close attention," Deryn admitted, his jaw tightening as Cal Canna began to clean the blood from Heth's face, revealing the extent of his wounds. He would carry these scars for the rest of his life.

"They are one of the world's great powers," Rhenna said, picking up the cloak she'd bought in Ter Drummond from where it had been puddled on the floor and wrapping it around herself. "It is claimed that the Radiant Emperor himself signed the treaty that brokered peace between our two peoples. The Tangle and all that lay south of that great jungle would forever belong to the zemani, while to the north were the lands of men. Even with his great power, Segulah Tain did not dare challenge the Scaled Queendom."

"It seems they have broken that agreement," Nek Tov grumbled.

"This was a raid, not an invasion," Rhenna said, tapping her chin. "They wanted something."

Nek Tov slammed his cutlass back in his sheath. "Something from the Kin. Eleven of my family are dead, with a dozen more wounded so badly that they'll be lucky to reach the Haven. And I need to go see to them. Cal Canna, finish up here quickly and then get to the others."

"Aye," Cal Canna replied distractedly, focused on drawing a filament of animal gut through one of the wounds on Heth's face with a needle.

"The rest of you," Nek Tov said, pausing in the doorway, the knuckles of his hand white from gripping the hilt of his sword so tightly. "Stay wary. We don't know if those things will come again before we can get somewhere safe."

9

HETH

The cat watched him from the branches of the cherry blossom tree, a small black shadow recessed among the pink and white flowers.

"Come here," Heth said, patting the gnarled trunk to show it the path down. "Cook will be looking for you."

"Meow," acknowledged the cat.

"Then you're not getting any fish tonight."

"Meow," lamented the cat.

Heth looked at the dried blossoms he was holding. If he wanted fresh ones for his mother, he'd have to climb the tree. But his father had beaten him the last time he'd done that, even though Heth had tried to keep it a secret. Somehow he'd known from the scrapes on his palms and the dirt on his shoes – his father was very clever.

Heth lifted his fistful of desiccated flowers to his nose and breathed deep. The smell was still sweet, though during the time they'd lain here, scattered among the roots, they'd also acquired a faint bitterness. He raised his face, shielding his eyes from the sun filtering through the branches. He could quickly scale the trunk, snatch a handful of just-blooming blossoms, and try to entice the cat to come down. Cook would be happy; she'd hug him to her flour-dusted apron and promise to sneak him some almond cakes later.

"*Heth.*"

A voice drifted down, thin and quavering. He glanced up past the gate of wrought black iron to the open window with its gauzy silken drapes stirring in the breeze.

His mother. His mother was calling for him.

"*I have to go,*" *Heth said to the cat, crouching to scoop up a few more petals. His mother loved the smell of cherry blossom flowers.*

"*Goodbye,*" *replied the cat, stretching to sharpen its claws on the bark.*

Heth dashed through the gate with its imposing iron pickets and along the path of blue-glazed tiles that led to the door of their manse. It had been left cracked open, and he turned his body to slip inside; he was just about to start on the broad stairs leading to the second floor and the bedroom where his mother was resting in her great canopied bed when Barnabas emerged from deeper within the house. The old servant cleared his throat loudly and Heth paused, his foot hovering over the first step.

"*Your father wants to see you.*"

"*I have to give something to Mother.*"

"*He said you must come now.*"

Heth gazed longingly at the second-floor landing. He hoped his mother would call out his name again, and he would have an excuse to run up the stairs and into her room; he would shut the door, closing them both off from the rest of the world. She would stroke his cheek softly with her pale hand and tell Heth that she loved him.

But there was only silence.

Heth reluctantly followed the stooped old man as he turned and shuffled into the manse. Barnabas brought him to the dining room, then inclined his head towards Heth solemnly before retreating.

His father was standing at the other end of a long table, his back to Heth. A fire was crackling in front of him, and his head was tilted as he contemplated the Su Canaav family sword hanging above the hearth. He sipped from a silver goblet, then spoke without turning around.

"*Heth.*"

"*Father.*"

"*You've been playing in the trees.*"

Heth hurriedly hid the hand that held the dried blossoms behind his back. "No, I haven't."

"Don't lie to me."

"Cook's cat got up in the branches again."

"I should have that thing drowned. It steals fish from the table and has never caught a mouse in its long, miserable life."

Heth's heart leaped into his throat. "No, please don't!"

His father sighed, his head dipping lower, as if Heth's outburst had disappointed him.

Motes of something were drifting up from the flames, black and indistinct. Cinder, Heth thought briefly, before he realized with a start that the little flecks appeared to be rising from his father.

"My own father sacrificed everything to give me what I have, and I have done all I can to make your position secure. Our family was always meant to have a great destiny, and you shall be the one to fulfill it, Heth . . . if you are strong enough to seize what should be yours."

"Father?" Heth murmured nervously as he slowly crossed the room. The number of specks rising from his father had greatly increased, and was now a blizzard of dark ash falling upwards. "Are you all right?"

"I am dead," his father said as he finally turned. Heth gasped. Half of the skin on his father's face had flaked away, revealing the sharp gleam of bone and glistening red tendons. And his eyes . . . they were empty wells of darkness, but deep, deep within their depths, Heth glimpsed the flickering of blue lights. His father brought his goblet to his mouth again, and the wine spilled out through the gap where his cheek should have been.

"I am dead, but you are not."

HETH CAME AWAKE with a shuddering gasp. Eyes that had been hovering just above his face widened – the color of pale jade, not blue ice – and then drew back. Golden hair, flawless skin, high cheekbones.

"Oh!" Alia breathed, fingers fluttering to her lips. "You're awake!"

"*Mmm*," Heth grunted, then groaned when he felt the lines of fire burning from his brow down to his chin. He reached up and found cloth bandages swaddling much of his head.

"No, no, don't touch those," Alia said, gently pulling back his hand.

"It hurts," Heth moaned, trying to understand where he was and what had happened. It looked like their cabin on the galley, but he had never seen it from quite this perspective, and then he realized that for the first time he was lying on the bunk – Rhenna had told them in no uncertain terms that they would be relegated to the floor for the entirety of their voyage.

"I know, I know it does," Alia replied. "But you have to let it heal."

Heth licked dry lips. Alia saw this and disappeared for a moment from his vision, then returned with a tumbler of water. She went to help him sit, but he shook his head and struggled on his own to push himself up until his back was against the headboard. He did let her put the small cup to his lips, as just the small accomplishment of sitting had already exhausted him.

"The zemani," Heth rasped as his memories started to return. "We fought them off?"

"Yes," Alia said, ducking out of sight again to return the tumbler.

Heth closed his eyes, and in the darkness he saw the great black lizard man swelling above him again. He flinched as he remembered the feeling of its claws striking his face, the flood of hot red agony.

"Is that monster dead? The zemani who did this to me?"

"I think so," Alia said, though Heth heard the uncertainty in her voice. "I didn't see, but apparently the turtle bit off its hand and it fell into the river. After that happened, the other zemani fled."

Heth sagged back against the headboard. It was no small amount of relief to know that the creature that had done this to him had been mutilated, if not killed.

He took a deep, steadying breath. "I'm hideous now, aren't I?"

Alia shook her head. "No," she said, and he couldn't tell if she was lying or not.

"My face—"

"There are scars," she said, interrupting him. "But Cal Canna did a good job stitching you up."

"The drunk?" Heth blurted. "They trusted him with a needle and thread?"

"There wasn't anyone else who had been trained as a healer," Alia explained. "The ship's healer was killed in the attack. Cal Canna was his apprentice; he has steady hands, and he kept the cuts from getting infected."

Heth turned his head to watch the wall. He didn't want Alia to see what he was feeling, though he knew he couldn't do much to hide it right now.

"Tell me the truth."

Her reply was a moment in coming. "You're still handsome."

His mouth twisted and he chuckled grimly, which pulled on his recovering skin and brought a stab of sharper pain. "*Ow*. I'm sure."

"Maybe less handsome," Alia admitted. "But just a little."

The door to the cabin opened and Rhenna swept inside. "Alia, I need—" she began, but then her gaze fell upon Heth and her eyes widened.

"Thank the blessed Mother of Darkness," she said, and the real emotion he saw in her face surprised him. The mask she maintained was usually impenetrable . . . his father had been the same way.

Heth frowned. Why had he just thought of his father?

"How do you feel?" Rhenna asked.

"It's painful, but I think I can get out of bed."

"Stay," Rhenna said, holding up her hands to forestall him. "Rest. We have a few more days until we arrive."

Heth blinked in surprise. "A few more days? How long have I been sleeping? I thought it would be weeks before we reached Karath."

"You've been in that bed for three nights and most of a third day. But we're not going to Karath . . . at least not yet. Nek Tov is insisting we stop somewhere else first."

"A place where the Kin congregate," Alia said when she saw his look of confusion. "He thinks the zemani who attacked us have been preying on his people. He wants to warn them . . . and see if he can get any answers as to why this happened."

Heth nodded, suddenly feeling a great weight pressing down on him. He was almost ready to allow his exhaustion to carry him away, but then something occurred to him and he struggled to sit up straighter once more. "Deryn! Is he all right?"

"He's fine," Rhenna assured him. "He has stayed by your side almost as much as Alia, but right now he's on deck practicing with his sword."

Heth settled back down again, relieved. "Good. He needs to practice; his footwork is still terrible."

Rhenna quirked a smile. "I'll let him know you're awake. He'll want to see you. And I'll have some food brought here; no doubt you're starving."

Heth suddenly realized how hungry he was, and the thought of eating something pushed back his tiredness. "Silver Shrike, please do that. I could eat an entire ox."

Alia blanched, and Heth had to fight to hold back a chuckle and the spike of pain that would have certainly accompanied it.

TWO DAYS LATER, Heth dragged himself from the bed despite Cal Canna and Alia imploring him to rest and limped his way out onto the deck. The galley had left the Belt some time ago, entering one of the tributaries that fed into that great, ponderous river as it made its long and meandering way to the Sea of Salvation. A marshy mire stretched into the distance on both sides of this new waterway; Heth hesitated to even call what they were on a river, as it was more like a huge, fractured wetland, hummocks of mud and reeds rising around them. There was little current here, and the sailors that remained healthy enough to pull the oars were laboring hard to keep *The Morning Dream* moving in the silty waters. It was much more shallow, and he could see ripples in the murky water where the Old Shell was keeping pace with the galley.

"Enjoying the fresh air?" Deryn's tone was jovial as he joined him at the railing, but Heth heard his concern.

"I was hoping it would be a bit fresher," Heth replied, wrinkling his nose. "Smells like rotten eggs. Still, it's better than the cabin. Cal Canna keeps slathering all these unguents and oils over my face and the air gets so thick with their reek that I can barely breathe. I feel like a courtesan from Ashasai perfuming herself to try to hide the Rot."

"Well, don't worry, you're not going to be mistaken for an Ashasai courtesan anytime soon."

Heth turned from the gray and brown murk hemming the river to stare at Deryn in surprise. Had he just made a jest? What was going on?

"I'm sorry, I shouldn't make light of things," Deryn said apologetically, ducking his head.

Heth snorted and clapped him on the shoulder. "Better than wallowing in misery," he admitted, and he meant it. The long days abed had forced him to confront the reality of his situation, and at first he'd been angry at the world for his disfigurement, but slowly he'd come to terms with what had happened. Yes, he was scarred, but many warriors boasted scars. And when Cal Canna had changed his bandages he'd looked into Alia's eyes and he hadn't seen disgust or pity. He'd seen concern, compassion . . . and maybe something else. He hoped something else.

"Where are we going? Rhenna said there's some sort of Kin village hidden out here in the marshes?"

Deryn nodded. "Nek Tov told us more about it last night. The existence of this place is one of his people's most well-guarded secrets, but after what happened on the Belt, I think we're trusted as much as anyone who hasn't been born on their boats. This village . . . they call it the Haven. It's an ancestral sanctuary for the Kin, a place to rest between trading seasons, and where the elders stay and help raise their children. It's also where they retreat in times of crises . . . which Nek Tov believes is right now. He's certain the zemani are hunting the Kin."

Heth frowned. "I thought of something while I was lying there with far too much time to think." He glanced around quickly to make sure none of the sailors were within earshot, then leaned in a little closer to Deryn. "Do you think those lizards might have been hunting *us*?"

Deryn pursed his lips as he considered this, then shook his head emphatically. "No. If those things had come up from the Tangle, they must have been traveling for quite some time. We might have still been at the Duskhold when they set out. There's no way they could have known we'd be on the Belt."

Heth ran his hands along the balustrade. "Unless they were already in the Middle Lands and were just waiting to be told where to go."

"You're getting paranoid. No one knows we are here. The ones who were after us – Cael Shen, the Ember, the Unbound King . . . they most likely think we died in the Frayed Lands."

Heth grunted. It seemed like wishful thinking to believe that the great powers hunting them lacked the resources to discover where they had fled . . . but it was also true that if any location was hidden from them, it would be this desolate place. He swept his gaze over the sprawling swamp – it was clearly not a land that saw many visitors.

Heth's attention was drawn to a sudden disturbance in the river. The peak of the great turtle's curving shell broke the water, and then its head lifted above the surface. Its long neck was straining forward as its speed quickened, and it had begun to pull ahead of the galley, causing the dark water to churn and froth.

"Something has gotten it excited," Deryn said, squinting into the day's brightness.

"I think we're almost there," Heth replied. Thin threads of smoke were rising from the wetlands ahead of them, and the waterway they were traveling on appeared to soon open up into a larger body.

A cheer went up from the sailors on deck as they passed into this lake. There were a few small islands scattered about covered in dense copses of mangroves, grasping roots fringing their shores, but clearly none of these were their destination because near the very center of this calm expanse was a fleet of river galleys. They were clustered together so tightly it almost looked like one could step between decks, and he frowned, confused by the decision to bunch together like this when the lake was more than large enough to spread out comfortably.

Realization dawned as they neared the boats. The vast majority of the galleys here were older and no longer river-worthy and had been lashed together to create something like a floating town. Wooden structures with doors and windows and bright strips of cloth fluttering from their roofs covered much of the decks, which were connected to their neighboring boats by arching bridges. Heth saw that soil had been laid down on some of the decks, sliced by neat rows of plants, along with trellises covered with twining vines speckled with fruit. As their galley drew closer, old men and women who had been working in these makeshift fields doffed broad hats of woven rushes and waved in greeting. A bell started to clang from deeper within this floating town, and soon a horde of children in mud-brown frocks boiled up from within the boats and rushed to the railings, shrieking and jumping in excitement. Heth noticed that quite a few sailors on *The Morning Dream* had stopped what they were doing to return the greetings.

Not all the galleys Heth could see had been converted into homes and farms – at least a dozen boats at the edges appeared not to be linked by bridges to the rest of the Haven and had sails on their masts. These must be the Kin galleys that still plied the Belt and the other rivers veining the Middle Lands. Heth realized that there must be quite a few Old Shells hunkered in the mud at the bottom of this lake right now, and he couldn't help but find that a little unsettling. A single huge turtle swimming in a river so wide you could barely see the shore was one thing, but the thought of many lurking just below them and watching the shadows of their hull pass above made him nervous.

They'd drifted close enough to the Haven that the rowers had stored their oars, a crowd having gathered to greet them. Several sailors had joined Heth and Deryn along the railing with long wooden poles, and they used these to keep the *Dream* from bumping too hard against the other hulls. Ropes were thrown, and another cheer went up when their galley was finally bound again to the Kin's floating town.

A plank was laid to bridge the gap, and the first to cross over from the Haven was an old man in a faded red-tasseled jacket that looked similar to the one worn by Nek Tov. He also wore a tri-cornered cap, though his sported a shimmering iridescent feather. He bounded across the plank with surprising agility for his age, then put his hands on his hips as Nek Tov clattered down the aft deck stairs. When his gaze passed over Heth, the old man's brow drew down in confusion.

"Nek Tov, you old pirate!" he cried, returning his attention to the *Dream*'s captain. "They haven't strung you up yet?"

"Still breathing, Vanac Hul. And you can be sure I'll be doing that long after your stubborn old spirit finally departs."

Nek Tov crossed to the Kin elder and clasped his hand in the same style that he had greeted Rhenna in Ter Drummond. "Good to be back," he said, then leaned in closer to confer more privately. Heth, with his Sharded senses, just managed to pick up what they were saying. "We have news," Nek Tov murmured.

"Why are there so many faces missing?" Vanac asked, also lowering his voice.

"We were attacked. Ambushed on the Belt. Lost many, and more are below wounded."

Vanac Hul's jaw tightened. "Who were they?" he hissed. "Three galleys have vanished without a trace. Everyone else got word to return here and did so – *The Morning Dream* is the last. You must have been far up the Havilas."

Nek Tov touched something on his chest, and for the first time Heth noticed that a long, curving claw dangled on a cord around his neck. "Zemani."

Surprise shivered the Kin elder's face. He clearly hadn't been expecting that answer. Then he shook his head and stepped back from Nek Tov, and his next words were proclaimed loudly for everyone watching. "Welcome brothers and sisters on your return to the Haven. Eat, drink, and make merry, for one day we will all lie in the mud!"

"But not today!" came the shouted response from the Kin, and then the sailors on the *Dream* began to surge across the plank.

Ignoring the swirling chaos of the reunion, Nek Tov took the arm of Vanac Hul and guided him over to Heth and Deryn.

"What are you doing bringing Soiled to our Haven?" the elder asked, frowning as he looked them up and down. One of his eyes was a milky white, and two fingers on his left hand ended in nubs of mottled flesh.

"They're the only reason we made it back here," Nek Tov answered gruffly. He inclined his head towards where Rhenna and Alia had just emerged onto the deck. "The raven-haired girl is a powerful Sharded."

This revelation seemed to agitate the old Kin even more, but after a moment, he schooled his face and sighed. "Aye, well, I know you wouldn't bring them here if you didn't trust them. Mistress," he murmured respectfully, lowering his head as Rhenna and Alia joined them. "Welcome to our Haven. I'm Vanac Hul. Thank you for the aid you rendered my Kin."

Nek Tov winced as a wailing carried to them from the mingling crowd, and then he sighed deeply like it was something he'd been expecting but dreading to hear. The joy of their return had given way to grief. Some of the children clutched at legs with stricken expressions, and a few of the older folk had collapsed into arms.

"I'm sorry we could not save everyone," Rhenna said. She looked like she was about to say more, but a commotion elsewhere on the galley interrupted her. Heth turned to see what was happening and a cold fist closed around his heart – the zemani Alia had captured had been dragged on deck by three sailors. They were straining at the end of the thick black chains wrapping the lizard man, faces red from exertion. It thrashed and snapped at them, claws gouging the wood – Heth hated himself for fearing this creature when it posed no threat to him now, but it was difficult to forget the feeling of talons tearing into his face.

Vanac Hul was staring at the zemani in open-mouthed surprise, as if he had not truly believed what Nek Tov had claimed until now.

"What will you do with that thing?" asked Heth, half-hoping they would just throw it over the side of the galley.

Nek Tov smiled pitilessly, eyes hard. "We're going to make it talk."

10

DERYN

"Mother's mud, I never thought I'd live to see the day when a bunch of *Soiled grassgrubbers* are allowed to be on the council!"

"They're not *on* the council," said the thin, gray-haired woman at the head of the table tiredly. "The Sharded are observing, as our guests. Now sit down."

The massive man with the waxed red mustache ignored her request, pointing a finger as thick as a sausage at Deryn. "It's been decades since anyone but the Kin has set foot in the Haven. And now we bring these outsiders here? What's stopping them from leading others to our home?"

Deryn shifted uncomfortably as the attention of everyone in the room focused on him. He glanced at Rhenna, unsure what he should do. Like him, she was seated on a stool at the council chamber's periphery. Alia and Heth were not here – Heth was with the best healers in the Haven to see if they could do anything more about his wounds, and Alia had wanted to explore this strange floating village before night fell.

The meeting room had once been the main berth of a galley, but the hammocks and posts where the sailors had slept had been removed to make way for a long table of red wood. A detailed carving of a river ran its length, complete with fish and snakes and – of course – enormous turtles frolicking among reeds and rushes. Fourteen men and women sat around this table, all past their middle years, all wearing the red-tasseled jackets that Deryn had come to learn signified their position as the captain of a river galley.

Rhenna looked like she was about to respond to this accusation, but before she could speak, Nek Tov rose from his chair. He was seated directly opposite the huge fellow who had challenged their presence here, and now he leaned forward with his hands on the carven table until his face was only a hand-span away from the man's glistening red mustache.

"We owe them, Berl Tac. Me and my people would be feeding the crabs if they hadn't driven off those lizards. And they don't get a vote about what happens here, so settle yourself down. It's also true we need answers, and the Sharded remember things the rest of the world has forgotten. The dark-haired girl told me she learned about the zemani in her hold. Might be she can give us some insights as to why they're preying on the Kin."

The red-faced man scowled and grumbled something unintelligible, but he sat back down, his chair groaning alarmingly. Nek Tov stayed standing for a moment longer, his gaze traveling up and down the length of the table, as if daring anyone else to challenge their presence. Then he also returned to his seat.

"Well, if that's all finished," the old woman said, picking up what looked to be a smooth, dark river-stone, "then I commence this council." She rapped the stone hard against the table twice. "Been nearly ten years since every boat was represented around this table."

"Not everyone's here," pointed out a sallow-faced man with a scar, nodding towards three empty chairs clustered at the far end of the table. "We don't know for certain what happened."

"The zemani got 'em," said a woman, her finger tracing the shell of one of the turtles engraved into the table. "Much as you don't want to believe it, Fen Pa. I know your sister was on Graj Mar's galley, and

I'm sorry. We have to consider all the Kin who were on those boats to be lost."

"But why?" bellowed the man with the red mustache, pounding his fist on the table. "What do those lizards *want*?" Raised voices erupted around the table, as if this unexpected outburst had swept away the dam keeping the emotions in the room restrained. Deryn glanced at Rhenna – such a chaotic display must surely grate on someone who had been raised in the somber decorum of the Duskhold, but she was just watching the scene unfold with pursed lips.

Movement in the corridor outside the council room drew Deryn's eye. An ancient bent-backed crone hovered in the doorway, leaning on a walking stick. The gray-haired woman at the table's head also noticed and motioned for her to enter, then rapped the table loudly again with the stone.

"You all know who this is?" she said into the silence that immediately descended.

Nods traveled around the table as the old woman shuffled into the council room, and a few of the Kin even looked embarrassed, as if they'd been caught misbehaving.

"Gram Neska," Nek Tov said, and Deryn could hear his respect. "What brings you to the council this evening?" One of the Kin closest to the old woman leaped from his chair and offered it to her, but she waved him away.

"Best if I stand, or I might not get up again," she said, her voice surprisingly strong. "Though thank you, Den Ras – you were always a sweet boy." Her gaze swept the room, pausing briefly on Deryn and Rhenna. "And to answer your question, Nek Tov – I came from the brig, where I just had a chat with our prisoner."

Surprised glances passed between the captains. "Pardon, Gram Neska," another of the Kin ventured, "but you're saying you can speak with the lizard?"

"I can and I did," the old woman answered primly, folding her hands over the top of her cane.

"But . . . how is that possible?" Nek Tov asked as mutterings started.

Another rap of the river-stone quieted the room. "Gram Neska was a member of the Great Expedition," the gray-haired matron explained. "I trust you all have heard of that, at least?"

"I have not," Rhenna interjected, causing most of the heads in the council room to turn towards her. "And I am curious. In the Duskhold, it is believed to be impossible for us to be understood by the zemani. Our physiology is just too different."

"Not impossible," the old woman said, clearing her throat. Then she cleared it again, more gratingly this time, before finishing with a sound that was something between a hiccup and a belch.

Deryn blinked in surprise when he realized she was apparently speaking the zemani tongue.

"Though I'm a bit rusty, it's true. After all, it's been about seventy years since I spoke it last."

"On the Great Expedition," Rhenna said, as if seeking confirmation that she understood correctly.

"Aye," the old woman said, and from her expression it seemed like she was viewing what had happened in the past again. "We went south, thirty of us led by that old rascal Hep Canna. It was his mad idea. I was the youngest, only sixteen, but I was known to have a way with languages. They've always just stuck in here, like boats on a mudflat at low tide." She lifted one hand from the top of her cane and tapped the side of her head. "The last male Old Shell had died the summer before. Our stories claimed we'd brought the great turtles out of the Tangle long ago, before even the days of the Radiant Emperor, when the gods still strode the land and immortals lived among us, and so we gathered supplies and went on a quest to bring back a mate for our lonely ladies." Rhenna was leaning forward on her stool, clearly interested in this tale. "There were trading towns on the fringes of the great jungle, for the zemani queen had a fondness for jewels and had also somehow acquired a taste for the great tree crabs of the northern forests. She bartered for these with eggs and artifacts scavenged from the ruins deep in her domain. We stayed in one of those towns for three months while I and another boy studied the lizard tongue. Then we went into the jungle."

"And did you find what you were looking for?" someone asked.

The old woman smiled sadly, shaking her head. "Half a year we explored the jungle. Hep Canna died after being bitten by a spider the size of a dog, and in the end, only seven of us emerged from the eternal twilight beneath those great trees. After all that, we had learned beyond a shadow of a doubt that there were no more Old Shells in the Tangle. They had died long ago. The last great turtles that would ever swim in the rivers of this world were right here, with the Kin."

Deryn sat back, surprised by the sadness he felt at hearing this.

"All right, so you can speak the tongue," said Nek Tov. "What did the lizard say, Gram Neska? Why are my people dead?"

The old woman turned her watery gaze to the captain of *The Morning Dream*. "They weren't trying to kill the Kin. Our folk were just in the way. Nor did they want our boat, or what you had in the holds."

"The turtle," Deryn said as realization struck, suddenly remembering how the zemani had hurled themselves from the galley and swarmed the Old Shell as soon as it had surfaced.

"The turtle's shell," corrected Gram Neska.

Berl Tac stroked his impressive mustache, his craggy face crinkling further. "The shell? Mother's mud, why would they want *that*?"

A far-away look entered the old woman's eyes, and when next she spoke, she sounded almost regretful. "A year in the Tangle and we never discovered what had happened to the Old Shells, why they had died out in the rivers where they'd first spawned. And now I've learned, seventy years too late." She shook her head sadly. "Hap Canna would have wanted to know, may the river soothe his soul."

"Do they eat the turtles?" asked the gray-haired woman at the table's head.

"No, they only want the shell," Gram Neska answered with a shake of her head. "If I understand our prisoner correctly . . . and if he isn't lying to me, the shells have some . . . religious meaning for them. The queen flaunts the shells to show that she is favored by the gods."

Nek Tov grunted. "If she already has some of these shells, why does she need to send her warriors up here to get more?"

"Because the queen that sent the raiding party that attacked your boat – and I'm sure those other boats that weren't so lucky to be carrying Sharded – doesn't have any shells. And it's apparently a sore spot for her."

"There's more than one queen?" blurted Rhenna, the shadows around her squirming. Only the gray-haired woman at the table's head noticed the darkness trembling, and though her eyes widened slightly, she said nothing. "We were taught in the Duskhold that there was only ever one."

"And this is what I always believed as well," Gram Neska said. "But this warrior-caste lizard claims that another queen has risen. His queen. The true queen, even though she sounds more like an upstart to me. There is a war raging in the Tangle between these two Scaled Queendoms, but the younger did not possess any shells before sending her warriors north. And she wanted some."

A heavy silence followed that pronouncement as everyone in the council chamber considered this. If the zemani queen desired the shells of the great turtles, and the last of those creatures lived along-side the Kin . . . then their very way of life was in peril.

"Why did the lizard tell you these things?" a small woman with dark hair asked.

Gram Neska sighed. "Because it considers us little more than animals. It does not care what we know, for in its mind we could never oppose its queen. I offered it meat in exchange for answers, and it took this bargain willingly."

"What if it was lying?" suggested another captain.

The old woman shook her head. "I don't think a warrior-caste zemani can even conceive of lying. Their purpose is only to fight and die, nothing else."

"Then the Old Shells must remain here," Nek Tov said slowly, his tone indicating his unhappiness with this idea. "They won't like it. I know Old Bassa gets mighty sick of this little pond very quickly."

"They can't stay at the Haven forever," said a captain who looked to be the youngest here, with only a few gray threads in her plaited braids.

The older woman tapped the river stone on the table thoughtfully. "And they won't. Just until this . . . infighting among the zemani concludes. Either the young queen's rebellion will be crushed, or the old queen will be overthrown."

Berl Tac snorted. "Is that a month? A year? A century? How long do zemani civil wars last?"

"We wait until it is safe for the Old Shells to swim the Belt again," the gray-haired woman said in a voice that brooked no disagreement. "They are far too precious to risk."

Muttered agreement rippled around the table. And it might have been Deryn's imagination, but he thought there seemed to be a general lightening in the mood. Perhaps the knowledge of *why* they were being hunted had brought some relief, even if the reason was horrifying.

"I have a question," Rhenna said loudly, quieting the room again. "The zemani that attacked our boat were led by one that was much larger and stronger – so strong, in fact, that its claws tore the flesh of a Sharded and very nearly defeated me. In my hold, the scholars told us of the *thul'ktan*, warriors that in the ancient stories were said to even be able to challenge the Sharded Few. We thought them to be only legend. but that creature must have been one. Do you know anything about this, Gram Neska?"

"I might," she replied after a moment of thought. "Our Great Expedition met with a delegation from the Scaled Queendom, and I remember one zemani being far more impressive than the rest. They called him something, perhaps it was *thul'ktan*, and when I asked what it meant I was told it translated roughly to 'prince-consort', and that he was hatched from the same royal clutch that gives birth to the queens."

The gray-haired woman at the table's head frowned. "If such

zemani are hunting the Old Shells – monsters that can stand against the Sharded Few – then we cannot even consider allowing the turtles to leave the Haven until we are certain it is safe." She looked around at the others. "And so are we all in agreement on that? If you must keep trading, fine. I know many of you have obligations. But don't take your turtles with you – let them stay hidden here." No one raised an objection to this, so the woman lifted the river-stone again and then brought it down with a sharp crack. The sound must have formally ended the council, as almost immediately most of the Kin captains stood up from the table. A few went to confer with Gram Neska and the woman with the river stone, while Nek Tov made his way over to where Rhenna and Deryn were seated.

"You heard her," he said, jerking his head in the direction of the Kin leader. "We can still take you to Karath, just without Old Bassa. It'll be strange being on the river, but knowing she's safe here will bring some comfort. And I don't think those lizards will bother us again if she's not swimming with us."

"How long until we can leave?" Rhenna asked, standing and smoothing down the skirt one of the Kin had given her to replace the clothes that had been shredded during the battle.

"Give us a few days to rest and mourn," Nek Tov said. "Lots of folk have lost friends and family."

"Of course," Rhenna said. She looked past Nek Tov to where a knot of Kin surrounded Gram Neska. "I'd like to go speak with your elder. I've never heard of anyone venturing deep into the Tangle."

"Aye, she's an interesting one," replied Nek Tov. "She used to tell all us youngins about her adventures when we were growing up. We believed her back then, of course – because what child doesn't believe the stories they're told – but when we got older, we decided they must have been tall tales told to make us quiet and go to bed." He shook his head ruefully. "And now that we're grown, we find out that they were true all along."

Nek Tov left to join other captains in discussing what they'd just learned, and Rhenna turned to Deryn. "Coming?"

Deryn rubbed at his face, trying to stave off the exhaustion that had been slowly building over the last few days. "I'm going to find my bed, though I'll be interested in anything you learn. She sounds like she's led a fascinating life."

Rhenna grunted agreement and began to cross the room, but then hesitated, turning back to him. "Get some rest. You look like you need it."

WHEN DERYN STEPPED out onto the deck of the hollowed galley used as the council meeting place, he found that night had fully fallen. An orange moon hung in the cloudless sky, surrounded by a vast scattering of jewel-bright stars. The air was musty, redolent of the marshes fringing the lake, and beneath the creaking of the ancient boats there was a faint thrumming that Deryn thought must be from the throats of countless tiny frogs as they called to each other in the darkness.

It was a beautiful night, but Deryn felt melancholy as he crossed over a bridge to another boat. There were no lanterns to light his way, and if he hadn't possessed his darkvision he would have been worried about turning an ankle or getting lost among the ancient fleet's shadowy labyrinth of masts and cabins and sharply rising foredecks. He could hear voices and see light flickering to his left . . . but instead, he turned right. He wanted to be alone right now.

Deryn picked his way across the decks of several more galleys until he arrived at the very edge of the Haven. He placed his hands on the railing and gazed out over the still and silent waters – the way the moon's ruddy light played upon the surface reminded him of his lessons in the cavern below the Duskhold, how the softly glowing stone of the ancient gazebo had reached across the underground lake with spectral tendrils. He wondered how Kaliss was faring. She must think him dead, slain by the flame-sharded. That deepened his sadness, and he hoped she had found someone else who could see past her prickly exterior. Perhaps Kilian had offered to become her patron. She would need one soon, given how quickly she had merged her first few shards, and Deryn knew that she would have no shortage of offers. Kilian would be the best choice; he was a good and honest man, and Deryn couldn't say that with certainty about very many in the Duskhold.

A mournful trilling carried to him from across the water. Some water bird looking for company, he supposed. It was hard to be alone, even for those like Kaliss, no matter how much she tried to demonstrate otherwise.

Deryn reached into his pocket and drew out a shard. It was a mote of deepest blackness in the center of his palm, but still it gave off a faint, dusky radiance. The darkness around it curled and billowed, like ink spilled in water. This had been a shadow shard. Yvrin's shadow-shard. Deryn had thought long and hard about which fragment he should merge next – his hoard also included wind-shards from the Crow and flame-shards from the servants of the Unbound King – but despite his misgivings, he knew which he would eventually settle on.

Yvrin had been a friend. She'd saved them – there was no doubt in his mind that they all would have perished in the Frayed Lands without her help. He had held other feelings for her as well, deeper feelings . . . and if she'd lived, maybe they could have shared a future together. A sharper pain cut through him at this thought. He'd never know what could have been. It would hurt, merging a fragment that had once been part of her, sensing her again like she was still alive, seeing her memories, however fleeting . . . but he had to. He had to.

Deryn licked his lips, steeling himself. Rhenna had been right – he was exhausted. And it was in large part because he had been channeling almost every waking moment since the zemani ambush. He had to get stronger to protect his friends. He was ready for his fourth shard – his pathways ached from all the *ka* he had been pushing through them, but otherwise he felt perfectly calm; he'd tamed the tempest.

It was time.

Taking a deep breath, he started to unbutton his shirt . . . only to pause when he heard voices. Hurriedly he slipped the shard back into his pocket, as the thought of trying to merge a fragment in public was not very appealing. It was the reason he'd made his way to these empty galleys farthest from where most of the Kin dwelled.

Two shadows had joined him on the boat, though they were down at its opposite end near the upswept prow. They didn't seem to have noticed him yet, deep in conversation as they looked out over the shimmering lake. Well, it wasn't exactly a conversation – one voice seemed to be dominating. A familiar voice, as Deryn recognized Cal Canna's cadence and the way the Kin man always tried so hard to sound charming. With a frown, Deryn suddenly realized who Cal Canna was standing with.

Alia.

The moonlight had turned her long hair into a silvery waterfall. She had her hands on the railing, and Deryn could just barely see a trickle of green radiance leaking from between her fingers to stain the darkness. Alia had tilted her body forward, as if trying to see something in the water below the boat. Cal Canna seemed to be interested in something else entirely, as he was very obviously leaning in her direction, his head almost brushing her shoulder as he talked.

Gritting his teeth, Deryn strode down the galley towards them.

"You know, I've always thought there were a lot of similarities between the Kin and those that dwell in the Wild. Freedom is so important to both our peoples. Freedom from the holds, from the cities . . . freedom to do whatever we want, whenever we want, with whomever we—"

"Fancy meeting you both here!"

Cal Canna jumped like a startled cat as Deryn clapped him heavily on the shoulder.

"Oh!" he cried, and Deryn thought he saw guilt in his face before he schooled his expression. "Deryn. You scared me."

"Hello," Alia said, still staring down into the depths. "Is the meeting finished already?"

"It is," Deryn answered. His hand was still on Cal Canna's shoulder, and he gave a squeeze that elicited a sharp intake of breath. "Turns out the zemani were after the Old Shell. The council agreed that the turtles will stay here in the lake until they know it's safe to return to the rivers."

"Ah, I see," Cal Canna said, subtly trying to extricate himself from Deryn's grip. After he failed to do so, he swept out his other arm to encompass the moonlit waters. "It's not so bad. The lake is beautiful . . . and safe. So safe, nothing bad can happen here. I, uh, I just wanted to show Alia what it looks like at night . . . you know, to thank her for helping me take care of Heth—"

"Oh, Heth!" Deryn exclaimed, finally releasing Cal Canna, who gave a little gasp of relief. "The healers have probably finished. We should go to him."

Cal Canna chuckled weakly. "You know, I think he should probably rest—"

"She's coming," Alia said, moving back from the railing as something disturbed the water. Deryn took a step forward to see what it was, then stumbled back as a huge black shadow rose smoothly from below.

"Silver Shrike," Deryn murmured hoarsely, reflexively grasping at his *ka*. Dark rivulets streamed from the craggy head of the Old Shell looming over them; most of its face was lost to shadow, though whatever hard substance formed its beak gleamed faintly in the moonlight. In his mind's eye he saw the beak snapping closed with startling quickness around the claw of the zemani prince-consort, and he knew if this great turtle wanted to it could just as easily pluck one of them from the galley's deck . . . but he also knew that this would not happen. The Old Shell regarded them calmly, motionless save for the water running down its head and the dilation of its massive nostrils as it breathed.

"Old Bassa," whispered Cal Canna reverentially.

Deryn felt awed by the great turtle and the intelligence he sensed in its measuring gaze. This truly was no simple animal. There was a wisdom here that had been hard-earned over centuries.

Alia approached the railing again, and Deryn had to restrain himself from pulling her back. She reached out a hand wreathed by the light of the seed-shard, and to Deryn's shock, the Old Shell lowered her massive head so that Alia could press a palm against her mottled cheek. The faint green luminescence of the shard played across the black wells of the great turtle's eyes. Bassa breathed out, stirring Alia's moon-touched hair, and then she pulled back from her touch and silently slipped once more into the water.

Deryn and Cal Canna looked at each other, then back to Alia. She was still standing at the galley's edge with her arm outstretched, though the light from her shard had vanished when she'd clenched her hand into a fist.

"She doesn't usually do that," Cal Canna said after a long silence. "The elders here say that once the Old Shells were more . . . friendly, but that a darkness now lies heavy on their souls."

A darkness. Yes, Deryn had felt that as well. "It's because she's old and she knows her kind are not long for this world," he said softly.

Alia stepped back from the railing. "She had a clutch of eggs inside her, waiting for seed."

"She will wait forever," Cal Canna murmured sadly. "There are no more male turtles – they died out long ago. She will lay those eggs, but they will never be filled with hatchlings; she will never be a mother again. The time of the Old Shells is almost finished."

"No," Alia said, shaking her head. "I quickened the eggs. They will hatch in the spring, four males and three females. Your people must make sure to protect them from predators; I do not know what dangers there are in these swamps."

Stunned, Deryn turned to Cal Canna. The Kin man had gone completely rigid at Alia's words, and Deryn almost nudged him to make sure he hadn't succumbed to shock. Then Deryn noticed that Cal Canna's face was glistening in the moonlight – tears were running down his cheeks, though he wasn't making any sound.

"Some of the other turtles might be carrying eggs as well. If they come to me, I think I can do the same again."

"It's your beckoning," Deryn murmured in awed wonder. "It makes things grow."

"Animals as well as plants, apparently," Alia replied with a shrug.

"I didn't know if it would work . . . but I could feel the new life sparking inside her. She will spawn, I'm sure of it."

At that, a wrenching sob finally tore itself from Cal Canna. There was no sadness in it, though. He fell forward onto his knees, clutching at Alia's hand and pressing his forehead to her wrist.

"Thank you," he gasped. "If it's true . . . my people will . . . will . . ." He rose, wiping at his face, and to Deryn he looked like a man who had just learned that the impossible had happened. "Come, we must tell everyone."

11

HETH

Heth had feared that when it came time to depart the Haven that many of the Kin would refuse, not willing to risk the Belt now that they knew the dangers. But to his surprise, there were so many volunteers vying to join *The Morning Dream* that Nek Tov was able to pick and choose the very best to replace those of his crew who had perished during the attack. This was because of what Alia had done – if before the Kin had been grateful for their help in throwing back the zemani, after the Wild girl had quickened the eggs lying fallow inside the Old Shells their attitude had become almost worshipful. They were treating her like a goddess made flesh, begging for her to touch their heads in benediction, and even grown men shed tears in her presence. Alia seemed more than a little uncomfortable with this behavior, and after *The Morning Dream* departed the Haven, she spent the first few days sequestered in her cabin.

This time Heth and Deryn had been given their own room, though they spent most of every day outside on the deck. In the mornings, Heth instructed Deryn in his swordsmanship, focusing on improving his footwork and introducing the more complicated forms. He was learning quickly, especially considering he had not spent his youth in sword-halls or under the gaze of tutors, but Heth feared his progress was still too slow. Right now only a Sharded weapon could harm Deryn, but in Karath their fragments would be nothing more than lifeless pieces of crystal, and a simple sword thrust from a child could kill him. He would be vulnerable, like any other man.

Heth also worked on sharpening his skills, which had grown rusty. He had asked for a sword to replace the one that had shattered on the scales of the zemani prince-consort, and the Kin had gifted him a weapon that would have been the envy of Flail's most celebrated Blades. Its balance was exceptional, the grip seemed perfectly fitted for his hand, and its steel was both lighter and more robust than any other weapon he had held, save for Deryn's strange white-metal sword. When Nek Tov had presented him with the blade, he'd said that it had once been wielded by a dervish of the Salahi. The oasis cities of the desert had perfected a secret forging technique that allowed steel to be folded many times over, and their swords were known to be the finest in the world. It was a great treasure, and Heth appreciated the gesture.

But still, he missed his family sword.

During the afternoons, Deryn became the teacher and helped guide Heth as he channeled and beckoned. He could sense that the once-raging *ka* inside him had been almost completely gentled, and he hoped he would be ready to merge his second fragment before they reached the City of the Dead. For this reason, most of his time was spent seated cross-legged up on the *Dream's* forecastle with his eyes closed, harnessing the *ka* flowing from his shard, pushing it through his body's pathways and then smoothing it as best he could. He did not neglect his beckoning, though – ever since that moment during the zemani ambush when he'd caused all the night lanterns to flare he'd been able to touch the light and make it fade or brighten. It seemed a poor ability when compared to how the shadow-sharded could give the darkness substance and use it to grasp things, or how Alia by touch alone could make life grow, but perhaps he was just scraping the surface of his capabilities. Rhenna had told him that the beckonings of shadow-sharded changed and grew more potent as they gained more shards, so Heth was hopeful that the power had not yet reached its full potential. He noticed that no matter how much brighter he made the light he was never blinded, and that at least had the potential to be very useful during a fight.

Just before dawn on their tenth day on the river, Heth woke from a dreamless sleep and fairly leaped from his bed, expecting to be able to spend the early morning refining his beckoning before Deryn joined him on the deck. But to his surprise, he saw that the other bunk in their cabin was empty and did not look like it had even been slept in. Deryn often stayed outside late into the night trying to deepen his understanding of the shadow elemental, but this would be the first time he'd never even come to bed. Slightly concerned, Heth threw on the tunic and trousers and slipped out onto the deck.

The sky was just starting to lighten, the ghost of last night's moon slowly fading. They were close enough to the river bank that Heth could see the shadowy outline of a town, thready wisps of smoke climbing as the early risers lit fires in their hearths. If the *Dream* had reached this place later in the day, they likely would have stopped, as Nek Tov had made it a habit to send a delegation into larger settlements – ostensibly to trade and replenish supplies, but Heth suspected the real reason was to ask for any news about zemani raiding on the river. Right now Nek Tov was still abed, and so the town slid away into the morning gloom.

Heth looked around and quickly found Deryn sitting near the prow of the boat. He made his way past the sailors of the last watch as they readied the galley for the day – adjusting sails, checking knots and extinguishing the night lanterns – and dropped down next to Deryn, who at first did not seem to realize he had company.

"Good morning," Heth said cheerily, and Deryn startled slightly.

"Morning," he mumbled, rubbing at his face. He looked exhausted, even more tired than Heth expected.

"Didn't sleep?"

Deryn nodded. "I was just about to go collapse into my bunk."

Heth glanced about, but he saw no sign of the little black cat . . .

though it was adept at hiding in the shadows of things, so it still might be near. "Shade keep you up?"

Deryn stretched out his legs with a groan. "No. I spent a long while last night channeling, making sure my pathways were ready . . . and then I merged my fourth fragment."

Heth had been searching for signs of the elemental, but that pulled his attention back to Deryn. He hadn't realized his friend was so close. "Congratulations are in order, then. Rhenna said she didn't know if we would be able to channel while in Karath, or what staying in the city would do to our *ka*, so that's great news. I've been worried what progress I've made will vanish if we're there for too long."

Deryn nodded absently, clearly distracted.

"Do you feel different? Stronger?"

"Not right now. Merging a shard is exhausting, both physically and mentally. I don't think I'll be able to train today, I'm sorry."

"It's fine," Heth said with a shrug. "Take a rest. Nek Tov said it will be another few days until we reach the Sea of Salvation."

He had been expecting Deryn to climb to his feet and stagger back to their cabin, so he was surprised when he stayed. His friend's brow was furrowed, as if he was considering saying something.

"The shard I merged . . ." he murmured finally, squinting into the early morning haze that had settled over the river. "The shard I merged was Yvrin's."

Heth glanced sharply at Deryn. He'd sensed long ago that Deryn had harbored feelings for the steppe girl. And now he had taken a fragment of hers inside himself . . . what was he feeling now? Heth shifted, unsure what he should say or do. Moments like this were always confusing for him. Did Deryn want a shoulder to lean on? Heth supposed he probably just wanted to be left alone, so he was contemplating saying something vague and comforting before going elsewhere, when Deryn suddenly spoke.

"It was like she was there again. I could feel her." Deryn rubbed at the dark circles under his eyes. "And there was this . . . this moment, this memory. She was standing in a golden field, grass shimmering in the day's brightness. The steppes, I suppose. She must have been young, because a man had been there that I think was her father, and he towered over her. He was leading a beautiful horse by its reins, and I felt what she felt at that time . . . love, a deep, powerful love for the man and the horse and that moment."

Deryn swallowed, lowering his chin to his chest. "It was just a glimpse of who she really was. Fleeting. But it was so bright, so pure . . . A daughter's love for her father. She was beautiful, so beautiful, in every way, and now all those memories, all those moments, everything that had knotted together to make her who she was . . . it's all lost." Deryn lapsed into silence, staring at something only he could see.

"She's not gone," Heth said slowly. "And she never will be, so long as you hold on to that memory."

A flock of red-winged birds burst from the trees lining the riverbank, shrieking as they surged into the sky. Heth wondered what could have disturbed so many at once, but he could glimpse nothing among the tangled skein of branches. They watched as the swirling cloud of birds coalesced into something more organized, then struck off in the direction the river was flowing. When they finally disappeared, Deryn sighed deeply and stood.

"I'm going to rest. Don't wake me unless we're attacked by another horde of monsters."

THE REST of the morning Heth smoothed the last few uneven patches in his *ka*-saturated pathways and practiced making the light reflecting off his Salahi blade flash brightly and then fade to nothing. Rhenna and Alia emerged from below deck just as the sun was cresting, and he started to get up to go to them, but Rhenna waved for him to sit again as they made their way over. She also beckoned for Cal Canna to come join them – he'd been up on the foredeck conversing with the steersman, and Heth thought he was pretending to not see Rhenna until a wisp of shadow slithered around his waist and forced him to turn in their direction. He gave a surprised yelp, flashing her a guilty smile.

"Deryn's not here?" Rhenna asked, scanning the deck with a slight frown.

"He's resting," Heth explained. "He merged his fourth shard last night."

Rhenna's face brightened. "Excellent. His progress has been remarkable."

"I think I'm also ready," Heth said, drawing himself up and lifting his chin. He glanced over at Alia as he said this, hoping she'd be impressed.

"More good news," Rhenna continued, lowering herself gracefully to sit cross-legged beside him. "Alia merged her second last night as well. It seems our time on the river has been very productive."

Heth just managed to school his face. Last to beckon, last to merge another fragment . . . why was he such a laggard? At least if there was anyone who was not going to lord her accomplishments over Heth, it was Alia. She smiled innocently back when she noticed him staring at her, and he hastily looked away. Rhenna must have sensed what he was feeling, because the corners of her mouth lifted in amusement.

"You should all be congratulated on your progress. Each of you would have caught the eye of the Duskhold's lords and been invited to join the elite *arzgan* and *sardor* as an adept." She twisted around to find Cal Canna, who was now hovering a dozen steps away, as if afraid to approach them. What was he so nervous about? He'd spent plenty of time in their cabin tending to Heth before they had arrived at the Haven.

"Cal Canna, come here and sit," Rhenna commanded, indicating an empty spot on the deck between Heth and Alia.

"Yes, my lady," he mumbled, hurrying to comply. As he settled himself, Heth noticed that he was taking some pains not to look at Alia. Curious.

"I have asked Nek Tov who among the Kin is most familiar with the – ah, *Soiled* cities, and he said there is no one more knowledge-able than you."

Cal Canna blinked, as if this was not at all what he had been expecting Rhenna to say. Then he licked his lips and offered a shaky smile. "Oh. Aha. Well, yes, old Nekkie's right. As usual. I've always enjoyed spending time with the soi—, uh, the people of the cities in which we trade. So many stories to hear and histories to learn. And there's no city that the Kin spend more time in than Karath."

"Which is why I summoned you down here," Rhenna said, brushing back a lock of dark hair the breeze had pushed across her face. "We need to know what to expect when we reach the City of the Dead. Its factions, its geography, its leaders. Can you do that?"

Cal Canna furrowed his brow. "Why are you going there if you know so little about the city?"

Rhenna smiled at him, but her eyes were flinty. "That is our business."

Cal Canna tilted his head to one side, understanding widening his eyes. "Oh. You're Sharded going to Karath, and you all have different fragments . . . you must want to join the Unbound King."

"I do not want to discuss this," Rhenna said, and the hardening of her voice pulled Cal Canna's attention back to her . . . and the patches of shadows around her that had started trembling.

He swallowed. "Of course. Of course. Apologies, lady. We owe you all a debt that can never be repaid, so I'll keep my questions to myself and just answer yours."

Rhenna nodded curtly. "Good. Then speak and assume we know nothing about the city."

Heth suspected that this was not true – Rhenna was the daughter of a hold lord, and Karath was one of the most important cities in the world. Perhaps she wanted to compare her knowledge with Cal Canna's, though it was also true that the Duskhold was about as far from the City of the Dead as was possible without falling off the edge of the map.

Cal Canna cleared his throat and sat forward; whatever else was bothering him, Heth could tell that he was excited to share what he knew.

"Well, the first thing you must understand is that Karath is not some den of lawlessness. Just because there are no Sharded – or I suppose I should say, the Sharded dwelling there are like any other man or woman – this does not mean the city is gripped by chaos. Once, that may have been true. I was told that centuries ago Karath was dominated by a few powerful merchant families, and that they were constantly striving against each other. But after a particularly deadly period of bloodletting a peace was achieved, and a council representing the five remaining families was established, called the Quinumvirate. They're still rivals, of course, but the days of warriors with different colored cloths wrapped around their arms clashing in the street are long since over. Each of those great families – the Valari, Chaim, Pulcras, Anellium, and Bharach – are still represented by a particular color, and many in Karath will identify with one of them by favoring this color in their dress. They even often refer to the families as the Blues or the Reds and so on. The leadership of the Quinumvirate rotates every few years, a position known as the Shield. It is the Shield that keeps the city safe from the predations of the Sharded Few, or so it is commonly claimed. Though this is not true. What keeps Karath independent is what lies beneath it and exists nowhere else in the world."

"Karathinite," Heth said when he noticed Alia's confused expression. Cal Canna had reasonably assumed that they were all familiar with that famous ore, but it must be unknown in the Wild. Heth had never seen the reddish metal until Rhenna had pointed out the shackles the Sharded masquerading as Vertus had been wearing atop the mesa.

"Of course," Cal Canna said, looking at him like there had been no need for Heth to clarify. "Karathinite. Bane of the Sharded Few. If Karath is ever conquered, it will be by steel and fire, not by any power granted by the shards."

"Then the city must have an army," Rhenna said, her tone suggesting how odd she found this very idea. In most other places, only guardsmen and magistrates would be needed to enforce the law and maintain order, as serious conflicts would be settled by the Sharded. What good would a troop of swordsmen do if they could be instantly swallowed by a column of flame or torn to pieces by a ravenous wind? The lone exception that Heth knew of was the Ifashan Jihad, when the sand-sharded had led a great force of Sharded and common folk that had swept away all before being defeated by the combined strength of the Flame, Storm, and Shadow outside the blood-sharded city of Ashasai.

"The city has an army," Cal Canna said with a nod. "The Wardsmen, led by the Sword, who is voted in by the Quinumvirate and is responsible for defending Karath from enemies both without and within. The Sword right now is Selavin Thiss, a mercenary who was once a Blade from the city of Flail. He's a right bastard." Cal Canna blushed when he realized what he'd said, glancing over at Alia. "Sorry, ladies."

Rhenna ignored the apology. "So that is who governs the city. Where does the Unbound King fit into this hierarchy?"

"I don't truly know," Cal Canna answered with an apologetic shrug. "It's not something that's commonly discussed in the taverns. I know he has a great manse in the richest area of the city, almost a fortress, and that the Wardsmen treat him and his lieutenants like they are a sixth great family."

"No doubt the leaders of Karath find that having a powerful group of Sharded beholden to them is useful," mused Rhenna. "After all, they must on occasion have to pursue interests beyond their city walls."

Cal Canna gasped as a shadowy snake slithered into the space between them. It undulated for a moment, then grew still.

"If this is the Belt," Rhenna began, and Heth realized she meant for her beckoning to represent the river, "tell me about the layout of the city."

"Karath is almost entirely to the north," Cal Canna said, eyeing the serpentine slice of darkness like it might lunge at him. "There are docks on the southern bank and a few buildings, warehouses and barracks and such, but mostly it is just the mines. The Wardsmen keep everyone else away." He hesitated, then leaned forward to sweep his hand along the length of Rhenna's beckoning. "Along the Belt, all the way to where the river empties into the Sea of Salvation, that's called the Nethers. It's where the poor folk live, or the ones with nowhere else to go. The Hollow who make it to Karath usually settle there, as most have nothing to their names when they arrive."

Heth glanced at Cal Canna. "The Hollow?"

"Aye, a fair number of them live in Karath. Pretty much any that manage to escape a hold end up in Karath eventually, because it's the only place in the world that is outside the reach of the Sharded Few."

He looked at Alia, and was not surprised to see that her jaw was clenched. She had not been Hollow, but she had been treated like one of them after the Shadow had refused her a shard, and the experience of being a slave had been so intolerable that she had tried to flee the Duskhold.

"There's one other community in the Nethers, though they don't really associate with anyone else. That'd be the sandbathers."

"The who?" Rhenna asked, frowning in confusion.

"Sorry, the Salahi. After the battle of Gerendal, the forces of the emir were shattered. Many of the survivors hurried south to defend the oasis cities, but the northern alliance arrived first and sacked the sand-sharded city of Derambinal. So the remaining Sharded desert warriors led refugees north, and they begged for solace within the walls of Karath. They were granted entrance and settled in the Nethers, turning it into a little slice of their homeland far away from the Salah."

"Tell me about the Erudinium."

They all turned to find that Deryn had quietly approached while Cal Canna had been talking. He was still pale, his eyes sunken, but to Heth, it looked like the rest had done him some good. The sadness that had wrapped him like a shroud earlier also seemed to have vanished.

"The Erudinium?" Cal Canna said. Heth noticed a slight flinch when he looked at Deryn, though Heth couldn't fathom why his friend would ever elicit such a reaction – Deryn was the kindest person he'd ever met. "The Erudinium is a place unlike any other, where knowledge and truth are valued above all else. Its scholars are the most dedicated in the world, and its library is said to be the most extensive ever gathered."

"You've been inside?" Deryn asked, settling beside Alia on the deck.

Cal Canna gave a humorless laugh. "Ha. No, of course not. Only the scholars and their trusted servants are allowed to walk its halls. One must first study for many years, swear powerful oaths, and don the umber robes." His tone was wistful, as if he had dreamed of exploring the secrets of the Erudinium. "There is a museum beside it where a curated selection of artifacts is on display. I always try to visit at least once when we are in port. It is where I saw other First Empire weapons made of palesteel, and the contents of this museum must be just a taste of what is locked away in the Erudinium's vaults. If it was not for karathinite, the holds would have marched in to loot these treasures long ago."

"But if we had a question," Deryn pressed, "a question the answer to which has been forgotten everywhere else, the scholars of the Erudinium would be the ones to ask, yes?"

Cal Canna shifted uncomfortably. "If anyone knows the answer, they would be within those blue-veined walls . . . but you don't seem to understand, you cannot simply saunter into the Erudinium, pull on the sleeve of a passing scholar, and ask your question. It is not open to ones such as us . . . even if you are Sharded." His expression was almost apologetic. "That carries far less weight in the City of the Dead."

"We know," Rhenna said tersely, then with a flick of her wrist obliterated the shadowy tendril representing the Belt. "You have answered my questions, and I thank you. If I have anything else to ask, I will come find you."

Cal Canna remained seated for a few moments longer, at first not realizing that he had been dismissed. Then he blinked and scrambled to his feet, nearly tripping over Alia's outstretched leg in his hurry to depart.

"You're welcome, my lady. It's been a pleasure!"

Heth watched Cal Canna flee, shaking his head in bewilderment. "I wonder what's bothering him?"

"I suppose we'll never know," Deryn said flatly, and Heth glanced at him suspiciously. Something had transpired that he hadn't been told about. He was about to ask more about this, but then Rhenna spoke.

"I hear congratulations are in order. Four shards in less than a year is an admirable feat."

A bit of color crept into Deryn's pale cheeks. "I'm sure if you had been under the same pressure to merge shards you could have done the same," he said, but there was a hint of pride in his voice.

Rhenna heard this as well, because the edges of her lips quirked upwards. "And has a new talent manifested?"

"Not yet," Deryn admitted. "But I'm still hopeful. I could not summon the Breath of the Mother until several days after I'd merged my third fragment."

"That is often what happens," Rhenna said with a nod. "One's *ka* becomes extremely unsettled in the aftermath of adding another shard, and it is not until you bring order to your pathways that a new ability can emerge." Her attention abruptly shifted from Deryn to Heth. "Now, I'm afraid it is time."

"Time for what?" Heth asked uncertainly, casting a questioning glance at Alia and Deryn.

Rhenna did not answer, instead drawing something palm-sized from her pocket that flashed as it caught the light. It was a small silver hand mirror, its border elegantly worked into a design evoking twining vines.

Coldness flooded Heth's insides and his hand went to the bandages wrapping his head. "Where did you get that?"

"I borrowed it from Nek Tov," Rhenna said, sliding closer to Heth. "It seems the good captain is a bit vain about his appearance. Or perhaps some long-lost paramour left it in his possession – I'll let you decide which you think is more likely."

"I don't want to see," Heth said with as much iron in his voice as he could muster.

"Heth," Alia said softly, laying her hand on his arm. "Facing our fears is the first step towards conquering them. My mother told me that."

If it had been anyone else, Heth would have jerked his arm away and stormed off in a huff. He had made it very clear that he didn't want to remove the wrappings and see what kind of monster he'd become. *Especially* somewhere like on the deck of the galley, with so many watching out of the corners of their eyes. But Alia's touch was gentle, and the concern in her face so genuine. She truly thought this would be best for him.

Heaving a deep sigh, Heth nodded his assent. Then he clenched his jaw as Deryn carefully unwound the wrappings, steeling himself to hear gasps of horror. His skin prickled as the breeze touched it for the first time in many days, but at least there wasn't any pain.

Rhenna held up the mirror and Heth forced himself to look at his new face.

He let out a low hiss. It . . . wasn't nearly as bad as he had imagined. Lying in bed unable to sleep he'd run his fingers over the bandages, feeling the strange ridges and contours beneath the cloth and conjuring all sorts of horrific visions. But this . . . his features were all intact – his eyes and lips and ears – though one of the scars traveling over his nose had carved away a small piece. The livid marks began at his brow above his left eye and extended down to the bottom of his right cheek – it almost looked like he had applied some primitive war paint, such as he had seen on the faces of the People of the Wind.

"You're still handsome," Alia said, and to Heth, those were the sweetest words ever spoken to him. "You just look dangerous now, too."

Dangerous. He could live with that.

12

KALISS

The day was too bloody bright.

Kaliss grimaced as she pushed through the tent's flap, blinking back tears as her eyes tried to adjust from the darkened interior to the brilliant morning outside. The sun – an unfamiliar sight after more than a year spent sequestered away in the Duskhold – seemed to be different here in the Fangs, as if these mountains lifted higher into the sky than the Firemounts ringing the fortress of the shadow-sharded. Which they might – it was obvious that the two ranges were nothing alike. This had surprised her. Kaliss's entire life had been shadowed by the Firemounts, first in the streets of Phane and then in the Duskhold, so she had assumed all mountains were the same – dark and brooding, bereft of vegetation, their summits either scooped out by past calamities or unspooling threads of smoke. But the Fangs had no fires in their bellies, at least that she could see. These mountains squatted like enormous giants, their ice-sheathed peaks glittering as if they wore silvery helms and their rippling lower reaches covered in dark forest like the pleated folds of a battle-kilt. And yet even though Kaliss had been told that fell cats and rethwings and wolves prowled between these trees, the depths of the Fangs felt just as stark and empty as the sere slopes of the Firemounts.

That is, except for the Ember.

It bulked against a sheer cliff-face like a black abscess growing from the mountain's flesh. The outer walls soared impossibly high, seemingly fashioned from single great slabs of rock, and beyond these ramparts an enormous bulbous fortress hunched, buildings and towers and battlements all hewn from the same dark stone. A gatehouse that by itself looked larger than the magistrate's keep in Phane controlled the only entrance to the flame-sharded's home, and its door was as tall as a dozen men and forged from a reddish metal purported to be a product of the First Empire's artificers.

Three times it had been laid siege to during the old wars between Shadow and Flame, and never had its mighty walls been breached.

The hold looked daunting. Impregnable.

It looks like the mountain is having a bowel movement.

"Be quiet," Kaliss muttered after quickly glancing around to make sure no one else was near. Only a few shadow-sharded were moving among the great sprawl of tents, as most of the warriors from the Duskhold were understandably hiding from the midday sun. Like her, they were unaccustomed to brightness and vast open spaces.

Tell me you don't see it.

"*You* don't see it – you don't have eyes." Kaliss said, starting to slog through the knee-high grass of the mountain meadow that separated the shadow-sharded from where their allies were encamped. The Storm's tents were far different – peaked instead of rounded, striped with bright colors instead of drab, uniform gray, and the pennants snapping in the strong wind were emblazoned with the sigils of the Windwrack's great families.

I see all and know all.

"You're a knife," Kaliss hissed through gritted teeth.

A sibilant chuckle slithered through her mind. *No, I'm not. You're simply mad, and I'm sorry to have to be the one to tell you this.*

"Silence." Kaliss's fingers twitched, and she had the strong desire to rip the dagger from the sheath at her side and cast it away. Despite what the voice in her head always claimed, she knew it inhabited the knife – she had first heard it when her hand had closed around the hilt as it lay in its box of carved black wood, and it had disappeared after she had returned to the underground lake where Leantha had gifted her the dagger and thrown it into the water.

What had happened after she'd done that was why she did not dare cast the haunted blade away now, though. She had returned to her cell in the Duskhold, relieved that the presence infringing on her thoughts was finally gone, and had fallen into an exhausted sleep . . . only to be woken soon after by a soft knock. She had known who it would be before she'd opened the door. Leantha, with her alabaster skin and glistening black hair, thin lips pressed together and dark eyes hooded. In her hands she had held the silver-bladed knife, the black skull in its ebony pommel grinning mockingly at Kaliss.

It had been perfectly dry, as if it had never been at the bottom of the lake.

"Do not discard this dagger again," Leantha had said, her voice shriven of emotion. "Keep it on you at all times – when you sleep, when you eat, when you bathe." Then she had handed the dagger to her and the ghost or demon or whatever it was had returned to her head.

And it had been with her ever since. If she did end up insane, it would be because of this damned thing and its incessant chattering. Or perhaps she *was* already mad. This dagger – this dagger that looked exactly like the one that had belonged to her old master in Phane, the one she had shoved into his belly just before the Hollow hound had found her and brought her to the Duskhold – this dagger couldn't be what it seemed. She had left that one in her master's corpse. It was impossible that it had found its way back to her.

On the edge of the storm-sharded camp was a huge, rounded tent of silver and azure, its cloth-of-gold flaps pinned open. The entrance was unguarded, for no one would be foolish enough to enter without invitation. The meeting that was about to start constituted perhaps the greatest concentration of power in the north.

But most of the others had not yet arrived. Only Leantha stood outside the tent, tall and wraith-like, her hands tucked into the long loose sleeves of her dark robe.

"Mistress," Kaliss murmured, ducking her head. Leantha did not acknowledge the greeting, turning away from her to enter the tent.

Kaliss followed. The interior was even larger than she had imagined, lit by a hovering sphere. Blisters of energy formed on its crackling surface before dissipating with a faint popping. The bulk of the tent was dominated by a great round table of white wood that drank the sphere's light and seemed to glow with its own pale radiance. High-backed chairs were arrayed around it, twelve in total. Six were carved from the same bleached wood as the table, and the rest were fashioned from what looked to be ebony, same as the dagger's hilt. Kaliss had wondered what the great wagons that had accompanied the storm-sharded army into this valley had been carrying, and now she knew. Tables and chairs.

Leantha's hands slipped from her sleeves, her fingers brushing the surface of the table as she came to stand behind the black chair situated the farthest from the tent's entrance. "Stay beside me," she said quietly. "And do not move or speak."

Kaliss did as Leantha commanded, though she felt foolish doing this in an empty tent. She was about to ask her mistress why she wanted her here for this meeting, but her words died in her throat as three young women glided silently into the tent and took up position behind the white chair across from Leantha and Kaliss. They each wore diaphanous dresses of pastel silk, and looked virtually indistinguishable from each other save for their hair – one had long golden tresses, another a pleated black coil, and the last was as hairless as Kaliss, though she was not Ashasai. They did not nod or offer greeting, simply staring at them from across the table with a vacant calmness that reminded Kaliss of the dead.

What delicious little things do we have—

The voice in Kaliss's head faltered as the gaze of the woman with the black hair suddenly sharpened. Her eyes darted around the room, as if searching for something.

She couldn't have—

The presence in her head vanished again as the woman's attention focused on Kaliss. The others turned to look at her, then as if something unspoken had passed between them their expressions once again grew opaque.

Kaliss risked a glance out of the corner of her eye at Leantha and noticed that the corners of her mouth had tightened, as if in annoyance. What had just happened?

It was a relief to feel that her mind belonged only to her once more, but this exchange had unsettled Kaliss. Who were these women? She remembered them from the delegation that had visited the Duskhold, although she hadn't given them much thought at the time. She had assumed them to simply be handmaidens to the Mother of Storms, but clearly they were much more than that. A droplet of cold sweat trickled down her back, and she fought down the urge to shiver. *She* would also be attending this council, as everyone knew that she was the true ruler of the Windwrack, even though it was her son who sat the throne.

As if summoned, Lady Khaliva swept into the tent.

She moved with the grace of a much younger woman, despite age having seamed her face and rounded her back. Her dress was shimmering silver and jewels dripped from her ears and neck; she did not radiate strength like other Sharded, but Kaliss would have wagered anything that she had as many fragments as anyone else in this valley, except perhaps Cael Shen. There was an aura of authority around her that could not come merely from her royal bearing – here was someone who had spent several mortal lifetimes refining her *ka*.

The Mother of Storms did not spare a glance at Kaliss or Leantha, settling into the white chair to the left of the three handmaidens. The dark-haired young woman leaned over and whispered something into her ear, and Lady Khaliva's brow furrowed briefly, but still she did not look at the shadow-sharded across from her. Then she raised a ring-bedecked hand and shooed the handmaiden away.

Kaliss's attention was drawn to the entrance to the tent as it was darkened by a massive shadow. She held her breath when the

Warden who had accompanied the storm-sharded delegation to the Duskhold strode inside, the huge shard set in his empty eye socket leaking wan light. He was clad in the same battered plate armor that Kaliss had seen him wearing before, and a war hammer that would have been impossible to lift for anyone not Sharded was strapped across his back. Before he lowered himself into another of the white chairs – which creaked alarmingly – he unslung this mighty weapon and leaned it against the table.

The next to enter was also someone she had seen before – tall and sandy-haired and dashingly handsome, with a golden sword at his side that crackled with latent power. Prince Lessian, the heir to the Windwrack and the man to whom Lady Rhenna had been betrothed to marry, if the cowardly flame-sharded had not ambushed their wedding party. Kaliss remembered him with laughing eyes and an easy smile, though today he looked solemn, his face as cold as the northern sky.

Two more warriors followed the prince into the tent – both were tall and broad-shouldered like the scarred Warden, but younger and leaner. One wore a shirt of copper-colored chain mail, curly blonde ringlets falling to his shoulder, and the other had a sallow, sunken face and a hooked nose, his eyes and hair dark. He was not wearing armor, but Kaliss knew he was one of the famed Wardens of the Windwrack – the sigil on the tabard over his doublet was a great bird with wings spread, a lightning bolt clutched in its beak. Geralth Chassain, the Falcon of the Fangs.

Kaliss was staring so intently at the storm-sharded that at first she didn't realize that a small, tonsured man in threadbare brown robes had also slipped into the tent until he sat in the white chair beside the Mother of Storms. There was a soft kindness to his face that reminded her of the priests of the Broken God in Phane who had spoken of love and mercy before casting stones at any urchin who lingered too long near their temples. Such gentle smiles, in Kaliss's experience, often hid something dark and vicious. She disliked him immediately.

"Where are they?" bellowed Bailen Khaliva as he stormed into the tent and threw himself into the last unoccupied chair. The lord of the Windwrack was a massive man, easily as large as the scarred Warden, but while the one-eyed Sharded looked hard as granite, Bailen was soft as sun-warmed suet, with a belly that had swallowed his belt and a great bushy beard which could not completely hide his rolls of neck-fat. He steepled thick fingers and glared at Leantha. "Did you hear me? Where is your master?"

"He comes," the White Spider of the Duskhold murmured, and Kallis blinked at the lack of any honorific. This man was the king of Flail, the lord of the Windwrack, and the master of the storm-sharded. There was no greater power in the north, even though any loyal shadow-sharded would be loath to admit this.

A few faces around the table darkened at this slight – the Lady Khaliva snorting a very unlady-like laugh – but before anyone could demand satisfaction for the insult, something behind Kaliss drew their attention. She turned just as the shadowed recesses of the tent spasmed and a jagged doorway formed of darkness swelled into existence.

Nishi Shen was the first through the rift, the heir to the Duskhold sweeping his gaze over the assembled storm-sharded before stepping aside to hold his Shadow Walking open for those who followed. His father was next, long white hair tied back in a topknot, the greatsword Night slung across his broad back. The lord of the Duskhold nodded gravely at Bailen Khaliva, then sat in the seat directly across from the Windwrack's master, the one Leantha was hovering behind like a ghost. Azil Shen passed into the tent next, and Kaliss noticed that he offered a far more respectful bow to Bailen and then an even deeper bow to the Mother of Storms, who smiled indulgently at him like he was a favorite nephew. The Black Sword of the Duskhold took the chair beside the huge Warden in tarnished plate, and he made a conspicuous show of leaning his fabled staff the Dark-bringer beside the storm-sharded warrior's mighty hammer.

Kaliss's heart leaped when the next shadow-sharded passed through the portal – Saelus, who had taught her channeling and beckoning and nearly everything she knew about the world. The old man hobbled to the chair in front of Kaliss and collapsed into it, never glancing at her. She couldn't help staring at the few wispy gray hairs left on his age-spotted scalp, wishing he'd turn around and smile at her the way he used to when she'd inevitably triumphed in one of the contests he'd set before the novices.

Joras Shen entered in much the same way Bailen Khaliva had, stomping through the rift and immediately filling the tent with the force of his presence – except while the lord of the Windwrack had glowered like the storm clouds perpetually wreathing his hold, the brother of Cael Shen wore a grin that seemed entirely out of place among the shadow-sharded. He threw himself into his chair and looked around like he expected serving maids to sweep into the tent carrying flagons of ale.

The last shadow-sharded to come through the doorway Nishi was holding open was the one Kaliss knew the least about, and also the one she found the most unnerving. Ilia Balenchas stalked into the tent like a predator, her sharp-featured face raised as if she was scenting the air, her unnaturally long limbs moving with a fluid grace. She was beautiful and exotic-looking, with strangely uptilted eyes and fiery red hair that the stories said had come from when her long-ago ancestor had gone exploring across the trackless eastern seas. The Balenchas were the second most powerful family in the Duskhold and the only real threat to the primacy of the Shens ... but with the killing of their scion Vertus – who had been appointed to lead Rhenna's wedding delegation to Flail – that rivalry had been set aside. Ilia was Vertus's older sister and the youngest *famdhar* in the Duskhold, and if it were not for the Black Sword, she would be considered the greatest prodigy of her generation.

With a curt gesture, Nishi closed the doorway to the shadowrealm and slipped into the vacant seat beside his father. Kaliss was expecting someone to speak, but the storm and shadow-sharded seemed content to spend a few moments taking the measure of the other. Silence descended, broken only by the buzzing and popping of the roiling ball of light hovering over the table. The power concentrated in the tent was making Kaliss lightheaded – there was a feeling like just before a summer storm, when the air was pregnant with what was about to be unleashed, and she could feel the tiny hairs on her arms – the only hairs she had – standing on end. The strength of the Shadow was also evident, as the darkness in the recesses of the tent seemed to roil and throb like a thing alive. Kaliss suspected it had been many years – perhaps since the war against the Sand – that so many legendary Sharded had come together like this. Among the Shadow delegation there were four *famdhar* – Azil, Ilia, Joras, and of course Cael Shen – when there were only seven such Sharded in all the Duskhold, at least that Kaliss knew about. She couldn't be certain who among the storm-sharded had risen to that august rank, but the Wardens of the Windwrack were known to all be *famdhar*. Bailen Khaliva had never attained a third-tier talent, and Kaliss had heard it was a sore spot for the Wrack's lord, but given the respect his mother commanded it was very likely she was an ancient and powerful *famdhar*. Age and wisdom were valued among the Sharded, but the number of fragments was of paramount importance.

Kaliss was not surprised at all when it was the Mother of Storms who eventually broke the silence.

"You know, you all could have just walked across the meadow," she groused, folding jewel-encrusted hands in front of her. "Would have taken you but a moment. Such a dramatic entrance has little effect on us, I assure you."

"We were not trying to impress you, Lady Khaliva," Cael Shen said, and Kaliss was surprised by the note of deference. "We were not in our camp, but higher up on the valley's lip, scouting the Ember's fortifications."

"And discussing what you all should say and how you should act in this meeting," Lady Khaliva continued, wagging a finger at the lord of the Duskhold. "Very wise – you don't want anything to happen that might abrogate our alliance."

Kaliss couldn't see Cael Shen's face from where she stood, so she was surprised to hear the amusement in his voice when he answered. "Of course. I think everyone here understands how delicate this situation is. The Shadow and the Storm have contested for centuries to rule the north. This wedding was supposed to build a bridge between our holds, but ancient enmities die hard. I know this. You know this."

"Well, we're here," interjected Bailen Khaliva, leaning his great bulk forward. "I've nearly emptied the Wrack, and it looks like you've done the same. This . . . this crime cannot go unpunished. Lord Char has doomed his hold."

"She was remarkable."

All eyes turned in surprise to Prince Lessian, who flushed under the sudden attention. He swallowed hard, forcing himself to hold Cael Shen's gaze without flinching. Not an easy feat, as Kaliss and everyone else from the Duskhold could attest. "I didn't know her well," he continued, and it seemed to Kaliss that his interruption had been spontaneous rather than planned. "But when we dueled atop your drum tower I learned how fierce she was and the strength of her will. I was . . . I was distraught when I heard what had happened." Finally he looked away, and to Kaliss's surprise he appeared overcome. Had he truly been in love with her after his brief visit to the Duskhold? That seemed impossible to Kaliss, but she had heard that the storm-sharded were passionate romantics. How in the frozen hells would he have ever paired with the cold and stoic Rhenna Shen?

"She was not the only one who died." Ilia Balenchas's voice was like ice, and there were visible indentations on the table where her fingers were placed.

The Mother of Storms held up her hand in acknowledgment. "Yes, of course. The Duskhold lost many that day." Her sharp gaze shifted to Cael Shen. "I had a question about that, though I hesitate to bring up such a painful memory. You saw the site of the ambush, yes?" She paused then, waiting for the shadow-sharded lord's slight nod. "What did you find?"

"Death," Cael Shen intoned. "Destruction. The Flame is a scourge that leaves little behind. Corpses that were more ash than flesh and bone. Charred scraps."

"You found your daughter?"

Cael Shen hesitated, then shook his head. "It was impossible to tell the bodies apart." There was a rawness to his voice that shocked Kaliss – the thought of the Duskhold's lord showing emotion seemed impossible, but if anything could elicit such a reaction, she supposed, it would be the death of his daughter.

"Then how do you know she is dead?" asked Lady Khaliva, leaning forward with her elbows on the table.

"Because she is not here," Cael Shen replied sharply. "If Rhenna had survived, she would have returned to the Duskhold."

"But what if she was taken prisoner?" the Mother of Storms pressed. "What if she is within the Ember as we speak?"

"Then Lord Char would have paraded her in front of our armies to keep us from assaulting the walls. He knows I would not dare attack whilst he holds her hostage."

"And that is what I don't understand," Lady Khaliva continued, playing with a huge star sapphire set in one of her rings. "Lord Char is brazen and impetuous, but he is not a fool. He must have known that by killing your daughter – my grandson's betrothed – he would bring about the end of his hold. And yet he made no effort to hide what had happened, leaving evidence that would point directly back to the Flame."

"He was maddened beyond reason by what he saw as a terrible insult," interjected Joras, gesturing emphatically at nothing. "The man was not thinking clearly. The thought of the Storm and Shadow united, of his realm hemmed in on both sides; he felt walls closing in . . . he suspected a threat to the Ember, and so he chose to strike first."

"And was he wrong?" the mousy storm-sharded in plain robes asked mildly. "Were there any other agreements reached – beyond the betrothal – when the Storm visited the Shadow?"

The Mother of Storms shot the man an irritated look. "Of course not. My visit had the purpose of bringing peace to the north, not war."

Several of the storm-sharded shifted and grumbled, also clearly annoyed that this brief exchange had shown cracks in their unified façade. Kaliss noticed a few quick glances between several of the shadow-sharded, but they at least managed to keep their faces unreadable. Apparently, the reputation of the storm-sharded as emotional was justified – Cael Shen would have unsheathed Night if anyone had dared question him in front of outsiders.

The tonsured man appeared unaffected by the exasperation of his fellow storm-sharded. Instead, he turned to Cael Shen, his expression placid. "I assume you consulted the shadows where the ambush occurred. Did you learn anything?"

"The Remembrance of Dust is one of my talents," Saelus said. "I tried to witness what happened that night, but the memories imprinted on the darkness there are jumbled and fragmented. Fire creates shadow, and there were so, so many fires that night. It was like sifting through a mountain of glass shards, each with a different moment frozen inside. I saw the Ember's warriors with their fragments burning in their brows; I saw shadow-sharded wreathed in flames as creatures fashioned from fire stalked among the burning tents. I did not see Rhenna . . . or Vertus." He added that second name quickly with an apologetic nod towards Ilia.

"Enough," Bailen Khaliva huffed impatiently. "The details of what happened are irrelevant. All that matters is that our two holds are here now, and we need a plan to tear down those walls, or else we will have come a long way for nothing. I shouldn't need to remind anyone that the Ember has survived many sieges by the armies of Storm and Shadow."

"Storm *or* shadow," corrected Lady Khaliva. "Not the combined powers of our holds."

"Whatever," Bailen said, scowling at his mother. "We still need a plan to breach those walls."

Kaliss has been wondering about exactly that. The black walls of the Ember were widely considered the greatest fortification ever constructed. Months ago, Saelus had spent an entire morning lecturing the novices about how dozens if not hundreds of shards had been set into the wall, making it what was believed to be the largest Sharded artifact in the world. Any Sharded who did not carry pieces of the Flame who tried to use their talents when outside the wall would combust spectacularly, a lesson painfully learned during those long-ago sieges. Even *famdhar* had allegedly fallen victim.

"What about your Shadow Walking?" asked the Warden with the head of golden curls. "Have you tried to simply bypass these defenses?"

"The histories teach us that the wall's influence extends into the shadowrealm," answered Saelus, his voice taking on the familiar cadence of a teacher imparting knowledge. "Others have tried to do the same and never returned."

"Siege weapons," rumbled the hulking one-eyed Warden. "We did not bring any with us, but trebuchets would be easy enough to build from the skyspear forests."

"The shards have the same effect on the stone of the wall as they do on our bodies," Lady Khaliva replied tiredly, as if disappointed to have to respond to such a foolish suggestion. "A rock hurled at the walls would shatter without leaving a scratch."

"Starve them out," offered the last Warden, the Falcon of the Fangs, his raptor eyes glittering.

"Surely they have supplies to last years," Joras Shen scoffed. "And I for one do not want to stay that long in these mountains freezing my buttocks off!"

The testiness of this rejoinder seemed to spark something, and voices swelled as the table deteriorated into bickering. The Lady Khaliva spoke sharply to the tonsured storm-sharded, while Bailen reprimanded his Wardens for their ill-thought out suggestions; even the shadow-sharded were not immune to the rising tension in the room, as Ilia Balenchas had leaned in closer to Cael Shen to converse in a quieter but just as angry tone, and Saelus admonished Joras for his lack of tact. Only the three maidens in their gauzy dresses remained silent, watching the proceedings without any outward signs of dismay or vexation.

All Kaliss needed was for the haunted dagger to start yammering away in her head again to complete the utter chaos of this moment.

"My lords." This new voice was barely more than a whisper, yet somehow it cut through the babble like a sharp knife sliding into flesh. Kaliss glanced in surprise at Leantha, who had stepped out from behind Cael Shen's chair and come to stand by the table, where she towered over those seated like she was in truth the most powerful Sharded in the tent. Bailen Khaliva's mouth fell open, his jowls quivering, and he blinked up at her like she was a piece of furniture that had just spoken.

"My lords, I have a plan."

13

DERYN

Deryn awoke well before dawn, surfacing from troubled dreams of dead wolves and talking severed heads. After he blinked away the last vestiges of sleep, he realized Heth was staring at him from across the cabin where he lay in his own cot. Deryn wondered briefly what had awakened both of them . . . but then he felt it. The world had changed. Despite the gloom, Heth should have been etched clearly in his darkvision, but Deryn could just barely make out his features. The cavalcade of sounds and smells that he'd adapted to live with since being granted his shard had faded, and as he lay there listening to his breathing he sensed them receding even further. The pulse of *ka* flowing through his pathways was just barely noticeable, a faint throbbing when once it had been easier to feel than his own heartbeat.

"I don't think I'm one of the Sharded Few anymore," Heth murmured.

"We're almost to Karath," Deryn replied. "This is what it's going to be like while we stay in the city." Or worse, he supposed. His Sharded strength was draining away, but he had not yet been entirely emptied. Soon he would be just as weak and helpless as when he had been indentured, and once more he would be at the mercy of cruel men with whips and swords.

"Shade?" he whispered, looking around their small cabin, and then felt a little swell of relief as a darker patch of shadow squirmed out from under his cot. It was hard to tell with his diminished darkvision, but he thought the elemental had cocked his head and was staring up at him in something like confusion. Deryn had been worried that whatever strange aspect of Karath limited the power of their shards would also hurt or even destroy the elemental, but Shade seemed unaffected . . . though perhaps a bit bewildered by all that was going on.

They slipped from their cots, dressed quickly, and then left the cabin. Deryn was not surprised when they emerged onto the deck and found Rhenna and Alia already standing by the prow, staring into the roiling mists. Only a few sailors of the night watch were moving about in the early-morning gloom, attending to their final tasks.

Karath's reputation as the City of the Dead seemed very well-deserved. A clotting fog hung heavy over the river, reducing the buildings clustered along the northern bank to vague shapes. The only people they saw were drifting like lost ghosts over the hummocks exposed by the tide, carrying satchels bulging with whatever creatures they were harvesting from the mud. It was an eerily silent scene, especially considering that they were on the outskirts of one of the largest cities in the world. Deryn could only assume that there would be a lot more commotion further on, closer to where the Belt emptied into the Sea of Salvation.

"It's strange, isn't it?" Rhenna said as they came up beside her, rubbing at her arms as she watched the city sliding past. "To feel the cold again. It's been years since I've been so chilled." There was a nervous edge to her words that Deryn completely understood. She had been Sharded for so long that feeling her power seep away must be unsettling . . . she was vulnerable again after having been protected by the Shadow for most of her life. How would this change her?

"At least all Sharded are affected equally," Deryn replied. "The Unbound King and his followers won't be able to use their talents either."

"But they will have experience with this . . . malady." Rhenna shivered, but Deryn didn't know if it was from the cold or the thought of what Karath was doing to her. She turned to Heth, who looked hungover, even though Deryn knew he hadn't had anything to drink the night before. "You will have to protect us, Heth. Deryn and I can fight, but we've been trained as members of the Sharded Few. You're a swordsman, and just like in the old, barbaric times before the Sundering of the Heart your ability to swing a sword is now the most important skill in the world."

Heth drew himself up straighter, though he was still swaying slightly and the effect was less than reassuring. Hopefully, their conditions would improve as they got used to this new reality.

"Good, you're all here."

Deryn turned to find that Nek Tov had joined them at the railing. The burly Kin captain drew in a deep lungful of the chilly air and then let it out slowly.

"Crisp day, eh? Don't worry, the fog will burn away soon enough."

"Will you be staying in the city long?" asked Rhenna, brushing back a lock of her mist-damp hair.

Nek Tov shook his head. "Nay. This trip was just to deliver you all here. There are a few trade goods we'll row over to the docks, but they'll be no dallying. The council made it clear that everyone should be hunkering down in the Haven until we know it's safe to ply the rivers again. And truth be told, I want to get back there just in case those scaly bastards come looking for where the Old Shells are hiding."

Rhenna nodded, thrusting out her hand. "Then I thank you for bringing us here. You've held up your end of the bargain."

Deryn noticed Nek Tov's slight hesitation, and the captain even winced slightly anticipating her strength before realizing it was no longer the same.

"You never need to say thanks to the Kin," he said gruffly. "You've already given us a gift we'll never be able to repay."

Rhenna released his hand and then reached into her pocket to withdraw the pouch that contained the jewelry scavenged from the flame-sharded, but Nek Tov quickly shook his head.

"And we certainly won't be taking that. In truth, I've a mind to return what you've already given us . . ."

"That's not necessary," she said with a slight smile. "You'll no doubt find a good use for the gold, especially since you won't be trading anytime soon."

Nek Tov bowed to her in gratitude. "Well, the least we can do is get you situated here in the city. The Kin keep a house just beside the river, and you're welcome to stay in it until your business in Karath is concluded."

Now it was Rhenna's turn to nod in thanks. "We will take you up on that offer."

The Kin captain clapped his hands together sharply, then looked to the sterncastle. Deryn followed his gaze and saw Cal Canna chatting with the man at the wheel, although he gasped and tried to hide behind the hulking steersman when he noticed Nek Tov's attention.

"Cal Canna! Come down here and get ready to take these Soiled ashore! They'll be staying with Mam Nar!"

DERYN HAD ALWAYS FELT a little guilty about how much the Kin reminded him of giant toads, with their grayish skin, broad features, and bulging eyes. During their weeks spent on the water together this association had gradually faded, until eventually he'd wondered how he had ever thought such a thing.

And then he met Mam Nar, and it all came rushing back. She had a complexion that was even darker than most other Kin, almost like fresh-turned clay, and some ailment she'd once suffered from had left her skin pebbled in places. She was nearly as wide as she was tall – though she barely came up to Alia's shoulder – and she even had a sort of waddling gait that would not have looked out of place at a pond's edge.

She seemed to be the sole inhabitant of a rambling old building, half of which hung out over the river like it was in the process of sliding into the water. A decrepit private dock allowed the Kin to enter and leave without interacting with any Soiled, and that was where they'd rowed to after leaving *The Morning Dream*. No one had met them when they arrived, and it hadn't been until Cal Canna had led them inside into a vast, raftered space filled with trestle tables and called out a greeting that Mam Nar had appeared.

"Cal Canna you rascal!" she cried, wringing her hands with a drying cloth as she stomped out of what Deryn guessed must be the kitchens from the brief glimpse he'd gotten before the door swung shut again. "Come to make more trouble for me?"

Cal Canna placed his hand over his heart and affected an expression of absolute incredulity. "What? Never, Mam Nar! You know I always behave when staying at this house!"

The frog-faced matron snorted. "I know nothing of the sort. Last time you blew through here I had a dozen Wardsmen coming around asking questions. Seems you caused a bit of a ruckus at *The Blind Pig*."

Cal Canna's expression became pained. "A misunderstanding, which I'd be happy to explain to the relevant authorities if they stop by again."

Mam Nar rolled her watery eyes. "I'm sure you would." Then, with a deep sigh and a shake of her head, she shifted her attention to the rest of them. "What do you have here? Friends of the Kin? They look like trouble if I ever saw it."

"And you would be wrong," Cal Canna assured her. He quickly explained what had happened ever since Nek Tov had agreed to take them on as passengers in Ter Drummond. Mam Nar gasped when he described the zemani ambush, eyed them in a new light as he told her of their Sharded nature, and by the time the tale was finished and he'd explained to her what Alia had done to the eggs of the Old Shells tears were running down her face.

"Most days I'd take your stories with a hefty pinch of salt," she said, wiping at her cheeks with weathered hands, "but you know that if you lied about something like this to me, there'd be no forgiveness." Mam Nar turned to Alia then, who stiffened in surprise as she swept closer and enveloped her in a fierce embrace.

"Thank you," she said. "If those eggs hatch, you'll have saved my people. We were staring at the end of everything we've ever known, and now that's changed. You can stay here for as long as you want, and I'll have hot meals waiting for you three times a day." She stepped away from Alia and flung out her arms, encompassing the eating hall. "Usually there's a galley or two staying here while trading is being done in the city, but no one has arrived for weeks. Now I know why." She wiped damp palms on her smock, leaving wet smears among the stains, then gestured at a set of stairs leading to a second-floor landing. "That means there's plenty of space for you all, and my stores are near to bursting. Find rooms you like and by the time you get back down here I'll have something ready to eat." After taking a deep breath to finish calming herself, Mam Nar spun on her heel and hurried back through the swinging door to the kitchen.

Cal Canna cleared his throat when she'd vanished from sight. "Ah, well, I should be getting back to the boat. I know old Nekkie wants to get going as soon as possible . . . and to be honest, the, uh, fiasco at *The Blind Pig* was perhaps a bit more serious than I just made it out to be."

"I'm shocked," Rhenna murmured.

Cal Canna's eyes widened as Alia stepped forward to enfold his hand with hers. "Thank you," she said. "For everything. I'm sorry we never had the chance to visit those secret places with the beautiful views of the moon you told me about."

"Wait, what secret places?" Heth asked, narrowing his eyes at Cal Canna, who was already backing away.

"Aha, ha-ha, yes, next time, I promise. And, uh, you're of course all invited – there are some simply spectacular little coves in the marshes where the moon just floats in the water . . ."

"Like a goddess's face," Alia continued, smiling innocently. "Almost as beautiful as my face, I believe you—"

"Well, then, I'm off," Cal Canna said quickly, interrupting Alia before she could finish. "Hopefully, we'll all meet again . . . but until then, goodbye!"

After a last jaunty wave, he turned and dashed through the doors back to the dock. Heth watched him flee, then turned to Alia. "What was that all about?"

"He was trying to woo me," Alia replied.

Even Rhenna seemed taken aback by the frankness of this admission. Deryn, for his part, had thought Alia completely oblivious to the Kin's romantic interest in her.

"Oh," Heth said, blinking in surprise. "Uh, did you, ah, like him?"

"No," Alia said cheerily, picking up the travel bag she'd placed on the floor earlier. "Now I'm going to go find a room with a window; I'd love to be able to see the stars tonight." Humming to herself, she then proceeded to skip up the stairs. The rest of them stayed staring after her until she'd turned down a corridor and disappeared.

"So it sounds like you still have a chance," Deryn said, unable to suppress his grin.

Heth punched him in the shoulder.

DERYN CLAIMED a spacious bedroom filled with ancient furniture that smelled faintly of must and mud, then collapsed on the lumpy cot and stayed there for quite some time staring at the mold-scarred wood of the ceiling. It felt strange not to feel the gentle swaying of the boat or hear the slap of the water against the hull, and he was tempted to close his eyes and let his exhaustion carry him away, but he knew Rhenna wanted to immediately start planning their next move, so he mustered the energy to sit up. Movement caught his eye, and he turned to find Shade dashing from one patch of shadow to the next, as if curious about what might be lurking within each. With a sigh, Deryn slid from the cot and returned downstairs, where he found his companions already seated at one of the trestle tables with a steaming tureen in front of them. Rhenna was slurping the thick white stew with a lack of decorum that would have no doubt shocked her family, and Heth surfaced from his own bowl just long enough to encourage Deryn to try some.

"Silver Shrike, it's good," he moaned. "I didn't realize how tasteless the gruel we had on the boat was until now."

"You're not eating?" Deryn asked Alia as he slid onto a bench and grabbed an empty bowl.

"I told Mam Nar I don't eat animal flesh and she's preparing something else," she explained, glancing yearningly towards the kitchen door. "Soon, I hope."

Deryn filled his bowl, then used one of the spoons that Rhenna and Heth had ignored to try a bite – the base was rich and creamy, laden with chunks of fresh fish and crab. It was just about the most delicious thing he'd ever tasted. They ate without speaking until the tureen was scraped clean, and for a while after stayed staring at each other in a daze, until Rhenna finally put her elbows on the table and leaned forward.

"It's time to get some answers."

Heth looked thoughtful as he ran his finger along the lip of his bowl. "Do you still believe in the plan you suggested in Ter Drummond?"

Rhenna nodded. "Yes. We need someone to infiltrate the home of the Unbound King and find out if those flame-sharded were truly sent by him. I doubt it's possible to learn whether my father was behind the attack, as I'm sure that would only be known by Xend an-Azith and his most trusted lieutenants, but surely everyone who serves here in Karath must know if a large number of flame-sharded had recently been dispatched on some errand." Rhenna's dark gaze settled on Alia. "And it has to be Alia. Her seed shard is rare, yes, but its existence is at least known about, and I find it likely that this exoticism will compel the Unbound King to take her into his service. She would undoubtably be an interesting addition to his menagerie."

"I've never heard of Treesworn leaving the Wild," Alia agreed. "I don't think there's another shard like mine within a thousand leagues of this city."

Heth grimaced and shoved his bowl forward with a clatter. "I still think it's madness."

"She only needs to stay until she discovers if the Unbound King ordered the attack. Just a simple, harmless question." Rhenna widened her eyes and looked around innocently. "Oh, where are all the flame-sharded?" she asked, affecting a terrible imitation of Alia's accent.

"Well, you see, we sent them off to assassinate the daughter of the most powerful man in the north!" Heth replied sarcastically, deepening his voice to pretend he was also someone else. "But in truth, he was actually the one who hired us to kill her!"

Rhenna's face darkened, and for a moment Deryn feared she was going to upend the soup tureen over his head.

"I can do this," Alia said, clearly speaking to Heth. "I'm not a child or a fool."

Heth had been about to say something more, but instead he closed his mouth so abruptly that Deryn heard the click of his teeth coming together. He looked crestfallen, like he'd been reprimanded when he'd only been trying to help.

"I know you want to protect me," Alia said, her tone softening. "And I appreciate that. But if I'm the one best suited to join this king's tribe, then I need to do it. And I'll be careful, I promise."

Heth flushed, the scars on his face growing even more livid. "So what are we supposed to do while Alia is in the lair of the Unbound King? Sit here drinking soup?"

"There was another reason to come to Karath," Rhenna replied, glancing towards the kitchen as Man Nar pushed through the door carrying a tray laden with plates heaped with glistening vegetables and mushrooms. "That old woman said we should find the House of Last Light because the one who dwelled inside had answers for us."

"The madwoman in the ruins?" Heth asked incredulously.

"That madwoman saved your life," Deryn reminded him. "Your flesh knit together after she poured out that potion."

"And she gave me my shard," Alia said, pulling off her glove to display her fragment. The emerald light that had previously leaked from her seed shard had vanished; it looked like a speck of vaguely green-tinged crystal sunk in the center of her palm, the tracery of branching black lines also having mostly faded away. She was focused so intently on her shard that she didn't notice Mam Nar approaching and jumped in surprise when the Kin woman placed the platter in front of her, then squeaked excitedly when she realized what had been delivered.

"Mam Nar," Rhenna asked as the old matron was turning away. "Have you ever heard of the House of Last Light?"

Mam Nar's face crinkled. "Nay. Never have. Doesn't mean there's no such place in Karath. This is a big city and I stay down here on the river. Might be someone knows about it up on the Skull or in that old library."

"The Skull?" Rhenna asked.

"Oh, that's the hill where the five families meet. The Sword and the Shield's fortresses are up at the top, and the richest folk in Karath live on the slopes. As you travel down, things get poorer and poorer until you come to the Nethers ... and then there's the river."

"Thank you," Rhenna said, and Mam Nar must have heard the dismissal in her tone because she ducked her head and made her way back to the kitchens. Tapping her fingers on the table, Rhenna leaned back on the bench, and when she spoke again her voice sounded like she was trying to work something out in her head.

"That old woman might be mad," she said, "but there's no denying her power. My father said she has wandered the world for centuries, at least – his own father had told him of her, about how she traveled around to the different holds, and everywhere she was treated with respect and reverence. She is a vestige of the old world – from before the Radiant Emperor, even. My father called her one of the Elowyn ... it means 'The Old Ones' or 'The Elders' in the Gilded Tongue of the First Empire. And she said we should find the House of Last Light in Karath."

"She said something else as well," Deryn said, trying to remember what that had been. "Something about a pale woman she saw in the Duskhold ..."

"I know who she was speaking about," Rhenna said. "I was there the night when she visited our hold."

"As was I," Alia said, popping a plump mushroom into her mouth. "I remember that feast, all those disgusting foods."

"She was referring to my father's advisor, Leantha Devoril. In recent years, he listens to her even over his own brother. This hardly seems to bother Joras, given how disinterested he is in matters of ruling, but Nishi and I found it concerning."

Deryn frowned, still trying to remember what the old woman had said in those chaotic moments after the blood-sharded had been pulled into the shadowrealm. "She said she'd seen Leantha before she visited the Duskhold, didn't she?"

Rhenna nodded tightly. "She did. She said . . . she said she recognized her from the great square in Derambinal, that the same woman – but wearing a different face – had placed the copper crown on Osmari an-Alams's brow and declared him shah of all the Salah. And not long after that, the armies of the desert had boiled forth and conquered the stone-sharded canyon city of Chan-Anok, then begun marching on Ashasai. If the holds of the north had not hurriedly joined forces, the First Empire might have been reforged under the copper crown of the Salahi."

"Wearing a different face . . ." Deryn repeated slowly, his thoughts churning.

"Yes," Rhenna said grimly. "If that old woman spoke the truth, then the one who returned to the Duskhold claiming to be Leantha Devoril might be an imposter. An imposter that can take the face of another." She let those words hang in the air, looking around the table meaningfully.

"A soul-sharded," Deryn murmured. "Like the man who took Vertus's face."

Rhenna pursed her lips. "We may have discovered pieces of the puzzle, but we don't know how it all fits together. I hope that the one who dwells in this House of Last Light – if it truly exists – can help us understand."

And perhaps make it clear if her father was truly responsible for what had happened. Deryn knew this was what was truly consuming Rhenna. Was Cael Shen just a piece in a game that was being played by others . . . that thought seemed impossible, but then again, Osmari an-Alams must have been a man similar in strength and stature to the shadow-sharded lord.

"So we will look for this House while Alia finds out what she can in the manse of the Unbound King," Deryn said.

Rhenna nodded, looking slightly relieved that she had convinced him. "Yes. This city is huge, and we have no idea where the House might be, so I believe it would be best to separate and search different areas."

"Cal Canna said the city proper was split into two sections," Heth said. "With the poorer part hugging the river called the Nethers. If we're dividing up Karath, I think I should stay here. It'll likely be rougher, more dangerous . . . and right now, I'm the one who can defend himself the best."

"That makes sense," Rhenna agreed. "And that leaves the rest of the city for Deryn and myself—"

"Let me go to the Erudinium," Deryn interjected. "It's the greatest library in the world. If anywhere might have knowledge of this House of Last Light, it would be there."

Rhenna opened her mouth, looking for a moment like she wanted to ask him something else, but then she shrugged. "Very well. And if the scholars do not entertain your requests for help, the next day you can join me in searching north of the Nethers." She laid both of her hands flat on the table, her gaze slowly moving between them. Her pale cheeks were slightly flushed, and there was excitement in her dark eyes. Deryn knew exactly what she was feeling – they had a plan and a purpose, and after the long, grueling journey from the Winter Palace in the Frayed Lands, the answers to the mysteries haunting them might finally be within reach.

"I propose we get some rest," Rhenna said, pushing herself away from the table and standing. "Tomorrow we will find out what secrets this city holds."

14

HETH

The next morning when they stepped from the Kin house they found that the heavy shroud of mist which had draped the city the day before had lifted, revealing the Nethers of Karath in all its decaying splendor. Once the buildings lining the riverfront must have been the abodes of the rich and the trading houses of wealthy merchants, but now their intricate stonework had been effaced by the elements, their elaborate entrances on the verge of collapsing, and some were even listing dangerously, leaning against their neighbors like drunks struggling to stay upright. Nevertheless, there was still quite a bit of activity – small boats plied the waters with nets hanging over their sides, and fishmongers hawked fresh catches from blankets laid on the road running beside the river's edge. Women with children clinging to their legs chatted as they hung laundry from crumbling porticos, and men lazed on steps playing a game of black and white stones or called out their trades to passersby in the hopes of finding work for the day.

Heth had retired to his room in the late afternoon and hadn't woken until well after dawn had broken, but he still felt a bone-deep weariness that he suspected had little to do with how much rest he'd gotten. Everything seemed hazy, like he was seeing the world through a veil. And his companions also seemed to be suffering – Rhenna looked wan, and she kept blinking and grimacing as if the brightness of the day was bothering her. For Heth, it had been a little under a month since he had gained his shard, and so returning to this drab and muted existence was far less debilitating. Still, Rhenna seemed to have accepted her situation, and Heth had to quicken his stride to keep pace with her as she started on the avenue leading north, away from the river and into the city proper.

They had decided over a breakfast of bread and cheese that before they all went their separate ways they would first make sure that Alia gained entrance to the Unbound King's manse. Her mission was the most important, and Heth thought it very likely that the rest of them might be on a fool's errand anyway, chasing down the imaginings of a madwoman. A strange and powerful madwoman, but a madwoman nonetheless. Heth suspected that this 'House of Last Light' did not even exist, or perhaps it had existed long ago, in whatever dim past that woman remembered . . . but he also knew that searching for this mysterious place would give them all something to do aside from worry about how Alia was faring.

And it would give him an excuse to explore the Nethers. Cal Canna had told them that a group of people lived here that Heth was very interested in meeting.

The Hollow.

He had been considered Hollow while serving in the Duskhold. No, not serving – *enslaved* in the Duskhold. His father had been a slaver, and Heth was very aware that the Hollow were not servants, as the Sharded Few claimed. Servants could leave their masters; they were not property, to be disposed of without consequence if they failed in their duties or tried to flee. Heth felt a flush of shame knowing that he had once treated Deryn like a slave, even though he had in truth been only indentured. He had acted like one of the Sharded Few.

The situation in the Duskhold had been monstrously unjust, and he suspected the Hollow were treated similarly in every other hold. Only here, in Karath, could they live freely.

But what if something else was possible? What if Heth was not unique? What if every Hollow man and woman could claim a fragment from the Light shard hidden beneath the Winter Palace? The thought was dizzying. It would upend the very order of the world.

Heth thought about the butcher boys he'd taught the sword back in the Duskhold. Yennick and Vinish and Mouser. Boys who – if he was right – should be channeling *ka* through their pathways and practicing Sharded talents, not hacking apart meat in the bowels of the Duskhold. They should be princes, not slaves.

If he was right. *If* he was not special, some strange anomaly. He needed to bring other Hollow to that hidden shard and find out the truth. Could he convince some of the Hollow hiding in this city to risk a journey halfway across the known world?

Vessel of the Radiance. You must bring others to drink deep, as you have.

Heth gritted his teeth, willing away the memory of bloody lips and cold blue eyes. That ... *thing* may have planted the seed, but the plans he'd been considering the last few weeks were his own.

"What's wrong with them?" Deryn muttered uneasily, pulling Heth back to the street they were walking down. He blinked, glancing around to figure out what Deryn was talking about.

Nothing seemed particularly out of the ordinary. Slouching buildings of two or three stories hemmed the way, pockmarked where bricks or tiles were missing, and the road bustled with gray-bearded men in threadbare clothes, ragged young children who appeared mostly feral, and young women with baskets of vegetables under their arms.

And then he saw it. An unsettling number of the older men and women had some deformity – a withered arm here, a badly twisted leg there, or a hand curled into a claw and stained black, as if afflicted with some kind of rot. The skin of many was strange as well, broken by patches of silver that gleamed iridescent, like the scales on a fish's belly.

"Some sort of plague?" Rhenna guessed, keeping her voice low as she gave a man with a pustule bulging from his neck a wide berth.

"What disease can cause so many different ailments?" Alia asked, frowning.

"I don't know," Heth replied, gesturing at a large group of people gathered up ahead where the street emptied into a plaza, "but don't get too close to anyone." He suspected that it wasn't contagious, though, as no one seemed to be very concerned about being near the afflicted.

"Is that a stage?" Rhenna asked, craning to try to get a better view of what was beyond the milling folk blocking their way.

"It's definitely a platform," Deryn answered, his pace slowing as they reached the outskirts of the crowd. "Perhaps a performance?"

"A performance?"

Heth turned at this new voice. A young man in a wine-colored tunic and frayed trousers was leaning against a wall, his mouth twisted into a bitter smile.

"It ain't a performance," the stranger said, then spat in the dirt at his feet. "Ten days after the full moon is the Tithing. The Wardsmen would never forget."

"Tithing?" Heth asked, standing up on his toes to get a better view of the low platform. A half-dozen guards wearing gray half-helms and chain shirts were arrayed across it, leaning upon halberds. A splayed black hand was displayed prominently on their white tabards, and Heth guessed that these were the Wardsmen he'd heard about. The hand must be their sigil.

The young man pushed himself from the crumbling wall, looking them up and down with interest. "You're all new here, then. And since you're in the Nethers ... you Hollow?"

Heth glanced at the others, unsure what to say. Would those dwelling here be more willing to talk if they thought them to be Hollow?

"Yes," Rhenna said, apparently deciding that this was indeed the best course forward. "We escaped from the Duskhold and are looking for a new life in Karath."

The man's eyes widened. "You came from the Shadow? I've never heard of anyone slipping away from the shadow-sharded.

They're the most vicious bastards of them all. Must be quite the tale."

"It wasn't easy," Rhenna replied tightly. "And not something any of us want to talk about anytime soon."

"Understood," the young man said. "I'm Nethers born and bred, like most here. Regan's the name. My parents were Hollow, ran away from Flail after my da did a poor job shodding Lord Jorel's horse and the stallion broke a leg. Others had lost heads for less, so they fled. Hounds almost caught them more than once." Anxious murmurings suddenly rippled through the crowd, drawing Heth's attention back to the platform. Two more guardsmen had now joined their fellows, faces flushed from carrying a huge barrel to the front of the stage. The top of the barrel was open and bristled with strangely shaped objects – after a moment, Heth realized that these were dozens of sword-hilts, all tightly packed together. As they set the barrel down, a few moans of dismay rose up from those watching.

"What is going on?" Rhenna asked the young man, who had sauntered closer to her. "What is the Tithing?"

"It's the way of things here in the City of the Dead," Regan explained. He'd laid his hand on her arm, and she glanced at it like she might have detached it from his wrist if circumstances were different. "See, this place ain't paradise for us Hollow. There ain't any other place we can go, and the Wardsmen know that. Us Hollow, we're the only ones who can go down into the mines and dig out the rock that makes everyone except us wealthy. Regular folk, they're dead within a fortnight. Hollow, though . . . it does bad stuff to us, given enough time down in the tunnels, but it don't kill us. Usually. Maybe an arm falls off or something. And you can always tell who has been down in the mines from the scale-skin."

Heth shared a quick glance with Deryn, who was frowning. One mystery had been solved.

"Now, of course, no one would willingly take the risk of losing a limb to fetch the karathinite. So we have the Tithing. Every month those who just reached their thirteenth name day have to come here and see if they're lucky. The ones that aren't . . . well, they gotta go across the river for five years, or until something happens to them that's so bad that they can't work no more. And then they . . . " Regan's voice trailed away, his mouth twisting into a bitter scowl. "Ah, that's him," he muttered darkly, staring daggers at a fat man who had appeared on the platform just behind the spray of sword-hilts thrusting up from the barrel.

"Who?" Heth asked, squinting at this new arrival. He wasn't wearing the helm or chain mail of the other Wardsmen, but a black hand was emblazoned on the surcoat straining to contain his ample belly.

"Daemonel Thiss, the Sword's nephew. He's the man who took my brother."

"Took him to the mines?" Deryn asked, his hand tightening around the hilt of his wind-sharded sword.

"Yeah. Lelant was Tithed last year. He's still got a long time to go down there before he can come back to me and my ma." He jerked his chin up at the toad-faced man, who had moved out from behind the barrel and was holding a scroll as he surveyed those gathered below. A deathly quiet had fallen over the crowd, and the man grinned, seemingly enjoying the rising tension.

"I don't know why I always come to these Tithings," Regan said, his words barely more than a whisper now. "I hate seeing Thiss up there, so smug." He shook his head, scowling.

"Citizens of Karath," the fat man cried, his surprisingly shrill voice echoing in the silent plaza. "We gather here for the Tithing, to see who among your children will dedicate themselves to ensuring the prosperity of our beloved city." He unrolled the scroll, studying whatever was written. "Now, I want no dallying if I call out your name, children – come up here and wait by the stairs. I'm certain we all have a great many things to do today, so let's make this quick." The man then cleared his throat loudly and began to read out a list of names.

"How do they decide who has to do this . . . Tithing?"

Regan spat again. "The Wardsmen keep careful records of births in the Nethers. It's just about the only time anyone up on the hill pays any attention to the Hollow living down by the river."

"And if they don't bring their children here on this day?" Alia asked, wrapping her thin arms around herself. She looked ill, as if the thought that parents would have to send their sons and daughters to toil under the ground was making her nauseous.

"Then the Wardsmen will break down the doors to their house and drag their children away. At least in the Tithing there's a good chance they won't be chosen."

A crowd of scared-looking children in ragged clothes were now clustered on the edge of the stage, staring at the barrel bristling with swords in dread. The fat man finished reading the names, though his plump lips kept moving while he silently counted the boys and girls who had come onto the platform.

"You!" he said, jabbing a finger at a thin waif in a flour-stained smock.

As the girl shuffled towards the barrel, a woman in the crowd started crying, great gulping sobs raw with terror and grief. Deryn looked pained, and Heth wondered if he was reliving some memory about his own mother and how she had been forced to indenture him to keep them both alive. Only Rhenna remained visibly untouched as the girl came to stand beside the barrel, though Heth had now known her long enough to suspect that strong emotions were churning beneath her stony exterior.

Everyone gathered in the plaza below the platform seemed to be holding their breath as the small girl slowly reached out and grasped a hilt protruding from the barrel. She strained to pull it up, but the sword only shifted slightly, and with an annoyed huff the fat man lurched forward, grabbed the hilt, and ripped it from the barrel.

Heth frowned. It looked just like any other sword, nothing remarkable that he could see. Evidently Fortune had turned her golden face to the girl, as somewhere in the crowd a woman gasped in relief. Daemonel Thiss scowled and tossed the sword aside, then motioned brusquely for the girl to get off the platform. Realization finally dawned in the waif's face that she had avoided being Tithed, her huge eyes widening further, and then she scurried away down the stairs to vanish into the crowd.

The next to approach the barrel was a stocky lad with the thick arms and shoulders of a blacksmith's apprentice, and he let out a deep sigh when he pulled forth another sword that to Heth looked perfectly normal. He was just about to turn and ask Regan what result would lead to a child being Tithed when a slight boy with a mop of dark curls stumbled back from the barrel holding a stubby sword – he'd yanked hard expecting something heavy, but this blade was less than half the length of what had been drawn forth previously. He stared at the sword in shock for a moment, and then let it drop to the wooden stage with a clatter. Horror replaced the surprise in his face, and he tried to make a dash for the stairs but two of the Wardsmen had apparently been expecting this as hands clamped around his thin arms.

From somewhere in the crowd came a terrible keening.

Deryn turned from the platform, jaw clenched hard. His hand was on the hilt of his sword like he wanted to draw it there and then.

"Come on," Rhenna said before he could speak. "We must go."

"They're taking that child," Deryn said tightly, his knuckles as white as the metal of his wind-sharded blade.

"And we can't stop them," Rhenna replied.

Heth studied the Wardsmen slouching on the stage. They didn't look particularly formidable, but without their Sharded strength he knew they had no chance of saving that boy. The same sense of frustration and powerlessness he'd once felt in the Duskhold rose in him again.

"This is not our place or our fight," Rhenna continued, then began to push her way through the fringes of the crowd, making towards the plaza's northern exit. The wailing had subsided into ragged sobbing after the boy had been dragged away, and up on the stage a small girl was approaching the barrel nervously, hands kneading the hem of her frayed smock. Heth forced himself to look away, and his gaze met Deryn's – he understood the pain and anger he saw in his friend's eyes, but he also knew that they could do nothing about what was happening. He shook his head to show he agreed with Rhenna, then plunged into the crowd.

THE SOUND of the Tithing faded away as they left the plaza behind, replaced by city noises – peddlers declaiming about the quality of the goods in their carts, the clopping of hooves and the clanging of iron, loud conversations, laughter, and the crying of children. None of them spoke about what they had just witnessed, though Heth knew from Deryn and Alia's expressions that they were thinking about the Tithing. Rhenna remained well out in front of them, striding down the street like she knew where she was going.

Which she didn't. Heth supposed she just wanted to get far away from the plaza, especially after seeing Deryn's reaction to what was happening. Maybe she also feared what Heth might do, but she need not have worried – he wasn't such a fool that he'd suggest trying to rescue those children. It might take Deryn a while to accept that he could no longer draw upon his Sharded strength and powers, but not Heth. He knew full well that a sword-thrust from one of those bored-looking Wardsmen would split his belly open.

He tried to avoid thinking about the terrible cries of those mothers as their children were dragged away, focusing on the city around them and noting how it changed as they moved farther from the river. The facades of the buildings became better maintained, the streets widened, and the clumps of night soil that had spotted the cobbles disappeared. The clothing of those around them looked finer, and there were no more ragged shadows hunched in alleyways or on crumbling stoops. They seemed to have passed completely out of the Nethers and entered a more prosperous district of Karath, and the hill with its ornate manses and soaring fortresses was looming larger and larger.

Rhenna's steps finally started to slow, and after a moment of apparent indecision at the choice of two streets she went over to a fruitmonger's stall. She returned soon after and handed a fist-sized purple fruit to each of them, though only Alia seemed excited – Deryn just stared at his dully and Heth also didn't feel much like eating.

"We're close," Rhenna said, wiping away a trickle of juice after taking a bite of her fruit. "He said that Xend an-Azith's house is up ahead, just at the base of the hill. We can't miss it, apparently. Just look for the shattered chains, as that's apparently his sigil."

"Strange to think that someone so hated by the holds can live so openly," Heth mused.

Rhenna gestured with her half-eaten fruit at the hill. "The Unbound King is a guest of those that live up there. We would do well to remember that."

Deryn sighed and shook his head. "All right, I understand. We can't change anything here."

Rhenna nodded, watching him carefully as he finally started to peel the fruit she'd given him, then turned to Alia. "And you're ready?"

"I think so," she said. "I just have to stick to the story. And once I know for certain if the flame-sharded came from here, I'll come back to Mam Nar's house."

"Good," Rhenna said, and to Heth, it looked like she was forcing herself to smile. "Then let's get you there."

THE HOUSE of the Unbound King was not what Heth had expected. Cal Canna had claimed that it was a fortress unto itself, and so Heth had been anticipating high walls with parapets patrolled by guards, perhaps a gatehouse with a portcullis.

Instead, it looked like the manse of a rich merchant in Kething's Cross . . . though this estate was a magnitude larger and grander than any in Heth's hometown. The encircling wall was white stucco veined by creepers and was topped by ornate crenellations that looked more decorative than functional. The buildings rising beyond this barrier were fashioned from the same material as the wall, with sloping, red-tiled roofs and balconies of wrought copper draped with greenery. An arched entrance was flanked by a pair of guardsmen in garishly bright livery and plumed, open-faced helmets – both were tall and broad-shouldered and sported the same ridiculous curling mustaches.

"I still don't like it," Heth said, eyeing the entrance from where they were loitering under the awning of a trader's tarp. The street here was one of the busiest they'd seen so far, with a constant flow of shoppers and trundling carts visiting the stalls lining the way. Rhenna had bought them flaky pies, and they'd been picking at their food while studying the Unbound King's house . . . though what they were waiting for, Heth wasn't exactly sure. Maybe Rhenna was having second thoughts about sending Alia in there alone.

"It seems like a nice place," Alia ventured. "Look at all those fruit trees inside the walls. This king has a whole orchard to himself."

"He's confident, I'll give him that," muttered Rhenna, her meat pie untouched on the table in front of her. "He projects the confidence of the Sharded Few, even though he's as vulnerable as the rest of us in this city."

"Perhaps there are some defenses we can't see," Deryn mumbled through a mouthful of pastry.

Rhenna grunted in agreement. "I'm sure there are. Xend an-Azith is the scion of an Ashasai bloodlord. The politics of the Sanguine City are more intricate and deadly than anywhere else, even the Duskhold – I cannot believe he would leave himself as exposed as it seems here. His entire family was murdered by a rival house, after all."

"Perhaps like father, like son," Heth offered.

Rhenna snorted. "Xend fled Ashasai with nothing but the clothes on his back and now rules his own twisted version of a holdfast. My father suspected he had as many Unbound Sharded in his service as there were shadow-sharded in the Duskhold – such a spectacular rise would not have been possible if he was a fool. No, the Unbound King is a formidable man, and his name is spoken with wary respect by even the greatest Sharded lords."

"And yet we're sending in Alia to treat with him alone," Heth muttered.

Rhennas gave him a sharp look. "He likely has hundreds of followers. He will accept her oath and then turn his attention to matters of far greater importance; I doubt he will say more than a few words to her. Alia will have to glean what she can about the flame-sharded who attacked us by asking his retainers some *discreet* questions." The emphasis she put on this word could not be missed as she turned to Alia. "Do you understand? Nothing that will raise any suspicions. If you must stay in there for a fortnight or longer before a good opportunity arises to find out what we need to know, so be it."

"I understand," Alia said distractedly, still staring at the fruit-speckled branches rising over the ornamental battlements. "Ask this Xend fellow as soon as possible where all the flame-sharded are."

"No! Are you even . . ." Her words trailed away when she noticed Alia's grin. "You're getting more and more insufferable, do you know that?"

"I'm learning from you all," Alia replied, sliding from her stool as she shouldered her travel bag. "I'm ready. And I'll be careful, I promise."

"Good luck," Deryn said, and Heth tried to echo this but found his mouth had suddenly gone dry. Instead, he attempted a smile that he suspected looked less than comforting. Rhenna rose and hugged her briefly, then stood back and nodded.

Something passed between them in that moment, but Heth couldn't be sure exactly what, and then without another word Alia turned and left the awning. She threaded her way through a flock of bleating, horned animals a drover was herding down the street and presented herself – rather brazenly, Heth thought – to the two flamboyantly dressed guardsmen. She said something that caused their faces to go slack with surprise, and then one of them looked her up and down in obvious disdain, no doubt taking in her drab, Kin-gifted clothing and matted blonde hair. He drew himself up so that he loomed over her, making a dismissive shooing motion with the hand that was not holding the haft of his polearm, but Alia held her ground and raised her arm to show him what was embedded in the center of her palm.

Its effect was immediate and gratifying. The smugness drained from their faces, along with most of the color. Bowing and scraping, they hurriedly ushered Alia through the entrance, and soon she had vanished from sight.

Heth watched where he'd last seen her for a long time, and when he finally forced his gaze elsewhere, he found that the others were still staring after her.

"I hope this wasn't a mistake," Rhenna said with a sigh, and if Heth hadn't already finished his meat pie he might have thrown it at her.

15

ALIA

The strangely dressed guards led her down a ceramic path wending through a garden she thought could only exist in stories. Swells of brilliant flowers rose around her like crashing waves, and recessed in their depths she could see animals and birds wrought of metal – there was a bronze heron, its beak glistening silver, and a little farther on hunched a great turtle, shell inset with gleaming jewels. From the limbs of slender trees with bark as pale and translucent as human skin dangled elaborate birdcages, their occupants calling out to Alia in sweet voices. Blossoms the color of bruises opened and closed as she passed, delicate tendrils unfurling to taste the air.

It was a garden of dreams. She had heard stories about how the rich and powerful in these lands relaxed in artificial wildernesses, but she was astounded by the effort it must have taken to gather all these flowers and arrange them so beautifully. She found it perversely compelling, this yoking of the world for the whims of men. She wished she could still touch the Seed inside her and through it the roots and petals and stalks surrounding her in such an overwhelming profusion. She could have coaxed them to burst forth from the prison the gardeners had so carefully constructed, consuming the twisting paths and the metal creatures and the white buildings with their red roofs . . .

"Lord an-Azith will be in the back," one of the guards muttered, and Alia returned to herself, blinking away the image of serpentine roots slithering up the sides of the manses. Strange, she had almost thought she'd felt an answering whisper from the Seed when she'd strained towards it, but it had been so faint, and gone when she'd tried to touch it again.

"Lord an-Azith? You mean the Unbound King?"

The other guardsman stumbled when she said this. "Don't call 'im that," he hissed at her. "He don't like it."

Alia shrugged. Strange that one would want to be called a lord and not a king – she suspected that she'd never fully understand these southerners.

She followed the guardsmen as they skirted the largest of the manses, and then sucked in her breath when she saw that the gardens behind the buildings were even more spectacular. The thickness of the growth and its tangled lushness almost reminded her of somewhere her mother had brought her to when she was a child, a grove that she had claimed had once belonged to the Treesworn, and where flickers of their power still coursed through roots and branches.

In the center of this garden a large open space had been cleared, and it was here that the Unbound King was holding court. At least, Alia assumed the man lounging on a cushioned divan was Xend an-Azith. She knew he was an Ashasai, like Deryn's friend and fellow adept in the Duskhold, Kaliss, as this man shared her copper skin and complete lack of hair. That was where their similarities ended, though. Kaliss had always been scowling, while this man was grinning. He was also flamboyantly dressed, with a ruffled silken shirt unbuttoned nearly to his waist, and billowing, bright gold pantaloons cinched by a crimson sash. A deep-red jewel glinted in the lobe of one of his ears, and a serpentine golden band twisted up his right arm. The color of the gem in his ear nearly matched the huge fragment sunk into his broad chest, although the latter seemed to drink rather than reflect the sunlight. Alia stared in awe at Xend's shard – it was much larger than Rhenna's, several times the size. Then she realized what she was doing and hurriedly averted her gaze, feeling the color in her cheeks rise.

Xend seemed not to have noticed her attention – or even her arrival. He had propped himself up on one elbow to better see what was happening in front of him, where a pit about half the height of a man had been scooped from the earth and layered with fine white sand. A young Salahi woman in a dark pleated dress was standing in this hole holding a large wooden box with bright blue markings and silver hinges. She looked nervous, Alia thought, her fingers tight against the red wood and her jaw clenched as she stared at the empty patch of sand at her feet. Clustered on the edge of the pit above her were several other Sharded, including three long-haired men wearing tasseled jerkins that were untied to display their fragments. From the intricate tattoos covering their dusky skin, Alia thought these must be wind-sharded warriors from the Frayed Lands. They were also focused on the sandy hole, and from the way they were grinning and jostling each other it seemed like they were expecting something to happen soon. The last member of the Unbound King's entourage was a severe-looking woman, her mouth set in a disapproving grimace. She was dressed like a man in a simple tunic and trousers, and her back was as straight as the sword at her side. Her face was smooth and unlined, but her hair had mostly turned steel gray, with only a few darker streaks hinting at what the color once had been.

The two guardsmen who had led her here hesitated at the edge of the garden, clearly unsure if they should interrupt whatever was happening. Before they could make a decision about this, Xend an-Azith's gaze flicked up from the pit; his brow creased slightly in surprise when he noticed Alia, and then he made a beckoning gesture for them all to approach. As they did, he sat up a little straighter and took a sip from the glass of wine that had been on a small table beside his divan.

"Jurgens! Malin!" he called out, drawing the attention of everyone away from the Salahi girl in the hole. "Who is this?"

One of the guardsmen cleared his throat nervously, casting a quick, imploring glance at Alia, as if begging her not to divulge their initial rudeness. "Ah, my lord, this here's Alia. She says she's Sharded."

Xend placed the wine glass back down with a satisfied smacking of his lips and then leaned forward, spreading his arms wide. "Well! Welcome, then, Alia. I always have room in my house for more Unbound. I'm sure you have quite the tale to tell, but I must ask you to be patient until our business here is concluded."

"Of course . . . my lord," Alia replied, inwardly wincing at the quaver she heard in her voice.

"But come," he said, waving her over enthusiastically. "This should be interesting. And you two – back to the gate. Who knows when another Unbound will turn up!"

The guards who had brought her to the garden hurriedly bowed and retreated, and Alia took a few tentative steps forward as the focus of the others shifted once more to the pit. The Salahi girl swallowed at their renewed attention, clutching the box tighter to her chest.

"Now, my lord?"

Xend settled back onto the divan, waving his glass languidly in her direction. "Please, Lyka. Let us take the measure of your master's latest offering."

The girl nodded, then squatted to set the large box down on the sand. She hesitated for the barest of moments before flipping open the lid, then without even a glance at the contents turned and began scrambling up the side of the pit. Her foot slid in the sand, and she gave a panicked little cry before one of the wind-sharded reached down and grasped her wrist. When he pulled her from the hole she collapsed in the grass breathing heavily, then twisted around to stare back into the pit with wide eyes.

Alia moved closer to better see what could have possibly inspired such a reaction. Something was shifting in the darkness inside the box, something most definitely alive, and then a long, jointed leg sheathed in a reddish carapace slowly emerged. Another leg followed, and another, and another, and after bracing these in the sand, a large, mottled shell finally lifted from the depths of the box.

Alia sucked in her breath. She'd encountered creatures like this before – it looked like one of the great tree crabs that had clung to the trunks of the skyspears in the woods she had settled in with her father after fleeing the Wild. If anything, this was a rather paltry specimen compared to the one Deryn had gifted her those many months ago, and there were other differences as well – its shell was covered with tiny spines, while the ones she'd seen before had been smoother and their coloration had better matched the forest.

The crab wavered, teetering on the lip of the box, and then it tumbled onto the sand. A collective breath was drawn by all those watching, as if in anticipation.

But what were they expecting? Surely this crab couldn't easily climb out of—

Alia jumped as a geyser of sand erupted, something that had been buried flinging itself at the intruder. Another crab, she realized, although a darker shade of red and its shell was laced with scars. It moved with startling speed, and in an eye blink the two crabs were locked in combat, claws and legs a frantic blur. Alia couldn't tell which one was winning until suddenly one of the crabs was on its back, legs flailing as its opponent jabbed its claws into its exposed underbelly. The audience exhaled as blue ichor flowed and the movements of the prone crab began to slow.

And then it was over. The victorious crab – it was the one with the darker shell that had been waiting in the sand – climbed atop the weakly twitching body of its defeated rival, as if preening for the crowd, and then it scurried back down onto the sand and burrowed out of sight once more.

The wind-sharded warriors congratulated the victor with shrill ululations, stamping their feet in the grass. Xend an-Azith grinned broadly and raised his glass towards the Salahi girl, who was looking dejected, her shoulders slumped.

"Lyka! My champion remains undefeated. Apologies you had to

come all the way out here for nothing, but I do appreciate that your master thought of me . . . and I hope in the future he'll still offer the very best of the new crop."

"Of course, Lord Azith," the Salahi girl mumbled, ducking her head.

"Green River Flowing," Xend called out, and Alia couldn't understand what he meant until one of the wind-sharded turned to him and she realized this must be his name, "retrieve dear Lyka's crab-box, if you would be so kind."

Another whoop came from the other two wind-sharded, apparently pleased not to have been the one commanded into the pit, and with a resigned expression and a few strong thumps to his back the man Xend had named Green River Flowing approached the edge. He hesitated, then leaped down into the hole, grabbed the box, and dashed up the side of the pit, legs churning in the sand. Above him, his compatriots hooted and hollered, but the crab must have been exhausted by its bout, as it failed to make a second appearance.

The scowling wind-sharded stomped over to the Salahi girl, shaking his legs as he tried to dislodge the sand that was clinging to his boots, then brusquely handed her the box. Xend an-Azith unfolded himself from the divan and stood, shaking his head and chuckling when Green River Flowing shoved one of the wind-sharded into the other, and then the Unbound King said something that Alia couldn't hear to the Salahi girl. Her eyes widened, and after a slight pause she bowed low while clutching the box to her chest, and then turned and made her way out of the garden. She kept her head down as she passed Alia, though she saw a slight smile on her lips.

"Now!" Xend cried, clapping his hands together loudly as he turned his attention to her. "Alia, thank you for waiting. Come closer, my dear girl. I promise you that fierce Mauler will stay down in his hole resting. He always sleeps after defeating a challenger."

"Mauler? Your crab has a name?"

Xend picked up a decanter where it had been lying in the grass and refilled his glass, then poured a healthy amount into another cup and held that out for Alia to take.

"He does. How else would the good citizens of Karath know where to place their bets?"

Alia frowned down at the churned sand at the bottom of the pit. "People bet on crabs?"

Xend sipped from his glass. "Indeed they do. The Salahi brought many interesting traditions when they settled in this city, but none of them were embraced as widely as crab-fighting. Now fortunes are won or lost betting on these fierce creatures. As someone who grew up watching brutal dramas played out in the bloodpits of Ashasai, I can assure you that this is a healthier obsession for a city." He smiled, displaying exceedingly white teeth. "But don't worry, despite Green River Flowing's theatrics, crabs do not attack people."

"Sometimes they do," Alia said.

Xend blinked in surprise at her interruption, his grin fading. "Pardon?"

"I saw a tree crab even larger than these sand crabs attack my friend. Well, he wasn't my friend at the time. He became my friend afterwards."

"A . . . tree crab?" Xend repeated, glancing at the gray-haired woman beside him.

"They live in the north, in the foothills of the Fangs," the woman explained. "I've heard they climb the trunks of the skyspears, great trees as tall as any tower in Karath."

Xend's expression became contemplative. "Those crabs are larger than the ones found in the Salah? And they're aggressive enough to attack *humans*?" He turned back to Alia, raising his glass. "Thank you, my dear. I will have to get my hands on a few of these crabs and try them out in the arena. You may have just made me a significant amount of money."

"You're welcome," Alia replied, unsure what she should say to this.

"Now enough about violent crabs," Xend said, dismissing the topic with a wave of his hand. "Tell me about yourself. Anytime a new

Unbound finds their way to my doorstep, it's usually an interesting story."

Alia realized that the three wind-sharded had drawn closer to hear what she had to say. She swallowed, slightly unnerved to be the center of attention for so many intimidating strangers, and quickly took a sip from the cup Xend had handed to her in the hopes that it would prove steadying. It had the opposite effect – the wine was strong, immediately making her lightheaded. "I came from the north," she finally said.

Xend swirled his glass before taking another drink. "Then it makes sense you know about these northern crabs. Did you escape the Ember? The Windwrack? Certainly not the Duskhold – the shadow-sharded clutch tightly to their slaves."

"No, the *real* north," Alia clarified. "Beyond the mountains. The place you call the Wild."

Xend coughed, nearly spitting out his mouthful of wine. After a moment he managed to swallow, pounding his chest to help it go down. The stern-looking woman and the People of the Wind looked just as surprised, sharing confused glances.

"The Wild?" Xend said when he was finally able to talk again. "What kind of Sharded are you?"

Alia raised her arm and unclenched her hand, showing him the dull green crystal embedded in her palm and the faded nest of black lines radiating outwards.

"Oh, my," Xend murmured, before taking another quick sip of his drink. "Now that *is* interesting."

16

DERYN

"You *must* stay out of sight. This is important."

To anyone passing by, Deryn knew he must have looked like a madman as he sternly admonished the shadows in an alley, but he at least could see the faint rippling in the pooled darkness as Shade preened himself like he actually had fur and a tongue – Deryn still found it so strange that the elemental seemed to absorb not only the forms of animals but also their mannerisms. He could only hope that Shade had not also inherited the legendary feline tendency to do whatever the hells they wanted, for if a shadow cat strolled into the Erudinium beside him this would surely cause an uproar. And if at all possible, he wanted to avoid drawing attention to himself. Go in, find whatever answers were within those walls, and get out. Word of a shadow elementalist appearing in the Duskhold might have already reached Karath, perhaps even that said elementalist had been killed when the Lady Rhenna's wedding procession had been ambushed.

"Are you listening to me? Do you understand?"

Shade did not reply, apparently still engrossed with licking himself clean of whatever could cling to an entity made of living shadow.

Deryn sighed. The elemental had demonstrated good sense in the past about when to stay hidden, so he would just have to trust that this continued. Turning away from the alley, he squinted into the day's brightness. Sunlight gleamed on the strikingly white walls of the Erudinium, which rose in broad tiers behind a more formidable wall than had girdled the manse of the Unbound King. Streaks of iridescent blue veined the stone of the great building, the design of which reminded Deryn of the shattered remnants of the First Empire he had encountered before. The Winter Palace had lacked these blue accents, but the purity of the white rock was very similar. He suspected that this abode of scholars predated the Sundering of the Heart and the formation of the holds.

Squaring his shoulders, Deryn left the alley's mouth and strode towards the only gap in the walls that he'd found during his circumnavigation of the Erudinium. No surprised gasps rose up around him, so he assumed that Shade was following him hidden in his shadow. A laughing child brushed past, pursued by an obviously exasperated mother – the sight made Deryn's stomach twist, for it reminded him of what he'd seen that morning. This Tithing had echoes of what had happened to him. His mother had sold Deryn into servitude so that they might survive the merciless winter in the cold northern forest, and the Hollow in Karath were also forced to give up their children so that they would not be cast out of the city and compelled to serve the Sharded Few. Even though he'd traveled the breadth of the known world, everywhere he'd found the same cruelty – the strong preyed on the weak, justified by tradition or law or temple.

The entrance to the Erudinium was surprisingly modest. A small gap in the high walls was filled by a table of black wood, behind which sat a man in umber robes with a silver bell near his folded hands. His cowl had been pulled back, revealing a cheery youth with flaxen hair. A small crowd had gathered on the other side of the table, and Deryn watched as the young scholar beckoned for an older woman in a faded dress to approach. He listened earnestly as she explained something to him, then without the slightest faltering of his broad smile he told her something that caused her shoulders to slump. Deryn arrived among these petitioners as the woman shuffled away, her expression downcast, and the scholar motioned for someone else to step forward, a weathered Ashasai man who was nervously twisting the brim of the broad straw hat he held.

As the Ashasai explained something about needing access to old maps to settle some boundary dispute, Deryn's gaze wandered over those gathered. Most seemed to be common folk, either tradespeople or poor students in simple robes, and he wondered if the rich had other avenues of accessing the wisdom contained within these towering white walls. He was surprised that there were no guards on duty, as he doubted very much that the fresh-faced scholar behind the table could stop anyone determined to enter the Erudinium's grounds. Deryn craned his neck, trying to see what was beyond this point – it seemed to be just a courtyard of white stone pockmarked by the occasional small tree, with men in umber robes seated on benches that had been situated to take advantage of the shade cast by branches.

"You, good sir! Come, please state your petition."

It took Deryn a moment to realize that the scholar had addressed him. He looked around in surprise, wondering why he'd been chosen when just about everyone else had been here well before he'd arrived, but then he gathered himself and approached the table. The scholar beamed up at him, hands clasped.

"Ah, yes, greetings," Deryn began, suddenly unsure how to proceed. He'd been rehearsing what to say ever since leaving the others, but his mind was suddenly a scrap of blank parchment.

"And greetings to you on this fine day!" replied the scholar. "Now, do not be nervous. What has brought you to our hallowed hall of wisdom?"

"I need to know something," Deryn said, then winced inwardly. Everyone here no doubt needed to know something.

"Of course. But why do you think the answer to your riddle can be found in the Erudinium?"

Deryn licked his lips. "Because it's hidden, or at least forgotten. No one has heard of this thing, but I was told I have to seek it out by someone very old and very wise." Well, in truth, she might be very mad. Despite the great powers the old woman had demonstrated, Deryn suspected this might be the truth of it.

Something sparked in the scholar's eyes, and he leaned forward. "Lost lore! A particular passion of mine."

Hope swelled in Deryn at the scholar's interest. "I was told to seek the House of Lost Light in Karath."

The scholar's reply was immediate. "Never heard of it!" he cried in that same disconcertingly cheerful tone. His eyes slid past Deryn as he gestured at someone else in the crowd. "You! You're next, come here please."

"Wait!" Deryn cried in alarm as someone large enough to wrestle aurochs shouldered him aside. "Just because you haven't heard of it doesn't mean it doesn't exist! Perhaps the Erudinium's archives hold the—"

"Enough," rumbled the massive fellow who had come to loom over the table, glaring at Deryn. "He told ye to leave."

"Yes, apologies," the young scholar said, though he didn't sound apologetic. "We simply don't have the time to chase down every old story—"

"Malachai!" Deryn shouted, wrenching his arm away from someone who was trying to drag him back into the crowd. "Malachai Gooth!"

The scholar frowned, glancing up from the runes etched into the ancient ax the large man had just laid on the table. "Excuse me?"

"Malachai Gooth!" continued Deryn hurriedly as a muttering began to swell behind him. "The physicker of the Duskhold! He sent me!"

"The physicker of the Duskhold . . ." the scholar said, tapping his chin thoughtfully. "I think I heard he studied here long ago."

"He did! He did!" said Deryn. "He was the one who sent me! He said he had old friends in the Erudinium who would help solve this mystery."

The scholar tilted his head to one side, regarding Deryn like he was seeing him in a new light. "The Duskhold. We do usually take requests from the Sharded Few seriously. But why have you come here, rather than making your request through the appropriate channels?"

Deryn felt the crowd's anger subside as they realized he had captured the scholar's attention. "It's because I'm not an official envoy of the Duskhold or Lord Cael Shen. This is a question that is of personal importance to Malachai."

The scholar tapped a finger thoughtfully on his dimpled chin, his gaze distant, and then he stood so quickly that the huge man on the other side of the table jumped backwards in alarm. "Very well! I shall escort you into our halls where you may relay your question to one of our Seekers." He plucked the silver bell from the table and rang it sharply, and in the courtyard behind him one of the scholars sitting on a bench under a tree leaped to his feet and hurried towards them. When he drew close enough that his face could be seen clearly an audible groan rose from the crowd – Deryn had to agree that he certainly did look far less friendly than the scholar who had just rung the bell.

"Follow me, shadow-sharded," the scholar said, motioning for Deryn to accompany him.

"Thank you," Deryn said as they strode across the courtyard. "I'm sorry to bother you – I didn't know there were official avenues that the holds used."

The scholar waved away his words. "It's understandable if you're not here at the behest of your lord. And I don't mind leaving my post – it gets tiring turning almost all these folk away. But it helps with the reputation of the Erudinium if we at least listen to their questions and problems, and every so often, something truly interesting comes out of these public hearings. I'm Seeker Rundtha, by the way. Of the second circle."

"I'm Deryn. Of the, uh, Duskhold." Rhenna would be annoyed that he'd shared where they had come from, but he'd been desperate to pique the scholar's interest and had said the first thing that had leaped into his mind. Hopefully these scholars would not be aware of Sharded intrigues happening far away. They certainly seemed lost in their own little world here, he thought, examining the other scholars as they headed towards the largest of the tiered buildings. All were dressed in the same umber robes, though most were far older than the scholar who had been stationed at the entrance. None looked at them as they passed, continuing to read the ancient tomes open in their laps or staring vacantly out into space, their watery gazes unfocused. They reminded Deryn of the old men who had drifted like ghosts through the ruins of the ancient logging-turned-crabbing camp.

Massive white-stone lions flanked the broad set of stairs leading up to the Erudinium's pillared entrance. Deryn was reminded of Heth's outlandish story of a white lion that had been guarding the Light shard beneath the Winter Palace, but these sentinels seemed to truly be statues. Still, Deryn kept an eye on them until they'd climbed the steps and passed into the gloom beyond the soaring, blue-veined pillars.

The entrance hall of the Erudinium was just as imposing as Deryn had suspected it would be from the outside. The high vaulted ceiling was inset with glittering stones that appeared to represent the night sky, and the floor was a vast swath of gleaming white that was empty of furniture save for another blackwood table. This one was piled so high with towers of ancient books that the small, sharp-faced man hunched behind it was nearly invisible. The scholar was so intent on examining an unrolled scroll of cracked golden paper that he did not look up when they crossed the great room, despite their footsteps echoing in the silence, and Seeker Rundtha had to loudly clear his throat when they finally stood on the other side of the cluttered table to get his attention. The older man glanced up in irritation at the sound, then leaned back with a deep, long-suffering sigh.

"Seeker Varish," the young scholar said, his cheeriness undaunted. "This is Deryn, an envoy from the Duskhold."

The seated scholar stiffened at this, his gaze sharpening.

Seeker Rundtha saw this as well and hastily continued. "Well, not an official envoy. He's here at the behest of the Duskhold's physicker, who once studied in the Erudinium. Malachai Gooth."

Seeker Varish relaxed, his annoyed expression returning. "Malachai Gooth? Yes, I remember him. A favorite of Seeker Chastine, spent all his time in the Arboretum. Left as soon as he realized he was one of the Sharded Few." His eyes narrowed suspiciously. "What answer is Malachai looking for? The Duskhold has an impressive archive, if I remember correctly."

"Uh, he came across a reference in the hold's library that he thinks might be of some importance," Deryn haltingly explained. "He wants to know if the Erudinium has any record of the House of Last Light in Karath."

Seeker Varish blinked in confusion. "In Karath? Why is anyone in the Duskhold concerned about something in *our* city?"

"I don't know," Deryn said with a shrug – he'd already decided that pleading ignorance seemed like the safest response to this expected question.

"How strange," Seeker Varish muttered, but he pulled out a scrap of parchment and scrawled out a quick message. He stared at it for a moment, reading what he had written, then glanced at Deryn. "The House of Last Light? Did I hear that correctly?"

Deryn nodded, and the scholar scowled again – which made him look even more rat-like – then made a beckoning gesture towards the arched doorway at the far side of the entrance hall. Deryn was expecting another scholar to emerge from this passage, but instead something seemed to detach from the smooth white wall. He sucked in his breath when he realized what had been lurking and listening this whole time, reflexively reaching for *ka* that was not there.

Claws clicked upon stone as a pale zemani approached the table. Slitted red eyes darted to Deryn, forked tongue tasting the air, and a rumbling growl started deep in its chest.

"K'Ral!" barked the seated scholar, waving the message he had just written in the direction of the creature. "What is wrong with you? This boy is no threat."

The zemani uttered a series of croaks, its head-spines quivering, and the scholar raised an eyebrow at Deryn. "He says you smell like *gthrenka*, whatever that is. Bad *gthrenka*."

Deryn tried to keep outwardly calm. He had seen what those viciously curving claws could do to flesh that was not hardened by the power of a shard . . . for the first time in months, he felt truly vulnerable.

"I'm not certain what that means, but I arrived in Karath on a Kin boat that had survived an ambush by zemani raiders. Maybe there's some lingering scent."

With a vexed grunt, the scholar heaved himself from his chair and smacked the zemani on the side of its scaled head with the rolled up message. "Stop making a pest of yourself in front of the guest or there's no fish for you tonight! Now, go deliver this message to High Seeker Ferman."

The nictating lids of the zemani's red-tinged eyes flickered rapidly, and its head-spines sank down until they again lay flat on its head. It looked almost sheepish, Deryn thought, but still it shot him a sharp glance as it took the proffered parchment, curling its claws around it with surprising gentleness. Then it was off, scurrying with a clicking patter down the passage it had been guarding.

"Willful creature," the scholar muttered as he watched it vanish into the dimness. Then he shifted his attention back to Deryn and the scholar who had escorted him here.

"Seeker Rundtha, return to the front gate. You're not getting out of petition duty that easily. And you," he said, and from his tone he had already forgotten Deryn's name, "sit over there and stay quiet. Deciphering written Gilded requires the utmost concentration."

"Sit where?" Deryn asked, looking around the otherwise empty hall.

"There," the scholar replied dismissively, gesturing vaguely as he sank down again into his chair, and Deryn realized he was indicating a rickety little stool lost in the shadow of one of the pillars. It hardly looked like a chair for honored guests, but the scholar was already shuffling papers and mumbling to himself as he returned to the golden scroll.

"Best of luck with your query!" Seeker Rundtha said, slapping

Deryn with surprising familiarity on the shoulder. "Shouldn't take more than a few days before you get your answer!"

DERYN WASN'T sure how long he waited, drifting in and out of sleep on the little stool, but when he was finally startled awake by the clacking of claws on stone he immediately realized that most of the day had drained away. The light slanting between the pillars and burnishing the white stone floor had deepened, casting much of the vast chamber into shadow, and while Deryn had been napping the scholar had placed a contraption of metal and glass on his table and kindled something inside to help him continue poring over the books and scrolls.

The white-scaled zemani marched up to the scholar and handed him another rolled message. This one was bound by a blue ribbon, and it took the frowning scholar a moment to unpick the knot. He read the message silently, then motioned brusquely for Deryn to approach the table. Deryn's legs and back protested as he heaved himself to his feet, and not for the first time he longed for the resilience of his Sharded body. He wondered if this was what it was like to get old, constantly pining for a time mercifully free of aches and pains.

The zemani's red eyes were fixed on Deryn once more, but this time it did not make any threatening sounds. Apparently, it had decided he wasn't *gthrenka* . . . or perhaps it simply didn't want to be chastised again.

"Regarding the matter of the so-called House of Last Light in the city of Karath," the scholar intoned, reading from the scroll. "There are no records of such a place. It is not mentioned in Anagogus's *Histories*, the civil records from before the founding of the Quinumvirate, or in the collected popular discourses during the Brocaded Age. Thus, I am confident in saying that this House does not exist, nor has it ever existed in our city. Please send my regards to my good friend

Malachai, and I hope this helps with his investigations. Signed, Ferman Ten-Amel, High Seeker of the Erudinium."

The scholar set down the message and looked up at Deryn with a faint smile, as if delivering the news that such a long journey had been in vain had given him more than a little satisfaction. "I'm sorry, young man. Return to your master and tell him the High Seeker's message. Whatever rumor or legend he stumbled upon in the dark corners of his hold has no basis in fact."

Deryn chewed his lip, trying not to show his disappointment. He had been certain that if the House of Last Light was anything other than the ramblings of a madwoman that the knowledge of its existence would be here. Perhaps that old woman *had* been speaking gibberish – it was not impossible, he supposed, that she was both a powerful immortal witch and also of seriously unsound mind.

The scholar was staring at him, clearly waiting for him to leave. Deryn glanced at the fading remnants of the day visible through the pillared entrance, weighing the implications of asking about the other great mystery he wanted answers to. Rhenna would almost certainly be angry if he broached this topic . . . but when would he ever have a chance like this again?

Deryn tamped down his misgivings and forced himself to meet the scholar's gaze. "There was something else. The Archivist of the Duskhold's library also asked me to see if the Erudinium has any writings on the true nature of elementals."

Surprise softened the scholar's sharp features. "Elementals? Why does he want to know about *them*?"

Deryn swallowed back the sudden dryness in his throat. "Because . . . because an elementalist has emerged in the Duskhold. And the Archivist has found precious little in the hold's library to help Lord Shen understand what they truly are."

The scholar's chair creaked as he sat back, studying Deryn with eyes that suddenly seemed more appraising. "An elementalist in the Duskhold . . ." he murmured, rubbing his chin. "That might explain it."

"Explain what?"

The scholar leaped to his feet, startling the white-scaled zemani that was still hovering nearby. "There is someone who would very much want to meet you."

DERYN HAD ASSUMED the curmudgeonly scholar was going to personally escort him deeper into the Erudinium, but instead he had written out a long message, folded it, and then entrusted this to the care of his zemani servant.

"Take him to High Seeker Helash," the scholar had told the lizard man, carefully enunciating this name, and then croaked something else. The creature blinked rapidly at whatever the scholar had said, then turned abruptly and with long, loping strides made for a different passage than the one it had gone through earlier.

"I cannot leave my post," the scholar explained, "otherwise I would be very interested in the High Seeker's reaction to what you've just told me."

"About the elementalist in the Duskhold?" Deryn asked, torn between trying to get more answers out of the scholar and hurrying after the zemani before it vanished.

"Indeed," the scholar said, then made a shooing motion towards Deryn. "Now, off with you. It's late in the day and though I expect Helash to work deep into the night, he'll be taking his supper soon."

Deryn bobbed his head in thanks and started jogging in the direction that the zemani had gone, but he need not have worried because it had paused at the threshold of the passage to wait for him. When he reached the zemani it narrowed red eyes at him, tongue licking the air as if tasting for something. "*Follow*," it grated roughly, and Deryn was so surprised to hear it speak that it took him a moment to realize what had been said. As he stood there dumbfounded, it passed through the archway and into a long, white-stone corridor lined by statues of men wearing the same robes as the scholars he had already met.

They traversed more galleries, up twisting stairwells, and through huge chambers with walls lined by shelves bursting with clay tablets. They encountered more scholars, some seated at long tables surrounded by open books, others in comfortable-looking chairs engaged in conversation, but none spared them a glance. There were servants as well, all dressed identically in simple gray uniforms, scouring the furniture of dust or pushing carts laden with ancient tomes. Deryn guessed that the Erudinium did not have a dedicated library – rather, every chamber seemed to have a selection of books and artifacts and tables where the scholars could conduct their studies. He was also surprised to see several more of the white zemani standing at attention – unlike the scholars who seemed utterly absorbed in what they were doing, the spines of the lizard men stiffened when they noticed him.

"*Smell you*," the zemani leading him growled, waving a clawed hand to stop one of its brethren from moving towards them.

"Smell me?" Deryn asked, trying to calm himself – the agitation he was causing among the other zemani was evident.

"*Smell wrong. Like the people, but not. Smell like gthrenka.*"

Deryn guessed that this term that the zemani did not know the word for referred to the warriors of the usurper queen who had ambushed the Kin boat. The zemani here in the Erudinium must have originated in the realm of the other queen.

"We were attacked by zemani on the way to Karath," Deryn explained, hoping his understanding of the situation was correct.

"*Yet you live.*"

"We killed many. Others got away."

The zemani made a strange crooning sound, and for a moment Deryn feared he had made a mistake, but when his guide spoke again there was a note of something almost like respect in its guttural voice.

"*Is good. Gthrenka deserve the long dark.*"

They continued on in silence for a time, passing beneath an intricate amalgamation of silvery threads suspended from the ceiling that looked like an enormous bird nest, until Deryn finally worked up the courage to address the lizard man.

"Are you all related? I mean, the color of your scales is the same."

The zemani glanced back at him, as if surprised by his audacity. "*All brothers. Same clutch. Cursed clutch. Can't stay in the home. Old agreement made with scholars, cursed must come to the cursed city.*"

"Cursed city?"

"*This place. Where the First Mother fell into the long dark.*"

"Here? In Karath? The first mother of the zemani died *here*?"

The click of the zemani's teeth coming together was its answer, and Deryn sensed that this was a topic it did not want to discuss further. With a sigh, he resigned himself to accepting that this was yet another mystery to which he would likely never find the answer. He pushed the rest of his questions from his mind and instead studied the long, faded tapestry lining the wall of the corridor. It showed an army unlike any he'd seen before, well-organized squares of infantry bristling with long pikes opposing some sort of monstrous, many-legged lizards. Winged creatures clotted the sky above the combatants, and Deryn wondered if this was a riftbeast and the dun-colored plains represented the Frayed Lands. He was interested to see what the other tapestries farther down the hall displayed, but before they could reach those the zemani halted at a heavy door of pale white wood.

Without bothering to knock, the lizard man pushed it open, revealing a large, round chamber with a sunken area in the middle. The walls were lined by tables and shelves cluttered with all manner of strange objects and apparatuses, but it was what was in the center of the room that made Deryn's breath catch in his throat. Ten containers fashioned from glass or some other transparent substance were arrayed in a circle, each with what looked like a copper flower sprouting from their closed tops. The stems ended in tangles of delicate root-strands that merged with the contents of these boxes – in one they were sunk into what looked like just a hunk of gray rock, while in another their hazy outline could be seen dangling into a pool of murky water. Roiling black mist filled the container closest to where Deryn stood in the doorway, occasionally lit by flickers of light, and blue-green flames crawled along the roots in the one beside it.

Stone. Water. Storm. Flame. Deryn's gaze swept all the containers and saw that each of the shards were represented. He was surprised when he noticed that the roots of one of the metal flowers disappeared into a heap of amber sand, because he had heard that the Sand shard had been destroyed after the defeat of the Salahi.

Deryn was so distracted by this bizarre spectacle that he did not notice the scholar in his umber robes until he materialized beside the zemani and plucked the note from between its claws. He was small and slight, with a complexion so wan it looked like he had never been touched by the sun and a shock of wild red hair that had not been washed or cut in quite some time. His lips moved as he quickly read the note, then he whirled to face Deryn in obvious excitement.

"The Duskhold!" he cried, clapping his hands together. The scholar released the note, as if forgetting he'd even been holding it, though the zemani snatched it from the air before it could flutter very far. "Excellent! I've been waiting for you! Oh, I have so many questions!"

"You . . . do?" Deryn asked, just keeping himself from flinching back as the scholar lunged at him and gripped his forearm.

"Yes! I'm High Seeker Helash, and I study the primordial realms." He swept out his arm to encompass the arrangement of glass boxes and metal flowers.

"Primordial realms?" Deryn mumbled as the scholar dragged him down the steps into the basin in the middle of the chamber.

"Well, not *all* of them," Seeker Helash amended, sounding somewhat apologetic. "Just the realms that brush up against our own."

"They do that?" Deryn asked, feeling dazed. Was this scholar mad? He certainly looked unhinged. Deryn glanced over his shoulder to see if the zemani could offer any assistance, but the lizard man had already vanished.

"Do what?" the scholar asked, briefly releasing Deryn's arm to fiddle with one of the gleaming metal stalks thrusting from a container.

"Brush our own? They do that?"

The scholar gave Deryn a confused look. "Of course they do. In fact . . ." His hand darted out, and Deryn almost cried out as Seeker

Helash's finger poked the shard under his shirt. "Ah, yes, there it is. As I suspected. The Duskhold wouldn't send a Hollow or any other servant on a mission of such importance."

"What are you doing?" Deryn asked angrily, slapping away the scholar's hand. It was considered quite the violation among the shadow-sharded to touch another's fragment without permission.

"Showing you where the other worlds infringe upon ours," the scholar explained, oblivious to Deryn's outrage. "Your shard is a link to the shadowrealm. In here"—Seeker Helash crouched to rap his knuckle on the outside of a box utterly bereft of light—"cosseted in darkness, lies another shard of the Shadow. A window to that very alien place."

"Then what is this?" Deryn asked, gesturing at the metal flower. Now that he was closer, he saw that in the center of the unfolding petals was a gap, which presumably meant the stalk was hollow.

"My attempt to open those windows!" Seeker Helash cried. He bent over, putting his ear to the hole. "I can listen to the frozen winds rushing through the realm, the susurration of things moving through the dark. Some may not believe me, but sometimes I can even hear strange piping melodies floating on the ethereal tides!"

Deryn glanced at the scholar in surprise. He'd also heard that same music . . . if you could call it music, and seen the Others dancing at the edge of his vision when he'd accompanied Nishi through the shadowrealm. Apparently, this scholar was not as mad as he seemed.

"So you've come to learn about elementals," Seeker Helash said, lifting his head from the metal contraption as he straightened to face Deryn again. "Because one has taken up residence in the Duskhold. That must have happened about a month ago."

Deryn was startled by the confident incorrectness with which the Seeker had made this statement. Shade's appearance had happened during his Delve several months in the past. "No, actually. The elemental appeared well before that."

Now it was the scholar's turn to look confused. "That doesn't make any sense – the Event happened much more recently."

"The Event?"

The scholar's gaze unfocused, as if he was watching a memory unspool. "Oh, you should have seen it. The darkness in my Harridan cage was absolutely *thrashing*, and I didn't even need my funnel to hear the *keening* of the shadow realm. It was chaos! Somewhere in the world, something momentous had happened . . . a rip occurred, the living darkness bleeding across the divide."

Deryn couldn't understand fully the scholar's babbling, but he had a strong suspicion that he knew what he was talking about. A month ago, Shade had opened a doorway to the shadowrealm in the ruins of the Winter Palace, and through it the Others had emerged to save them from the blood-sharded hunting Rhenna. *That* must have been what caused the agitation the scholar had witnessed.

"What's your name?" Seeker Helash suddenly asked, leaning in so close that it became painfully obvious that he had not bathed in quite some time.

"Deryn."

"And what are you? *Sardor*? *Arzgan*?"

"*Kenang.*"

The grip on his arm tightened. "*Kenang*! How interesting. The lord of your hold – wait, what's his name again?"

"Cael Shen," Deryn offered quietly, unable to believe that there was anyone in the world who did not know who ruled the Duskhold.

"Yes! That's right, Cael Shen. He must be very interested in this elemental to send a *kenang* all the way here and risk losing you to the City of the Dead." Seeker Helash rubbed his hands together, almost gleefully. "A new elemental in the world. How interesting! What does it mean? What do *they* want? If its emergence was not what caused the Event, what *else* has happened?" His gaze sharpened on Deryn. "You've seen it, I take it? This elemental?"

Deryn swallowed nervously, hoping that Shade would not seize this opportunity to show himself. It would be just like the elemental to leap out at such a moment – Deryn suspected the scholar would at least faint, if not succumb then and there to a fatal shock. "Yes, I've seen it. The . . . the elementalist doesn't know why he was chosen, and that is why I've been sent here. To see if the scholars of the Erudinium have any answers."

"So it hasn't attempted to communicate? Nothing at all?"

"He . . . *it* may have spoken a few words, but it doesn't seem to be able to converse."

"Interesting, interesting," Seeker Helash murmured, releasing Deryn's arm and tapping his finger on his lips as he meandered towards another door. He gripped the heavy iron handle and pulled, revealing a room that might have been about the same size as the chamber they stood in, but so cluttered with overflowing bookshelves that it appeared much smaller. The scholar swept out his arm to encompass this jumbled mess, turning back to Deryn.

"Here I've collected much of the known literature on the other realms. And though it has not been my exact focus, there is also quite a bit of information about elementals and their . . . owners. I give you permission to see what you can discover, so long as you share your findings with me." The scholar hesitated, his brow creasing as something occurred to him. "You can read, can't you?"

"I can read," Deryn murmured, his throat suddenly dry. If the answers he sought were anywhere in the world, they were in this room.

He felt his shadow shiver, as if Shade shared his excitement.

17

HETH

Heth grimaced as he swallowed the last bitter dregs at the bottom of his cup. He didn't know what they put in the drinks here in Karath, but every tavern he'd visited in the Nethers had served him something with the same unwelcome flavor, regardless of what he'd ordered. Beer, wine, mead, and now ale – all that was left to try was hard liquor, and if the same silty residue was at the bottom of whatever watered-down spirit they brought to him, he'd know that it was inescapable. Although he wondered if what was served north of this district was different – he'd ask Rhenna when next they saw each other at the Kin house, though he found it likely that she had not indulged during her own investigations.

Outside of the odd additive in his ale, this drinking house was otherwise very similar to the grotty establishments he'd grown up frequenting in Kething's Cross. As the son of a rich merchant, he'd spent most of his time at *The Bull*, with its gilded candelabras and furniture intricately carved of skyspear wood, but he'd also regularly gone down to the drinking-dens along the banks of the Havilas, half of which had been listing so badly that they'd seemed to be on the verge of toppling into the river. This Nethers tavern could have been drawn from his memories: low ceilings, grimy windows, a floor sticky with spilled beer and other, less salubrious substances. Patrons sullenly playing cards or protectively hunched over their drinks. And of course there was the drunk passed out at one of the tables – here, it was a massive Salahi, one of the largest men Heth had ever seen. What hair he had left was gray, but the shoulders that were gently rising and falling as he snored were still powerfully broad. Some kind of laborer, Heth guessed. He'd seen quite a few Salahi in their colorfully patterned dresses during his exploration of the Nethers, but usually in groups, and they seemed to avoid interacting with the other denizens of the district unless shopping at the ubiquitous street-side stalls. This was the first of the desert people Heth had seen in any of the taverns he'd visited.

"Another one?"

Heth looked away from the sleeping Salahi to find that the thin, freckled boy who seemed to be the only server in the tavern – he'd already forgotten the name of this place, though he thought it had something to do with flowers – was standing next to his table.

The unpleasant aftertaste of the ale had almost fully vanished, but Heth still wasn't feeling very inclined to continue drinking. After all, if he left soon he might be able to visit another spot before returning to the Kin house. Maybe the fifth time would be the charm, and he'd finally find a decent drink in the Nethers.

He shook his head, then remembered why he was here in the first place and reached out to touch the boy's arm as he moved to collect Heth's cup. "Wait. I had a question I wanted to ask you. I'm looking for the House of Last Light. You heard of it?"

The boy's face scrunched up as he considered Heth's question. "Is it a tavern? Sounds like a tavern."

Heth shrugged. "I don't know. Could be."

"Ain't in the Nethers. Place with that name sounds fancy. Very ladee-da. I'd look around the Skull, if you want my advice."

Heth grunted his thanks, letting go of the boy. The wave of pleasant numbness that had been building was just starting to crest, and the memory of his less-than satisfying cup of ale was fading. Perhaps he'd rather enjoy his final drink of the night here. As the boy had said, this House of Last Light was probably in the district Rhenna was searching. Good chance she'd already found it, if it even existed.

"All right, another one," Heth said, and the serving boy bobbed his head before turning away. He leaned back in his chair, tamping down a moment of panic when he heard the old wood creaking, and let his gaze travel again over the common room. He was suddenly feeling a fair bit more affection for this place. Maybe the trio of gray-beards in the corner would be willing to teach him the card game they were playing, or perhaps the freckled girl polishing glasses behind the bar who almost certainly was the older sister of the serving boy would be interested in hearing about his exploits in the sword-halls back in the Cross . . .

The door banged open, drawing the groggy attention of a few patrons, though most of the rest remained lost in whatever stupor they'd sunk. Heth glanced over to see who had entered with such disregard for the comfortable tranquility of the tavern . . . and stiffened. The fat man who had just swaggered inside brandishing a meat skewer was familiar. His surcoat with the emblazoned black hand was now covered in grease stains, and at some point since this morning he'd acquired a heavy copper chain that was draped around the folds of his thick neck. Heth felt a swell of dislike, and he wasn't the only one – most everyone who had noticed his entrance was now staring at the Wardsmen captain with unabashed hatred.

Daemonel Thiss did not seem to care about the mood in the room as he made his way to an empty table and heaved his bulk into a chair. He wasn't alone – two other Wardsmen followed, helmets tucked under their arms, laughing at some jest. The sound grated in the previously subdued tavern like a rusty blade being drawn across stone, and the patrons stirred in annoyance.

Daemonel ripped the last hunk of meat from his skewer and then slammed it point-first onto the table, where it stuck, quivering. "Boy!" he cried, lifting his surcoat to wipe away the glistening juices running down his chin. "Bring us wine! And none of that Stormlands swill. We want the good Ashasai stuff!"

The girl behind the bar had apparently been anticipating this request, as she had already placed a dark red bottle on the counter, and at Daemonel's command the serving boy began pouring its contents into three tarnished goblets. Then he hurried across the room clutching the cups by their stems, weaving between tables and chairs with practiced efficiency. The attention of the Wardsmen had shifted to a set of black dice that Daemonel had spilled onto the wood with a clatter, none of them bothering to look up as the boy arrived.

"Oh!" the freckled youth cried, bumping against his hip against a chair. He lurched forward, and since the Wardsmen were intent on the outcome of the first throw of the dice, none of them saw how he practically flung the goblets he'd been carrying at Daemonel Thiss.

"Gah!" the fat man cried, nearly upending the table as he lurched to his feet. The black hand on his previously white tabard was now submerged in a sea of purple, and some of the wine had even splashed his face.

"I'm so sorry, lord!" the boy stammered, edging away from Daemonel. He looked on the verge of fleeing, but before he could escape one of the Wardsmen seized his wrist.

"It was an accident!" he continued, now almost shrieking as he strained helplessly. "My lord! An accident!"

Daemonel dragged his sleeve slowly across his stained face, his glittering black eyes fixed on the squirming boy. "Was it?" His voice was hard, edged with an anger so intense that Heth immediately knew that the boy was in serious trouble. Everyone else in the common room had gone silent, holding their breath in anticipation of what must be coming.

Realization suddenly struck Heth. Jogan. The swaggering arrogance, the casual cruelty, the disgusting personal habits . . . Daemonel reminded him strongly of his father's fat overseer. He remembered trading barbs with the man over glasses of wine in the ruins of the old lumber mill before watching him casually backhand a slave who had dared request a crutch after a fall from a skyspear tree.

He'd hated Jogan.

"I'm going to snap your clumsy fingers off," snarled Daemonel, grabbing the front of the serving boy's tunic and starting to drag him towards the tavern's entrance. The boy thrashed wildly, but the other Wardsmen had each clamped a hand on his shoulder and were forcing him along. Every patron in the common room watched with sullen gazes – even the massive Salahi had lifted his graying head from the table – but they made no move to intervene.

Heth shoved his chair back and stood. "Let him go," he said loudly, and the two Wardsmen stopped in surprise. The boy twisted about, his eyes widening when he saw who had spoken, and Heth could have sworn he saw a hint of a smile.

Daemonel turned, though his scowl faltered when he drank in the sight of Heth standing there with his hand on the hilt of his Salahi sword. Uncertainty replaced outrage, his beady black eyes fixed on Heth.

What was he—

Oh, of course. His scar. The anger that had kindled in Heth flared hotter.

"Do you know this boy?" Daemonel snarled, thrusting out his chest like he was trying to establish dominance. Heth wasn't fooled, though. There was a quaver in the man's voice and fear behind his eyes.

"He served me wine," Heth said simply, taking a few steps towards the Wardsmen.

Daemonel frowned in confusion. "Then he means nothing to you. Don't throw your life away, stranger. He has insulted an officer of Karath's watch, and he must be punished."

"It was an accident," Heth replied, his fingertips playing upon the pommel at his side. "Let him go."

Daemonel's fat face twisted in indignation. "*I* am the law in this city. How dare you?"

Heth shrugged. "I dare. Now, I'm going to give you to the count of five to leave this tavern."

"You bluff," Daemonel spat, but his gaze flicked nervously to the other Wardsmen, both of whom looked unnerved by this sudden turn of events.

"One."

"My uncle is the Sword of Karath. He'll have your head on a pike." Daemonel's words were full of bravado, but Heth heard their false-ness. He'd had plenty of experience with bullies, and this one was not to be feared.

"Two."

"The boy threw that wine at me," Daemonel whined, his tone abruptly changing. "I know it. They hate me down here."

"Three."

"Mern! Valis! Leave the boy. My uncle will be annoyed if we cause a scene. He's always saying the Nethers is looking for an excuse to riot."

The relief on the Wardsmen's faces as they released the boy almost made Heth smile. Almost, as he wasn't sure how much doing so would detract from the sense of menace his new scar was evidently imparting.

"This isn't finished," Daemonel hissed, jabbing a finger at Heth before hurriedly retreating to the door. Then he was gone, moving surprisingly quickly despite his paunch. The other Wardsmen followed without sparing any glances back, as if they feared Heth might still yet decide to come after them.

"Cowards!" slurred one of the old men slouched at the bar as the door banged shut. Voices echoed this in agreement, and the paralysis that had gripped the common room vanished; conversations swelled again, the clatter of dice being spilled across wood returned, and moments later it was like the interruption had never happened.

Heth wended his way between the tables to the freckled boy, who was patting himself down like he was surprised to find himself in one piece.

"Are you all right?" Heth asked. The boy's eyes were mismatched, Heth realized, one blue and the other green. How had he not noticed that before?

"Very good," the boy said, offering such a gleeful smile that Heth was taken aback. Hadn't he been just about to lose his fingers?

"You don't seem too concerned about what almost happened."

The boy shrugged sharp-boned shoulders. "Was never gonna happen. I would've pulled free once we got outside and gone into the warren, led them on a merry little chase. But I'm not mad at you for ruining my fun – it was worth it watching Thiss piss himself." His smile broadened when he realized what he'd just said. "Thiss piss. Haha."

The tension inside Heth had by now fully drained away, replaced by annoyance. "So you did dump the wine on him. I thought I'd imagined that."

"Course I did," chortled the boy. "If there's anyone who deserves gettin' soaked, it's Daemonel and his cronies after a long hard day of stealing the Nether's children."

"That's what this is about, then."

"Aye, he's a right bastard," the boy said, then laid hold of Heth's arm and began to steer him towards the bar. The old men crowding its length moved to open up a space for him, hands slapping at his back. "Come on, drinks on the house." The boy gestured at the freckled girl, who was already pouring him a cup of ale from one of the barrels. When she stumped closer to set it down in front of him, Heth realized that one of her legs was withered like a dried-out sapling, and only an elaborate splint was keeping her upright.

"Family?" Heth asked as the boy slid onto the stool beside him.

"My sister," he replied as the girl dipped her head at Heth. "Three years in the mines. Thiss was there the day she was Tithed."

"*Hm*," Heth grunted, returning the nod before hefting the cup and taking a long draught.

"I'm Jerik. My sister is Ferra. This here's our place."

"You seem a little young to own a tavern," Heth remarked, wiping the foam from his lips.

"Used to be our mother's. She couldn't stand the thought of Ferra down in the dark – her heart was already weak, and the Tithing made it worse."

"Sorry to hear that," Heth murmured. He noticed the girl was watching him with lips pursed, as if considering something. But she hadn't said anything, or made any sound at all – was she mute, as well as crippled? "I'm Heth. Just arrived in Karath yesterday."

"And you're already making enemies of the Wardsmen," Jerik said, flashing that impish grin again. "I think you'll be popular down here in the gutter, Heth. Welcome to the Nethers."

THE STREET WAS SLITHERING.

Heth placed his steps on the rain-slicked cobbles with care, waiting for the way in front of him to cease its annoying undulations. The cauldron of libations churning in his belly sloshed alarmingly, and he closed his eyes to steady himself. He shouldn't have allowed himself to be talked into that third bottle of Serisian black. It had been free, but so what? Rhenna had enough gold to buy a tavern in a better neighborhood.

Rhenna. Heth grudgingly opened his eyes, and was relieved to see that the street stretching in front of him had finally settled. He wasn't looking forward to seeing Rhenna when he finally arrived at the Kin house – he could already imagine her pursed lips and judging gaze. After all, he should have been out searching for the House of Last Light, not getting drunk in a Nethers winesink. Maybe he could sneak up to his room without her knowing he'd returned. Then again, what right did she have to be disappointed with him? After all, what better way to learn a city's secrets than in the taverns? Drinks loosened lips. Of course, no one had known anything about this mysterious house, but that was hardly his fault. It probably didn't even exist. They were chasing the ramblings of a madwoman while Alia was treating with the Unbound King, one of the most dangerous men in the world, feared by kings and Sharded lords. Heth shook his head, which made the street sway sickeningly again. There was no use dwelling on that now. He just had to get back to the boarding house, pass out, and he could worry about Alia when he woke up tomorrow—

Heth came to a sudden halt, his surroundings sharpening. He looked to his right, at the facades of buildings looming over him. Then to his left, where the great black expanse of the river unraveled into the dark. Above him, a sliver of an orange moon was visible behind shreds of clouds. He listened. Distant voices carried to him, raised in discordant song. The creak of shutters opening, followed by the sound of something soft and wet splattering on stone. The night noises of a city grumbling in its sleep.

What was bothering him? He concentrated, trying to assemble his fractured thoughts into something coherent. He was . . . He was . . .

He was being followed.

Cold clarity flooded Heth. He resisted the urge to turn around – if his pursuers knew he was on to them, they might immediately attack. Heth slipped his hand into his other sleeve and pinched himself hard. He needed to sober up. Was it a thief, trailing him in the hopes of emptying his pockets when he passed out in an alley? Or perhaps it was one of those old gaffers who had bought him a round after saving Jerik, making sure he arrived home safely.

No. Heth swallowed, tasting the last sour dregs of the Serisian black ale. It was Daemonel Thiss and his cronies. He must have hidden outside the tavern, waiting for Heth to stumble away so he could prepare an ambush where the streets were empty and the river flowing past could swallow up a body . . . Heth's hand slipped to the hilt of his sword. Here. This was where Daemonel would come at him. Well, at least the bastard wouldn't catch him unawares.

Heth whirled around and set his feet in the Mountain form as he drew his sword, the ring of steel clearing its scabbard sharp and sweet.

A man stood in the center of the empty street. It was not Daemonel or one of the other Wardsmen, but Heth knew him, even though his face was lost to the darkness. His shoulders were powerfully broad, and he must have overtopped Heth by at least a head.

The Salahi from the tavern.

"The sound of the *araskin* blade. Like music, even after so many years." The Salahi's voice was deep and slightly hoarse, as if he had not spoken in quite some time.

"Who are you?" Heth called out, shifting his stance slightly, though he did not lower his sword. "Why are you following me?"

The Salahi stepped closer, seemingly unconcerned by what Heth was brandishing at him. "I could not believe my eyes when I saw your hand fall on it in the drinking hall. But it is true. Its song is so pure."

"Stay back," Heth warned, retreating before the Salahi's advance. The man looked to be unarmed, but there could be weapons hidden within the folds of his loose, billowy dress. Was this a madman? Heth would rather not cut him down in the middle of the street, but he wouldn't hesitate to defend himself if he was attacked.

The Salahi was showing no sign of slowing. Heth gritted his teeth in dismay at what he was being forced to do, then lunged forward, trying to land a shallow slash on the man's arm, something that wouldn't be fatal but still demonstrate Heth's resolve.

He missed. Heth stumbled forward, unbalanced, as a huge hand clamped down on his wrist. His surprise at the speed of the Salahi's movement was washed away by blinding pain as his arm was twisted. His hand spasmed, the hilt slipping from numb fingers.

Metal clattered on stone. Heth reeled away in shock as the Salahi released his wrist and bent to retrieve the sword. He picked it up almost reverentially, staring into the dark blade as if Heth were no longer there.

Should he run? He'd never seen anyone who was not Sharded move so fast. And given the Salahi's size and strength . . . this was a warrior unlike he had ever faced in the sword-halls of Kething's Cross. With a sinking feeling in his gut, Heth knew that if he ran, he'd be caught almost immediately.

But the Salahi did not turn the sword on Heth. His craggy features, shadowed by the faint light spilling from the street lanterns, remained intent on the curving steel. Hoping not to pull the Salahi's attention to him, Heth began slowly backing away.

"Hold," the huge man rumbled, and despite his every instinct begging him to flee, Heth found his legs unwilling to move. In the tavern the man had seemed an aging drunk or a common laborer, with his grizzled face and stained clothing, yet here he loomed like a lord and his voice was heavy with authority. "This belonged to an *araskin*. A . . . dervish, a champion of the desert. Where did you get it?"

His tone was mild, but Heth heard the danger. "It was given to me by the Kin."

"The Kin?" The Salahi finally pulled his gaze from the depths of the sword, turning to Heth.

"River people. Traders. I traveled with them on the way to Karath. My family sword was shattered while defending their boat from an ambush, and they gave me this one to replace it."

The Salahi grunted. "And how did they get one of the sacred swords?"

"I don't know," Heth answered quickly. "As I said, they are traders. Perhaps they bartered for it with one of your people."

"No!" the Salahi snarled, and Heth's resolve came close to breaking. It took an effort of will not to start running. "None of the *araskin* would ever barter away their blade, even if they were starving. This sword was stolen from a corpse."

"Then I apologize," Heth said, trying to calm his thundering heart. "Take it back. I did not know it had been stolen, or that it had such importance to your people."

"The excuse of ignorance is not satisfactory," the Salahi replied, flourishing the sword as he took a step closer. Heth gritted his teeth, preparing to hurl himself out of the way if the desert warrior struck at him.

But instead the Salahi reversed the sword, holding out its handle. "You must apologize to my *bhalgras*. Come to my *qenari* in Karath and present yourself with this sword. Abase yourself and beg forgiveness for sullying this blade."

Heth reached out slowly and grasped the hilt. With a grunt of satisfaction, the Salahi let go of the sword and stepped back.

"Do this on the morrow."

"I'll come," Heth replied softly. The Salahi nodded curtly, and then without another word he turned away and was quickly swallowed by the night.

18

ALIA

The clanging of a bell woke Alia. Blinking away the last dregs of an unsettling dream – stuttering images of fleeing through a forest of thin dark trees, pursued by something that grunted and bellowed – she pushed herself from her cot and stood. The clothes she'd discarded before throwing herself down last night were still in a crumpled heap on the floor, and she quickly dressed as the sound of the bell came again, drifting through the open window. She noticed with some surprise that a platter of bread and eggs was on a small side table – one of the Unbound King's servants must have entered the room and left it while she was sleeping.

"Unfettered!" came a woman's voice, nearly as harsh as the bell. "I want you down here now! There is plenty of room in the mines if you can't follow orders quickly enough!"

Alia made her way to the window. Was she talking to her? The gray-haired woman who had been with Xend an-Azith in the garden yesterday was standing in the courtyard below, one hand on the reins of a beautiful bay stallion and the other holding a large bell like drovers tied around the necks of their cattle. She had donned armor of chain mail and tarnished gray metal, and she looked more at ease in this garb than in the clothes she had been wearing yesterday. Her gaze found Alia and she let go of the reins to make a curt beckoning gesture.

"I see you, Sharded! Stop staring like a halfwit and join me or by the tears of the Broken God I'll make you regret your clod-footed slackness!"

She *was* talking to her. Alia stepped back from the window, out of the armored woman's sight. There was a hot little worm of indignation squirming inside her at being ordered around so brusquely – it reminded her of the way she had been treated in the Duskhold after the Shadow had rejected her – but hadn't Xend told her yesterday that this was a fellowship, not a hold where she would be expected to bow and scrape? And they called each other Unfettered, which she'd learned meant to be free of chains. Perhaps this was just the woman's way.

The bell sounded again, if anything more impatient and insistent than before. With a sigh, Alia made her way over to the door, though she paused to stuff a few pieces of still-warm bread in her pockets. She considered taking her travel bag as well, but decided that it was unlikely she would not return – the girl who had showed her to this bedchamber had made it sound like it would be hers for as long as she chose to remain.

Alia slipped outside and hurried down a long corridor. This rambling old villa reminded her of the grander inns she'd stayed at with Kilian Shen when first traveling to the Duskhold, and she wouldn't have been surprised if that was what it had once been. Now it served as home for the newly Unfettered, as the serving girl had also explained to her. She would get food and a bed and a monthly stipend for so long as she promised to follow Xend an-Azith and the other leaders of his order.

One of whom was waiting for her and no doubt growing more annoyed the longer Alia failed to appear. She dashed down a broad set of stairs and through a confusing tangle of passageways, then burst out into the courtyard and discovered that she was not the only Sharded who had been summoned.

There were three, all very different in appearance but sharing the same wary expression: a tall, reedy boy with a pronounced apple in his throat; a young girl with black hair tied back in a topknot who looked to have been browned by long days in the sun; and a man somewhere in his middle years with ash speckling his dark hair and beard. His eyes were heavy-lidded and a startlingly pure shade of blue, like the northern sky in summer. None of them had brought travel bags, so Alia must have guessed correctly that they would be returning here later.

"A sorry lot, but I've forged decent swords from uglier pieces of iron."

The older man smirked at the gray-haired woman's words, as if he knew what game she was playing.

"Now," she continued, swinging herself up smoothly into her saddle. "I'm Palimas Jorel, lieutenant to Xend an-Azith. He has entrusted me with learning what you new Unfettered are capable of, and helping you develop your Sharded abilities."

Alia noticed the gawky boy glancing in surprise at the armored woman when she announced herself.

"We're headed north," she said, shifting in her saddle to gesture at the fortress-topped hill rising over the city.

"To the Skull?" the bearded man asked, shielding his eyes as he squinted into the day's brightness.

The woman shook her head. "Nay. We're going outside Karath, to the hills beyond the city."

Alia peered into the far distance, just able to make out the hazy swells that Palimas must be referring to.

"And what's there?" the man continued mildly.

"That's for you to find out," the silver-haired woman replied, then wheeled her stallion around so that she was facing the large set of double doors which opened out onto the street. Another horse – this one obviously bred for work, not war – stood in the shadow of the wall, hitched to a cart. "Hurry up and get in; it's a long journey, and I want to arrive before the sun finishes climbing."

"YOU'RE FROM THE WILD, aren't you?"

Alia blinked, focusing on the lanky boy sitting across from her in the cart. She'd been lost in thought, staring at the forest flowing past as they climbed into the hills, and his question had surprised her. No one had spoken since they'd left the city gates, where Palimas had engaged in a ribald exchange with the Wardsmen guards.

"I am," Alia replied, scratching at her palm through the leather. The fragment in the center of her hand had been feeling strange, almost itchy; she was tempted to peel off her long glove, but it still felt odd to be so open about her Sharded nature. Though, of course, if any folk were going to be comfortable with that, they were the ones sharing this cart with her right now.

"Thought so," the boy said, leaning back with a satisfied smile. "I've only seen eyes that green from those that live beyond the Fangs."

"You've met others from the Wild?" Alia asked, surprised. To her knowledge, her people rarely left the northern forests and tundra.

"Didn't meet 'em," the boy admitted. "But I saw 'em from a distance a few times. My da had a stall in Flail's biggest market square and traders would come from over the mountains with furs and rare woods and gems."

Alia nodded at this. It made sense. She'd seen Wild warriors wearing intricate armor and wielding steel weapons that looked far too fine to have been made in the simple forges set up in most villages.

"What are you doing this far south?" the boy asked, leaning forward with his elbows on his sharp-boned knees. There was an earnestness about him that appealed to Alia.

"You don't have to tell him anything," drawled the man with the heavy-lidded eyes from where he was ensconced in the corner of the juddering cart. Alia had actually thought he'd been sleeping, but now she realized he'd been watching them all the whole time. "It's one of the tenets of the Unbound King. When you join with him, your past is forgotten . . . if you want it to be."

The lanky boy's face colored in embarrassment. "I wasn't trying to pry."

"It's all right," Alia said quickly. "I don't mind." After all, she and Rhenna had spent quite a bit of time concocting a false history – it would be a shame if it were never used. "My father was one of the Treesworn. Seed-sharded. He fell in love with my mother, who was the daughter of a clan chief. This was forbidden, and they fled south, into the foothills of the mountains you call the Fangs. I was born there, and we lived peacefully for many years, but the Treesworn never stopped searching for us. One morning spear maidens attacked our homestead. My mother was killed, and it sent my father into such a rage that despite being terribly wounded he defeated all of the hunters. He made me promise as he lay dying that I would take his shards . . . his seed, as the Treesworn call it, and flee the Wild to find solace in the south. And so that's what I did. I quickly learned that there is only one place in all the lands outside the Wild safe for those without a hold . . . the city of Karath, and the hall of the Unbound King." Alia settled back against the side of the cart, trying to keep herself from looking too pleased by how well she had relayed the story.

"That's an incredible tale," the boy said, his eyes wide. The quiet, dark-skinned girl had turned toward Alia and was studying her now with pursed lips.

"An incredible story," repeated the bearded man, then snorted. Alia's good mood evaporated – did he know she was lying? Why was it so difficult to understand the people of this land?

"Tell me . . ." the boy asked, leaning forward. "What is a Treesworn? And a spear maiden? They sound like names from the old stories."

"Dey mus' be the seed-sharded," the girl said softly. She had a strange, lilting accent, unlike anything Alia had heard before.

"No one has seen a seed-sharded in ages," the bearded man scoffed. "They're all as dead as the frozen monks at Kara Dum."

Alia slowly pulled off her glove and held up her hand, palm

outward. Silence fell, broken only by the creak and crunching of the cart's wheels as they ascended the rocky path.

Alia lowered her arm, breaking the spell. The boy blinked and shook his head, as if waking from a dream. "A seed-sharded. How incredible. I'm Markis, by the way. Markis Fereeth."

"Alia. And you said you were from Flail?"

"Aye," the boy answered, the apple in his throat bobbing. "I grew up in the old town with my da and ma, and then when a hound found me I went up to the Windwrack. Stayed there for three years. That's how I know her." He jerked his head in the direction of Palimas, who was sitting straight-backed in the saddle as her stallion picked his way along the trail a little ways ahead of the cart.

"Oh? You know her?" asked Alia.

"Know her name. She said she's a Jorel. That's one of the oldest and most storied families in the Wrack. Don't know why she's here, though."

"I heard they don't allow women to fight," Alia mused, remembering something Rhenna had ranted about on more than one occasion. "And she looks like a warrior born."

"So, you're seed-sharded and I'm of the storm. And you?" he asked, turning to the tanned girl, but she only regarded him in stony silence.

"She's from the Whispering Islands," the bearded man interjected. "I know that accent. She's likely wave-sharded."

"Sea-sharded," the girl snapped at him, dark eyes flashing. "Wave-sharded is what yea all named us, to belittle our shard's true power. The sea is vast an' deep an' ancient."

The bearded man chuckled, closing his eyes as he stretched out on a bench. "Most definitely an island girl."

"And where are you from?" Markis asked, but the man ignored him, turning away.

Alia made a dismissive gesture towards where he sprawled and focused on the sea-sharded girl. "What's your name?"

She glanced at Alia, her expression guarded. "Sharl," she finally said. "I dunna want ta talk about why I'm here."

"That's fine," Alia assured her. "But that doesn't mean we can't be friends."

This earned her a surprised look, which a moment later gave way to a tentative smile. The tangled knot that had been sitting in Alia's stomach began to loosen – the Unbound weren't all vicious deserters who had fled after committing crimes, like Rhenna had intimated. They were just folk searching for a haven in a world where it was a death sentence to be Sharded without a hold. She shouldn't have been so nervous. Alia put her elbows on the side of the cart as she leaned back, returning her attention to the sparse forest. It looked different from a few moments ago. Lusher, infused with a verdant radiance. And sounds were spilling forth from the trees in a discordant rush of chitters and buzzes and rustling. How had she not heard them earlier? It was like something missing had been returned to her, as if . . .

Oh.

"My shard," she said in wonder. Markis and the island girl glanced at her in surprise, while the bearded man smirked as he cracked open an eye.

"Just feeling it now?" he said. "You must be an *arzgan*. I noticed quite a while ago that our strength was returning."

Markis raised his hand, then gasped as sparks began to drift from his fingers. "You're right," he murmured. "We must have gone far enough outside Karath."

Alia turned inward, reaching for that skein of roots at the center of her being. For days she had vaguely sensed it deep inside her, but it had remained impossible to grasp. This time, though, she closed mental finger around a gnarled tendril and power flooded her. Swallowing back the dryness in her mouth, Alia placed her ungloved hand on the side of the cart, pressing the shard sunk into her palm against the wood. Sprigs of green immediately emerged, curling upwards as their stalks thickened, tiny yellow blossoms unfolding.

Alia felt like she was floating, carried along in a swift-rushing stream. The power flowing from her shard was intoxicating – it pulsed from her fragment, winding through her twisting pathways, diffusing into her blood and bones. She could feel herself growing strong again. Hard.

She didn't know how long she remained fixated on her *ka*, but when she finally returned to herself, the forest had thinned even more. The path was nowhere near as steep as before, and they seemed to be approaching the top of the hill they'd been climbing. She looked to the others and found them still lost in the rush of their returning power, eyes half-closed and lips slightly parted. Then the cart lurched to a halt, and they rose from their stupor, blinking as they turned to find out where they had finally arrived.

The summit of the hill was bereft of trees, providing an unobstructed view of the city below and the serpentine river slithering into the Sea of Salvation. That expanse of water was so vast that Alia's breath caught in her throat – she had thought the Frayed Lands would never be equaled, but this dwarfed even those plains, endless swells rippling into the far horizon until finally joining with the sky. Alia was so struck by the view that at first she failed to realize that the top of the hill was not empty. Crumbling remnants of ancient buildings were scattered about in the long grass, walls and foundations so eroded by time that nothing even reached past her waist.

Palimas had dismounted and was waiting for them with a booted foot resting on what might once have been a statue's plinth. "Wake up, Unfettered!" she said loudly, waving at a glittering cloud of insects that had risen from the grass. "Time to gather round and find out why I've dragged you all up here."

Alia hopped down from the back of the cart and approached the gray-haired woman, trying not to stumble under the onslaught of her newly returning Sharded senses. In every blade of grass whispering against her legs she felt a thread of life extending into soil thrumming with insects and worms and other burrowing things, which in turn were inhabited by even lesser creatures, a dizzying progression of life that folded itself smaller and smaller seemingly without end . . . Alia shook her head, trying to focus on what Palimas was saying.

" . . . as I'm sure you've realized, this place is beyond the boundaries of Karath. The earth is empty of the karathinite that robs our shards of their power. And since it is possible to arrive here in the span of a morning, it is a useful spot to refine our strength."

Palimas paused, apparently seeing something in one of their faces. "Are you surprised? We Unfettered cannot spend the entirety of our lives in Karath. We will be sent out into the wider world to contest with the Sharded of other holds. Therefore, we must channel our *ka* and tame our pathways, so we might add more fragments and gain the talents necessary to stand against our enemies. You all will come here nearly every day – or to another of the spots we Unfettered frequent ringing the city – to either channel or hone your martial skills."

Palimas abruptly turned, staring at the city spread below with her hands clasped behind her back. The wind gusted, stirring a few loose strands that had escaped her pleated braid. "But before I turn you all loose to begin gentling your no-doubt unsettled pathways, I'm afraid there is something else we must attend to. You see, I know that one of you is not what they claim to be."

Coldness flooded Alia – Palimas was talking about her. They knew that she had joined under false pretenses. Her heart thudded in her chest, her hands suddenly slick and clammy.

What could she do? She didn't even have a talent yet. If she tried to entangle Palimas with the roots running beneath their feet, she'd snap them effortlessly – Alia wasn't sure how many shards the armored woman bore, but if she was a lieutenant to Xend an-Azith, she must be formidable indeed.

Alia opened her mouth to beg for mercy and plead for Palimas to hear her story when something huge hurtled past her head.

Palimas whirled around, striking out with a fist wreathed by crackling lightning. The huge chunk of ancient masonry exploded into a cloud of gray dust. For a moment Alia lost sight of the Unbound Sharded, and then she strode from the murk with a grim smile.

"You didn't disappoint—" she began, just before a barrage of rocks and chunks of earth ripped from the ground pelted her from every direction. Most vanished in flashes of light as they struck some sort of invisible barrier, but a few slipped through. Fresh dents appeared on her already battered armor, and a few stones rebounded off her flesh, though none drew blood. Any normal woman would have had her skull staved in under the force of those impacts, but she only looked mildly annoyed.

Alia gasped as the bearded man flung himself at Palimas. The Unfettered captain must have been surprised by this aggression, as he managed to land a blow on her chin that snapped her head back. Another flurry of strikes followed, far too fast for Alia to see clearly, but Palimas recovered with a speed that shocked Alia and managed to deflect every attack with the vambraces sheathing her arms. Stone hands erupted from the ground to clutch at Palimas's legs, but she easily broke free and kicked out viciously, her boot connecting with the bearded man's midsection. He gave a pained grunt as he was tossed a dozen paces backwards to nearly collide with Sharl. The sea-sharded girl shrieked in panic and threw herself out of the way, ending up in the arms of Markis.

The bearded man groaned, pushing himself with some effort to his hands and knees. In the chaos, he must have been struck in the face, as a long rope of blood unspooled from his mouth.

"Tell me who sent you and I might spare your life," Palimas said calmly, striding towards him with fists crackling. She appeared unhurt, though dust smeared her face and armor.

"Abyss take you," snarled the bearded man as he struggled to his feet, swaying. "I'd rather die—"

"Very well," Palimas said, her hand flashing out to close around the man's throat. He tried to say something more, but only managed a mangled gargling as he pried desperately at her grip. The lightning crawling over her hands flared brighter as a pulse of energy traveled from Palimas into the writhing man. For a frozen moment, Alia thought she could see his bones etched under his skin.

His eyes briefly flashed with radiance, and when this light dwindled, his sockets were only blackened pits. He went limp, and Palimas let him fall in a heap. The power swirling around her faded as she stared down at the corpse, and then she sighed and shrugged.

"Perhaps I should have tried harder to get him to talk. Ah, well." She turned towards Alia and the others, who were gaping at her. The fight had only lasted moments, but a man Alia had just been conversing with now lay dead, and the air crackled like during a violent thunder storm.

"Oh, Silver Shrike," whispered Markis, pushing away Sharl just before doubling over to spew out the contents of his stomach.

Palimas raised an eyebrow at this, then nudged the man's body with her toe. "Don't feel sorry for this one."

"Who were he?" asked Sharl, her voice surprisingly steady. She had recovered much faster than Markis, who looked like he might be sick again.

"An assassin," Palimas said, crouching beside the man and ripping open his tunic to expose his chest and the gray fragment embedded in his flesh. "Sent to kill the Unbound King. Luckily, Xend is very good at sniffing out such threats."

"If you knew he was dangerous, why bring him here?" asked Alia, wrinkling her nose in disgust as the smell reached her.

Palimas pressed her hand where the man's fragment was embedded, and the flesh rippled strangely. She grimaced, as if straining against something, and then pulled the fragments forth with a wet ripping sound that made Alia wince.

"I wanted the practice," Palimas said, studying the shards in her palm. "Though I don't know why I bothered. Only four – he was never a threat to me." The light of the shards vanished as she slipped them into a pouch. "He was brave, though. I thought I'd have to goad him into a fight, but he threw himself at me like he actually expected to win." She looked up at them. "I also wanted to teach you something. We are outcasts. Hunted. All the holds want us dead, and only by joining together can we survive."

"He was stone-sharded," Sharl murmured.

Palimas nodded, standing again. "Yes, although I don't think it was the Council that sent him. Of all the Sharded factions, Xend is on the best terms with the stone-sharded of Chan-Anok. Most likely, he had sworn himself to someone else. A bloodlord, perhaps. Xend has old, old enemies in Ashasai." She frowned, as if something had just occurred to her. "Or maybe it was the Ember."

"Why the Ember?" Alia asked quickly, then silently chided herself as Palimas glanced at her sharply.

"They have cause to oppose us recently," the gray-haired woman answered vaguely, then made a gesture as if to dismiss this line of conversation. "Enough. Let us find somewhere a little less . . . spoiled. I'm interested to know what you all are capable of doing."

19

HETH

"An *araskin* blade?" Jerik raised a disbelieving eyebrow and leaned forward to get a better look at the sword Heth had laid on the pitted wood. A little way farther down the bar his sister Ferra was also watching as she crushed some pungent spice with a mortar and pestle, though with far less interest. The tavern was almost empty, just a few grizzled old men beginning their drinking before the sun had reached its zenith.

"You've heard that name before? *Araskin*?"

Jerik gouged something from his ear with his finger, examined it critically, then flicked it away. "Nope. The Salahi live in the Nethers, but they keep to themselves. Mostly. Old Zayin is one of the few we see around here. He works down on the docks and comes here to drink every pay day. Drink and sleep, usually."

"And that was the Salahi who was in here last night?"

"Aye. He's never said more than three words to anyone before, far as I know. Strange he would go and threaten you, always seemed quite harmless. A gentle giant, if you will. A few times some rowdy boys who don't like the desert folk tried to annoy him, but he didn't do nothing."

"Lucky for them," Heth murmured, sliding the curving sword

back into its sheath. "I've never seen anyone move so fast who wasn't Sharded."

"He might have once been one. Sharded, I mean. Lot of the older Salahi were in the army that lost that big battle. They had to run here before the northerners killed 'em all."

Heth considered that. It was hard to remember, sometimes, that anyone he met in this city might bear a shard. There was just no way to know. "This *qenari* he said where I should bring the sword. It's close to here?"

Jerik blinked his mismatched eyes in surprise. "You're actually going to return it?"

Heth stroked the hilt. It would be a shame to lose such a fine blade . . . but he'd thought long and hard about what the Salahi had said to him.

"I had a sword that was very important to me," Heth finally said. "It was my family's sword, passed down from my grandfather. He'd been a Hollow in the Ember, and it had been given to him after he'd saved the life of old Lord Char's daughter. It was taken from me and I was so angry knowing it was in another's possession . . . Zayin feels the same way about this sword. I should return it, if it means that much to him and his people."

Jerik tilted his head to one side and gave Heth a look like he didn't fully believe what he'd just said. "Also, he's big and strong and scary."

"Well, yes, that too," Heth admitted. His wrist still ached where the Salahi had grabbed it last night.

"I just thought you might decide to flee," Jerik continued, his fingers tapping out a rhythm on the bar top. "You're new here, yeah? Easy come, easy go. Hop a ship for the Whispering Isles or head east to Ashasai. Not hard to get lost there if you're trying to disappear."

Heth knew Jerik was fishing for information about his past. "You know why I'm here. I asked you about it last night."

"Ah, yes. The House of Last Light."

"Maybe the Salahi know something."

"It's possible," Jerik said with a shrug. "Anything is possible."

"So you'll take me to them?"

"To the *qenari*?" Jerik said, suddenly looking pained. "But I'm so busy here – just look at everyone I need to take care of." He motioned expansively towards the three old men huddled in the corner. One raised his head from his cup and blinked blearily, his chin painted with foam. The other two appeared to be sleeping.

"Ouch!" Jerik cried as his sister smacked him in the back of his head. He turned to her with a hurt gaze and then flinched at her expression as she jerked her head in Heth's direction, hands on her hips. Jerik sighed, and then with a long-suffering sigh dragged his gaze back to Heth.

"I suppose I can spare a little time. Let's go."

Jerik set a quick pace through the Nethers, taking twisting side-streets and shadowy alleys without hesitation. He was evidently well-known in the district, as more than a few folks called out or waved when they passed, though Jerik did not slow or even acknowledge their greetings. It was quite obvious that the boy wanted to finish this errand and discharge the debt he owed to Heth as fast as possible.

"Up ahead," Jerik said, jerking his head at a collection of crumbling buildings that looked much like the rest of the Nethers. The only strangeness was that up ahead the street they were walking down became covered by an awning of pale pink fabric where it disappeared between two of these buildings. Well, that and the proportion of the people who were Salahi had shifted dramatically – elsewhere in the Nethers they were a very visible minority, but here most everyone were desert-folk, tall and willowy and with skin so black it almost seemed to gleam in the bright sunlight. Both the men and women wore brightly patterned dresses that nearly brushed the cobbles. The buildings in front of them did not seem to be occupied, as the doorways and porticos were filled with stalls selling all manner of goods – bolts of colorful cloth, heaps of gnarled black nuts and red peppers, and strangely shaped implements that might have been weapons or tools. One large man in a green-stained apron was chopping stringy-looking meat with a massive cleaver, dead lizards larger than dogs dangling by their tails from his stall. Among the shoppers browsing the goods were also many who were not Salahi, their pale skin and drab clothes starkly contrasting with the people of the desert.

Jerik's hand flashed out as Heth began to make his way towards the covered alleyway, grabbing his arm. "Wait," the boy hissed, his swaggering confidence gone. "Hold. You can't just walk in there."

"Why not?" Heth asked, glancing around the makeshift market. He couldn't see any guards or anything else to suggest that the *qenari* was forbidden.

"You just can't," Jerik said in exasperation. "The desert folk don't take kindly to visitors."

Heth indicated the sword at his side. "I was asked to come here by one of them. They'll let me in."

Jerik made a skeptical noise in the back of his throat, but he let his hand fall away. "Fine. But if they truss you up by your boots and drop scorpions down your pants, don't blame me."

"They're known to do that?" Heth asked, to which Jerik nodded emphatically.

"So my, uh, acquaintance was caught trespassing this one time—" Jerik began, but Heth never heard the rest of the story as he had already turned from the boy and was striding towards the covered passage that seemed to be the entrance to the *qenari*. At first he thought he was going to be able to walk right in, but a lanky Salahi youth who had been leaning against one of the pockmarked walls moved with a languid grace to intercept him. Heth felt a little shiver of recognition watching this Salahi – there was a perfect balance to his gait, one of the marks of a master bladesman. No hilt protruded from the sash at his waist, though Heth supposed there could still be something short and sharp secreted in the folds of his pleated, dress-like robes.

"*Halatha*," the Salahi said, his voice muffled by the cloth wound around the lower half of his face. "That place is not for you."

"I was invited," Heth said, feeling the attention of the other Salahi around him sharpen.

The one who had come to block his way shook his head slowly. "Only the *bhalgras* may issue such permission, *halatha*. Have you spoken with her?"

"I have not," Heth continued, resting his hand on the pommel of his sword. He sensed a stiffening from a few of the Salahi eavesdropping, but the guard who had challenged him did not seem the least bit concerned. His eyes did drop to the hilt, though . . . and then widened in recognition.

"*Araskin*," he murmured. "You would dare come here bearing that?" To Heth's surprise, he sounded more incredulous than angry.

"It's why I'm here," Heth said, quickly holding up his hands to show he hadn't been about to draw the sword. "I've been told to return this to your *bhalgras*. And beg forgiveness."

"By whom?" the guard asked, his tone sharp as whetted steel.

"Zayin."

The Salahi was perfectly still for several heartbeats, and Heth fully expected him to demand the sword before denying him entrance, but at long last he tilted his head, as if listening to someone whispering at his shoulder.

"Follow," he commanded, then turned on his heel.

THE QENARI WAS NOT what it had appeared to be.

From the street outside, it had looked just like all the other crumbling blocks of buildings that filled the Nethers. Ancient facades boasting stonework that once must have been beautiful, now long since eroded. Collapsing porticos and rotting, vine-twined balconies with missing balustrades. The vestiges of a once-wealthy district, long since fallen into ruin.

That was not what Heth found as they passed into the covered alleyway. Beyond the buildings rising around them was . . . nothing.

The foundations of what had once stood here were still evident, great stones sunk into the earth, but the walls that should have risen around them were gone. In their place were great swaths of rippling canvas, a labyrinth of rounded embroidered tents. Some were so small a tall man would have had to stoop to stand inside, and others were nearly the size of a stable. Heth had heard that most settlements in the Salahi were migratory, vast collections of tents that moved from oasis to oasis, and it was as if one of these desert towns had been transported inside Karath.

The flaps of many of the tents had been drawn closed, but Heth glimpsed the interior of a few as they passed. Figures huddled in the gloom, some tending to glowing coals and others sitting cross-legged on intricately braided mats as they conversed quietly. Most details were lost to the semi-darkness, but he noticed that many of the inhabitants shared the same sort of ailments that afflicted the rest of the Nethers — withered limbs, gnarled, claw-like hands, and strange lumps rising beneath their loose robes.

The Salahi were apparently not exempt from the Tithing.

Heth was expecting exclamations of surprise as he was led through the encampment – or at least some sort of reaction – but the ones who caught sight of him merely stared, dark eyes hooded and expressions guarded. They were mostly older men and women, Heth realized, with a sprinkling of youth. Only a few were of the same age as the guard he was following, and it was in these younger faces that he saw the most emotion – a hardening around the mouth, or narrowed eyes.

The Salahi were not what he had been expecting.

Heth had been raised on stories about the peerless warriors of the silver sands who had swept out of the desert and won every battle they fought until that bloody day on the plains of Gerendal. In truth, Zayin had matched the image built up in his mind . . . but these Salahi looked – if not broken – at least diminished by the city where they had been forced to beg refuge.

They stopped in front of a pale green tent lacking any decorations to set it apart. Heth was wondering if this was a detour on the way to somewhere more impressive when the graceful Salahi youth drew back the flap.

"*Bhalgras*," he said loudly, as if whoever was within was hard of hearing. "A *halatha* has come. He asks for an audience."

"And it is given." The response was immediate, and from the slight widening of his eyes even the Salahi who had brought Heth here was caught off-guard. He composed himself quickly, though, inclining his head in the direction of the opening he had made.

"Go inside," he said, and Heth nodded thanks before stooping to enter the dimly-lit space.

The four Salahi seated on the ground around a low table of lacquered wood turned to stare at him. Three were women of wildly varying ages and the last was a heavyset man with a fringe of graying hair. The man's mouth fell open at the sight of Heth, and then he glanced in surprise at the others in the tent. The oldest woman – a hunched crone with a face deeply fissured by wrinkles, lifted a steaming cup from the table and watched Heth calmly with glittering black eyes, while the younger woman beside her scowled, jaw clenching. The last Salahi was only a girl, perhaps a few years younger than Heth, and she shrank away from him. Something had happened to her face, as the flesh was mottled and one of her eyes was nothing but a milky white.

"Who is this?" snapped the woman in her early middle years, her hands gripping the edge of the table tightly.

"A *halatha*. I brought him here." The tent flap rustled as the Salahi guard also slipped inside.

"I can see he is one of the sullied," the woman said, now glaring at the ancient woman who had given permission to enter. "But that does not answer my question."

"He said Zayin bade him come. To return an *araskin's* blade."

"An *araskin's* blade," the woman repeated, her gaze flicking to the hilt at Heth's side. "Is it possible? Mother, did you know about this?"

The crone ignored the question, indicating for Heth to sit. He hesitated for a moment, unnerved by the thrumming tension in the tent, but then sank to the ground.

"Adil," she murmured, setting her ceramic cup down carefully on the table. "Bring Zayin here. If he is not in the *qenari*, find him in the *halatha* taverns he frequents. Tell him to join us."

"*Bhalgras*," the Salahi man said, hurriedly climbing to his feet. "I will be swift as the wind." Heth noticed the questioning look he gave the guard as he brushed past him, but the Salahi who had brought Heth here only shrugged imperceptibly.

"What has that old fool done?" the younger Salahi woman spat, turning her blazing eyes to Heth once more. "How dare he invite an infidel here? And to take it upon himself to summon him to an audience with you, Mother? The *halatha* drink has curdled his mind."

The old woman appeared unmoved by the anger in her daughter's voice. Her expression was placid as she fixed her gaze on Heth.

"It has been many turnings of the moon since a prodigal sword returned to us."

"Let me see it," the younger woman commanded. "Is it truly *araskin*? Perhaps Zayin was mistaken."

"In this he could not be wrong," the old woman said quietly. But still she released her cup and gestured towards the sword. "Still, I would see it."

Heth fumbled with the buckle of his sword-belt and then laid the sheathed blade on the table. The crone leaned forward, gnarled fingers closing around the hilt. She pulled on the sword, revealing a hand-span of silvery metal, then sighed and sat back.

"Is it true?"

The words were barely more than a whisper, spoken by the scarred girl. She shrank back when Heth glanced at her, her hands clutching at the hem of her robes.

"It is," the crone said, closing her eyes. "I heard the howling of the desert winds when it was drawn forth."

"Thief," the Salahi woman snarled, startling Heth. "How did you come by the sword? Did you come here looking to sell it? It is ours and always has been. Your life was forfeit the moment you touched its sacred metal, *halatha*."

"Calm, Fayraz," rumbled a familiar voice from outside the tent. "I hear the crackling of the fire inside you, but this one does not deserve to be cast into that furnace. *Bhalgras*, may I enter?"

"You may, *araskin*," replied the old woman, and a moment later the giant Salahi who had confronted Heth on the street slipped into the tent. The Salahi guard who had receded into the shadows after ushering Heth inside bowed his head low as the old warrior stepped past him to find a spot beside the child.

"Oh, *now* you show respect," the woman he had called Fayraz muttered.

"I always respect our *bhalgras*," Zayin replied, and Heth caught a hint of annoyance in his tone.

"Then do not bring a *halatha* into—"

"Enough." The old woman's command clanged like iron, silencing the tent. Fayraz's throat worked like she wanted to say more, but instead she slumped backwards, glowering at Zayin.

"We have been so long in this city that we forget our manners. A *halatha* has answered our invitation and you show him your teeth, daughter? Such behavior would never have been permitted in the desert." She turned to Heth. "Do not fear, you are our guest. Now tell me, who are you and how did you come by this sword?"

Swallowing back the dryness in his throat, Heth introduced himself and gave a stuttering retelling of the zemani ambush and the bestowal of the sword by the grateful Kin. When he had finished, the old woman cocked her head to one side as if weighing the truth of his words, then nodded slowly.

"Many of the sacred swords were lost in the dark days after the war. The blood of the desert was spilled into the black earth outside the city of the leeches. It is rare to see one of the missing blades again – the secrets of their forging, of the countless foldings that went into their steel, vanished when the Shahnate fell."

"You speak of respect, mother," Fayraz muttered, emerging from her sulk. "But I know the old traditions as well. No *halatha* may touch an *araskin* blade and live."

Zayin shifted and looked like he was about to say something, but the crone held up her hand to forestall him. "Surely you must have noticed that we no longer dwell in the desert. You have never even seen the silver sands, daughter."

"And whose fault is that, *mother*?" snarled Fayraz, climbing to her feet. She glared at the old woman, then turned her blazing eyes at Heth and spat on the ground. "The halatha have taken everything from us. I will not say 'thank you' when one returns something that was *stolen*."

"Mother . . ." whispered the scarred girl, reaching out towards Fayraz, but she was ignored as the woman stalked angrily from the tent.

Silence rushed in to fill her absence. Heth wanted nothing more than to flee as well, all the way back to Jerik's tavern so he could soothe his jangled nerves with a few flagons of black ale, but Rhenna would certainly throw up her hands in frustration if he missed this opportunity to ask about what they sought. It surely wouldn't come again.

"Grandmother," he ventured, and the old woman turned her tired eyes towards him. She looked diminished, as if watching her daughter storm from the tent had drained away something vital. "May I ask a question?"

"You may."

"I seek the House of Last Light. Have you heard of it?"

The old woman frowned, her brow drawing down. "That name is not one I know."

But there was something in her expression, and Heth sat forward, hoping it wasn't his imagination.

"What is it?" he asked.

The old woman waved a gnarled hand, as if to dissuade him from reading too far into what she was about to say. "Nothing. This place you call the House of Last Light means nothing to me. I am just remembering a story I heard when I was much younger, not long after I had led my people to take refuge here."

Heth glanced at the girl recessed in the shadows, distracted by the faint sounds of her weeping. What was wrong with her went beyond the scars she carried, he realized.

"A story?"

"A legend, told to me by one of the wise-men of my tribe who had visited Karath long before Osmari an-Alams donned the copper crown. He had traveled to Karath as a young boy to visit the Erudinium, but he'd been ambushed by thieves and left for dead in an alley. He awoke healed of his wounds in a great house whose only inhabitant was a young Salahi. There were no servants, no animals, just a single Salahi boy who looked to be barely a man, yet spoke like an elder. He spent a day wandering the halls of this manse, never finding an exit. Eventually a great tiredness came over him, and after laying down on a bed he fell asleep again . . . only to wake up back in the alley he had staggered into after being stabbed."

"Did the wound make him delirious?" Heth asked, his excitement ebbing away. For a moment he'd thought he'd discovered something.

The old woman shrugged, the layers of beaded necklaces she wore rustling. "Perhaps . . . but he showed me the scar he claimed was healed in that manse. He never mentioned anything about a light, though, the last or any other."

Heth nodded. Disappointing, but not unexpected. He had come to the conclusion some time ago that this search was almost certainly a fool's errand.

The crone reached out towards the sword on the table, gnarled fingers closing around the hilt. Steel hissed as she drew the blade from its sheath, showing a strength that belied her apparent frailty, and a ripple of brightness passed down its length as it caught the light spilling into the tent from outside. There was a faraway look in her clouded eyes, as if she was recalling something from long ago.

"Go now, *halatha*. I accept your apology for touching our sword."

Heth blinked at the old woman's words – he couldn't remember ever actually asking forgiveness, but he supposed if that was what was required to assuage Salahi pride he'd just pretend he had. A hand was on his shoulder, and he turned to find the guard who had brought him to this tent standing behind him.

"Come. It is time to leave."

Heth climbed to his feet slowly, tempted to ask some of the other questions that were on the tip of his tongue. Why didn't the Salahi living here return to the desert now that the war was decades in the past? How many of those living in the *qenari* were Imbued or Hollow or still members of the Sharded Few? Yet as he studied the crone and the grizzled warrior, how they slumped at the table staring at the *araskin* blade as if lost in bittersweet remembrances, he found he couldn't bring himself to ask anything more. Instead, he let the guard lead him from the tent and back into the day's cleansing brightness.

"Quickly," the Salahi warrior grunted as he began to wend his way through the maze of fabric. "You must realize many do not want you here."

Heth hurried to follow him, trying to ignore the feeling of being stared at from the darkened depths of the tents. He now realized the danger he had put himself in by coming to the *qenari* – if the beliefs of the *bhalgras* daughter were widespread, some of those watching him might believe he deserved to be murdered simply for daring to step foot into their community. Heth couldn't help but feel indignant about this. It wasn't his fault that—

"Azavel."

The guard Heth was trailing stopped abruptly as a voice called from the shadows between two of the tents. He glanced back at Heth with something like sorrow, and it almost seemed like he came close to telling him to flee, but then he closed his eyes in what might have been resignation.

"*Bhalgrasi*," he muttered as Fayraz stepped forth. She had donned black robes cinched by a silver sash, and from their bulk Heth thought that she might be wearing armor underneath. Streaks of red paint had been hastily daubed beneath her eyes, and bracelets of dark metal hung loose around her wrists. Her hands were resting on the handles of long curving daggers thrust in her sash. Two more Salahi in similar garb came to stand beside her, their eyes hard and glittering above their veils.

Heth's fingers twitched towards the sword that was no longer at his side. He might have turned and run right then if the young warrior he'd been following had not moved to interpose himself between Heth and Fayraz.

"Step aside, *araskinal*."

"But your mother—"

"Are you refusing my command?"

"I do not want to, *bhalgrasi*," the young warrior replied, his tone almost pleading. "But this one was named guest and your mother—"

"My mother is old and her thoughts are not as clear as they once were," Fayraz snapped. "You know the old way. He held a sacred sword stolen from an *araskin*, looted from the corpse of a desert son. A price must be paid—"

"And it should be paid to an *araskin*, not a *bhalgrasi*."

Heth turned. Zayin filled the narrow passage between the tents, his shoulders nearly brushing their sides. The gray-haired warrior was looking past Heth, his gaze fixed on Fayraz and the veiled Salahi flanking her.

"Tradition—"

"We are no longer of the desert," continued Zayin, folding his massive arms across his chest. "And we are no longer beholden to the old way. I am one of the last *araskin*. If anyone is owed blood for what happened to my brothers, it is me. But I do not claim that right. I will show mercy to this one, who did not know what it was he carried until I told him."

Fayraz's eyes flashed, but she did not challenge Zayin. Heth noticed the two warriors accompanying her sharing a quick glance, as if unsure what they should do now.

"I understand your anger," Zayin continued, his tone softening. "You have every right to hate the *halatha* who hurt Yari. But this man was not one of them, this I know."

"You know *nothing* of my anger, *araskin*," hissed Fayraz. "I would *burn* this cursed city and everyone in it who is not of the People. There are no *innocents* here." Then she whirled and vanished among the tents, moving with a grace that suggested she knew how to wield the daggers at her side. Her companions did the same, though they took a moment to incline their heads respectfully in the direction of the old Salahi before following.

No one moved for several long heartbeats. The younger Salahi was staring at Zayin, and the older warrior's attention was fixed on the corridor between the tents where Fayraz had disappeared.

Heth had nearly worked up the courage to thank the old warrior when Zayin spoke again.

"She grieves."

"Yari . . . was that the girl in the tent? The one with the scars?"

"Her daughter," Zayin said. "Her moon and stars. She was taken two years ago and returned just yesterday because she can no longer toil. She was broken in the darkness, like many others have been."

"She was Tithed," Heth whispered.

The giant Salahi grunted affirmation. "You are the first *halatha* she has seen since Yari was brought by the Wardsmen to the gate of the *qenari*. She has always had the hot desert wind inside her, so unlike her mother, but now it is a whirlwind. It cares not what it scours . . . I should not have asked you to come here at this time. I brought this about." He touched two fingers to his craggy brow in what Heth could only assume was a gesture of apology.

Heth tried to think of a response to this, but could not.

"*Araskin*," began the young guard, a note of warning in his voice, but Zayin silenced him with an upraised hand.

"I know, Azavel. There is danger here for this one. Remove him from the *qenari* quickly, but make sure you watch the shadows while doing so. Fayraz still desires blood." The gray-haired warrior shifted his stance to look Heth in the eye. "And you, *halatha*. Stay far away, if you value your life."

20

THE CLERIC

A thousand points of light glimmered in the hazy gloom.
Awakened Falin walked the temple's main hall with slow and solemn steps, the sacred flame writhing in the basin he held with cupped hands. Tiers of candles rose up around him like canyon walls, and when he noticed where one had been extinguished, he paused to relight it while murmuring the Vigilant Prayer of their Lord.

"Kindled flame preserves
The souls of all that cleave
To the truth behind the stars.
That when this age withers
And the heavens crack and crumble
What has died will rise again."

"What has died will rise again," he repeated softly, but without the traditional cadence of the prayer. This was a habit he'd had since childhood, ever since his mother had brought him to a temple to pray that the candles of her parents remained forever burning. Young Falin had been awed that his mother's devotion kept the flames lit, eternally flickering in this vast, soaring chamber, but old Awakened Falin now knew that the priests of the Broken God had labored hard to ensure those candles had always been burning when he and his mother had visited. It was a monumental task, keeping the souls of the faithful from disappearing into the darkness, yet it would be worth it when their Lord finally returned and ushered them all into the Forever Lands.

As Falin stooped to exchange a listing lump of wax for a fresh candle from his satchel he noticed a heap of tattered clothes huddled beside a low stone bench ablaze with glimmering lights. Sighing, he approached and laid his hand on what he thought was a bony shoulder.

"Mam Relga," he said soothingly, and gave a little shake in the event that she had fallen asleep. She often did these days, and then would wake confused and scared and calling out the names of her husband and children. They were all here, dancing right in front of her . . . though, of course, they would never answer her cries. They couldn't, until she laid down for her final rest.

Mam Relga turned to stare up at him so suddenly that Falin took an instinctive step back. The candlelight had fissured the crone's wrinkled face and turned her eyes into pools of darkness. She clutched at the silvery hem of his sleeve, her breathing labored.

"Awakened!" she rasped. "Ye shouldn't have dun that. My Jaks was speaking ta me."

She *had* been dreaming – Jaks had been her eldest son. He'd gone south during the war to fight the Salahi and never returned.

"He's probably telling you that it's time to leave for tonight," Falin said soothingly, restraining himself from jerking his arm back as her claw-like fingers tightened on his robes. "The temple is closing, Mam Relga. Jaks will be waiting for you on the morrow."

"Nay!" she said, shaking her head vehemently. "He says the day is coming!"

"The day always comes," Falin continued gently, unhooking her nails from his sleeve. If she put holes in his vestments, he'd have to stay up late tonight with needle and thread. "Night cossets the temple now, but when the first rays of our Lord touch the dome, I promise you the doors will open again, as they always do."

"*The* day, Awakened! The Reckoning! The return of Algeroth!"

Falin grimaced. Where had she heard that name? It was not supposed to be spoken, even by the faithful. Their Lord was the Broken God until he returned – only then would he reclaim all that He had once been, including His true name.

"I will tend to Jaks and the rest of your family," Falin assured her. "Now, you know you must leave. None but the Awakened may stay in the temple after dark."

A shudder went through Mam Relga, and when it passed she released him, looking around and blinking like she was surprised to discover where she was.

"Aye, Awakened," she mumbled as Falin helped her to rise. "I'll be back on the morrow. Wouldn't want my Jaks to get lonely."

"I know," he murmured, guiding her through the maze of flickering souls to the rounded doors that served as both entrance and exit to the temple. Gently he drew the sun of their Lord on her brow, then ushered her outside into the warm night. Her home was only a few streets over, and he knew she could find her way. She had done so many times before.

Falin watched her shuffle away until she merged with the darkness, then swung the heavy doors closed and barred them. The thought of anyone trying to rob the temple seemed absurd, but he wouldn't want Mam Relga or any of the other faithful to wander inside tomorrow before he could make sure all the candles were still burning.

As he turned back to the glimmering constellation that filled the main hall, he realized that he must have set down the basin with the sacred flame when he'd approached Mam Relga. Shaking his head at his negligence, he wended his way through the passageways made by the terraced benches covered with candles, glad that his old teacher, Awakened Varlden, was not here to cluck his tongue and shake his head disapprovingly. The flame was supposed to be carried at all times once it was taken from the ever-burning pyre. Since Awakened Varlden's body had been given over to that same blaze after his death, he might in truth know that Falin had committed a small blasphemy by abandoning the sacred flame . . . though of course, he wasn't likely to say much about it. Well, unless the Reckoning really was—

Awakened Falin stopped abruptly, frowning. He circled the bench slowly where Mam Relga's family flickered, his confusion deepening. He'd left the basin with the sacred flame right here, he was sure of it. Had it tipped over and rolled under a bench? Or had he placed it on one of the shelves among the candles?

Relief flooded him when he caught the familiar pale light dancing at the edge of his vision, hovering well off the temple floor. He'd put it on a shelf and somehow forgotten. How careless—

Awakened Falin fell to his knees.

"Radiant Lord," he gasped, clutching at the golden sunburst hanging around his neck.

Something huge loomed among the tiers of candles. His panic subsided somewhat when he realized that it must be a man, it must be, though he was far taller than anyone Awakened Falin had ever met before. Despite his height, his back was hunched and misshapen, a shadowy swell rising behind his cowled head. The stranger held the basin with the flame in his huge palm as he glided out from among the candles, and Falin felt his bowels loosen. The fingers curled around the basin were unnaturally thin and long . . . and certainly looked to have an extra knobby joint.

"*Awakened.*"

The voice was beautiful. So pure, like the ringing of the temple's silver prayer bells. His eyes were watering, Falin realized, and he hurriedly wiped away the tears before they could fall.

It would not be fitting to weep in the presence of an angel.

"My . . . my divine lord," Awaken Falin croaked, bowing his head. It had to be. The scriptures said that the speech of the Adored could gentle the fiercest beast and make believers of the most blasphemous infidel.

"*You were the one who spoke into the ice?*"

Falin nodded, trying to hide his trembling hands deeper within the sleeves of his robe. "Yes, lord." They had heard. Far away in the holy house of Kara Dum they had heard him whisper into the black ice. He'd wondered many times if they were indeed listening when he spoke, as the messages had only gone the other way before. "The words of the Senders issued from the ice for a full day, so I knew the matter was of great importance."

"Tell us what happened."

Falin swallowed, praying to the Broken God that he would not stammer. It was an affliction that had bedeviled him since he was small and had nearly kept him from donning the vestments of an Awakened. It had been much better in recent years . . . but he had never spoken with an angel of their Lord before.

"A visitor came to the temple. We get many here, since we are one of the last towns before the Belt reaches Karath. Merchants and travelers. She was of the Kin, river traders. There aren't many of that people who are of the faithful, but still a few come to the temple every season. The message from the ice . . . it said to question any that entered our hall about whether they had encountered a Sharded who could shape light like other Sharded can control fire or blood or darkness. This woman . . . she said her river galley had brought four Sharded down the Havilas and onto the Belt, going to Karath, and during the journey one of the Sharded had made every lantern on the boat shine like the sun." *Like the risen sun of the Lord*, Falin realized. A light-sharded appears, followed by a visitation by an angel. Again he heard Mam Relga's raspy voice, remembering the way her fingers had clutched at his robes. *The day is coming! The Reckoning!* Could it be? He felt light-headed, and he had to close his eyes for a moment to steady himself.

When he opened them again the angel of their Lord was gone, as if it had never truly been there at all.

Except that on the floor, glimmering in the light of a thousand candles, lay the golden basin. But now it was dark and empty, for the sacred flame he had nurtured and kept burning for decades had finally gone out.

21

KALISS

Don't look down.

Kaliss's fingers skittered over the glass-smooth surface, hunting for crevices where the great slabs of rock had been fused together. There. The tiniest crack, barely wide enough for her to wedge her nails inside. Taking a deep, steadying breath, she pulled herself higher, carefully placing the climbing spike into the gap and using her Sharded strength to secure it.

Be careful. We must be at least thousand span up – that thing pops out and you're nothing more than a stain for the Flame to gawk at tomorrow morning when the sun rises.

Shut up shut up shut up, Kaliss thought fervently as her foot sought the spike her hand had been clinging to a moment ago. If she hadn't been busy keeping herself alive, she would have been sorely tempted to rip the dagger from its sheath and toss it away. Would it scream all the way down before shattering on the rocks? The thought was surprisingly satisfying, and she allowed herself to indulge in it for longer than she probably should have before turning her attention back to the climb.

Kaliss gritted her teeth and pressed herself flat against the stone as the wind gusted again, clawing at her as it sought to fling her out into the abyss. Down below it had felt like barely more than a breeze, but up here it was as if a constant river of air was coursing between the Fangs. It didn't help that the object strapped to her back was long and thin and seemingly perfectly shaped to help the wind pry her from the wall.

How had Leantha convinced her to attempt this madness?

A raspy chuckle filled her head. *She could talk the sun out of setting. Don't let it bother you, my little gosling, you were never going to deny her anything. You saw how she bent the greatest among the Storm and Shadow to her will.*

That was true. Kaliss had been awed by how the squabbling Sharded had united so quickly behind Leantha's plan – she had expected at the very least for the Mother of Storms to show skepticism, but she had seemed the most enamored with the outlandish idea. It was all very disorienting . . . though, in truth, what was even more disorienting was her patron's knowledge of Kaliss's past. She'd never told anyone at the Duskhold about how she'd been plucked from the streets by Mazim Chain, the Black Hood of Phane, and trained to be his apprentice. More than just his apprentice – his assistant. Hushed speculation about how the Hood magically transported himself inside the fortress-like manses of Phane's merchant princes would fill the city's taverns and salons after every assassination – was he an Unbound shadow-sharded who could step through the darkness? A master lockpick capable of opening doors without leaving the faintest of scratches behind on the metal? Kaliss had never heard a rumor that approached the truth – which was that Mazim had trained children to climb the walls and squeeze under the gates of those thought-to-be impregnable manses and then simply open a door for him. No one alive should have been privy to this secret, because – as Kaliss had found out later– the Black Hood ensured that none of his apprentices grew up.

And yet, Leantha had known.

The thought that she had offered Kaliss her patronage because of this seemed impossible. She had approached her less than a day after the news had broken that the Ember had murdered Rhenna Shen and her wedding party. She surely couldn't have formulated this plan in that brief moment when the entirety of the Duskhold was reeling in shock. It must have just been coincidence that Kaliss alone among all the shadow-sharded boasted the exact skill upon which her plan hinged.

It must have been . . . because the alternative was honestly too frightening to consider.

Kaliss couldn't help but notice that the voice in her head had gone conspicuously silent.

Just enjoying the moment, little gosling. I've never experienced the world from such a rarified vantage. The light of the stars cuts like a blade this far up. And the wind! So bracing. But you know that already, of course. Your fingers are so numb you can barely feel them.

Quiet, Knife, unless you want to tell me what you are and why Leantha gave you to me.

A heavy sigh gusted through her head. *Believe me when I tell you that I wish I could. But our part is just to perform our roles to perfection and not to question the direction. We are pieces and not players, as someone somewhat wise told me long ago.*

Whatever, Kaliss thought with all the force of a falling portcullis, then turned the entirety of her attention back to the climb. It was rank madness to be arguing with a voice in her head when one poorly sunk spike or carelessly placed toe would result in a thousand-span plummet into oblivion.

Reach. Inspect. Place. Pull. Kaliss fell once more into the rhythm of the climb. Every once in a while she risked a dizzying glance at the sheer expanse of black rock thrusting above her and the gleaming stars beyond. Was she drawing closer to the top? It certainly didn't seem like it. She had been given specific instructions *not* to clamber over onto the battlements if she did ascend the entire height of the wall, as there would be powerful flame-sharded patrolling its length. No, she was supposed to find some other ingress into the Ember – a window or a murder hole large enough to squeeze through. There were a few such openings speckling the upper sections of the wall, or so she had been assured. Whether she could resist the temptation to scramble onto flat ground again if she did reach the ramparts was a question that would only be answered if it happened.

What was not in question was the existence of flame-sharded waiting above her. Every so often light would briefly wash over her as a massive orb of churning fire was tossed from the battlements – the first time, she'd twisted her head around to watch its blazing arc as it tumbled down to splatter just short of where the Shadow and Storm had encamped. The amount of raw power to summon such a fireball had made Kaliss's mouth go dry – it had to at least be a *kenang* with over a dozen shards, if not a *famdhar*. Either would tear Kaliss apart in an eye blink if they found her.

She couldn't help but wonder what she would do if she reached the top before arriving at any other way inside the fortress. Scale the Ember sideways like a spider scuttling along a wall in the hope of stumbling across an entrance? At some point even her Sharded muscles would give out from the strain of the climb; indeed, she could already feel a pulsing ache in her arms. The nagging doubt that Leantha had been wrong about there being windows up near the top had nearly strengthened into a full-blown panic before Kaliss finally caught sight of a lip of black stone hanging above her – the first imperfection she had encountered in the otherwise smooth and flat surface.

From below, it looked very much like a window sill. Heart hammering and fingers burning, Kaliss scrambled up the last few spans until her head was nearly brushing the jutting rock. Then, taking a deep breath, she reached and found a good grip on the ledge before slowly pulling her head up to see what she'd found. It occurred to her, just as she did this, that the object strapped to her back would already be visible before she could see inside. She tensed, half-expecting to hear incredulous curses or other exclamations of surprise, but her luck held and when she raised her head over the edge she saw that it was indeed a window she had reached and that the chamber beyond was uninhabited. It was also empty of furniture, except for rows of waist-high pots emblazoned with the sigil of a dancing flame. Oil, she supposed, or some other flammable substance. If an invader attempted to scale the Ember without using Sharded powers – say, with impossibly tall ladders or some great siege towers – this would be one of the defenses employed. There must be dozens of these windows speckling the wall up here, and by her great good fortune they did not seem to be guarded.

Kaliss froze as a noise came from the passage outside the little room, the scuff of boots on stone. She hunkered behind a row of the pots, trying to get low enough that the thing she had carried all the way up here could not be easily seen, and then watched from a gap between the clay containers as a shadow slipped across the floor when someone walked past the open doorway. Probably one of the Ember's Hollow, set to keep watch. There was no way such a menial task would have been entrusted to the Sharded Few. That was her hope, at least – if it was indeed a Sharded walking these halls, it would be very hard to remain undetected, given the sharpness of their senses.

After the sound of footsteps had faded, Kaliss eased herself from behind the oil pots and crept into the center of the small room. She fumbled for a moment with the straps securing the object to her back, then gently laid it down on the stone. It looked fragile – like a piece of black glass, and jagged as if it was just a shard of something that had once been much larger – but Leantha had assured her that it would not break, even if Kaliss dropped it from the top of the Ember.

"Do something," Kaliss whispered, staring down into the depths of the unfathomably dark object.

Patience, whispered the voice in her head. *You have done well, little gosling.*

Kaliss clenched her fists, nails digging into her palms. She should have pressed Leantha harder about what this thing was and how it worked. What was she supposed to do now – clamber back down the wall and ask? The very thought made her want to be sick. Her task was complete. She'd delivered the artifact inside the Ember, and now she could either stay here waiting for *something* to happen or—

An arm reached up out of the gleaming blackness.

"Mother Dark," Kaliss murmured, stumbling back a step. Her leg bumped one of the pots, causing it to rock dangerously, but Kaliss was too focused on the arm that was now groping for purchase on the stone floor to worry about what might spill forth if the container tipped over. The hand was nearly as black as the emptiness from which it had emerged, but it was most definitely flesh and blood and not the spectral limb of some creature from the shadowrealm.

And so she was not surprised at all when Azil Shen pulled himself out from within the object. The shadows thickened and writhed around the Black Sword as he silently climbed to his feet, the great staff Darkbringer slung across his back. His gaze slowly traveled around the small room, finally settling on Kaliss. She rose from where she crouched, gesturing towards the open doorway and the passage outside.

"Lord Shen, there's a guard—" she began to whisper, but fell silent when he laid a finger to his lips.

A head crowned by a shock of red hair next broke the surface of the blackness. Azil extended his hand, but Ilia Balenchas ignored the proffered help as she climbed forth. She wore close-fitting armor of black scales, and bracelets of gleaming silver covered the length of her bare arms. Her strangely uptilted eyes passed over Kaliss like she was invisible, her lips curling in distaste as she took in the chamber.

"Kaliss says we are not alone," Azil said softly, inclining his head towards the doorway.

Ilia's sneer turned into something more vicious, and then her edges rippled and twisted like she was made of smoke. Darkness rushed in to swallow the details of her face and form, and for a moment Kaliss thought she had used one of her talents to teleport away. But there was still something where Ilia had been, a shadow with unnaturally long limbs ending in curling claws. It flowed from the room without a sound, pulsing briefly when it passed through the light spilling in from the corridor.

Others were emerging from the artifact. A man with dark hair and cruel eyes above a nose hooked like a raptor – Geralth Chassain, the Falcon of the Fangs and the most infamous of the Windwrack's Wardens. In the meeting tent he had been unarmored, but here he wore blood-red plate, twin swords sheathed in golden scabbards at his side. He met Azil's gaze and nodded grimly. The last to rise from the depths surprised Kaliss – she had been expecting another Warden, perhaps even one of the Khalivas, but it was the older man dressed like a monk, his tonsured scalp fringed by gray. He wore the same worn brown robes and carried no weapons that Kaliss could see, though she knew that mattered little if he bore as many shards as she suspected.

"That was an experience I hope to never have again," he murmured, blinking as he gazed about the small chamber. "Oh, someone comes," he continued mildly, shifting his attention to the doorway. Azil's hand closed around the Darkbringer, azure power crackling along the staff, and Geralth had half-drawn his red-bladed swords before then releasing the hilts. A vaguely woman-like shape molded from fractured darkness stalked into the room, dragging behind it two limp bodies. Both had been eviscerated, as if mauled by a wild animal, and their glistening entrails dragged on the stone. The shadow tossed the corpses away like they weighed nothing, then dwindled and thickened to reveal Ilia Balenchas.

"These were the only two close by," she said. "Both Hollow. There are others on patrol, though, and they could come this way soon. Some might be Sharded or have ways to alert the Flame that the Ember has been breached."

"Then there is no time to waste," the older man said mildly, motes of energy drifting upwards from his suddenly glowing hands. "We must strike quickly."

Azil strode over to the small window and gazed out into the black. "We are far from the gatehouse. And we do not know the way, nor what guardians we shall encounter. Gather your *ka*, *famdhar*, for this will be a difficult night."

"I can perhaps help," murmured the tonsured storm-sharded as he went to crouch beside one of the sprawled bodies. Taking a deep breath, he pressed his glowing hand to a bloodstained brow, and a moment later the corpse spasmed, its limbs juddering. Kaliss had to stifle a shriek of surprise as the dead Hollow's eyes flew open, staring sightlessly at the ceiling as a spray of sparks erupted from between his slightly parted lips.

"A talent I have never seen before," Azil said, staring at the twitching body with some interest.

"Third-tier, and very rare," murmured the older Sharded through gritted teeth. From the sound of it, whatever he was doing required quite a bit of exertion. "And it is why Bailen chose me instead of Warden Harath or another more . . . adroit warrior."

"What is this?" asked Ilia suspiciously, narrowing her strangely shaped eyes. "Necromancy?"

The storm-sharded shook his head, sweat beading on his scalp. "No, Balenchas. Though I suppose it may seem like that. You see, as it turns out, the mind crackles with the same power that infuses the Storm, and upon death this . . . *energy* lingers for a time. I am mining this poor creature's memories for all that we need to reach the gatehouse."

"Interesting," Azil said. "And I suppose it works on the living as well."

"They do not stay alive," the storm-sharded replied, removing his hand from the corpse. Immediately, the dead man stopped his movements, wisps of smoke rising from his mouth and ears. "Which is why I prefer to use the talent on the recently dead. Though you cannot wait overlong, or the mind degrades too far." He turned to the Falcon, wiping his brow with the frayed hem of his sleeve. "I know the way and what defenses we will encounter. Potent, but with four *famdhar* we should not worry overmuch. A larger problem will be how to get the gate mechanism working. This one does not know."

"There will be more minds to flay," said Geralth, a harsh sibilance sounding as he slid his twin blood-red blades from their sheaths. The fragments set into the hilts of the swords flashed like rubies, and tendrils emerged from the pool of blood that had collected beneath the bodies to reach towards the Falcon. Kaliss felt her pulse quicken unnaturally as the red metal tasted the air – the swords were extremely puissant blood-sharded weapons.

The Darkbringer crackled in Azil's grip, and curving claws of glistening shadow were growing from Ilia's hands as the telltale shimmer of Ghost Chitin formed over her black-scale armor.

"What should I do?" Kaliss asked, realizing with a sinking sensation that the *famdhar* she had delivered into the Ember were making ready to depart . . . and that they would move far too quickly for her to follow.

The champions of Storm and Shadow turned to her, and for a moment she could not breathe under the weight of their gazes. The power pulsing in this tiny chamber was enough to make her eyes water.

"Wait here," Azil said, not unkindly. "Hide. Either we will win through and open the gate for our forces . . . or we will be consumed by the Flame. You will know if we succeed."

Azil touched the Darkbringer to his temple solemnly. "For Rhenna," he said to her, and then he was gone, the shadows writhing at the speed of his departure.

THE NIGHT CRAWLED past with agonizing slowness. Kaliss stayed hunkered in the small chamber behind the oil pots, certain she would soon hear a commotion outside when someone finally came looking for the Hollow guards who had disappeared. To distract herself, she spent the time gathering the *ka* flowing through her pathways, preparing herself for the inevitability of her being discovered, and practiced summoning the talent that had manifested after merging her third shard. She shaped the darkness around her into a Winnowing Spear, taking what comfort she could from the cold heft of the shadow javelin.

What do you think their chances are?

Kaliss grimaced as the unwelcome question wormed its way into her head. "They are four of the strongest Sharded in the north."

Four famdhar surrounded by a hundred Sharded enemies. The Ember has their champions as well, you know.

"I would not wager against a vengeful Azil. Rhenna was his sister."

He is an interesting one. He reminds me of someone I once knew in Derambinal—

The voice fell silent with an abruptness that surprised Kaliss. "Hello? Spirit? What happened?"

Did you feel that?

"Feel what?" she asked, though now she sensed what the knife must have noticed first: a faint trembling welling up through the stone. "Oh."

I believe that is something very large opening below us.

"Mother of Dark," Kaliss breathed, rising and going over to the window. The success of Leantha's plan had seemed improbable, a wild throw of a die. And yet out there in the dark she saw a stirring as the army of storm-sharded surged towards the Ember, glimmering like a sea of fallen stars. The fortress's massive doors must now be opened if they would dare such an assault, and the shadow-sharded were also streaming forth from their camp in a sluggish black tide. Kaliss watched breathless as this army merged with the charging storm-sharded, light and dark coming together, the Storm and Shadow united for the first time in living memory.

"Ah!" Kaliss cried, stumbling back as a terrible brightness flared, consuming her vision. She blinked frantically, trying to clear the pulsing spots.

And so it begins, the voice murmured.

Outside the window it was raining fire. Countless balls of flame were tumbling down from the top of the Ember, staining the sky red and orange. The amount of raw *ka* that was being shaped and released in this hellish volley was staggering.

She wasn't sure how long she'd been standing there in a dazed stupor when the voice in her head finally roused her. *Someone will be coming soon to pour that oil out the window.*

Kaliss swallowed, wiping away the sweat on her brow. Her gaze darted to the two Hollow corpses she'd hastily stuffed behind the pots, one with wisps of smoke still rising from its eye sockets. "You're right."

Any ideas?

Kaliss chewed on her lip, considering. She could try to descend the Ember's walls... though the fire raining from above – and also the flaming oil soon to be dumped out the windows – made that seem suicidal. She glanced at the sheet of black glass lying on the chamber's floor. Perhaps...

I wouldn't risk climbing in there, warned the voice. *Stronger Sharded than you have become lost in that abyss. I'm honestly surprised all four of the famdhar survived their time inside.*

"Then what would you suggest?" Kaliss muttered in frustration.

Go find someone's sleeping chamber and hide under the bed until—

"You there!"

Kaliss whirled. A man stood framed in the doorway, the shard embedded in his brow glowing crimson.

"What are you doing, Ashasai?" he cried. "They're attacking! Start pouring the ... the ..." He frowned, staring at the Winnowing Spear she had forgotten she was still holding. "Godsflame!"

Kaliss hurled the spear, and the flame-sharded staggered as it pierced him just below the collarbone. He blinked in shock at the glistening haft and reached to pull it out, but as his hands closed around the spear it dissipated into shreds of shadow.

She didn't wait for him to recover, leaping across the small chamber to slam her hand into the wound. The flame-sharded shrieked in pain, reeling backwards, but Kaliss's hope for a quick victory was dashed as a wall of flame erupted between them, forcing her to recoil.

He's escaping.

"I know," she snarled, summoning and tossing another Winnowing Spear at the shadow of the retreating flame-sharded. When it struck the flames, the javelin melted away like it had been made of ice.

If he tells his friends you're here, you're dead.

"I know!" Kaliss screamed, then threw herself into the wall, desperately hoping that this flame-sharded wasn't so much stronger than her that she would be immediately incinerated.

To her relief, after a rush of searing pain she found herself on the other side and standing outside the chamber. The flame-sharded was limping down the passage, clearly suffering from the numbness caused by the Winnowing Spear. He glanced over his shoulder and hissed in fear, then redoubled his pace as he shouted for help.

When Kaliss charged after him he whirled around, flames wreathing his hands, but these sputtered and died as she shoved the damnable talking dagger into his belly. His eyes widened, and then to Kaliss's surprise he began to *wither* – his skin tightened over his bones, as if the blood and muscle were being drained from his body, his flesh fading to the color of ash. The flame-sharded tried to scream, but only a hoarse rattling emerged, and then he collapsed in a heap of bones and parchment-dry skin.

Kaliss stood over the body, gaping at what she had done. He had been a healthy young man a heartbeat ago, and now he looked like a corpse that had been sealed in a tomb for centuries.

Delicious.

"What did you do?" Kaliss whispered in horror.

The dagger's ebony handle pulsed in her hand. *What you wanted me to. Unless you expected a different result after stabbing a man in the stomach.*

"You *ate* him!"

I did. Not all of him, though. I would take his shards, if I were you.

Moving as if in a dream, Kaliss crouched beside the jumble of stick-like limbs. As soon as her fingers touched the gleaming shard in the corpse's brow it popped loose, separating into two fragments of about equal size.

Let's go find more of these delicious fools, the voice said in her head. It might have been her imagination, but Kaliss thought it had grown louder.

She shoved the dagger back into its sheath, unable to suppress a shiver of disgust. What was this thing? Why had Leantha given it to her? To know her thoughts? It made sense, she supposed. It would be impossible for Kaliss to betray her with this spirit or demon of whatever it was inhabiting her mind.

I'm here to help you, little gosling.

"Help me be useful to your mistress," she corrected through gritted teeth, slipping the shards into a pocket and wiping the ashy residue clinging to her fingertips that had moments ago been living flesh onto her robes.

Your mistress as well, lest you forget.

A faint screaming carried to Kaliss from somewhere inside the fortress, and brightness made her glance back to see that the fiery cascade from above had strengthened.

"What should I do?" Kaliss whispered, suddenly feeling very small and vulnerable. This chamber was clearly important to the Ember's defense, and others would come soon. She needed to get somewhere safer.

And quickly.

Ignoring the babbling advice in her head from the gorged dagger, she began working her way deeper into the Ember. The walls and floor of the twisting corridors were like black polished glass, the same sort of stone as the outside wall. Flames roiled in ornate metal sconces growing from the rock, and Kaliss was not surprised that she couldn't see anything fueling these torches. If there was one place in all the world where fire had been tamed, it would be the Ember.

The gleaming black hallways and these flames resulted in plenty of skittering shadows, and she used her beckoning to cloak herself in darkness as she dashed through the passages. Kaliss suspected she could have remained nearly invisible even without her Sharded powers – she had spent much of her childhood skulking in alleyways and slipping through pitch-black streets the lamp-lighters had feared to enter. After all, a street rat of Phane didn't last long if they couldn't disappear into the shadows. Kaliss shook her head in bewilderment. . . that life was so far behind her, and yet the skills she had been forced to learn then were now what were keeping her alive. She had been a fool to think that she could ever escape her past. Her finger traced the skull carved into the dagger's pommel. Time was a circle. The first man she had ever killed she'd used this knife . . . her old master. And now she had used it to kill again, except in the intervening years it had somehow been inhabited by a very annoying and very blood-thirsty spirit.

It was all so strange, like a dream pieced together from the shattered fragments of her past.

Kaliss flitted through tangled corridors sloping downwards that reminded her of the labyrinthine depths of the Duskhold – narrow and low and worn smooth by the passage of centuries. It felt like home, even if she was constantly afraid that she would turn a corner and collide with a flame-sharded, but she realized that this skein of passages was only the outermost layer of the Ember when the way suddenly opened up into a vast hall that stole her breath away. The Ember, it seemed, was hollow.

She stood on a balcony overlooking an enormous space, a switchback stairwell leading down to where an army of mighty pillars of dark stone marched into the distance. Ropes of frozen flame hung between these pillars like burning strands of spider-silk, illuminating the dwellings clustered around the bases. It was like a city had been transported into the depths of the mountain – there were buildings and streets and stables, all bathed in the ruddy glow of the fiery filaments draped overhead. Light was also spilling from massive red jewels sunk into the black stone of the pillars and walls and the facades of many of the houses below. It was an awesome sight, made all the more striking by the panic that had engulfed the Ember's inhabitants. They rushed to and fro, some carrying children and others clutching valuables. Shards flashed in the brows of a few older men and women, but most must have been Hollow or Imbued, like those who served the shadow-sharded. Kaliss couldn't help but wonder if this was what would happen if the Duskhold was breached – chaos, and a mad stampede to escape. She couldn't blame them, as there was absolutely nothing that those without Sharded strength could do if threatened by the Few.

A prickle spreading across her skin finally pulled her from the churning chaos below. Frowning, Kaliss glanced back the way she had come, and was immediately hit in the face by a wave of heated wind. It did not dissipate, but grew even hotter, and her eyes watered as the air itself began to shimmer.

"Oh, Mother of Dark," she hissed, throwing herself down the steep stairs leading to the underground city. A popping sound came from behind her, and Kaliss twisted around just as a flower of flame bloomed where the balcony had been a moment ago. Heat buffeted her, scalding her skin and nearly sending her tumbling from the steps hewn into the rock.

The flame-sharded were flooding the passageways with fire. And while they would of course be immune, the Hollow and Imbued dwelling in the Ember were not, as evinced by the screams rising from the city below as another gout of flame exploded into the hall. If any of them had been inside that warren, they had just been immolated.

Her bare feet slapped the stone as she hurried down the steps. Kaliss briefly feared that someone would notice her descending and wait for her at the bottom with weapons ready, but she soon realized that those in the hall were far too focused on more pressing concerns.

Like how they were going to survive this night.

Kaliss didn't envy them – unless there were secret escape tunnels leading outside, they were trapped in here during a battle between three great Sharded armies. They might scurry around in a mad panic like ants after their hill had been overturned, but where could they go? Perhaps the fighting would not reach this hall. Perhaps—

Kaliss grimaced as that possibility was suddenly dashed to pieces. New light sources had appeared in the hall, balls of crackling energy slowly drifting among the burning strands. In a blinding flash, lighting lashed out to strike one of the black pillars, sending a spray of stone cascading onto the city. The crowds – already terrified – became even more crazed by fear, any small semblance of order that had remained instantly evaporating. And these lightning balls were only the vanguard for the invaders. Roiling black clouds floated behind them, their depths lit by pulses, the figures clustered at their edges staring down at the city spread below.

The storm-sharded had entered the Ember.

Panting, Kaliss finally reached the floor of the great hall. Should she try to make it known that she wasn't an enemy? Surely they wouldn't start indiscriminately killing Hollow, which were valuable to all the holds.

"Oh, no," Kaliss murmured as dozens of blazing figures rose into the air atop pillars of flame. There were also flame-sharded in the city . . . which meant that things were about to get terrible for anyone without a shard.

And possibly also for a *sardor* like herself, with only three shards.

Lances of molten flame erupted from the Ember's defenders, passing through the clouds to strike the crackling shields of the storm-sharded. Other flame-sharded summoned great serpents and birds shaped by fire and sent them hurtling towards the clouds – Kaliss had heard about this ability to create and control beings forged from flame, but her imagination had not done these creatures justice. They crashed against the clouds with blazing talons and burning coils, seeking to rend and crush, and that was not all the storm-sharded had to contend with – balls and whips and sprays of fire erupted in a torrent of destruction. Much of this flood of fire then dripped down in great gobbets onto the city, and even though the buildings were made of stone, pockets of flame quickly took root and began to spread.

I wouldn't advise seeking shelter there.

"Thanks for the suggestion," Kaliss growled, hugging the wall as she skirted the edges of the great hall. A massive archway promised escape from the devastation, although she wondered uneasily why the inhabitants of the city weren't fleeing in this direction. When she'd been on the steps, she'd seen a stream of people rushing towards the opposite wall, but none had been trying to seek refuge beyond this arch. Kaliss frowned, eyeing the exit speculatively, then flinched as a great sword-stroke of lightning rent the hall. Whatever the passage beyond led to, it had to be safer than where she was right now.

She passed under the looming archway, her gaze lingering on its elaborate carvings: huge entwined serpents that must have been balewyrms, horned giants wielding enormous swords, and filling the keystone at the very top was what looked to be a jagged rock wreathed in flames.

Where did this lead?

A massive hallway sloped downwards into darkness, lined by statues carved from the Ember's gleaming black stone. Each was at least three times her height, and they were all men, designs representing shards incised into their brows – some were clad in armor, while others wore flowing robes. The ones closest to the entrance looked almost fresh-hewn, but as she continued, she noticed that cracks had appeared in some, and on others the features had been effaced by time. These must have been the masters of the Ember, down through the ages. The most recent would be the ancestors of old Lord Char, but Kaliss remembered from her lessons that his clan had come to power only a few centuries ago, after the Wildfire Rebellion. She had long forgotten the name of the family from which these older Sharded hailed.

The ground shook, making her stumble. Kaliss glanced over her shoulder at the now distant archway – it was pulsing with light like the sky during a thunderstorm. A massive battle was raging in that hall, but had the trembling come from behind her . . . or in front? She couldn't tell. This looked like the way towards the Ember's inner sanctum, and there was a strong chance that powerful flame sharded were waiting there for the Storm and Shadow. Or had they gone out to meet the invaders in battle? Kaliss summoned a Winnowing Spear, trying to keep to the darkness as she continued on. The power being unleashed in the battle for that underground city could easily tear a lowly *sardor* like her apart; she had to stay out of the way until the fighting was finished, or her paltry few shards would be claimed off her corpse by whoever was still standing at the end. If only this war had broken out a few years from now, after she'd attained the rank of *kenang* or *famdhar* . . . then she could be out there, exacting revenge for what the Flame had done to Deryn without worrying that a stray fireball or strike of lightning would obliterate her.

A second archway appeared, just as grand and ornate as the first. Kaliss could tell that the space beyond was large, but still she sucked in her breath when she crept close enough to peer beyond the graven columns. The entrance where she hovered was situated near the top of a vast, circular chamber. Tiers of stone cascaded down the sides of the room, a hundred rows at least, and at the bottom was a floor of dusky crystal veined by deeper strands of darkness. Thousands could have filled these benches – not only every Sharded in the Ember, she suspected, but also all the Hollow and Imbued who dwelled in the underground city.

At this moment there were only four in the meeting chamber . . . though they seemed to fill the space entirely. A young man in crimson robes stood at the center of the crystal floor. He was not Ashasai like Kaliss, but still he looked to be utterly hairless, his face smooth and unlined. Perhaps it was his shard that had caused his baldness – it occupied most of his brow, a huge, glittering red fragment throbbing with light. Below that shard . . . Kaliss hissed in surprise and unease. Even from this distance she could see that his eyes were a pure, milky white, like the blind men who used to beg for valanii outside the temple of the Broken God in Phane. But this boy was no cripple. His hands were folded into the sleeves of his robe, his expression utterly bereft of emotion – no fear or anger marred his youthful features, even though he was surrounded by those who had come to shatter the shard at the heart of the Ember.

Azil Shen stood just in front of the lowest tier of benches, holding the Darkbringer in a defensive stance. Blue light coruscated along the length of the staff, crackling and popping with the power of a dozen shards. The robes of the Duskhold's Black Sword were tattered and pockmarked where flames had charred the cloth, but he otherwise looked unharmed. To his left, forming another point of the triangle enclosing the young flame-sharded, Ilia Balenchas seethed. She stared with a fierce, unblinking hate at the boy, panting like a wild animal that had just run its prey to ground. Wisps of darkness slithered around her, and a steady drip of what could only be blood was falling from her long, glistening black claws. The Falcon of the Fangs was the last, and he appeared to have suffered more than his companions since Kaliss had seen him last – his armor was so battered that it looked on the verge of falling apart, and half of his scalp had been reduced to burned, mottled flesh. Only one of his swords remained, and he brandished it towards the serene-seeming boy like he expected an attack at any time. The red substance of the blade had changed since Kaliss had first seen it drawn – now it flowed sluggishly, like blood seeping from a shallow wound, though somehow the shape of a sword remained.

Of the tonsured old storm-sharded there was no sign.

Can you feel that? the voice whispered in her head, sounding both awed and wary. *The power?*

Kaliss could. It was like when she'd climbed the tallest peak in the Firemounts and felt a pressure rising in her ears and behind her eyes. Except this was *ka* thickening the air.

That boy is no longer entirely human the spirit in the dagger said, and Kaliss had the sense that it was talking as much to itself as it was to her. *He has begun to merge with the outside, with what dwells in the primordial realms. This is a rare thing . . . and dangerous.*

"What are you talking about?" Kaliss murmured, beginning to descend the steps. "He may be *famdhar*, but so are the others. And Azil is one of the strongest Sharded in the north. The flame-sharded is doomed."

There are famdhar . . . and then there are famdhar.

"What does that mean?" Kaliss replied, ducking behind one of the basalt benches when she saw movement below.

But it was just the flame-sharded slowly withdrawing his hands from his sleeves and letting his arms fall to his side. He held nothing, though there were some odd markings etched on his wrists – Kaliss frowned, suddenly realizing that these were his veins, black and swollen. She bit down on her lip, wondering what they were all waiting for. Perhaps during their assault on the gatehouse they had emptied themselves of *ka* and were frantically refilling their reserves. Or perhaps—

It began.

Azil vanished, reappearing behind the flame-sharded, the Dark-bringer crackling as he lashed out with the staff. The blow should have caved in the boy's skull, or at least sent him sprawling, but without turning around his arm flashed out and he *caught* the legendary Sharded weapon with his bare hand. A crack like a thunder clap echoed in the chamber, and the flame-sharded grimaced slightly. For a brief moment, everything was frozen.

And then the stillness shattered.

They moved so fast that Kaliss had trouble understanding what was happening. Ilia flowed across the crystal floor, talons flashing as the Falcon screamed a war cry and took flight like he was a bird in truth, blood-sword roiling, lightning burning in his eyes. The flame-sharded hurled the Darkbringer at the Windwrack Warden with Azil still clinging to it, though the Black Sword Shadow-Stepped away just before they collided. The Falcon had briefly arrested his momentum as Azil tumbled towards him, throwing up his free arm to protect himself, and when the Black Sword vanished a lance of molten fire hurled by the boy struck him in the chest, shattering the remnants of his breastplate and sending him flying backwards. Kaliss hadn't even seen the flame-sharded summon that talent – she'd been watching Azil being tossed through the air in numb shock – and when she turned her attention back to him, she found that he was locked in combat with Ilia Balenchas. They traded blows in a frantic blur, far too fast to follow. The boy's hands were now glowing red, and no longer looked to be flesh and blood. Kaliss glimpsed long black claws raking the flame-sharded's arm, shredding his robes but scraping harmlessly against his burning skin, and then an open-palm strike slammed into Ilia's chest, staggering her. Her strange eyes went wide as she coughed up a mouthful of blood, but before the boy could land another blow, Azil was suddenly between them, smashing the Darkbringer into the huge shard set into the boy's brow. The flame-sharded shrieked in pain, clawing at his head, then rose into the air on a pillar of fire.

A Black Disc spasmed into existence beneath Azil, and he shot upwards in pursuit. Fire washed over him, but he burst through the deluge apparently unharmed and lashed out at the boy again. The pillar twisted like a swaying serpent and the crackling staff stuck nothing. The Disc and Pillar wove together in a dance as the two *famdhar* lunged to attack and then quickly drew back; this physical exchange was only part of the battle being waged, as shadowy snakes were slithering around the flame-sharded, trying to wrap him in their coils, while monstrous creatures forged of flames flung themselves at Azil.

Into the haze wreathing the flame-sharded Ilia suddenly appeared, leaping at him with claws upraised. The boy seized her even as she raked his face, opening lines of blood, and then hurled her down with such force that a whole section of the amphitheater collapsed.

"Get up," Kaliss murmured, but nothing emerged from the billowing cloud of dust. From her vantage she could see that a crater had been formed by the force of the impact, and this awed and terrified her. She hoped that Ilia was lying at the bottom stunned, not with every bone shattered, her flesh pulped beyond recognition.

Kaliss's attention returned to the battle above her as Azil seized upon the flame-sharded's momentary distraction to leap from his Disc, bringing the Darkbringer down in a killing blow. Yet somehow the boy's burning hands caught the staff again before it collided with his face, though the weight behind the strike sent both him and the Black Sword plummeting. They struck the crystal floor with a terrible crack, and then surged to their feet, still wrestling for the Darkbringer. Kaliss could *feel* the titanic struggle in the very air around her, and she whimpered, hunkering so low that she could barely see over the bench. She moaned in dismay when she saw that the flame-sharded was now holding on to the staff with only one burning hand; the other was clutching at Azil's chest, and the shadows writhed in a mad panic as the Black Sword grabbed the boy's wrist, desperately trying to stop him from digging his fingers through his robes and into his flesh.

Cold disbelief filled Kaliss when she realized the flame-sharded was trying to rip out Azil's shards.

Before she could think about what she was doing, Kaliss leaped to her feet and hurled a Winnowing Spear at the boy's head. Her aim was miraculously perfect, the shadowy point striking him in his milk-white eye. She could not have thrown it any better . . . but it did not matter. The javelin dissolved like it was a drop of rain falling on stone, though the flame-sharded did toss Azil aside without ripping out his shards, instead turning towards her.

She saw her death staring at her from the emptiness of his eye sockets. His expression was once again unnaturally serene, despite the bloody slashes Ilia had left across his face.

Kaliss flinched as light flashed and a tremendous boom echoed, blinding her and making her ears ring. She frantically rubbed at her eyes, shocked that she was still in one piece, and as the brightness began to fade from her vision, she was able to make out a vague shape struggling with the flame-sharded.

The Falcon of the Fangs. Most of his hair had been burned away, and his face was seared red. He'd shed his shattered armor, and must have lost his Sharded sword of roiling blood after he'd first been struck, because he was desperately grappling bare-handed with the flame-sharded. He looked like a madman, grinning wildly and eyes burning with the power of the Storm, the tendons visible in his neck and arms as he strained. For a brief moment, it looked like he might be able to subdue the boy . . . and then the flame-sharded's lips curled into a vicious smile as he broke the Falcon's hold, his burning hands finding Geralth's face. He pressed his thumbs into the storm-sharded's eye sockets and there was a *shriek* of pain that made Kaliss's breath catch in her throat.

Hands crackling with lightning beat frantically at the flame-sharded, but the boy ignored the blows, pressing down harder. His thumbs disappeared, gouging deeper . . . and then the Falcon's head split open.

"Seven hells," Kaliss whispered.

The flame-sharded let the corpse fall, then raised his hands to inspect the sizzling gore. He seemed to have already forgotten about Kaliss, as if she was an insect, though perhaps she was even less than that to him – some insects could at least sting. She was nothing, not even worth a sliver of his attention. He did glance up, though, when the radiance around him flickered.

The Darkbringer smashed into his side, sending him flying across the chamber. Azil was on him immediately while he sprawled dazed on the crystal floor, bludgeoning him over and over again, stuttering flashes of blue light exploding with every strike. Azil's robes had almost been entirely burned away, and the Salahi looked like one of the Ember's black-stone statues come to life, his body etched with corded muscles as he swung again and again and again.

Fire enveloped the boy, and the Darkbringer passed where he had been a moment ago to crack the crystal. He reappeared a dozen paces away in an identical burst of flame, his battered face smeared with blood, gobbets of what looked like tar dripping from the whiteness that filled his eyes. The boy bared red-stained teeth and thrust his hands into the floor beneath him. Another crack formed, but this one quickly widened into a crevice that Kaliss feared would split the chamber asunder; it was wide enough to swallow a dozen men and lit from within by a hellish glow.

Azil had not leaped after the boy to press his advantage – he was staring at the spreading chasm with a look of horror, as if he couldn't believe what was happening . . .

Coal-black talons as long as scimitars curled over the edge, and then a nightmare heaved itself out of the disintegrating floor. Gnarled red hide glowed like a bloody dawn as a monstrous head reared, resembling something between a horse and a man, horns curving from its brow. Broad and powerful shoulders burst forth, wide as a gatehouse. Was this a creature summoned from the deep places, those fiery pits that churn endlessly? Or something created and given life by the flame-sharded? Those shapings back in the city had been crudely sketched and compelled into awkward, juddering motion. This . . . this looked real.

The thing threw back its hideous head and roared, slamming its fists against the floor. The crystal splintered as fractures appeared in the walls of the great chamber, and a massive chunk of rock tumbled from above, obliterating a section of the benches near Kaliss. She was thrown down as the stone beneath her feet shook, landing flat on her back, and then she could only raise her arms and scream as a larger swath of the ceiling crashed down upon her.

A VOICE CAME, drifting in the emptiness.

Wake up, little gosling.

Kaliss fought her way out of the clotting dark. Her eyelids scraped open to find a different kind of blackness – there was a substance to it and a terrible, terrible heaviness . . .

Things were pressing down on her. Sharp edges and rough, uneven harshness. Stone. She was buried under stone. How much was on top of her? It was so quiet, like the outside world had ceased to exist. But maybe that was because she was down so deep beneath the Ember. Her panicked breathing quickened. Miraculously nothing had crushed her head – the way the rock had fallen had created a little pocket for her upper body – but how long would the air last?

Calm, girl. Someone is coming for you.

"How do you know?" she whispered hoarsely, dust coating her throat. She began to claw at the surrounding stones, cold shivers wracking her body.

Because I know, came the whip-crack response. *Now do not touch anything, unless you want to risk bringing this mess down on your bald little head.*

Fighting back the urge to scream, Kaliss forced herself to stop prying at the darkness. She had to keep her wits. Maybe she could find a gap and try squirming her way out . . .

Other voices traveled to her. Faint, muffled by the rock, but most definitely not in her head.

"Help!" she cried. "I'm here! I'm here!"

She couldn't make out what those far-away voices were saying, but they seemed to be growing more excited. Slivers of light appeared as something above her shifted – a rumbling crack, and those slivers became a flood. A dark silhouette stood framed in the emptiness that moments ago had been filled by stone.

"Azil!" she gasped, nearly sobbing in relief. "I mean, Lord Shen. My apologies! I just . . . I just . . ."

"You were just buried alive," the Black Sword said, pulling away the slab of stone that had fallen across her lower body with ease. Kaliss stared in shock at her miraculously whole and undamaged legs – she had been expecting nothing but a smear of blood and bone, but it seemed her Sharded strength had protected her. "I forgive your momentary lapse of propriety," Azil continued. What had happened after the ceiling had come down? Why were they not all dead? The Black Sword leaned over, his strong arms sliding beneath her, and then she was lifted like she weighed no more than a feather.

"I can walk, my lord," she murmured. After a moment's hesitation – in which Azil seemed to be weighing the honesty of this claim – he set her down atop the great pile of rubble. Her legs wobbled slightly, but she managed to stay standing as she took in the sweep of the devastation surrounding them. Much of the ceiling had come crashing down onto the tiers of benches, but the crystal floor had somehow been spared. Most of that was still gone, though, having disappeared into the canyon splitting the room. There was no sign of the fiery giant that had tried to climb out of the depths.

"My lord, where is that . . . that thing?"

"It fell," Azil said as he began to pick his way down the mound of shattered stone. "Back into the chasm, after my father slew it. Or perhaps he only wounded it – what matters is that it did not return."

Cael Shen. Kaliss swallowed away the dryness in her throat and tried to stand up straighter. Yes, she could see that the master of the Duskhold was down below on a fragment of the crystal floor that looked to have survived unscathed. She recognized him from his long white hair and the glistening black blade of his greatsword. And he wasn't alone. A short, rotund man in shining silver armor stood nearby, next to a massive warrior in battered gray armor leaning on an enormous war hammer. Kaliss stumbled when she realized that this was Bailen Khaliva, the lord of the Windwrack, and another of his legendary Wardens. Cael Shen was also not alone – a gaunt and hunched shadow of a man hovered at his side, wisps of white hair clinging to his scalp. Saelus. What was he doing here in the Ember? He was a scholar, not a warrior, and as ancient as any shadow-sharded alive. Surely he should be waiting back at the camp.

Another old man kneeled on the dusky crystal with his head bowed and his hands bound behind his back, long gray beard brushing the floor. Only one flame-sharded would bring the Storm and Shadow together in this place, at this moment . . . Lord Yanith Char, the ruler of the Ember and the guardian of the Flame. If he had been captured, then the assault must have succeeded. Leantha's mad plan had somehow worked . . . and *she* had been instrumental to its success. The thought was dizzying.

"Who was that flame-sharded?" Kaliss asked as they crossed from the rubble to what remained of the crystal floor. "I never imagined anyone could have such strength."

Azil paused for a moment, prodding the fractured expanse of crystal in front of them with his staff to make sure that it was still sound enough to bear their weight. "We had heard rumors that a prodigy had been born in the Ember, a boy who had attained the rank of *famdhar* before he could even grow a beard. I had thought it was just a story."

"And yet you defeated him."

Azil grimaced. "I struck the final blow. But it took three of the most powerful Sharded of our holds. If Ilia and Geralth had not been here, he would have bested me and torn out my shards." He glanced at her, inclining his head slightly. "In truth, if you had not distracted him, I would be dead and he would have gone to help the Ember's defenders battling in the great hall. I'm not sure that we would have won the day, even with my father's arrival. You were important to our victory in more than one way, Kaliss."

Kaliss tried to calm the butterflies flooding her stomach. The Black Sword of the Duskhold was expressing gratitude to *her*? She swallowed again, trying to think of what she should say to this. "Ilia, is she . . . ?"

"She's alive, thank the Dark Mother," Azil answered. "Broken bones and wounded pride, but she'll recover fully, or so I've been told. I know she'll be angry she missed this moment, though. She would have asked my father to be the one to swing the sword."

The sword. Kaliss's gaze returned to Cael Shen's greatsword. Its black blade did not look like it was made of steel, or any other metal. There was a depth to its churning blackness that suggested it was an abyss unto itself . . . almost like the pane of dark glass that Kaliss had carried during her climb. Deryn had once told her how Cael Shen had cut the head off a novice and after that execution, Lord Char had manifested in the flames to angrily denounce the new alliance between Storm and Shadow. If he had seen through his Fire Sending, he very likely had noticed the headless corpse in the Duskhold's hall. And now . . . and now he was poised to meet the same fate as that poor boy. Such strange patterns were woven in Fate's tapestry.

"Kaliss."

The voice startled her, and she whirled to find Leantha. She hadn't been there a heartbeat ago.

"Mistress," she murmured, ducking her head. Kaliss glanced at Azil and noticed a slight hardening around the corners of his mouth as he also turned to his father's favored advisor. She looked like she had not been involved in any of the fighting that day, as her dress was immaculate and her alabaster skin – so striking, especially beside the Salahi-born Azil – was unblemished by grime or gore.

"You did well. I am pleased."

"Thank you, Mistress."

Leantha brushed a cold nail down Kaliss's cheek. "And you have something of mine. I would like it back."

Panic stabbed Kaliss. "I'm . . . I'm sorry, Mistress. Forgive me. I left the artifact you gave me in the room where I entered the Ember. I was afraid I would be discovered if I stayed, and it was so cumbersome to carry—"

"That is not what I was referring to," Leantha said, holding out her pale hand.

She means me, little gosling.

"Oh," Kaliss murmured, fumbling with the buckles securing the sheath at her side. She wanted the knife? Would she finally be free of the thing scurrying around in her head?

Yes, until she needs you again. You did well . . . very well. So this will be farewell . . . but perhaps not for forever.

Her fingers closed around the hilt, and she could have sworn the grin of the carved skull had widened. Trying to keep herself from showing too much excitement at finally divesting herself of the haunted blade, Kaliss handed over the knife. Almost immediately it felt like the splinter that had been lodged in her mind had vanished. She was alone, for the first time in months.

It felt wonderful.

Leantha did not even glance at the knife before secreting it in the folds of her robes. She turned to Azil, and Kaliss had the distinct impression that she had been dismissed.

"Come, Azil. Your lord father wants to finish this."

Kaliss hesitated as the Black Sword and the White Spider began to move once more towards where the lords of the north had gathered.

Azil noticed this and turned back to her. "Come," he said. "There should be witnesses."

Swallowing, Kaliss followed, her pulse quickening.

Something was going to happen. Something that would shake the world.

"You have lost, Lord Char," Cael Shen said after Azil and Leantha had come to stand around the defeated flame-sharded. "The Ember has fallen and your hold is ruined. Your crimes will be avenged."

Slowly the old man raised his head. Kaliss sucked in her breath – one of his eyes had been torn out, leaving a bloody pit. To her surprise, the huge fragment in his brow remained, which meant that the shackles binding his wrists must be forged from karathinite. If they were not, she had no doubt this chamber would right now be filled with swirling flames.

Lord Char bared bloody teeth at the lord of the Duskhold, then spat on the crystal floor. Rage blazed in his one remaining eye. This man was broken but not bowed, Kaliss realized.

"You're a bastard, Shen," he hissed, then shifted his burning gaze to the fat man in his gleaming plate armor. "And you too, Khaliva. You've always wanted to destroy my house."

"You know why we came here," Bailen replied, his face wrinkling his disgust. "You had his daughter murdered. My son's betrothed."

A ghastly grin spread across Lord Char's face as he shook his head, making the long, matted locks of his gray hair sway. He grated a laugh that caused Kaliss's jaw to clench.

"You're a fool, Khaliva, if you—"

"Silence," Cael Shen commanded, hefting his greatsword. "We cannot tarry here too long. The fight still rages."

"Damn you to the hells, Shen," Lord Char snarled as Night swept down like darkness rushing to fill a room after a light was extinguished. His head bounced on the floor as his body slumped forward, great gouts of blood flowing forth. Kaliss took a quick step back as the redness slid across the crystal, thought Azil seemed not to care when the blood pooled around his boots. His mouth was set in a grim line, but his eyes were triumphant as he gazed down at the corpse of the man who had ordered Rhenna's death.

The massive Warden in the battered armor reached down to grasp the head of Lord Char by its long hair, then held it up for all to see. The shard set in his eye socket flickered, shreds of power leaking forth and making the air around his head shimmer.

"It is done," he rumbled gravely.

"I will carry the head to where the fighting is fiercest," Cael Shen said, striding towards the giant warrior with his hand outstretched. "Give it to me."

The Warden nodded agreement, offering the lord of the Duskhold the bloody trophy.

Cael Shen reached out to take it . . . then suddenly brought his greatsword up, driving Night's glistening point into the middle of the Warden's breastplate.

"No!" screamed Bailen Khaliva as the Sharded sword parted the ancient steel like it was paper. An arm's length of the roiling black blade emerged from the Warden's back, sheathed in blood. The warrior's one good eye opened and closed in shock, staring at the sword impaling him, and then Cael Shen withdrew Night smoothly and the Warden toppled forward, his armor clanging when it struck the crystal floor.

"Shen!" the lord of the Windwrack cried, lightning crackling around him, his face flushing in rage. Kaliss had heard he wasn't a *famdhar*, but she could feel the power he was gathering and it made her want to burrow down under the rubble again and hide. "You bloodless—"

Bailen grimaced, the lightning wreathing his head evaporating, then shook his head, as if confused. The ample flesh of his jowls began to dwindle, as if he were somehow wasting away from starvation in the span of a few moments. His eyes sunk into their sockets, and his hair became brittle and gray, falling out in clumps. He was withering . . . and it was something Kaliss had seen before.

A death rattle issued from his cracked lips, and then the Lord of the Windwrack collapsed next to the headless body of his greatest rival. Behind him stood Leantha, the ebony skull set into the hilt of the dagger she held grinning madly. Again there was no blood on the blade.

"Father!" croaked Azil, stumbling towards the corpses in disbelief. "What have you done?"

"What needed to be done," Cael Shen said calmly, returning Night to the sheath across his back.

"But we fought beside them!" Azil cried, his voice cracking. "The Falcon saved my life!"

"The holds have no friends," Cael Shen said simply, wiping away the blood spattered on his hand with the hem of his dark robe. "Only allies of convenience. And when the chance comes to reach out and seize a greater prize . . ." He turned to Leantha, and for the first time

Kaliss saw her smile. "We must not hesitate." The coldness in the White Spider's beautiful, upturned lips made Kaliss shiver.

"This was your doing!" Azil cried, jabbing a finger at Leantha. The shock in his voice had given way to anger. And pain, Kaliss realized.

"Saelus," Cael Shen said, ignoring his adopted son as he turned to her teacher. The old man's lips were pursed, but he did not seem surprised by what had just happened. "Send Dark Whispers to every *famdhar* and all the *kenang* you can find. Tell them the Storm is now our enemy and to leave none alive."

"Father!" Azil cried again, aghast, but the lord of the Duskhold again pretended not to hear him.

Cael Shen then shifted his attention to Leantha. "And you. Find Bailen's son and mother and make sure they never see the dawn. They are far too dangerous to let live, especially the Mother of Storms."

"As you command," Leantha murmured, and then she was gone, the darkness rising up to swallow her. Kaliss stared numbly at where she had vanished, unable to fully comprehend what had just happened.

Finally, Cael focused on his son. Azil's hands were clenched, shadows writhing around his fists.

"My son," Cael said, and the gentleness in his tone surprised Kaliss. "This is a joyous moment. The Shadow has fallen over the north, as it was always meant to be." He extended a blood-stained hand. "Come. I need your strength in this moment. And your support – it was not easy for me to keep this from you, I promise."

The Black Sword of the Duskhold could have been carved of stone. Then a wrenching shudder passed through him, as if he was trying to forcibly expunge whatever his soul was wrestling with. "We do what we must," he whispered, and stepped forward to take his father's hand.

22

ALIA

Alia leaned back against the gnarled bark of the banyan tree, her fingers kneading the thick grass. She'd finally found a comfortable nook in the nest of slithery roots, shaded by the thick canopy. If she closed her eyes and concentrated, she could imagine she felt the heartbeat of the tree, the thick lines of life pulsing through the trunk. But that was just in her mind. Here, in the City of the Dead, the shard that connected her to all living things was cold and dark, little more than a chunk of green crystal.

This was still her sanctuary. Many of the Unfettered who served the Unbound King lived in a collection of townhouses that had once belonged to a vanished merchant family, and at the center of this estate was a garden that looked to have been ignored for decades, maybe centuries. Alia wasn't even sure if it was truly a garden anymore, since by her understanding that term presupposed the existence of a gardener. No one had tried to tame this wildness for a long, long time, and while it lacked the exotic blossoms and songbirds that filled the private retreat of Xend an-Azith, she far preferred this place. For one thing, there was rarely anyone else here, even though the great houses fringing the garden were filled with Unfettered. She could retreat into her thoughts without fear of being disturbed. And second, the unkempt beauty reminded her of the forests of the far north, bringing back memories of slipping through sunlit glades and splashing across cold streams with her father and mother.

Alia was lost in just such a remembrance when the noise first came to her. It was faint and rhythmic and most definitely did not originate from anything that usually inhabited this garden. She opened her eyes and stood, brushing dirt and twigs from her trousers. She wasn't scared – whatever it was must have passed through the buildings she could see even now around the garden, slices of their canted, red-tiled roofs visible through the branches. Nothing dangerous could find its way in here. Still, she was curious, so she found an overgrown path she thought might lead towards the sound and began following it, the grass pushing up from between the stones tickling her bare feet.

Someone was sobbing. A grown man, she thought, and that surprised her. There were a few southerners she'd met who showed their emotions openly, like Deryn – sensitive souls, forthright and kind. And then there were many, many others who kept their faces closed and thoughts guarded. An example of this was the different way in which Deryn and Heth spoke of their parent's deaths. There was pain in Deryn's eyes whenever he mentioned his poor mother, while Heth's jaw tightened and his gaze turned flinty at talk of his father. Alia could never be sure if he was sad or angry or even uncaring. In the Wild, folk did not hide behind such carefully woven masks. To hear this stranger weeping now, so openly . . . Alia approached cautiously, unsure what she would find.

He sprawled upon a cracked stone plinth that might once have held a statue, his arm flung over his face and chest heaving. His skin was dusky, only a shade lighter than Sharl's, so Alia thought he might also have come from the Whispering Isles. The simple gray trousers and tunic he wore looked like the clothing that filled the dresser in her own chambers.

"Why? Why? *Why*?"

Alia flinched at the pain in the man's voice, so raw and wrenching. She spared a glance behind her, wondering if she should slip away because it felt like she was spying on a very private moment. But what if he needed help?

"I *told* him!" the man screamed, beating his fist against the plinth's stone. "I told him it was a terrible idea! The Shadow does not forgive! It does not *forget!*" Whatever he meant to say next dissolved into sobbing, and Alia retreated farther into the underbrush, grateful that she had been taught how to disappear among the trees.

A convulsion wracked the man, his arm slipping from his face. Alia had to stifle a gasp, her gorge rising, for long, deep scratches covered his cheeks, and in the center of his brow was a bloody hole, as if something had been gouged out. Alia's breathing quickened. She had seen something like this before, when Rhenna had pulled the fragments from the heads of the fallen flame-sharded atop the mesa. But this man wasn't dead – who or what had removed his shard? It almost looked like he'd done it to himself. But why?

Perhaps he was a madman. Even if not, he clearly was not in his right mind, and that meant he might be dangerous. She should go find help and let someone know that he was here before he hurt himself further ... or others.

Alia dashed along the twisting path, now heedless of the sounds she made. The man behind her was far too distraught to care, even if he heard her. He was flame-sharded, she was sure of it – or had been. For a moment she considered stopping, maybe even returning to the man. That was her mission here, after all, to determine if the Unbound King had dispatched the flame-sharded assassins, and that fellow slumped back there *must* know the truth. But the thought of trying to approach him after he had ripped apart his own face ... no, he needed help from someone with more authority and experience than her.

She burst from the garden path and onto a verandah extending from the rear of one of the Unfettered manses and found a group of men and women standing in a knot arguing under the gabled roof. She hadn't seen them before – these were not new recruits like her and Sharl and Markis – but they did look to be Unfettered.

"Excuse me," Alia gasped when she ran up to them, and the

conversation stopped. Most looked bemused at the interruption, though one hulking man with a bristly beard scowled at her like she had broken an important rule.

"What is it?" he growled, folding huge arms across his barrel chest. "You're one of the new ones, aren't you? Palimas's whelp. We don't have time to hold your hand or put you back in your crib."

"She ran from the garden," said a woman with flaxen hair that reached past her waist. "And from the look of her, she's probably seen Ontos." The other two men – both tall and thin and so close in appearance they might have been twins – nodded at this.

"Ontos," Alia said, finally managing to catch her breath. "He's flame-sharded?"

A quick glance passed between the Unfettered. "Aye," the burly man muttered grudgingly. "We're searching for him. His chamber was torn apart and there was . . . blood."

"He's hurt," Alia said quickly. "It looked like he scratched his own face . . . and . . . and tore out his fragment."

"Silver Shrike," murmured the golden-haired woman, long fingers fluttering to her mouth. "Why would anyone do such a thing? Do you think . . . do you think *it* happened?"

The bear-like man pulled at his beard in agitation. "Xend knew the risk . . . oh, by the Broken God. It'll be like the Sand all over again . . . this will change the north."

"It will change the world," one of the tall men said grimly.

"What are you talking about?" Alia asked, glancing back at the overgrown garden. That man was in pain! How could they just stand here? "Please, just follow that path and you'll soon hear him! He needs help!"

"We can't give him what he needs," the other tall man replied, running a hand through his dark hair. "No one can."

"But we *can* keep Ontos from tearing his own eyes out," snapped the woman, striding quickly towards where Alia had indicated. "Hurry, all of you. Xend will be disappointed if we let him hurt himself further."

"This is *his* fault," the bearded man muttered under his breath as he pushed past Alia. The two lanky Unfettered – brothers, Alia had to assume – shared a quick, inscrutable look, then followed the others.

Alia watched them all disappear into the tangle. She hoped they would find that flame-sharded before he did anything more drastic. She could go with them, she supposed, but she doubted she would be of much use . . . and now she had something to tell Rhenna. There was at least one flame-sharded among the Unfettered, or there had been. Alia began to skirt the edge of the gardens, heading towards the manse where her chambers were located. She knew the way to Mam Nar's house from that location – if she tried to find her way from else-where, likely she'd end up wandering for half a day. The city was confusing, as all the buildings and streets looked the same to her, especially in the Nethers.

Alia was so lost in her thoughts that she didn't hear her name being called until a hand fell on her arm. She jumped, and turned to find the Flail boy, Markis, grinning at her. Sharl was at his shoulder, looking as solemn as usual.

"We've been looking for you!" he said, grinning like a simpleton. A loveable simpleton . . . but a simpleton nonetheless.

"And why's that?" Alia asked, pulling her arm away gently and fighting back the urge to rub the spot where he'd grabbed her. She'd learned that Markis was much like a big dumb hound – exuberant and loyal, but he sometimes didn't know his own strength.

"We're going out," he explained proudly.

Alia frowned. "Out?"

"Outside. To explore the city."

"Palimas told us to stay at the estate, at least until we finished our first month of training."

Markis waved a hand, as if to dismiss what Alia had just said. "That's only a few more days away. What could change by then? And anyway"—he leaned in closer, glancing around as if to check that no one was eavesdropping—"we know you've been sneaking out. And we're jealous."

Alia felt the color rise in her cheeks. It was true, she had been slipping from the manse some nights to visit the Kin house when most of the other Unfettered were asleep. She'd thought her little excursions had gone unnoticed . . . but apparently not.

"And we have to celebrate!" Markis cried.

"Celebrate?" Alia echoed, looking at him blankly.

"We heard," Sharl said, finally joining the conversation. "We heard ye manifested a talent."

Alia thought her face must be burning up by now. Word had gotten around quickly after she had merged her third shard up at the ruins outside the city where they trained, but she'd only told Palimas about the Sharded power that had come to her the next day while channeling.

"You have to tell us all about it," Markis demanded. "But not here. Let's go to the Lanthium."

"The . . . what?"

"It's another old ruin like up where we go to channel," Markis said excitedly. "But just one big building. It's on the Skull, the hill where the rich people live, and it's also the most famous food-hall in the city. I've heard there are stalls selling things from all over, even spiced frog legs like the kind we used to eat in Flail." Markis's eyes grew distant. "Silver Shrike, I've missed those . . . "

Alia's stomach twisted at the thought of eating frog's legs. Sharl noticed her expression because she hit Markis on the shoulder.

"Swallow yer words, fool. Haven't ye noticed by now dat Alia nay eat flesh?"

Markis blinked. "Truly? I thought you just loved mushrooms."

"I do love mushrooms."

Markis tapped his finger on his chin, looking contemplative. "You know, if you think about it, mushrooms are really just the flesh of the forest."

Sharl made an annoyed sound in the back of her throat, pushing Markis away. Then she turned to Alia. "Come on. We're going an' I want ye ta come."

"Oh," Alia said, unable to keep her lips from twitching up into a smile. Markis and Sharl had kept her from feeling lonely these long weeks, and she did want to spend more time with them. Their relationship as fellow newly sworn Unfettered had deepened into being friends. "Then I'll go."

She needed to tell the others about the flame-sharded, but no one would even be at the Kin house at this time. Rhenna would be searching the upper city for clues about the House of Last Light, Deryn off in the Erudinium studying with the scholars, and Heth . . . Heth would probably be drinking somewhere in the Nethers. Perhaps she could stop by Mam Nar's house later.

MARKIS MOVED through Karath like he had been born in the city, leading them confidently through the twisting streets and even taking a few shortcuts down narrow alleyways. He ignored the calls of the touts and the merchants and the beggars huddled in the shadows, though he did gift a small piece of fruit that Alia recognized from their breakfast platters this morning to a grubby-faced waif who had been staring forlornly at a baker's display of steaming pies. Alia knew he had lived most of his life in Flail, and she could only assume that the great cities of the world shared enough similarities that it had been easy enough for him to adapt to living in Karath. Sharl, on the other hand, looked as skittish as Alia felt, jumping when things moved unexpectedly or someone declaimed too loudly about the quality of their wares. Alia had no idea what life was like on the Whispering Isles, but she doubted there were any cities the size of Karath.

The cobbled streets climbed steadily upwards, the hill at the center of the city looming larger and larger. From the Nethers – or even the manses of the Unfettered – the top of the Skull had appeared crowned by a jumble of large buildings, but as they ascended Alia was able to discern where one great pile of stone ended and another began. The two most impressive structures rose on opposite sides of the hill's peak, thick towers topped with imposing battlements, each surrounded by a smaller but equally well-fortified wall. When Alia had asked who lived there, Markis told her that one was for the Shield – the leader drawn from the council of five merchant families that ruled the city – and the other belonged to the Sword, who led the Wardsmen and was responsible for defending Karath. Situated at the very top of the hill but dwarfed by these two fortresses was the tumbled remains of an ancient structure, its white stone bronzed by the lateness of the day. Unlike the ruins on the hill outside Karath, this building was still mostly intact, mighty pillars supporting the tattered remnants of a roof. This must be the Lanthium – Alia could see colorful streamers snapping in the wind, and its broad steps were crowded with people.

"Is dis a festival day?" Sharl asked when they finally reached the hilltop. Alia had been wondering the same thing: musicians were perched on stools plucking at instruments, and a troupe of children dressed in motley were performing feats of acrobatics for an appreciative audience. No, not children – these were grown men and women, but smaller than any she had seen before. She was about to ask Markis about them, but a plume of fire made her gasp and flinch back. A sweat-slicked Ashasai, naked to the waist, grinned at her and showed blackened teeth as he dipped whatever he had used to conjure these flames back into the smoking container at his feet.

"We can watch the performers later," Markis promised, beckoning for them to follow as he approached the Lanthium's pillared entrance. "I can already smell those frog legs."

They hurried up the ancient steps, pushing through the press of people, and then paused after passing between crumbling pillars. Spears of afternoon light pierced the pockmarked roof and illuminated the interior of the Lanthium, which was hazy from the smoke billowing from the dozens of grills and cookpits and fires. Long benches and trestle tables had been placed in the center of the hall, and these were so crowded that many patrons had been forced to sit on chunks of fallen masonry as they ate.

"By the First Seed . . ." Alia breathed, overwhelmed by the raucous din and heady smells.

"This is even grander than the great market in Flail," Markis said, somewhat grudgingly. "I've never seen such a mix of people."

Alia had just been thinking the same. There were men and women of all colors milling in the food hall – ebony Salahi, copper Ashasai, dusky islanders, and some who even looked pale enough to hail from the deepest reaches of the Wild.

"Let's sit dere," Sharl said, indicating a slab of stone surrounded by rocks that could serve as chairs. "Markis, go find yer frog legs. We'll meet later." Then, without waiting for his response, she laced her fingers with Alia's and began pulling her towards where a woman who shared her dark skin was fanning things laid out on a long charcoal grill. There were all kinds of fish with crisped skin, clams that had been cracked open and stuffed with garlic and cooked onions, and a few strange-looking animals that looked to Alia like they had been drawn from her nightmares.

"What's that?" she asked, pointing at a charred, many-limbed creature.

"Squid," Sharl answered, giving her hand a reassuring squeeze. "My father used ta catch dem wit' his bare hands. He would jus' lean over the side of his boat and snatch dem from the water. But nay worry, I don't bring you here to eat one of those. I want ye to try *dat*." The excitement in Sharl's voice surprised Alia – the island girl was usually so reserved . . . but now she was grinning as she gestured towards strips of what looked like some kind of plant, blackened by the grill.

"What is it?" Alia asked as Sharl handed over a few coins to the woman tending the flames.

"Seaweed," Sharl replied, almost bouncing up and down as the islander scooped up a generous helping of the green ocean grass and dumped it onto a broad leaf, then sprinkled a pinch of salt and a few other spices over its top. "Dere are forests of it growing under the water. Not all is good ta eat . . . but I know dis one. Right delicious."

She led Alia back to the makeshift table and they found Markis had already returned, bringing with him a heaping platter of red-dusted frog legs. Alia did her best to avoid looking at these as she found a seat. Sharl settled beside her, then placed the leaf with its tangle of seaweed on the stone between them. Alia picked out a strand and took a tiny nibble . . . and then shoved the rest into her mouth.

"Good, eh?" Sharl asked with a smile.

Alia could only nod, cheeks bulging.

"When you can speak again," Markis said, stripping a little leg and tossing the bone onto the floor, "you have to tell us what it what like merging another fragment."

"You've never done it before?" Alia asked after she'd finally managed to swallow.

"I only have one," Markis admitted sadly, tapping his chest. "I think I might be ready soon, but shards are hard to come by. I'm hoping Palimas will share from the Unbound King's hoard after this first month of training is finished."

"Was it how dey claim?" Sharl asked, lowering her voice as if they were discussing something forbidden. "Did ye actually see someone's past?"

Alia shifted uncomfortably. "Yes, but the memories passed by in a flood, too quickly to understand."

"Tell us!" Markis begged, leaning forward in interest.

"There was a big black fortress in the mountains . . . then fleeing through a forest, chased by something terrible. And a great fire, alive with monstrous shapes."

"They must have been a flame-sharded," Markis murmured, eyes wide. "Maybe they tried to flee the Ember and perished. They could have been trying to get here and become Unfettered, like us. Perhaps in a way you completed their journey."

Alia said nothing, peeling another piece of charred seaweed from the pile. In truth, the shard she'd merged had been one of the ones Rhenna had torn from the heads of the Sharded who had attacked them in the Frayed Lands. There was a very good chance that they had once lived in Karath as Unfettered . . . perhaps even eaten in this same food hall. She found that thought a little sad.

"What's yer talent, *sardor*?" Sharl asked. "An' how did it manifest?"

Alia blinked at her for a moment, then remembered that this was one of the odd terms used to differentiate between the Sharded Few.

"It's my skin," Alia said, holding up her pale, thin arm as if she could show them what had happened. "I'd been channeling for a few days after merging the fragment, trying to calm my *ka*, and then I just *knew*. It was no harder than adding a simple sum in my head . . . and then my body was different, dark and hard, like the heartwood of a tree in an ancient forest. When I told Palimas, she had me demonstrate, then slapped me without warning. I barely felt anything, and she said it was like striking stone."

"I believe I said steel."

Markis coughed at the unexpected voice, spraying bits of frog onto the stone table . . . which had suddenly been cast into shadow. Palimas stood over them, her arms folded across her chest, silhouetted by the last drops of light leaking through the roof. Alia saw that braziers were being lit throughout the hall, but it seemed they would not get to experience what the Lanthium was like at night.

"Captain Jorel!" Markis said, quickly rising and attempting an awkward bow. "Uh, welcome! What a coincidence to meet you here!"

Alia couldn't see the expression on Palimas's shadowed face, but from the way she was standing and the tone of her voice it wasn't hard to imagine.

"It's no coincidence. I tracked you through the city after I found you missing. Actually, I had *them* track you." She waved vaguely in the direction of the Lanthium's entrance, and Alia saw the three wind-sharded who had attended Xend in his garden were now standing amongst the pillars. They seemed oddly alert, watching the bustling crowd with their hands on their hilts of their stubby swords.

"We're sorry," Alia said, trying to sound as earnest as possible. Seeing that so many had been dispatched to find them concerned her. "We should not have left."

Palimas let out a deep sigh. "You all disobeyed me . . . though it's true that usually I would care little about such minor defiance. But something has happened."

"Ontos," Alia blurted, but Palimas only cocked her head quizzically at this outburst.

"Ontos? What has happened to him?"

Alia swallowed, wishing she had remained silent. "He . . . he clawed out his shard. I found him weeping in the garden, covered in blood . . . I thought someone would have told Lord an-Azith by now."

"I'm certain someone has informed him," Palimas said in a strange tone. "But I did not know about Ontos because I have been tracking *you* all afternoon."

"Why?" Sharl asked.

"Three Unfettered have vanished over the last few days."

"Vanished?" Markis exclaimed. "What do you mean, vanished?"

"I mean we can't find them," Palimas snapped, clearly running out of patience. "Now, enough questions. On your feet and come with me. We're returning to the estate and you are all staying there until we know what is going on." Without another word, she turned sharply on her heel and began striding towards where the windsharded were waiting, clearly expecting them to follow.

Alia shared an uncertain glance with Sharl, then rose. Palimas had said the Unbound King had many enemies – the stone-sharded assassin she had confronted at the training grounds was proof of that – but Alia hadn't thought that she'd be in any real danger inside Karath. This was going to make telling Rhenna about the flame-sharded more difficult. There probably would be guards posted now at the manse if Palimas was this worried.

They emerged from between the pillars just as dusk was settling over the city. In the gloaming, Karath was a scabrous, shadowy expanse rippling all the way to the edge of the softly-glowing Sea of Salvation. As Alia watched, the last slice of sun vanished below the horizon . . . and in that moment, something else drew her attention. It had come and gone so fast she'd barely noticed. She frowned, searching again for what she'd glimpsed. The last red ray reaching across the water had struck something in the city below and flared strangely bright.

"Alia, lass?" Sharl asked, shaking her arm. "Are ye all right?"

"Yes," she whispered, then forced herself to start descending the crumbling steps. Palimas was already waiting at the bottom with her hands on her hips, surrounded by her equally impatient wind-sharded entourage.

Alia's thoughts were racing. Surely it was nothing, just her imagination forging connections where none could possibly exist. Surely . . .

But what if . . .

She had to go talk to Rhenna. And soon.

23

DERYN

The ancient book's spine crackled as Deryn gently laid the tome open on the table, a wash of musty air rising up from the yellowed pages. This made his eyes water and nose tingle, and he had to fight back the strong urge to sneeze. After he had finally collected himself, he returned his attention to what was before him. The book had been scribed by someone with an ornate but cramped handwriting, which made it difficult to separate the words from each other. Beautiful illustrations of twining vines and cavorting animals had been inked inside the margins, making the pages seem even more cluttered. Deryn suspected it would have been difficult to read even if it had been written in a modern script . . . which this mostly definitely was not.

"The strang'r arriv'd on the seventh day of the husk'd month, not longeth aft'r the lasteth of the wyrms hath returned to the deepness to spawn. That man wast tall, dark of hair and eye, and bore the lasteth marketh of the Fallen yond ev'r seen in our carn. That man hadst been known by anoth'r nameth the lasteth timeth he collied this hall, bef're that man had ventur'd beyond the edge of the w'rld, but anon that and did refuse to answ'r to yond nameth. That man hadst lost it, he claimed, in the depths *of the realm wh're stone liveth and breathes, and that man hadst been given anoth'r nameth, though he wouldst not sayeth what it wast."*

Deryn leaned back on his stool, sighing. Trying to understand books like this, from before even the days of the First Empire, quickly brought on a splitting headache. He often found his eyes glazing over, and many times he'd reached the end of a page and realized he had absolutely no idea had he'd just read. When that happened, it was time to leave this cluttered annex and go wandering in the Erudinium, as the pain in his temple usually abated after sitting under one of those flowering trees in the courtyard for a little while. Still, he could at least tease out some meaning from these old books. Many of the ones written later, during the zenith of the empire, were completely indecipherable. The scholars and nobles of that time had developed an entirely new dialect they'd called the Gilded Tongue to converse and write in, apparently to ensure that they remained apart and aloof from the common rabble.

Deryn had decided he hated them for that.

For all he knew, the secret as to why elementals entered this world and the reasons they chose who to bond with were contained in those texts. He had naively hoped when he'd first begun searching through the Erudinium's collected writings on the other realms that he would be able to restrict himself to somewhat modern books, since the Sharded Few had only emerged after the Sundering of the Heart. But in the very first scroll he'd unrolled from the age before the Radiant Emperor he'd found a reference to what could only be an elemental, a living serpent of water that had dwelled with a sorceress in a cave beneath the sea. He suspected now that these creatures from the other realms had been visiting this land long before a reed had first been used to make marks on clay.

Deryn rummaged through his satchel and pulled out the book that Archivist Devenal had given him not long after Shade had appeared. The librarian had said it was the journal of the last shadow elementalist, Gehart Othakis, but Deryn had no idea if that was true. He traced the strange, gnarled object set in the center of the lacquered cover, then flipped the book open, studying the squirming symbols filling the pages. He liked to glance over the bizarre writing at least once a day, so it was fresh in his thoughts if he did happen to stumble across a similar character in another book. That had never happened, though. He'd nearly accepted that the journal was the concoction of a diseased mind, and that there was no meaning which could be derived from these scribblings. Still, he was clinging to a tiny sliver of hope that this was not the case. After all, if the last elementalist of the Duskhold had gone insane, was that eventually going to be his fate, as well?

"What do you think about that?" Deryn asked, nudging the puddle of shadow curled under the table with his foot. "Will you make me go mad?"

The darkness rippled as a vaguely feline head lifted to regard him with the annoyed disdain of a disturbed cat.

Deryn sighed and returned to his reading, gingerly turning the brittle page. On the other side was inked a detailed but faded illustration of the 'stranger' mentioned earlier meeting with a trio of what looked to be zemani – except that these lizard-men were dressed in flowing robes and wore intricate jewelry, diadems on their scaly brows and thick bracelets encircling spined wrists. Deryn couldn't help but compare these pictures to the savage monsters daubed in red war-paint who had attacked the Kin boat. Had the zemani fallen from a more civilized state? Perhaps he'd ask one of those white-scaled lizard men who served the scholars here – although he didn't expect a very warm reception. Bared fangs and alarmed hisses usually resulted when he got too close to the zemani of the Erudinium, and he assumed this was because they could catch a whiff of the spoor still clinging to him after the ambush on the river.

What surprised him most during his search through these ancient texts was how different the world had once been. The Sharded Few and the holds had sprung into existence after the Sundering of the Heart. Before that, the First Empire of Segulah Tain had persisted for only a few centuries. There was a vast history preceding the empire that stretched into the mists of time, but the few books and scrolls and tablets that had survived were almost indecipherable and on the verge of crumbling to dust. Deryn's interest was often piqued by off-hand references to places he had never heard of – the Red Triarchy of Thes, the Murmuring City, Gel-Anath. And these long-ago people had worshipped strange gods . . . although, to his surprise, he recognized a few of these. Belandria was mentioned several times in a book describing the journey of a young woman to different temples. She was asking to be cured of some rare ailment, which is how Deryn had made the connection, for the strange sorceress who had healed Heth had poured a substance she'd called the 'tears of Belandria' over the terrible wound inflicted by the blood-sharded. Deryn remembered a sound like water striking red-hot iron – a hiss, and then a froth of bubbles that when brushed away had revealed pink, unbroken skin. And there was one other name that had caught Deryn's attention.

Algeroth.

The old woman had mentioned it as well, though Deryn couldn't remember the exact circumstances. But at that time it had lodged in his mind like a splinter, because he'd actually heard it before . . . well, in a way. It had once echoed in his thoughts like the reverberations of a terrible drum as the ancient balewyrm searched its lair for him. Every moment from that terrifying ordeal was still etched with sword-sharp clarity in his memories.

'HIDING, LITTLE GODLING? THOU ART NOT AS BRAVE AS THY FELLOWS. THEY FOUGHT AND DIED AND THE PIECES OF DREAD ALGEROTH THEY CARRIED NOW ADORN ME'

HE'D SEEN GLIMMERING shards embedded in the scales of the balewyrm, but he wasn't sure if that was what the monster had meant by 'pieces of Algeroth'. And dread? From the ancient histories Deryn had been reading, Algeroth had been the god of the sun, his name invoked fondly to mark the passage of the day. 'Algeroth had awoken' was often used to describe the dawn, and the night was 'Algeroth slumbering'. This was a mystery, but not the one Deryn was supposed to be investigating, so he tried to put it out of his mind.

Deryn jumped as the door to the small library banged open. High Seeker Helash stood framed in the entrance, looking like he'd just seen the risen dead, his face pale and eyes wild.

"What is it?" Deryn asked, rising from his stool in concern. The Seeker ignored him, hurrying through the maze of rickety shelves and tables piled high with books.

"High Seeker?" Deryn pressed as Helash arrived at the only other door in the small chamber and began fumbling with a ring of black-iron keys. "Are you all right? What's happened?"

The scholar rarely entered this little library, spending most days outside fiddling with his strange contraptions and the metal flowers growing out of the captive shards. His visits were so infrequent that Deryn had even stopped worrying about the Seeker discovering Shade.

He certainly wouldn't notice the elemental at this moment, as his attention was entirely focused on finding the key that fit into the door's elaborate lock. Deryn had wondered many times what was beyond that door, because the wood was banded with iron and looked formidable, and he had eventually assumed that inside were artifacts so ancient they needed to be kept well-protected.

High Seeker Helash gave a little cry of triumph as one of the keys finally turned in the lock. He hauled the door open and then vanished into the darkness beyond, not even bothering to take one of the glass globes filled with glowing mist scattered about the chamber.

Movement from under the table drew Deryn's attention. Shade had risen from where he'd been curled and was now very obviously interested in the room where the Seeker had gone. A sound came to him, the rustle of moth wings, and then a high-pitched mewling. Whatever was inside the room had interested the elemental.

Deryn scrambled to his feet as Seeker Helash burst through the doorway again, flames writhing in his cupped hands.

"Silver Shrike!" Deryn cried, fear washing through him that the scholar was going to blunder into one of the bookshelves and start a conflagration. Seeker Helash, however, seemed unconcerned by the writhing fire as he strode with purpose past the gawping Deryn and back out into the chamber where he was conducting his experiment. There had been no pain in his expression, no fear at what he was holding, only grim determination.

What was going on?

Glancing again at Shade – who was still rigid, staring at the door the Seeker had left open – Deryn followed Helash. The Seeker had gone over to one of the glass boxes that contained a shard and crouched beside it.

"Seeker Helash," Deryn said softly as he came to stand beside where the scholar was hunkered staring into the glass. "What's going on? Please, talk to me." Now that he was closer, Deryn saw that the flame he held was not touching his flesh; instead, it was set atop a thin disc of black stone. The flame was acting strangely – there was no wind, so it shouldn't be moving very much, yet the crimson tongues were swaying as if to an unheard melody.

Something else surprised him as well. Every time he'd passed through this chamber while coming and going from the small library – and he'd done it dozens of times in the past month – this particular glass container had been filled with crackling flames. But now the only thing inside was a heap of crumbled charcoal and the twisting, blackened roots of the copper flower.

"Why has the fire gone out?" Deryn asked uneasily.

This was the question that finally got through to the High Seeker. Helash twisted around, looking surprised to see Deryn looming over him.

"By the Book, Deryn. Do you know what this means?"

"No, most definitely not."

The Seeker rose and placed his ear to the unfolded petals of the copper flower, then stepped aside, motioning for Deryn to listen as well.

He did, bending down until the still-warm metal touched his skin. "I don't hear anything," he finally said, straightening.

"Exactly!" Seeker Helash said, brandishing the flame he held like it proved the point he thought he was making. "There's nothing! The window has been closed!"

"The . . . window?"

"Yes!" the scholar, thrusting the fire so close to Deryn that he had to jump backwards. "The window to the fire realm! Or the Infernal Kingdom, as the flame-sharded call it. It's shut!"

"You know that because the flames in there went out?" Deryn asked, eyeing the crumbled charcoal dubiously.

"Not only that!" Seeker Helash cried. "This fire I hold now? It is no ordinary flame. This is a piece of the Infernal Kingdom, brought into our world by someone who visited that primordial realm. It does not behave like the flames we are familiar with. It will never extinguish or spread, but always remain exactly as it is now. The flame-shard within my Harridan cage . . . it should be flaring at this moment like when grease is thrown onto a fire. But there's nothing!" He paused, then took a deep breath. "The shard inside is dead."

"This shard is . . . dead?" Deryn asked, peering through the glass.

"No . . . no. *The* Shard is dead. The flame shard that sat at the heart of the Ember. It has been destroyed, severing our world's connection to the Infernal Kingdom."

Deryn rocked backwards. "But that means . . ."

"Every flame-sharded has lost their powers. Their strength is gone, their powers snuffed out." Seeker Helash had a far-away look on his face, as if he was trying to imagine what had just happened. "Like a douter placed over a candle's burning wick."

"But how . . ." Deryn began, feeling unmoored. He didn't finish his question because he realized he knew the answer. The Shadow had done this. For centuries, the Ember and Duskhold had been twined; always rivals, but at times allies against the Storm and the Sand. And now the Shadow had destroyed its sometimes-enemy. How could the Shadow even exist without the Flame? Their history had been knotted together, and it had seemed like they would always exist side by side . . . and now it was finished forever. The Flame had been extinguished.

"I will keep the shard here, in its Harridan cage," High Seeker

Helash was saying, but to Deryn the words were floating to him from very far away. "Just as I did with the sand-shard after the Sand was destroyed. I wonder what reaction the inert fragment will have if placed beside this piece of the Infernal Kingdom? I suppose I should find out . . ."

Seeker Helash's voice faded as Deryn left the chamber in a daze, stepping once more into the library. His gaze drifted over the over-stuffed shelves and piles of books scattered across the tables. How many of those books referenced the Flame and the Ember? He felt like he had just witnessed a moment that would reverberate down through the ages. A hold's Shard had been destroyed, for the second time in the last thirty years. That made him pause as he considered this. The Sundering of the Heart had been a thousand years in the past, and up until very recently, none of its pieces had been lost. Contact with the monastery of Kara Dum had been severed long ago, but to his knowledge there was no evidence that the Ice Shard had been shattered. And now two orders of the Sharded Few had been ended in the last few decades . . . and one new Shard had been discovered.

Deryn sat heavily on his stool, his head spinning. His shard was itching as if it sensed something was different. What had Cael Shen told Azil that day the lord of the Duskhold had summoned Deryn to his chambers so he could interrogate him about his elemental? *The pulse of history has suddenly quickened.* It was true.

Deryn surfaced from his thoughts as Shade flowed across the table to rub against his arm. Was the elemental part of all this? Could there be some connection—

Deryn frowned, his gaze alighting on a strange object that had appeared on the table. It resembled a sliver of dark glass, maybe as wide as his hand and twice as long, like a piece from a broken window. It was lying across the pages of a book that Deryn had no recollection opening – the diary of Gehart Othakis. Frowning, he leaned closer to better see what this thing was . . . and then gasped.

The piece of dusky glass was just transparent enough that he could see the writing on the pages beneath . . . writing that was no longer a cavalcade of illegible symbols.

"The umbral dukes did manifest upon the flensing plains," Deryn whispered, reading out loud what had been revealed, "and the last shreds of the rebels fled before their might. Or so it was told to me by the darkness, whispering in my ear as I slept. And in my dream, I saw them towering black and terrible above the churning lands, and I knew that the purpose of my beloved no longer existed, and I wept, for they would now be coming for her."

It sounded like the ramblings of a madman. Deryn grimaced, scratching at his chest again. His shadow shard – which, here in the City of the Dead, he sometimes forgot about for days at a time – was prickling strangely, like it was trying to pull itself free of his flesh. As if . . . as if it wanted to go to the sliver of dark glass that had somehow translated the elementalist's journal.

Oh.

Deryn looked at Shade, preening himself with an air of self-satisfaction, and then to the still-open door that the High Seeker had just unlocked. Helash had gone in there to fetch a spark of what he'd called the Infernal Kingdom. The only conclusion Deryn could draw right now was that the dark glass that had appeared while he'd been in the other chamber was a piece of the shadowrealm . . . and that *Shade* had found it in that room and brought it here and placed it on the open journal.

This thought was staggering, for several reasons.

Deryn stared at the entrance to the chamber where the High Seeker was still absorbed by what had happened to his flame shard. How quickly would he finish? Eventually, he would return the piece of the Infernal Kingdom to the storeroom, and there was a good chance he would notice that the sliver of the shadowrealm was missing. Deryn's fingers drummed on the table, his mind racing. He could return the dark glass while Helash was occupied and the scholar would never know. Or . . . or . . .

Deryn gently scooped the piece of the shadowrealm from the table, shivering as a prickling coldness sluiced through him. His shard was pulsing like a second heart, making him lightheaded as he slipped the shadowy substance – he should really should stop thinking of it as glass, since it clearly was not – into his satchel, along with the elementalist's journal.

Then, heaving a deep breath, Deryn left the small library. He had an explanation for his abrupt departure prepared, but High Seeker Helash never even noticed him leaving because he was so intent on scribbling notes in a small book.

"I'm sorry," Deryn whispered, taking a last look at the scholar before hurrying down the corridor, Shade rippling in his shadow.

24

HETH

A haze filled the Hollow eating hall, redolent of stewed meat and stale beer. Once this had been the cellar of a rich merchant's house in the Nethers, perhaps even a family crypt given the intricate stonework and smoke-blackened statues set in niches, but someone had knocked down all the interior walls. Long trestle tables now filled the torch-lit space, and rushes that hadn't been changed in far too long were scattered across the floor. Heth assumed that the food must be prepared upstairs, in the deteriorating husk of the mansion proper, because he saw no cookpit or fire. Probably wise, given the lack of windows or other ventilation.

"In the back," Jerik said, nodding towards the farthest reaches of the hall. The table there was crowded, although not much else could be seen in the dimness. "Come on, I'll introduce you."

Heth followed Jerik as the boy made his way across the hall. Communal tureens of soup were on every table, the benches filled with Hollow families slurping from bowls or helping themselves to steaming hunks of meat piled on platters. It was loud and boisterous, and Heth could sense the good cheer. However difficult life was in the Nethers, this was where the Hollow came to feel safe and happy. They could not entirely escape the Tithing even here, though, as he saw many men and women and children with withered limbs or skin marred by the strange scaling that was brought on by long exposure to the raw ore before it was refined into karathinite.

Jerik was clearly liked, as several men raised their glasses as he passed, and more than a few children squealed greetings while clutching at his shirt. He slapped their hands away playfully, then sent them into shrieking hysterics by lunging at them. Heth smiled at a pair of little girls who had attempted to touch Jerik, but when they saw him, they flinched back fearfully and reached for their mother.

Oh yes, his scar. It had its uses – he could stroll through the most dangerous parts of the Nethers without fear of being accosted – but his days of making friends with children were probably over. That saddened him, though it was true he'd rarely given children much attention in the past. His youth had been spent fighting in sword halls and wooing girls and downing good northern ale in the taverns of Kething's Cross. Frivolous pursuits, he now realized.

"Caden Vars!" Jerik exclaimed when they arrived at the table pushed up against the far wall. A cowled stone statue with arms outspread loomed over those seated, as if bestowing its blessing upon the grizzled men beneath, all of whom had been thickened by labor and tanned by long days in the sun. Playing cards depicting various beasts – some real, some Heth believed to only exist in stories – were scattered across the pitted wood, along with quite a few coins.

A heavyset, balding man with a thick ginger beard looked up from the cards on the table when Jerik spoke. His gaze flicked from Jerik to Heth, and then he motioned for them to approach. Groans erupted around the table as another player slapped down his hand, and Heth had to jump back as a man with over half his face covered with gray-green scales lurched to his feet cursing.

"Jerik," the bearded man said as the boy slipped onto the bench beside him. "Good to see you, lad. How's your sister?"

"Pissy as always," Jerik replied amiably, reaching to pour himself a tankard from one of the jugs on the table. "Things are well with you, Caden?"

The big man shrugged. "The usual. I'm enjoying watching Yerl lose the allowance his wife gave him."

"Bugger off, Cade," snapped a scrawny fellow, his beady eyes fixed on the cards he was holding so close to his face they were nearly touching his nose.

Caden chuckled and turned to Heth, his eyes shrewd as he looked him up and down. "And this is the one you told me about?"

"Aye," Jerik said, wiping foam from his upper lip. "Scared the fat Thiss and sent him running."

Caden grunted, motioning for Heth to also sit. "Wish I could have seen it. What's your name, stranger?"

"Heth."

"Well met," the bearded man said, reaching across Jerik to clasp his arm. "I'm Caden."

Another loud exclamation of disgust rippled around the table after more cards were revealed. "I heard you're the big man around here," Heth said.

Caden shrugged, then withdrew a pipe and began filling it from a pouch on the table. "I'm *a* man. Do my best to make the Nethers a decent place. You been here long?"

"About a month."

"*Mmm*," Caden murmured as he finished packing the bowl. He rummaged in his pockets and drew out a thin piece of rolled paper, then held it out for Jerik. "Here, lad, go light this taper for me, will you?"

"'Course, Caden," Jerik said, plucking the paper from between his fingers and rising. After he'd left, Caden motioned for Heth to take his spot, then leaned even closer so that the others at the table couldn't hear what they were saying.

"You looking for work? Jerik says you know how to swing a sword. I need a few boys to guard some cargo that's coming in soon from the Whispering Isles. Just a few days, until my mates from Chan-Anok are ready to pick it up."

Heth understood how Caden had become a leader in the Nethers. He had a way of talking that made others feel relaxed; he wasn't speaking down like Heth was a servant, or trying to cajole him to do something he didn't want to. It was like they were old friends, even though they'd just met.

Still, he shook his head. "I came here about something else."

Caden leaned back as Jerik returned bearing the smoldering taper. He held out his pipe, and then took a long draw after the boy lit it for him.

"Something else," he said, blowing out a stream of smoke. "Could this something make me money?"

Heth shook his head again.

Caden tilted his head to one side, regarding him quizzically. "You don't want to work for me, and you don't have an opportunity to discuss. What's this about, then?" He turned back to Jerik, still hovering at his shoulder. "Give us a bit, lad."

Heth hesitated as Jerik dutifully moved away, unsure how to continue. He'd rehearsed this moment a dozen times, preparing for how to respond if the Nethers bossman was hostile or indifferent or wary . . . yet, for some reason, his amiable disposition had left him floundering.

Finally he swept out his arm, indicating the Hollow filling the eating hall. "It's not an opportunity just for you. For them as well."

A shadow fell across Caden's face, the warmth in his eyes fading. He sucked on his pipe, regarding Heth through the curling smoke. "Are you Hollow, lad?"

The question surprised Heth, though he'd expected he'd be asked it at some point. "Not exactly."

"Not exactly," Caden repeated, his tone growing heavier. "Well, either you are, or you aren't. And if you aren't, then I don't think you have much to offer my people."

"My grandfather was Hollow in the Ember," Heth explained, holding Caden's measuring gaze. "He was freed and rewarded for service to the hold. I grew up in the Twelve Towns, under the Shadow. Hound came to my town and found I was Hollow as well. Dragged me off to the Duskhold."

Caden squinted at him. "And you're running, because the Shadow doesn't let its slaves go."

"I'm not Hollow," Heth said quietly, tapping his chest. "Sharded."

"Are you playing with me, boy? Or are you mad?"

Heth turned himself so that the rest of the table couldn't see what he was doing, then briefly pulled down the front of his tunic to show Caden the fragment embedded in his chest. The light that had infused the shard outside of Karath was gone, but still there was no denying what he was.

"So you're Sharded. Unbound?"

Heth shrugged. "I don't belong to a hold, but I wouldn't call myself Unbound."

"One of Xend's Unfettered, then?"

"No."

Caden sighed, pinching the bridge of his nose, the stem of his pipe clamped between his teeth. "Speak plainly, lad. You said you were Hollow, yet now you're Sharded. Everyone knows that's impossible."

"It's not," Heth said, trying to demonstrate the importance of what he was saying with his tone. "I found a shard. And I don't mean what I just showed you . . . much larger, like the ones at the hearts of the great holds. It gave me my fragment."

"Madness," Caden snorted, but there was something in his eyes.

"It's not," Heth insisted, reaching out to grasp the bearded man's arm. "In an ancient ruin in the Frayed Lands, I found the Light. I was a Hollow and it made me Sharded. I swear to you on the souls of my mother and father."

Caden shifted uneasily. "Even if I were to believe you – which I don't – why are you here telling me this?"

"Because I'm not special. If other Hollow come with me, they could become Sharded as well."

"Doesn't make sense," Caden muttered.

"Doesn't it?" Heth shot back. "Think about it. This Light shard has been hidden since the Heart was destroyed. Ever since the Sundering, the Hollow have served the holds. We're immune to the power flowing from the great shards, but why is that? Maybe we were *supposed* to be Sharded. We just weren't brought before the right one."

"We're not Imbued," Caden said tersely, and Heth could tell he'd unsettled the big man. "The Hounds sniff and they know we have no chance to claim a shard. They know we're just Hollow."

"Maybe that's because we are different from other Imbued. Special."

"What do you mean?" The sharpness had disappeared from Caden's voice. Now he sounded curious, although Heth suspected he still wasn't close to believing him. Maybe he just wanted to know more about this strange fantasy Heth had concocted.

"I found the Light shard in an imperial ruin. A palace. What do the stories call Segulah Tain? The Radiant Emperor. Maybe the Light was special to him. Maybe . . . maybe we're of his blood." Heth's hand slipped from Caden's arm, surprise washing through him. What had he just said? Where had *that* idea come from? It had just slipped out; he'd never even considered such an outlandish possibility before.

Caden grinned around the pipe in his mouth. "Descendants of the emperor, are we?"

"I . . . don't know," Heth admitted, shaking his head to clear it of a strange feeling that had suddenly come over him. "It's just a guess. All I know is that I was Hollow, and now I'm one of the Sharded Few. And I think you could do the same. They all could." He swept out his arm again, indicating the other Hollow.

Caden removed his pipe and tapped out the bowl onto the table. He stayed quiet for a long time, staring at the ashes, and then shook his head. "Lad, you're either a madman, the greatest liar I've ever met – and I've met quite a few – or you're telling the truth." He sighed deeply, then rubbed at his face like this conversation had exhausted him. "Let me have a think about what you just told me. Talk with some of my people, see what they say."

"You have to keep this a secret," Heth implored. "If any of the holds found out, they'd hunt me down and torture me until I told them where the shard is."

"I'll keep it tight," Caden promised, sounding a little hurt that

Heth would worry about such things. "The Sharded Few are the last bastards I'd betray anyone to." He leaned over, grunting as he fished for something under the table.

"Good," Heth said, forcing himself to try to relax. Had this meeting been a terrible mistake? Silver Shrike, he hoped not.

He then flinched as Caden slammed a jug of dark liquid down on the table. It looked like something that had been homebrewed . . . which, in Heth's experience, usually meant it was bordering on poisonous.

"Drink with me," Caden said, straining to unstopper the container. "You can't really get to know a man until you've gotten good and wet together." The cork pulled free with a pop, and a moment later Heth's eyes began to water as fumes wafted forth from whatever vile brew was contained within.

"Jerik!" Caden barked, and the boy turned from the pair of pretty, wide-eyed maids he had been regaling with some story. "Two cups, lad!"

HETH CAME to himself swaying in the middle of a darkened street. He staggered, trying to remember the sequence of events that had brought him here. Had he been drinking with Jerik in his tavern? He could see the boy laughing as they struck their cups together, a disconcertingly brown liquid sloshing out to stain his tunic . . . that drink. Oh, that drink. Heth groaned, holding his head to try to stop the city from spinning. Bogwater, the grinning bearded man had called it. Caden. Caden Vars. One of the big men in the Nethers. He'd gone to the eating hall to talk to him about the Light shard, and how it could be the salvation for the Hollow of Karath. Then they'd been drinking, and there was singing, and maybe even some dancing on the tables . . .

Ugh. Heth hunched over as whatever was churning in his gut strongly considered an escape. With his hands on his knees, he contemplated the faint outlines of the cobbles, wondering how he was going to make it back to Mam Nar's house. Perhaps he should drag himself out of the street and sleep until morning . . . he turned his head, searching for a suitable spot to collapse. An alley's mouth yawned invitingly to his left, promising sweet oblivion. He took a stumbling step towards it, but then paused, blinking. Had that been movement in the shadows? His hand went to the sword he'd bought to replace his Salahi blade, but then he realized it was only a dog. He released the hilt, wondering if it was friendly. He hadn't seen any other stray dogs in Karath. And this one was huge, at least the size of the sheep hounds kept by the shepherds in the hills above the Cross.

"Hello, doggy," Heth mumbled, then tried and failed to whistle. "Come, boy. Can you share your alley with me? I promise I'll be nice."

The bogwater chose that moment to make a triumphant return, driving Heth to his hands and knees as it climbed out to splatter on the cobbles. He gasped, wiping at his lips and wishing he could gargle literally anything else to get this taste out of his mouth. He turned his head towards the alley, but his performance must have spooked the dog, because it was nowhere to be seen.

"Sorry, boy," he slurred, lowering himself to the stone and then rolling onto his back. Above him, the stars danced a merry jig, almost as merry as Jerik had been with those two lasses, one tucked under each arm . . .

A shadow loomed over Heth, blotting out the stars. "Doggy?" he murmured, and then something hard smashed his face and he tumbled into a deeper blackness.

25

DERYN

"The Shadow does not forgive . . . the shadow does not forget. You're sure that's what you heard?"

Alia looked up from the huge leaf overflowing with crisped green vegetables she was holding. Her face was dusted with some red spice and her lips glistened from whatever sauce had been drizzled over this edible weed that Alia claimed had come from the sea.

"That's what Ontos said," she said, wiping her mouth with the sleeve of her gray tunic.

"And you're certain he was flame-sharded?" Rhenna asked, drumming her fingers on the side of the strange object she held, a thin wooden tube with pieces of glass fixed at both ends. When you looked through it, things that were far away suddenly appeared much closer. Deryn had found it at Mam Nar's house, some navigation tool that a Kin sailor had left behind, and Rhenna had decided to bring it along after Alia had told them about what she'd seen.

"There was a hole right here," Alia said, touching her brow with a spice-speckled finger. Deryn wondered if she knew she'd just left a smear in the middle of her forehead.

Rhenna grunted, gently slapping the seeing device into the palm of her other hand. She was standing on a chunk of stone at the edge of the hill, using the vantage to improve her view of the city spread below. A bloody sun was descending, staining the Sea of Salvation crimson. Soon it would slip below that thin seam where water joined with sky, and they would find out whether this trek to the top of the Skull had been for naught . . . or if the House of Last Light would reveal itself at the day's end.

"Have you heard anything else? If the flame-shard has truly been destroyed and the Unfettered know, then this must be all anyone is talking about."

"No," Alia said through a mouthful of her seaweed. "But no one talks to me. Well, except Sharl and Markis, but they don't know anything, either."

"They may be trying to keep it quiet," Rhenna mused, putting the device to her eye and focusing on the fortified tower rising on one side of the hill, the bastion of either Karath's Sword or Shield – Deryn wasn't sure which. "The shattering of a shard would shake the foundation of the world. Everything has changed, if this is true."

"What happens when a shard like that is destroyed?" Deryn asked, trying to imagine how this could even be accomplished. He remembered when he'd been brought before the Shadow under the Duskhold, the sense of something impossibly vast and ancient looming over him, peeling away his flesh and peering into his mind to determine if he was worthy to bear a shard . . .

"It has only happened one time, to my knowledge," Rhenna murmured, sweeping the object she held across the city below. "After the fall of Derambinal, my father used his greatsword Night to split the Sand shard into three parts, each of which was claimed by one of the victorious armies. These great fragments were hauled back to the Windwrack, the Ember, and the Duskhold and merged with the shards under those holds. Saelus told me that when the chunk of the Sand shard joined with the Shadow, every Sharded in the Duskhold felt themselves grow stronger."

Deryn frowned, touching his shard through his shirt's fabric. He wondered if he would experience this strengthening if it had indeed been the forces of Cael Shen that conquered the Ember. He likely wouldn't be able to tell, given where they were right now.

"There are new Sharded in our house, and I think Palimas put them there to keep an eye on us. I can ask them if they know why the flame-sharded was in the garden."

Rhenna shook her head. "No. You've already learned what we need. The Unfettered know that it was the Shadow who destroyed the Flame, which means they were involved in fomenting this conflict. Xend *must* have been hired by my father."

"You seem . . . at peace with that," Deryn said, shielding his eyes from the brightness of the setting sun. If anything was going to happen, it would be soon.

"I've had a lot of time to accept this possibility," Rhenna replied, lowering the object so she could get a broader view of the city.

"What should I do now?" Alia asked, staring down forlornly at her empty leaf.

"Come back to the Kin house," Rhenna said matter-of-factly. "Things have suddenly become more dangerous."

Alia's head came up, her jade eyes widening. "I can't leave without saying goodbye to Sharl and Markis!"

Rhenna sighed. "You'll have to leave them soon anyway, because —Mother Dark!" She fumbled with the close-seeing device, raising it again to her eye.

Deryn had glimpsed a flash as well, just as the sun slipped below the horizon. *Something* had caught that final ray of light – he thought it had been fairly close to where the Erudinium bulked, down at the edge of the Nethers.

"Did you see where it came from?" Alia asked, hopping up onto the chunk of stone beside Rhenna.

"I think so," Rhenna said slowly, frowning. "I recognize a few of the buildings in that neighborhood – a mansion with a collapsing turret, another with minarets in the Ashasai style. But I think the light came from a smaller house."

"Do you think it could be the House of Last Light?" Deryn asked, extending Rhenna a hand to help her down.

"No," she replied, ignoring his offer as she stepped off the stone. "But there's only one way to find out."

THE HOUSE WAS NOT what he had expected. Given the brightness of the flash, Deryn had imagined a massive, many-paned window, or perhaps that a huge metal decoration had been fixed on the façade. Instead, Rhenna led them to a humble dwelling squeezed in between much more impressive manses. It did not even seem to be made from stone, unlike its hulking neighbors – the white walls were rough and uneven, pitted in places. Some kind of clay, Deryn supposed, though he'd never seen such a material used for building before.

"You're sure this is the place?" he asked dubiously, turning back to squint at the Skull rising over the gabled roofs. Night had fallen during their descent, and now the hill was just a dark mound swelling over the city, though scatterings of light illuminated the Lanthium and the fortresses of the Sword and Shield.

"I'm not certain of anything," Rhenna replied, sounding annoyed. "But it doesn't look like a sorcerer's abode, or whoever it was the old woman wanted us to go find. It doesn't look old enough, for one thing."

"I think the house is old," Alia said, crouching down to pet Shade, who was sprawled between her legs. Hopefully, anyone watching would think the elemental was a friendly little stray looking for a handout. "Just well cared for."

Deryn found himself agreeing with her – the white walls were speckled with small holes, but they weren't crumbling like the masonry of the surrounding manses. The door was small and simple and made of red wood, with an iron knocker crudely shaped into the head of some large animal. A bear, perhaps, though Deryn couldn't tell exactly from where they were standing across the street. The lamplighters kept this neighborhood bordering the Nethers well lit, perhaps unsurprisingly, but the night still obscured many small details.

"So, what should we do?" Deryn asked, looking at Rhenna. She had her arms folded and was staring at the red door like she could pierce the wood with the intensity of her gaze.

"We should be cautious. In the small chance one of these Elowyn actually lives here—wait, Alia, what are you doing?"

"Oh, frozen hells," Deryn muttered. Alia was marching across the street, Shade scampering beside her. Deryn shared a quick glance with Rhenna, and then they both hurried after her.

"Don't—" Rhenna began, but whatever she was about to say turned into a deep sigh when Alia raised the knocker and rapped it sharply against the door. The crack was surprisingly loud, echoing up and down the empty street.

"You shouldn't have done that," Rhenna hissed, though she sounded more exasperated than angry.

Alia shrugged. "What were we going to do, climb the walls and sneak in through a window?"

"No, but—" Rhenna fell silent at the heavy thunk of a bolt being drawn back. She threw one last scowl at Alia, then forced a smile and drew herself up straighter. Deryn guessed that if the inhabitant of this house was truly an ancient sorcerer, she wanted to make a good impression.

The door swung open. In the entrance stood a small Salahi boy dressed in a simple dark blue robe trimmed with gold, similar to what Deryn had seen the other desert people wearing in the city. He looked to be maybe twelve or thirteen, though there was some faint webbing at the corner of his eyes that suggested he might actually be older than he appeared. Behind him was a corridor, its walls made from the same material as the outside of the house, and farther on this opened into a larger space lit by a soft, welcoming light.

"Yes?" he said, raising an eyebrow. He seemed surprisingly unsurprised to find the three of them on his doorstep this evening. A very well-trained servant, Deryn assumed.

Rhenna must have thought the same. "Is your master home?" she asked, craning her head to get a better view of what lay at the end of the entrance hall.

"Usually visitors introduce themselves," the boy admonished her, and Deryn was surprised to see Rhenna blush.

"Ah," she said, focusing on the unsmiling Salahi boy. "We have come a long way to find the House of Last Light. We were instructed to do so by an old woman who I was told is one of the Elowyn. Is this . . . is this that house?"

The faintest of lines creased his forehead. "This is not that house," he said simply, and then began to swing the door shut.

"Wait, wait," Alia cried, sticking her foot out to keep the door from closing. The boy paused, staring at her in what Deryn thought might be bemused interest. "What's that?" Alia asked, pointing at a bracelet the boy was wearing. It was made of irregularly shaped chunks of what looked to be bone, threaded together on a piece of red twine.

"That is none of your concern," the boy replied, a slight edge to his voice, and for a moment Deryn feared that he was about to slam the door on Alia's toes.

"She was wearing the same thing," Alia blurted hastily. "The old woman. A bracelet of bone. I'm sure of it."

The boy cocked his head to one side, as if studying her in a new light. "It is traditional among my people to bear such trinkets. Now, I must bid you all goodnight."

"She said to tell the master of this house something," Rhenna said quickly, also stepping forward to wedge herself in the entranceway. "About Leantha Devoril, the advisor to Cael Shen, lord of the Duskhold. She said she'd seen her before . . . placing a copper crown on the head of Osmari an-Alams and declaring him shah of all the Salahi. She said their faces were different, but she was certain they were the same person."

If the master of this house was in truth a simple merchant or craftsman, Deryn thought, then this boy must now think them utterly mad.

"And what does that mean?" the boy asked, sounding genuinely curious.

"That the soul-sharded are plotting something," Rhenna answered, meeting the Salahi's calm gaze.

The boy blinked, as if taken aback by this response, then opened the door wider. "Please enter the chamber at the end of this hall and make yourself comfortable. You will be joined shortly."

26

HETH

ake up.

Heth stirred, slowly returning to himself. The first thing he noticed was the pain – his cheekbones throbbed, and it felt like his scar might have split open, as dried blood covered much of his face. His arms ached from being lifted above his head and bound together at the wrists with shackles, and his feet were just barely brushing a stone floor scattered with rushes. Something was also wrapped around his ankles, making it impossible to move his legs. He forced open his eyes, wincing as the brightness of the flame in the brazier set in from him made the pounding in his temple worse.

Where was he?

What had happened?

The room was large, its farthest reaches lost to shadows. From the silence and the lack of windows, he could only assume he was underground. He swallowed away the thickness clotting his throat, trying to focus on something other than the dancing flame The stone wall he was hanging against was damp and cold, but the waves of heat were somehow even more uncomfortable, making his flesh tingle and his tunic damp with sweat. A wooden rack had been placed near the brazier, filled with all manner of sharp implements. As his gaze traveled over those glittering blades and hooks and points, the fear that he had been trying to keep firmly clenched threatened to squirm free. Heth's breathing quickened as he strained against his bonds . . . but the metal was firmly welded to the wall. He doubted he could have broken free even if he still had his Sharded strength.

The sound of a door creaking open came from somewhere beyond the light shed by the brazier. Footsteps approached, growing louder, and then a familiar man emerged from the darkness.

Daemonel Thiss.

A grin split his fat face when he saw that Heth was awake, his porcine eyes gleaming. He'd shed his Wardsman uniform and its surcoat with its black hand, and was instead dressed in a stained leather jerkin that must have been fitted for him before he'd reached his current girth. Heth realized what those splotches on Daemonel's clothes were, and for a moment he lost himself to panic, thrashing against his restraints.

"*Shh, shh,*" Daemonel murmured, holding up his hands as if trying to calm a panicked animal. "There's no use making a fuss."

"What are you going to do to me?" Heth asked, finding his voice.

Daemonel's grin twitched wider as he wandered over to the rack, running a finger over one particularly long, curving dagger. "Torture," he said brightly, picking up a smaller flensing knife and testing its edge. "And then eventually I'll kill you."

"Why?" Heth asked, trying to keep the fear from his voice. "Because I embarrassed you in the tavern?"

Daemonel nodded vigorously at this, then flinched as the knife he was testing pricked his skin. "That's right. If you hadn't decided to come to that boy's defense, you certainly wouldn't be here." He raised his finger, studying the trickle of crimson as it flowed into his palm. "But you did."

"Bastard," Heth snarled, yanking at his chains. "Stealing children and sending them to the mines."

Daemonel shook his head, chuckling as he pulled on a thick, fire-blackened glove. Then he held the small knife over the flames until its metal glowed red. "Such spirit. Some beg immediately, but I have to admit I always prefer rage and indignation. It makes what comes later all the sweeter."

Daemonel stepped closer to Heth and pressed the flat side of the blade to his arm.

Pain.

Heth screamed as his flesh blistered and smoked, his vision blurring. Giggling with delight, Daemonel skipped back a step as Heth vomited up what little was left in his stomach.

"Oh, this is going to be fun."

The door bangs open, letting in a gust of wind that makes the candles flicker and the tapestry stir on the wall. Outside, the hissing rain strengthens as the night pulses with lightning. The room is humid, almost febrile with the way the air trembles, and smells like black rot mixed with blood.

In one hand Heth holds a goblet full to the brim with dark wine, and in the other he grips a flail's handle. The braided leather cords coiling on the wooden floor are stained black. A boy is slumped in front of him, his wrists secured around a hitching post, his bare back laced with cuts.

There's so much blood.

It has pooled beneath the boy where it has not drained between the poorly joined floorboards. Heth hadn't struck his head, but he can see that the boy's hair is sticky and matted. He looks dead, although every once in a while his leg will spasm weakly.

Heth's gorge rises. He wants to vomit, but instead he forces himself to take a sip from his goblet. His hand is trembling so badly that he spills wine down the front of his tunic, and an exasperated sigh comes from behind him.

"You must be stronger."

"Yes, father," Heth murmurs, though he wants nothing more than to throw aside the flail and the glass and flee out into the storm shaking the old mill.

"*Again. Hit him again.*"

Heth manages a shaky nod, raising the whip as he steps forward. He hesitates as the boy stirs, lifting his head slightly.

"*Heth . . .*" *the boy croaks.* "*Why . . . ?*"

"*Deryn?*" *Heth murmurs, letting the leather handle slip from his suddenly numb fingers.*

"*He gave away one of our crabs,*" *his father says, voice heavy with anger.* "*He stole from us. From you. Pick up that flail and show him who is the master.*"

"*No,*" *Heth says, stepping back in horror.* "*He's my friend.*"

"*He is a slave! And you are the Light bearer!*"

"*I'm what?*" *Heth asks, his hand going to his chest. Beneath his damp tunic, he feels the hard outline of the shard embedded in his chest.*

"*The blood of kings flows through you. The blood of Algeroth's chosen!*"

"*What are you talking about?*" *Heth says, finally turning to face his father.*

Who is not there. A stuffed divan crouches in the middle of the room, its cushions frayed. Ornate, decaying chairs are scattered around a table covered with the splayed carcass of a deer. Boots and hunting bows are set on the floor beneath the tapestry, wet and glistening.

The tapestry.

Picked out in faded threads is a man with a shard set in his brow thrusting his spear through a monstrous boar. The light spilling from his fragment is the color of white-hot flames. Beside him, his Hollow servant holds a spare spear, but he's not facing his lord . . . no, he has turned his head away to stare at Heth, and deep within his eyes glimmer motes of deepest blue . . .

"Do you know what you've done, you fool?"

Heth floated on a black tide, cosseted by pain. It felt like a thousand burning insects were crawling all over him, jabbing barbed mandibles into his flesh. The bones in his shoulder ached like his arms were about to separate from his body, and his lips were cracked and bloody. His eyes fluttered open, and he fought to focus on the shapes in front of him.

The brazier had been reduced to glowing embers, and most of the chamber's light was now coming from a pair of armored men holding lanterns. In front of where they stood, the rack had been largely emptied, torture implements strewn across the rushes. Daemonel Thiss stood nearby with his head hanging low, as if embarrassed. His leather jerkin had acquired fresh stains and dangling loosely in his hand was the hilt of a cleaver, like what butchers used to chop meat.

Meat. He was the meat. Heth moaned, rolling his head to one side, and this drew the attention of the others in the room. A small, slight man in gray leather stood next to Daemonel with his arms folded. He wore a long dark cloak with its cowl pulled back, revealing a man well into his middle years. His graying beard was tightly cropped, and only a trace of stubble fringed his scalp. The brooch securing his cloak was a white circle set with the outline of a black hand, and a jeweled sword hilt hung at his side.

"Well, what do you have to say for yourself?" the man in gray asked, frowning. Despite his expression, his voice seemed entirely shriven of emotion.

"I didn't know," Daemonel muttered, glancing at Heth. "How could I know?"

"A stranger appears in Karath, swaggering about like he is not beholden to the laws of our city. As if he is accustomed to not fearing mere men, even if they have swords. You are saying you could not have possibly guessed?" Despite the man's mild tone, Daemonel's face was ashen.

"Selavin . . ."

The man in gray silenced Daemonel by raising his hand and then bringing it down sharply. "Enough. Let me think, nephew, about how this situation can be salvaged."

Selavin. Heth recognized the name. This was the Sword of Karath, commander of the Wardsmen and protector of the city. What in the frozen hells was he doing down here in this dungeon talking about Heth like he was someone important? A shiver of pain went through him, and Heth groaned. It was too much effort to keep his head raised, and so he slumped in his shackles, a ribbon of red unspooling from his mouth. His tunic was nothing but tatters, his shard clearly visible in the center of his chest. Suddenly, he realized what they were talking about. They hadn't known he was one of the Sharded Few until now. But why did they care? He was just a man in this city. Another shudder wracked Heth, and he writhed in agony. He felt like he was drifting again, the room beginning to recede. Desperately, he tried to cling to consciousness . . . and then hissed in alarm.

Something crouched in the darkness beyond the light shed by the lanterns. It was huge, bestial. He could hear its ragged panting and its corpse-smell filled the room. How could they not notice it? Heth struggled in his bonds, his gaze locked on where the creature had wrapped itself in shadows. It was looking at him, he knew. Those cold points of light were burrowing into his soul, laying bare his darkest secrets . . .

He didn't realize he was screaming until Selavin Thiss was suddenly in front of him, blocking his view of the thing.

"Be quiet," the Sword of Karath commanded, pulling off one of his chain mail gloves. Metal struck Heth hard across the face, sending him tumbling once more into the black.

A WAVE of freezing water brought Heth awake. He gasped and spluttered, blinking as the coldness coursed over his face and down his bare chest, trickling into the ragged remnants of his trousers. A wide-eyed boy in servant garb was in front of him, holding an empty bucket. He flinched when he met Heth's eyes, then glanced over his shoulder to where Selavin Thiss was standing. Wardsmen were clustered behind the Sword, along with a miserable-looking Daemonel and an older man in the umber robes of the Erudinium.

Heth suddenly remembered what he'd glimpsed before Selavin had struck him unconscious, and his gaze went again to the darkened corners of the room. Relief flooded him when he saw that there was nothing huge and monstrous hunched in the shadows – it had just been a phantasm conjured by the pain.

The pain. To his surprise, the burning had greatly lessened. He still hurt, but for the first time since Daemonel had pressed that red-hot blade to his flesh, he felt like he could think clearly.

"Good," Selavin said, dismissing the servant with a gesture as he stepped forward to stand beside the now-dead brazier. The boy ducked his head and scurried away, but not before casting one last fearful glance at Heth.

"You're in better spirits, I see," Selavin said, addressing Heth. "No more screaming."

Heth opened and closed his mouth, trying to tell if his jaw had been seriously injured by the blow the Sword had given him. It ached, but the bones still seemed to be in the right place.

"I feel wonderful," Heth rasped.

"I find that unlikely," Selavin said, the faintest of smiles touching his thin lips. "But I have no doubt you feel better than before." He swept out his arm to indicate the scholar. "I've paid for one of the finest healers in the city to treat your wounds and make a balm for the burns my nephew gave you. Though there may be scars, I'm afraid." He dipped his head slightly towards where Heth hung. "And for that, you have my apologies."

Heth blinked at Selavin Thiss. The Sword of Karath was saying *sorry*? For throwing him into a dungeon and letting his bastard of a nephew torture him?

"Accepted," Heth finally croaked. "Now, just let me down and I'll be on my way."

This elicited a dry chuckle from the Sword. "You have pluck, I'll give you that." He took a deep breath, his fingers stroking the green jewel set in the center of his sword's hilt. "And I'm certain that pluck was what brought you to the attention of my nephew. He does so hate to be embarrassed."

"We could still kill him," Daemonel suggested, sounding sullen. "Xend doesn't know he's here."

Selavin scowled and turned to face his nephew. "Are you so certain?"

"He's not Unfettered," Daemonel muttered, staring at the floor as his boot made patterns in the rushes. "My men were watching. He spends his days in taverns and eating houses. He's just an Unbound, probably running from something he did in his old hold."

"Xend very likely knows about him," Selavin snapped back. "That man has an uncanny knowledge about the Sharded in this city. He might have been waiting to approach him and offer a place in his service . . . perhaps one of his damn wind-sharded was even watching when your Wardsmen dragged him away."

"Are you really just going to release him?" Daemonel whined, glaring at Heth.

"No," Selavin said, shaking his head. "You and I are going to deliver him to the Unbound King."

27

DERYN

The chamber at the end of the hallway appeared to be used for receiving guests – it was well-appointed and cozy, with several cushioned chairs and divans intricately carved of dark wood surrounding a low table inlaid with mother-of-pearl twining blossoms and birds in flight. Shelves were set into the walls, filled with leather tomes and an assortment of odd knick-knacks – a lacquered red skull with only a single eye-socket, two small jeweled urns, a silver statue of a woman with upraised arms. Fire crackled in a white-stone hearth, which seemed odd to Deryn, because when they were outside he'd looked for smoke rising from the house to tell if anyone was home and seen nothing.

It was a comfortable room, and despite the modest exterior, the owner was clearly a man of some means. Deryn's mother had worked in several of the finest houses in Kething's Cross, and this reminded him of the reception room of a well-to-do merchant.

Alia and Deryn each claimed one end of a divan, while Rhenna lowered herself into a chair. She looked tense, Deryn thought, frowning as her gaze traveled over the contents of the shelves.

"Be careful," she murmured when she caught Deryn looking at her. "And don't believe your eyes. This place is not what it seems."

"What do you mean?" Deryn whispered, leaning closer to her.

"I made note of the house's size from the outside," she replied softly. "And I'm sure that we should have already stepped through its back wall."

"That's impossible. You must be mistaken."

Rhenna settled back in her over-stuffed chair, her pursed lips and flat gaze conveying her annoyance at being doubted.

"Or not," he said with a sigh.

A door opened, and the Salahi servant boy entered bearing a tray laden with steaming cups and a pile of biscuits. He crossed the room and placed the tray on the mother-of-pearl table, then made a gesture inviting them to partake.

"Please," he said after no one moved.

"When will your master be joining us?" Rhenna asked, leaning forward to inspect the offerings. Deryn did as well – the liquid in the cups was clear, and had a faint floral aroma. Tea of some sort.

The Salahi moved over to one of the chairs and sat gracefully. "I am the master of this house."

"But you're just a boy," Alia blurted. "How can you have a house like this?"

For the first time the Salahi smiled, sitting forward as he took up one of the earthenware cups. He blew away the steam, regarding Alia from over the rim.

"I look young, but I am not."

"You're one of the Elowyn," Rhenna said, also reaching for a cup. She didn't drink from it, though, holding it away from her like it was something that might be dangerous.

"I am," the boy said, nodding. "You may call me Menahla."

"Menahla," Rhenna repeated slowly. "That does not sound Salahi."

"Perhaps it is not a common name now, but I was born in the Salah."

"The other Elowyn we met would not give us her name," Rhenna said. "Why are you different?"

Menahla's gentle smile faded. "I doubt she even remembers her name."

"Why?" Rhenna asked. "What happened to her?"

The sound of crunching drew Deryn's attention. Alia looked like a squirrel who had been nut-gathering, her cheeks bulging as she reached for another of the crumbly brown biscuits. Horrified, Deryn glanced at Rhenna. Who knew how dangerous it was to partake in food or drink here? Rhenna's fingers were curled around the chair's arm rests tightly as she glared at the Wild girl happily munching away.

"Oh, these are delicious," Alia said after she finally managed to swallow.

"Thank you," Menahla said, looking quite pleased with himself. "It is my own recipe."

Alia paused before stuffing another biscuit in her mouth. "What are in these?"

The Salahi boy chuckled, smoothing out the folds of his blue robe. "Do not fear, seed-sharded. Just flour, butter, oats and honey, with a pinch of salt." He leaned forward and lowered his voice, as if sharing a secret. "Cinnamon is the special ingredient, from the Isles."

"Cinnamon," Alia repeated softly in wonder, as if trying out the feel of this unfamiliar word.

"You say you are one of the Elowyn—" Rhenna began, then gave a little hiss of surprise as a shadow leaped up onto the Salahi's lap. Shade made a few small circles, as if trying to find the most comfortable spot, then curled up. Deryn's mouth fell open. The Salahi did not even glance at the elemental in his lap, but he began to stroke the rippling darkness. The ensuing shocked silence was soon broken by a low rumbling.

Shade was purring.

"You came here with very interesting news," the boy said. "Terrible news, if I may be blunt. And while I am not in a position to directly oppose what is happening, perhaps I can still help you in my own small way. Ask your questions."

Rhenna swallowed, still staring at Shade. "Who is she? The one who has ensnared my father. The soul-sharded."

Menahla sipped again from his tea. "Her birth name was Aerith."

To his surprise, Deryn realized that name was familiar. He'd seen it somewhere in the Erudinium's archives. She had been someone important long ago.

"You recognize that name," the Salahi said, looking at Deryn with new interest. "You must be something of a historian. She has worked hard to erase all knowledge of herself from the memories of the holds." He scratched behind the little nubs of darkness that were Shade's ears, his gaze growing distant. "I remember her birth, though. The celebrations lasted for a month, with every city in the empire rejoicing at the news."

"I think I remember now," Deryn said slowly. The book had been memorable because it was one of the few texts from the days of the late empire that had not been written in the Gilded Tongue, some treatise on festival days . . . the most important of which had been the birth of Aerith Tain, the child of Segulah Tain.

Coldness flooded Deryn.

"What?" Rhenna asked in frustration. "*Who* is Leantha?"

"The daughter of the Radiant Emperor," Deryn murmured.

Rhenna snorted. "Impossible."

"She has been known by many names," Menahla said. "But she was born Aerith Tain seventeen years before the Sundering of the Heart. It was a momentous occasion in the empire, because Segulah Tain had reigned for over three hundred years without fathering a new heir."

"She was young when the Heart was shattered and her father . . . defeated." Deryn had almost said 'slain', but then he'd remembered the monstrous wolf in the Frayed Lands.

"She was the one who betrayed him," Menahla said, reaching for one of the few honey biscuits that had survived Alia's attentions. "What could mere men do against the power of the Radiant Emperor? No, she was brought into the conspiracy because she was the only one who could get close enough to slip the poison into his drink that would render him insensate."

"But why?" Rhenna asked. "Why would she do this to her own father?"

"Love," Menahla said with a sigh, then took an almost dainty nibble of the biscuit. "She was wooed and seduced by one of the most powerful rebels, Imperator Valus Shen of the Steel Legion."

Rhenna fumbled with her tea cup, nearly dropping it. "Valus Shen?"

"Yes. Your ancestor. The founder of the Duskhold and the first shadow-sharded. He, along with a cabal of the most powerful men and women of the empire, shattered the Heart while the emperor was unconscious. The power unleashed consumed Segulah Tain and sliced open reality itself, allowing things from far-flung realms to seep into our world. Most of the Heart's shards were claimed by the leaders of the rebellion, who fled the unfolding cataclysm to found their holds and kingdoms in distant lands."

"Aerith must have taken the soul shard," Deryn guessed.

"No. Despite her importance to the success of the plan, she was far too young to demand such a prize. And her only concern at that time was to please her beloved. So she went with Valus Shen east, as his concubine – for the Imperator was already married – to the Fire-mounts where he would found his kingdom."

"She'd been to the Duskhold before," Rhenna whispered, her eyes wide.

"She was there when they delved into those first tunnels and beat back the balewyrms that laired in the deep," Menahla said, dusting his hands free of crumbs. "He built for her a sanctuary made of white stone to remind her of the Summer Palace in Gendurdrang."

"Oh," Deryn breathed, remembering endless mornings listening to Kaliss's lessons in the white-stone gazebo in the middle of the underground lake.

"But she was truly her father's daughter," Menahla continued. "She wanted to be given the chance to stand before the Shadow and claim a shard, but Valus Shen refused. Why, I cannot say, but I suspect he feared the daughter of the Radiant Emperor. Perhaps he never even had truly loved her . . . only needed her. That is a secret he would later take to his grave, if it is true. So denied by her lover, the cloth finally fell from Aerith's eyes, and her ambition drove her from the Duskhold to seek out the other pieces of the Heart. But at the gates of those other freshly built fortresses and newly minted kingdoms she was turned away. They no doubt shared Valus Shen's concerns about the blood in her veins." Menahla rose, Shade pouring from his lap to puddle on the floor. The Salahi boy wandered over to the hearth, watching the flames with his hands clasped behind his back. "Only one hold offered her entry. The hidden home of Gethanakis Chorn, who had once been the spymaster of Segulah Tain. He had known Aerith since she was a girl, had even introduced her to the dashing Imperator of the Steel Legion. And he had been the one who fled the dying, convulsing Gendurdrang with the soul shard." Something popped in the hearth, accompanied by a shower of sparks. "Aerith was not the first to bear a soul-shard, but she quickly became the greatest. The fears of what power she could wield if granted a shard proved justified. I believe she may have reached *famdhar* before any other Sharded in the world, gaining the first third-tier talents ever. And one of those talents was what came to be called Core Migration."

"Mother Dark," Rhenna murmured.

"All soul-sharded can change their appearance to look like another," Menahla continued, still staring into the fire. "It is their form of Beckoning, and in truth is merely a form of illusion. But Core Migration is different. With this talent, a soul-sharded can shift her memories into a new body, pushing out the mind of the old. And since she also retains her mastery of the shards, she can easily merge as many fragments as she had before, quickly regaining all her power."

"A thousand year old Sharded . . ." Deryn said, awed by the implication. How strong could a Sharded become with that much time to channel their *ka*?

"What does she want?" Alia asked, drawing surprised glances

from Rhenna and Deryn. A good question, and perhaps the most pressing.

"To realize something that she has been working towards for a long time. She attempted to do it at least once before, when she convinced Osmari an-Alams that it was his destiny to unite the world under his rule. And now she whispers in the ear of Cael Shen, driving him onwards."

"She wants to recreate the Heart of the World," Deryn guessed. "So first she must conquer all the holds." He looked at Rhenna with wide eyes. "The Sand. The Flame. She will spur your father on to conquer the world and make himself emperor."

Menahla snorted. "Her ambitions are far greater than that. She serves now, because it suits her purpose. But Aerith desires to become what her father once was: she would crown herself the Radiant Empress and make herself master of all there is."

28

HETH

Heth felt every jarring bump as the carriage clattered through the streets of Karath. He could only hope that Selavin had been telling the truth and Daemonel had not inflicted any permanent damage – the unguents smeared on his body were dampening the pain he would otherwise be feeling, but he could sense it was still lurking in the background and would make its presence known later. When a wheel slipped into a hole and the carriage lurched, there would be a sharp flash in his ribs or back, a promise of things to come.

The fact that he had been blindfolded and gagged amplified his discomfort. If he could have concentrated on the city outside – or if there were no windows, at least the Wardsmen sitting in here with him – he might have been able to distract himself from the pain. But instead, floating in the darkness, he could only think about how uncomfortable he was in this moment. That, and where they were going.

The Unbound King. The man who had almost certainly sent assassins after Rhenna. A man who would take one look at his shard and immediately know it was something new, something momentous. Would he resume where Daemonel had left off, torturing Heth for the location of the Light shard? Or would he drag Heth outside the city to pull the shard from his flesh and try to merge it himself, curious what the flood of fragmented memories might show him? Would his sudden appearance endanger Alia? It was almost more comforting to dwell on the pain pulsing through his body than the possibilities that awaited him at Xend an-Azith's manse.

He lurched as the carriage abruptly halted, grimacing as a hand pressed to his chest stopped him from falling forward. Heth heard the carriage's door being unlatched, and then noises that had been muted spilled inside. Laughter, the hum of many conversations, and the faint, merry sounds of strings being plucked.

One of his guards gave voice to what Heth was thinking.

"Looks like the Unbound King is having a party."

A party. In the city they had been enjoying a night of revelry and good cheer while he'd been hanging from a damp wall being tortured.

"Out with you, then," growled another Wardsman as rough hands grabbed Heth and guided him out of the carriage. The warm night air carried the smell of roasting meat and beneath that something more subtle, a sweetness that might have been exotic blossoms in bloom. Heth remembered his view of the Unbound King's manse from the street outside, the flowering trees and gardens visible beyond the walls.

No one removed Heth's blindfold or gag as he was prodded forward, a hand staying on his arm to keep him walking in the right direction. The uneven cobbles beneath his boots were soon replaced by smooth flagstones, and Heth assumed that they had left the street and entered the manse's grounds. The sound of minstrels swelled, and he even heard snatches of conversations as he was led along stumbling.

". . . there's not a fresh crab in the city, the river trade has completely dried up. None of those Kin boats coming down from the north recently, I hear . . ."

". . . Lady Chamoneth was spotted at the theater with one of the

Valari scions. Lord Pulcras must be incensed to have his youngest daughter seen in such company . . ."

". . . they said it was still in his brow, but there was no spark, nothing. Like it was just a piece of rock . . ."

The voices faded again, then disappeared entirely, along with the rest of the night's noises. Heth would have known they had passed into a building even without the sound of their footsteps echoing in the silence. He was surprised by how few seemed to be coming with them, and he thought he could even guess who was who by their stride. That one to his left, heavy and plodding and with labored breathing – that must be Daemonel Thiss. And then on his right – steps ringing with sharp precision – Selavin. Behind him, he heard the jangle of armor and the scuff of boots. The hand that had been on his arm had moved to his back, guiding him along until eventually it clutched at his shoulder to bring him to a halt.

"Sword. So you decided to accept our invitation after all?" The voice was low and husky, but distinctly feminine.

"Aziza. I'm afraid your invitation was lost on the way up the hill. More's the pity, for it's refreshing to see so many distinguished members of the families mingling without rancor." This elicited a guffaw from Daemonel. "Now, go run and tell your master that I have important matters to discuss with him."

"Someone has already been dispatched," the woman he'd named Aziza murmured. "So I would bid you wait here for him to arrive."

"Of course," Selavin said, sounding almost annoyed.

"Refreshments? Victuals? What may I offer you gentlemen? We have unsealed a cask of the finest aged Ashasai red, and then there is also a delicious blue from a vineyard in the western Fangs."

"Nothing," Selavin replied curtly.

"Very well. Xend will be with you shortly." Heth heard the crack of heels on stone, and then a heavy door opening and closing. Silence descended in the wake of the woman's departure.

The feel of the hand on Heth's back vanished, and then fingers fumbled with the blindfold's knot. He blinked as the cloth fell away, averting his eyes from the brightness of the torches illuminating the great chamber. Colorful frescoes covered the curving walls, scenes of sordid excess that Heth had never imagined would be displayed so brazenly. Naked men and women writhing together, or sprawled on divans with decanters of wine watching warriors in the famed barbed armor of the Ashasai bloodpits stab each other with knives or be mauled by beasts. In the background of some of these scenes loomed the tiered black pyramids of the Sanguine City, while others were dominated by the fortresses that crowned the Skull of Karath.

The large chamber looked to be for receiving guests – the space where they stood was empty of furniture, but there were steps in front of them climbing up to a dais where an ostentatiously orna-mented chair was flanked by two low couches. Alia had told them on one of her infrequent visits to the Kin house that Xend an-Azith rejected the title of the Unbound King . . . but this certainly seemed like an audience hall. As Heth had guessed, Daemonel Thiss stood on his left, his stained leathers traded for a frilled tunic that made him look like a white-feathered chicken, and Selavin was to his right, still in his simple gray garb, a silver medallion engraved with the image of a sword around his neck. There was a mosaic under their feet made of red and black stones, and it took Heth a moment to realize what it showed, given its enormity: links in a chain, shattering as they were pulled apart.

Heth glanced up from the floor as the huge silverwood door behind the throne swung open. Two warriors who were very clearly People of the Wind entered first, spears in their hands and with faces empty as the Frayed Lands. They took up position on either side of the entrance just before an Ashasai man strode into the room. Heth knew who this was immediately – he wore his authority like a mantle, even though his clothes could have just as easily attired a commoner. His billowy trousers were secured by a thick crimson sash, and the buttons were undone on his simple vest to display a broad, hairless chest and the massive shard embedded in his flesh. It was the color of a garnet . . . or perhaps, more fittingly, a freshly scabbed wound. The amount of jewelry he wore surprised Heth – in the north, only women draped themselves with their wealth, but a ruby glittered in the lobe of each of his ears, a jade pendant lay just above his shard, and an intricately carved silver band encircled his powerful forearm.

Heaving a deep sigh, the Unbound King threw himself into the chair, tossing one leg over a gilded armrest.

"Selavin Thiss!" he cried, spreading his arms wide. "I can't say I'm pleased to see your dour little face tonight. You've pulled me away from some very entertaining frivolities."

"Lord an-Azith," the Sword of Karath called up, his arms crossed tightly. "Apologies for disturbing you at this late hour. Though it certainly doesn't seem like you were on the verge of retiring any time soon."

Heth had been so overwhelmed by the appearance of the Unbound King he hadn't noticed that an Ashasai woman had also entered until she leaned over and whispered in Xend's ear. She was tall and slender and so beautiful that she looked to have been sculpted from copper-colored stone. Xend cocked his head to listen to what she was saying and then focused with new interest at Heth.

"I see you've brought a prisoner before me," the Unbound King said, swinging his leg off the armrest and sitting forward. "Does that mean you've caught our killer? He does look fearsome."

"Killer? Are you so sure your missing Unfettered are dead?" Selavin asked, sounding honestly curious.

Xend frowned. "The men who disappeared . . . they would have returned by now, if it was at all possible. So I must assume they are dead. And if this one is not responsible . . . why is he here?"

Out of the corner of his eye, Heth saw the Sword's nephew cast his uncle a quick look that spoke volumes.

"He is one of the Sharded Few," Selavin explained. "We did not realize this until we began . . . questioning him about his activities in our city."

Xend rested his chin on his knuckles, looking bored by this explanation. "And *why* were you questioning him?"

"He made a disturbance," Daemonel interjected hastily. "Me and some of my fellow Wardsmen were out at a tavern and he threatened us and stopped us from doing our duty. There was this brat, you see, he spilled wine on—"

"Quiet," Selavin snapped, glancing sharply at his nephew, and Daemonel immediately fell silent. "The circumstances that brought him to our attention are irrelevant. The long and the short of it is that once I realized he was Sharded, I knew we must bring him to you. The agreement is very clear on that. What you do with him now is up to you. I am simply fulfilling my end of the bargain."

Xend was obviously amused by the tone Selavin had taken with Daemonel; apparently, he held no affection for the younger Thiss. The Unbound King raised his hand and made a lazy gesture towards Heth. "Well, let's see his shard. Not to question what you've claimed, Sword, but there have been a few who pretended to be members of the Sharded Few."

Selavin must have communicated something to the Wardsmen behind Heth, because one of the guards suddenly came around and began cutting away the tattered remnants of his tunic. Heth's pulse quickened as swatches of fabric fluttered down to settle on the mosaic floor, exposing his shard. What would their reaction be? Would they realize that this was something they'd never seen before?

He got his answer when the Wardsmen finished and stepped away. The Ashasai woman stiffened, her dark eyes growing even larger, and shock passed across the faces of the wind-sharded. Xend, however, showed no surprise, his slight grin never wavering. Heth did notice Selavin's gaze sharpen on him, as if the Sword hadn't expected these reactions from the Sharded on the dais.

"He is certainly one of us," Xend drawled, still sounding bored with the proceedings. "I accept your apology for anything you did to him. And it certainly looks like you were enjoying yourself, Daemonel. You naughty fellow." The Unbound King made a tutting sound and shook his head. "We'll extend to him the same invitation all newly arrived Unbound are offered. He may choose to become Unfettered, or he can try to survive without our protection and assistance. I thank you, Sword, for bringing him before us." Xend sank back in his throne, hands resting on the elaborate arm rests.

"Now, I have a party to return to. If there's nothing else, I shall bid you gentlemen good night."

"Very well, Lord an-Azith," replied Selavin. He was still looking at Heth strangely, like he knew he had made a mistake, but wasn't sure exactly what it could be. "I shall continue my investigations into your missing Unfettered."

"Do that," Xend said, abruptly standing. Then he turned to face the Ashasai woman hovering at his shoulder. She had recovered from her initial surprise, but her copper complexion was still paler than a moment ago, having lost some of its luster. "Aziza, please find comfortable accommodations for our new guest. Oh, and perhaps have a bath drawn for him as well. I'm curious what he looks like when he's cleaned up."

29

DERYN

"I will kill her."

Rhenna's words were cold-hammered iron. There was no bravado in what she'd said, no boasting. She sounded like she was simply speaking about what would come to pass. "Leantha . . . or Aerith, or whoever she is . . . she has bewitched my father, and so she must die."

Menahla turned from the crackling hearth, regarding her solemnly. "If only it were that easy, daughter of Shadow. She cannot be killed. Even if you were to destroy the body she now inhabits, her essence would persist. It is a talent that all soul-sharded *famdhar* gain – their souls become bound to what they call a phylactery, a hidden object that has great meaning to them. So long as this artifact exists, their essence remains tethered to this world, and in time, they will gather the strength to inhabit another body."

Rhenna's hands were clutching the armrests so tightly that Deryn was certain the wood would have shattered if she still had her Sharded strength. "Then I will find this . . . object and cast it into the rivers of flame beneath the Duskhold."

"How could we find this thing, it could be anywhere," Deryn said, the enormity of such a challenge making his heart sink. "It might look like anything."

"Someone knows," Rhenna said, rising to her feet. "Leantha knows. And there are other soul-sharded, like the one who pretended to be Vertus. They might know. We'll force them to scurry out from behind whatever face they're hiding and inflict such pain that even one who cannot die will be compelled to tell us."

"They do not fear death as much as they fear Aerith," Menahla said, gliding across the room to inspect the one-eyed red skull staring at them from its shelf.

"Then what can we do?" Rhenna asked, her fists clenched.

"Do *you* know where this thing is?" Alia asked, brushing biscuit crumbs from the front of her shirt. Deryn was certain Menahla was going to shake his head – why wouldn't he have already told them, if he did know – but to his great surprise, the Salahi boy nodded gravely. Deryn shared a surprised glance with Rhenna, who then took a step towards the Elowyn. Menahla still had not turned around, reaching up to trace the outline of the empty socket set in the skull's brow.

"Tell us," she pleaded.

"It will be your end," the Salahi boy said tiredly. "Even a host of *famdhar* would fail such a quest."

"I have to try," Rhenna said, the iron returning to her voice. "For my father and my hold."

"And the world," Deryn murmured.

"And the world," Rhenna agreed, nodding. "You said she wanted to destroy the shards, claim their power and make herself the Radiant Empress. That cannot happen."

Menahla sighed, finally turning from the skull's leering visage. In that moment, he did indeed look the age he claimed.

"I will tell you, but if you follow this path you will only find death." He returned to his chair and sat down heavily. "In the far south, on the eastern flank of the Breakers, lies the ancient citadel of the soul-sharded. I believe this is where Aerith and the other powerful *famdhar* of her order store their phylacteries."

"Good," Rhenna said, and Deryn heard the resolve in her voice. "Then that is where we will go."

"It is not so simple," Menahla said, steepling his fingers in front of his face. "That mountain range is impassable. The only way to reach the hold of the soul-sharded is to enter the Tangle and brave its dangers."

"The zemani," Deryn murmured, remembering that black-scaled monstrosity holding Heth's broken body.

"And things even more terrible," Menahla warned. "Some of the creatures inhabiting that place were spawned by the First Mother of the zemani . . . others were warped by her presence, twisted into terrible perversions. Even though she perished thousands of years ago, some of them persist, hiding in shadows beneath a canopy so thick it has not been pierced by daylight since the age when gods strode these lands."

"The dark does not frighten me," Rhenna said, her lip curling.

Menahla sighed. "I suppose not. You are like him, you know. Valus Shen. And in the end, he triumphed against impossible odds, so who am I to doubt a child of his line?"

"Who *are* you?" Alia asked. "You're talking about someone dead hundreds of years ago, aren't you? How could you have known this man?"

"A thousand years in the past," Menahla said softly, taking another sip of his tea. "But that is only half my age. The woman who told you of my House is older still. She was chosen by Belandria long before I became Calyxes's favorite."

Those names resonated in Deryn's memory. "Belandria . . . she was a goddess in ancient times. And Calyxes was a god as well, wasn't he?"

Menahla inclined his head towards Deryn. "I am again impressed, young shadow-sharded. Few remember the old gods. Yes, Belandria was the goddess of healing. Calyxes was mostly seen as a trickster god, associated with the shifting sands and mercurial storms of the Salah."

"Did these gods grant you and your Elowyn brethren your

immortality?" Rhenna asked, a disbelieving edge to her voice as she sank down into her chair again.

"At first, our immortality was through their will," Menahla admitted, ignoring her tone as he set down his cup with a soft clink. "We were chosen to be their avatars, lifted up to represent them in the realms of man. The gods had great difficulties comprehending the minds of mortals, you see, as they were entities not entirely of this world." Menahla sighed, shaking his head. "Although, in the end, perhaps they were always more like us than they ever would have admitted."

"But the gods are gone, aren't they?" Deryn asked, struggling to accept that their host, this little Salahi boy, was in truth an immortal. "And yet you still live."

Menahla raised his arm and shook it, making his bracelet of bone clatter. "This is our secret and our shame."

"Whose bones are those?" Alia whispered.

"These?" Menahla said, giving his bracelet another shake. "I do not know. I like to believe they belonged to Calyxes, but it was difficult to tell. The gods were . . . melting together when I found them."

"This is madness," Rhenna said forcefully, as if trying to convince herself. "The gods were false, as the Radiant Emperor proved when he abolished their temples. The Heart of the World is the fount of power, not imaginary beings that demand prayer and sacrifice."

Menahla graced her with a sad smile. "You are right, in a sense, though the gods and goddesses did not care if they were worshipped. Men abased themselves before them, of course, but the concerns of the gods transcended this world . . . all except for the Betrayer." Menahla hesitated, his face clouding over. "Should I tell you the story of creation? We Elowyn have kept it secret for so long, but I am tired . . . we are all tired, or sinking into madness. After all, what is the point of keeping secrets now? What am I protecting? My existence? My brothers and sisters? Perhaps we Elowyn should have embraced oblivion long ago." Deryn saw the resolve harden in his young face. "Yes, yes. Demerial told you of my house, so she must believe you have a part to play in what is coming ... and thus, you deserve the gift of knowledge."

Menahla swept his arm out wide, and in its wake the air squirmed like a thing alive. Deryn sucked in his breath, every instinct screaming at him to flee this place, but he found his limbs frozen and his breath had caught in his throat. Only his eyes could still move, and when he looked at Rhenna and Alia he saw that they were rigid as well, staring at the Salahi sorcerer.

"We must start at the beginning," Menahla said, the light in the chamber abruptly dimming as the flames in the hearth subsided into embers. And in that new darkness something began to form above them. It looked like several roiling patches of mist, each a different color and texture, and they undulated almost organically, like things living but mindless, uncoiling limbs towards the other shimmering pools of color before withdrawing when they brushed together.

"This is how I choose to represent the All," Menahla said, sounding awed by what he had summoned. "Though of course, the reality is no doubt very different. But it will do for my purposes – without some sort of visualization, I do not think any of us can appreciate what happened at the dawn of this world." He pointed at a shifting red mist, and it pulsed brighter. "That would be what the blood-sharded have come to call the Crimson Sea. A vast, sluggish ocean of blood just as teeming with life as the oceans we know ... Though the creatures that inhabit that place are in the end unfathomable to us, as are all the denizens of these realms." He moved his hand to indicate a blotch of writhing darkness. "This would be the Shadowrealm, which I am certain some of you have glimpsed as you skirted its borders. There is the Infernal Kingdom. And there the Undine Abyss. The Living Skein, an unimaginably vast labyrinth of knotted vines and devouring blossoms. The Deepness, where philosophers of stone contemplate existence. Of course, it was humans who named these places from the brief visions and visitations they were afforded." The patchwork of colored mists had by this time expanded to cover the ceiling. "Scholars even today call these places the primordial realms. They are worlds in their own right ...

but they are also the *ingredients* of worlds. The boundaries of these elemental realms are fluid, and at times they brush up against or even collide with each other. Such effects can be cataclysmic – imagine the endless water of the Undine Depths pouring into one corner of the Infernal Kingdom. Now, much rarer is what we came to call a Confluence. That is when any number of primordial realms meet at the same point, which then stabilizes – what emerges is something new, a place that contains aspects of all the other realms. Ours is one such world." A point of light flared into existence where many grasping arms of mist intersected. "You may wonder where we came from, along with all the other life that shares our home with us. I have no answer to this, but my belief is that *we* are also products of the realms mixing together. Our bodies contain blood, of course, and water, and our bones share more than a passing similarity with stone. The storm-sharded discovered long ago that our minds crackle with the same power that pulses in the clouds. Our breath is the wind and inside us wells a heat like rises up from the desert sand. And of course, our nature is forever torn between the light and the dark. But this, as I said, is just my speculation."

Movement at one of the chamber's entrances briefly pulled Deryn's attention from the billowing mists. If he had command of his limbs, he would have gasped and scrambled to his feet, for a massive white lion was poised at the room's threshold. Silver eyes regarded what was unfolding with calm disinterest, and then with a swish of its tail the lion moved on, disappearing from sight. Menahla had never even glanced in its direction.

"But this is all just preamble to what is truly important," Menahla said. "For soon after our world was forged, other things emerged. At the point where each primordial realm joined with this creation, an entity was birthed. They had no parents to guide them, no teachers to instruct them about how to act. They were of this world, but also not. They yearned to travel to the primordial realms, yet they were bound here. Confused, upset, curious . . . they spent thousands of years growing and maturing. These were what men came to worship as gods. Twelve beings, each with an aspect that hearkened back to the primordial realm that had given them life. Over time they became more and more like mortals, but still they had trouble understanding and interacting with us. So each chose a single avatar, granting these men and women – who became known as the Elowyn – a small sliver of their power." Menahla's expression turned contemplative. "None of us that remain are the original Elowyn. Even though we do not age, we could perish from other dangers, or because the divine grew bored or dissatisfied with us. Haelthius, god of flame and rage, was famous for casting his Elowyn into the Infernal Kingdom, demanding that they try to make contact with the things that inhabit that realm. None returned. That was the great irony of the gods – they were spawned by the primordial realms, but they could not leave this world. They were fascinated by those places, but they could not communicate with the great powers that dwelled in them. And they wanted to, very badly. For there they thought the mysteries of their own existence resided."

Deryn felt numb, untethered from his body. Menahla's words washed over him like waves of cold water as he struggled to accept what he was hearing. It was incredible ... impossible.

"At first, the gods rarely cooperated or even treated with each other ... though there was one great exception when the world itself was imperiled." Menahla spread his arms wide again, then indicated the floor beneath their feet. "The spot where this city was built bore witness to that moment. You see, ours is not the only Confluence that exists. There are worlds beyond this one, created by the mixing of other primordial realms. As I understand it, we are separated from them by a gulf that is both unimaginably wide and as thin as paper. Sometimes the inhabitants of another Confluence will find their way into this one – either accidentally or intentionally, I do not know. Surely you have heard stories of the riftbeasts that enter our reality from the gashes that were torn in the veil? Ten thousand years ago, a far more dangerous being found its way here. The gods united to slay this beast, and only just succeeded. This is where it fell, and over time the earth rose up to cover its bones. A great temple was built to commemorate the victory over where its skull lay – and now those ruins have been repurposed as an eating hall, or so I understand."

The Lanthium, Deryn realized. And that would mean the hill it was on, the Skull . . . oh, Silver Shrike. Something else occurred to him, disparate knowledge slotting together in his mind. A terrible being had died on the grounds that became Karath, or so Menahla claimed . . . and his zemani guide in the Erudinium had told him that the First Mother of its people had fallen into the Long Dark here.

"This enormous grave, the site of their greatest victory, became where the gods gathered to discuss matters of importance. The Godsmeet, it was called. We Elowyn would travel here every few centuries to help mediate between our immortal patrons and the mortals who worshipped them. And it was here – thousands of years after the death of the creature that had invaded – that the greatest of all crimes was committed, a transgression that would forever change this world." Motes of light appeared and drifted together, forming the image of a shining man. "Algeroth," Menahla murmured, and the name sent another shiver of recognition through Deryn. "Birthed where the Effulgent Wastes poured their endless radiance into our forming world. Worshipped as the god of the sun, most beloved in all the realms of men. But being the most beloved was not enough for him." Menahla gestured sharply, and the radiant figure dispersed again into countless glimmering specks. "Of all the divinities, Algeroth was most like a mortal. He dwelled overmuch on his standing in the pantheon, and he had always burned with pride and jealousy towards his brothers and sisters. Finally, he could no longer stand being first among equals." Menahla's voice was heavy with an old sadness. "He sent a message to the others, asking them to imme- diately join him at the Godsmeet, for something terrible was about to happen. We Elowyn were caught off guard as our patrons rushed to this place, concerned that another world-devouring beast was about to appear. Instead, they found Algeroth, bearing a weapon unlike anything they had ever seen before. A god-killing weapon. Algeroth turned it on his brothers and sisters, slaughtering them like animals lured to a watering hole. I was hurrying here when it happened – I felt Calyxes die. It was like my heart had been ripped from my body and torn to shreds . . . there was only a yawning emptiness in my breast, and I could feel myself falling into this chasm. As Calyxes sank into the endless dark, the tether connecting us was pulling me along as well . . ." A shudder passed through Menahla, his hands tightly clutching his chair's armrests. "I managed to will myself the last short distance to where this city now stands. The gods . . . their bodies were dissolving into the earth. In desperation, I scrabbled for the last of their remains before they sunk out of sight . . . and to my surprise, when my hands closed around a bone, I found that the howling abyss inside me had quieted, and the fog obscuring my thoughts had lifted. Somehow, being in contact with these remnants of the divine staved off my own death." Menahla raised his arm, studying his bracelet of bone. "And for over a thousand years, this is what has kept me alive. The other Elowyn . . . they had not been so close to the Godsmeet, and they could not escape the taint of madness or the piled years that had suddenly come crashing down on them. I searched and found four of my brothers and sisters and bequeathed bracelets like I had fashioned for my own salvation. But among the Elowyn, I was the only one who remained as I had been before, uncorrupted and whole. Even so, if I leave this place where the gods died without this relic I would be affected. For you see, this ground we stand on changed when the essences of the divine seeped into the soil. It is what made this the City of the Dead. Even the seams of ore beneath the surface were altered, becoming what is now known as karathinite. This place . . . this city . . . is the graveyard of the gods."

30

HETH

"You'll have to forgive Lord an-Azith for not meeting with you immediately," the beautiful Ashasai woman said as she led Heth down well-appointed corridors lit by torches in elaborate sconces. "Selavin pulled him away from some very important guests. It is our mid-autumn fete tonight, you see. A good number of the most important people in Karath are here celebrating."

Heth would have responded, but no one had yet removed the strip of cloth filling his mouth. And for that reason, he wasn't sure what he was, a guest or a prisoner. Xend had made it sound like he would be treated like the former, but the two People of the Wind flanking him certainly suggested otherwise. There was no warmth in their faces, and the ends of their spears made muffled thumps on the carpeted floor. Heth had tried to sneak a few glances at the swirling tattoos that could be glimpsed beneath their tasseled vests, wondering if he would recognize the sigils. He thought he remembered the designs inked onto Crimson Grass, the Falcon clansman who had carried them on his Wind Dragon to the Duskhold, and the memory of the sneering Crow warriors who had ambushed them in the Frayed Lands was still vivid, but these two wind-sharded must be from yet another clan, as their tattoos were very different, sharp and angular instead of flowing.

They arrived at an imposingly solid-looking silverwood door and the Ashasai spent a moment fiddling with a key ring. Finally, a click sounded and she pushed the door open, motioning for Heth to enter.

If he was still a prisoner, his circumstances had markedly improved.

The chamber was spacious, with a canopied bed and a finely woven rug patterned with red and black diamonds. There was a heavy desk of black wood with a matching chair, and a beautifully carved wardrobe that resembled the one that had been in Heth's own room at his manse in Kething's Cross. This looked like the quarters for a visiting dignitary, not a man who had just come from a dungeon.

Remembering what had been done to him sharpened the pain that had been lurking. The effect of the numbing salve that the scholar had slathered on his burns and cuts had faded, and he staggered, dizzied.

"Come, sit down," the Ashasai said, taking Heth's arm and guiding him to the chair. He collapsed into it just before his legs gave out, groaning through the cloth in his mouth.

"And let's take that out," she continued, undoing the knot securing the gag and letting it flutter to the floor. "Now, I am Aziza an-Valin and I suppose you could consider me Xend's right hand in most matters, at least while my brother is away. Who are you, and how did you find yourself the guest of the Sword's idiot nephew?"

Heth worked his sore jaw for a moment before answering. "My name is Heth Su Canaav. Daemonel was about to hurt a boy for spilling wine, so I stopped him."

Aziza's thin lips quirked in amused surprise. "Then he told the truth to Xend. Why did you intervene?"

Heth raised his bound hands. "First, I want to know if I have traded one prison for another."

In reply, a dagger appeared in Aziza's hand, and she deftly sliced his bonds. "Let us say you are our guest . . . although you're not allowed to leave until Xend speaks with you. There will be no more torture . . . at least, let us all hope not."

That wasn't entirely comforting, but Heth nodded, rubbing at his aching wrists before wiping a shaking hand across his blood-crusted lips. "I stopped that fat toad because I don't like bullies. I saw what Thiss did during the Tithing. He's a monster."

"That he is," Aziza agreed, gracefully perching on the edge of the bed. "But he is one of the monsters – like his uncle – who keeps this city from tearing itself apart. The strong must keep the weak in order, or there will be chaos."

Heth frowned – he'd heard almost the same words from his father. And ever since that night in the old mill when he'd watched his father die, he'd wondered if the idea of the strong and the weak was just an illusion, a matter of perspective. If all it took to be strong was a sword, why not give a blade to the weak and see what happened? He glanced at the two People of the Wind, who had taken up position guarding the door. They looked impressive, their lean bodies strengthened by training sessions with those spears they were brandishing. Heth had seen the Wardsmen up close and watched them scurry away at his challenge. Were the Sword's soldiers really 'the strong' here in Karath?

"I will send a tailor here so you can change out of those disgusting rags," Aziza said, rising. "And a healer as well. If we were to take you outside the city, I could make you whole in an eyeblink, and I might even be able to address that unfortunate blemish on your face . . . but such gifts would require your cooperation, Heth Su Canaav, so I would advise you to give Xend what he wants."

"And what would that be?" Heth asked, though he suspected he knew the answer.

Aziza had already begun to move towards the door, but now she paused and turned back. "An answer to the riddle about what is in your chest, of course."

31

DERYN

"That crime changed our world forever," Menahla said, dissolving the churning vortexes above them that represented the primordial realms with a wave of his hand. "But not how Algeroth had anticipated. After his brothers and sisters had fallen to his dark spear, he ripped out their hearts . . . or what we might call their hearts, as every one of the gods had at their core a shard linking them to the primordial realm from which they were birthed." Twelve points of gleaming light appeared in the air over Menahla, each a different color. "Algeroth took these shards, then cut open his chest and fused them with his own fragment of the Effulgent Wastes. And thus the Heart of the World was birthed." The dozen motes drifted closer, then with a flash merged into one larger, many-colored crystal.

"Algeroth had what he wanted – he was the only god of this world, and he had absorbed the power of his siblings. But before his endless celestial reign could even begin, something happened." Cracks formed in the Heart of the World, and from these a blackness began to spread. "Algeroth proved unable to contain the power that now seethed inside his breast. It poisoned him. Broke him." The hovering jewel was now almost completely dark, covered by the expanding stain.

"And thus, we finally come to Arenkinas. Later, he would promulgate the story that he had been merely a shepherd who had stumbled across Algeroth's catatonic body. In his tale, the Heart of the World had pushed its way out from the divine flesh and now lay there glistening in a field, waiting to be claimed. This, however, is not true, because he and I had known each other well in the centuries before the death of the gods. Arenkinas was Algeroth's Elowyn, and I have always believed that some of his own ambition and ruthlessness seeped into his patron during their long bonding. Rather than try to save Algeroth or bring him back to life, Arenkinas claimed the Heart for himself, abandoning his dying god. He found that the near limitless power of the primordial realms could be harnessed through the Heart, and so he became Segulah Tain, the Radiant Emperor. He conquered the old world, sweeping away the kingdoms and city-states and autarkies that had persisted for thousands of years, forging their ruins into his First Empire . . . though, in truth, many empires had existed before him. He destroyed as much of the old histories as he could find, effacing the memory of the gods from the world. Arenkinas wanted his ascension to be remembered as our world's first recorded moment." Menahla shook his head, as if disgusted by the audacity of such a desire. "He did allow one remnant of the past, though – despite Algeroth's death, Arenkinas created a new religion worshipping his memory. And it has persisted to this day, even after the cataclysms consumed the First Empire and Gendurdrang. The cult of the Broken God, as Algeroth is now known, waits patiently for a resurrection that will never come. For Algeroth's true heart, the Light shard that connected him to the Effulgent Wastes, was lost after the Sundering. I believe it was shattered, like what happened to the Sand shard which was once my own patron Calyxes's heart."

No! Deryn wanted to shout, but his throat was still frozen. *It wasn't destroyed!* How could he know something so important, while this ancient immortal with all his power did not? He glanced at Rhenna and saw the same question in her eyes.

Menahla rose again from his seat, and now he seemed much taller, his presence filling the room. "There, that is what Demerial wanted. She told you of my House and claimed that here you would find answers – and I have given you them, somewhat against my better judgement . . . though I suppose I can see her reasoning. Who else could oppose Cael Shen but his daughter? And with an elementalist at her side?" He shook his head, the movement so slow it was almost dream-like. Deryn realized that everything was growing hazier – either smoke was filling the chamber, or the solid objects around them – the chairs, the table, the oddities lining the shelves – were somehow unraveling, turning to mist. "I have given you a direction, Rhenna Shen. My warning still stands – Leantha and her soul-sharded are dangerous enemies, and far beyond your ken. Then again, your ancestor managed to throw down the Radiant Emperor even before he claimed the Shadow and became one of the Sharded Few, so who am I to doubt your blood?" Menahla was barely visible now, a giant looming over them. "I bid you farewell, children of the Heart." He raised his arms, and the chamber was plunged fully into darkness, the sourceless glow that had illuminated it suddenly and violently extinguished.

Panic rose in Deryn at his blindness, and he fought the paralysis that had wrapped him ever since the Elowyn had begun his story. He strained, willing his limbs and tongue to move, straining towards a point of light that had suddenly appeared in his vision. It swelled larger and larger, until suddenly he was able to thrust himself into this consuming radiance . . . and he came awake sitting up in his bed in Mam Nar's house, drenched in a cold sweat, his heart pounding. Shade lifted his head from where he was curled at his feet to stare at him for a moment, then settled down again.

"Rhenna!" Deryn cried, throwing aside his blanket as he leaped from the bed.

32

HETH

"Do you know what is best about residing in the City of the Dead?"

Heth came awake groggily, and the first thing that swam into focus was the late-morning light infusing the gauzy canopy above him. His body ached, but the pain was more a lingering soreness than the sharp stabbing from the night before. Wincing, he struggled to prop himself up in the bed, silken sheets sliding away from his naked skin.

Xend an-Azith sprawled in the blackwood chair, a silver decanter and a bowl of grapes beside him on the desk. The Unbound King was dressed only in a shimmering shawl of iridescent feathers that was secured at his waist by what looked to be the same thick crimson sash he'd been wearing the night before. The shard in his chest was visible like a second heart, and he had divested himself of all his jewelry except for the huge rubies in his ears. Xend's eyes were heavy-lidded, as if he was having trouble opening them fully.

"Wine," the Unbound King continued, finally answering his own question. He raised the goblet he'd been holding loosely by its rim and shook it, sending droplets flying. "And I have to say it can also be the worst thing, like on mornings such as these. Do you know why?"

Heth shook his head, still struggling to accept that he'd awakened to find one of the most powerful Sharded lords in the world in his bedchamber.

"It's our Beckoning," Xend said, taking a sip of wine. "We blood-sharded, I mean. Ours is passive, unlike most of the abilities granted to the other Sharded. We heal constantly. For a newly Sharded *arzgan*, this means a nosebleed will stop slightly earlier. A *famdhar*, though, can have their hand lopped off and yet be sporting a new one within a fortnight. It also means that our bodies are nearly immune to the effects of alcohol. Outside of Karath, we cannot enjoy the warm pleasure that wine brings . . . but also, we never suffer what arrives the morning after we've indulged too much." Xend sighed, refilling his goblet. "I've decided the best solution is to simply stave off the effects by continuing to drink. Would you like a cup? It's always more enjoyable to drink with others."

"No, my lord," Heth replied, hoping he wasn't causing insult. Whatever was about to happen, he wanted his wits about him.

"You're missing out on a good northern blue," Xend warned him, picking up the decanter and making its contents slosh around. "Don't tell anyone I prefer blue to red. It would be quite the scandal in Ashasai – they might send a new cohort of assassins after me if they learned of such heresy."

"I think I need to recover a bit before I start drinking," Heth said, and this was true. He felt lightheaded from his tribulations, and the patches on his body where Daemonel had burned him were starting to itch, despite the cooling unguents the physickers had applied.

"Very well," Xend said, smacking his lips together after taking another sip. He didn't sound offended, which relieved Heth. "I do hope you're feeling well enough to answer a few questions, though. I have to admit I'd likely have stayed abed if it were not for my burning curiosity."

Heth swallowed. "I . . . I appreciate you saving me," he murmured.

Xend waved his hand dismissively. "No need for thanks. I would not allow any Sharded to be treated in such a way in this city. Of course, I also most likely would not have given them a room in my own manse, but I believe you know why I've extended such an invitation to you."

"I suppose I do," Heth said softly. He couldn't remember taking off his small clothes before collapsing on the bed, and was suddenly very aware that he was naked under the silken sheets. It made him feel all the more vulnerable, even though Xend did not seem to be carrying a weapon and his imposing wind-sharded guards were nowhere in sight.

"So," Xend said briskly, setting down his goblet and clapping his hands together. "Your shard. What is it, and where did you get it?"

Heth's mind churned frantically as he tried to think of something, anything, that would satisfy the Unbound King without telling him the truth.

"Oh, come now," Xend sighed, rolling his eyes. "I can see you frantically trying to come up with a lie I'll believe. Don't bother, it will only make me annoyed." He popped a grape into his mouth, smiling as he chewed.

"I am light-sharded," Heth said after a drawn-out silence.

Xend swallowed the grape, then plucked another and began peeling it. His expression was unreadable. "Light-sharded," he finally said before tossing the skinned grape back into the bowl. "How interesting."

Heth said nothing.

"When I first saw it in your chest last night, I wondered if I was already drunk. Then I thought it must be one of the lost shards, perhaps from the Ice. You don't look like a monk, but maybe you'd found some poor brother who had died on a pilgrimage." He shook his head. "After all, we had a seed-sharded find her way to my house not long ago – why not one of the ice shards?"

Heth tried his best to keep his face empty of emotion, even though his pulse had quickened at the mention of Alia. Xend was back to contemplating his wine cup, though, and did not seem to notice Heth's sudden agitation.

"But the color is wrong – I've seen an ice-shard up close, held it in my hand before merging it with my own. My next guess was that I had caught one of those slippery soul-sharded. Not to alarm you, but I kept several spears trained on this chamber's door last night, and a few more pointed at your window. I thought if you were soul-sharded, you'd certainly try to escape, despite your injuries. But Aziza was quite certain you are something else. Something new." He rubbed his hairless chin, looking at Heth speculatively. "Light-sharded, eh? I have to admit, like many over the years, I have wondered why there was no light if there was shadow." He leaned forward, his attention sharpening. The movement was almost preda-tory, and Heth had to stop himself from flinching back. "So now I must ask you something very important. And I beg you, do not lie, for I would like to keep our relationship cordial." Xend paused dramati-cally, as if to reinforce the importance of what he was about to ask. "Where did you get this shard?"

"I found it in a ruin of the First Empire," Heth replied quickly. It was an answer he had prepared for just this sort of moment – not a lie, but also not the full truth.

It almost looked like Xend relaxed slightly at this answer. "Then you were not given your fragment by the Light shard. There is no secret holdfast of light-sharded hiding out in the world."

"There isn't," Heth replied immediately.

Xend's black eyes were piercing now. "You answered so quickly. How interesting. For if you'd found the shard in a First Empire grave or treasure room, you should have no idea if other light-sharded exist. Yet you are quite certain. Tell me, did the Light give you your frag-ment? Were you granted your shard at the source?"

Heth felt like he was drowning. What could he say? And by virtue of his hesitation, surely Xend already knew the answer. "It did," he finally managed.

Xend sank back in his chair, and Heth suspected that the aston-ishment he saw in his face was the first genuine emotion the Unbound King had shown him so far. "You know where the Light shard is," he said, sounding almost awed. "Tell me."

Heth briefly considered concocting a falsehood, but then discarded the idea. He had no illusions about his ability to fool one such as Xend an-Azith. Instead, he kept his mouth tightly shut, hoping that this wouldn't result in him finding his way into whatever passed for a dungeon in this manse. He tensed, expecting an outburst that would summon whoever was waiting outside the door.

"Wise," Xend said, wagging a finger at him. "Very wise." He grinned as if amused, and Heth nearly gasped in relief. "Such knowledge is of tremendous value. In truth, it may be worth more than any other secret in the world. To think, the foundation of a new hold is out there, just waiting to be claimed . . ." Xend shook his head. "The thought is staggering. Is it possible we could, in the span of a few weeks, both lose and gain an order of the Sharded Few?"

Heth blinked in surprise. Lose an order? What was he talking about?

"Oh, you didn't know?" Xend said distractedly, his mind clearly still on the implications of what he had just learned. "The Flame has been shattered by the Shadow and the Storm, just as once happened to the Sand. Every flame-sharded has lost their powers . . . they are merely Imbued again, and their only hope to return to the ranks of the Sharded Few is to merge a different kind of shard." He tapped his chin thoughtfully. "A new shard in the world that is not already controlled by one of the holds . . . this is quite the opportunity. It could be the salvation of so many Imbued and once-Sharded."

And Hollow. Heth thought, but he kept this suspicion to himself. He should try to hold as much information back as possible – it might be his only leverage.

Heth jumped as Xend clapped his hands together again. "So. Heth. I must know the location of the Light. Either we can reach some sort of agreement, a trade perhaps, or I will have you tortured until you tell me. I would prefer not to do that, of course! But this knowledge is simply too important."

"I won't talk," Heth said, but he could already feel a cold knot of dread forming in his belly.

Xend sighed. "Everyone always says that. And perhaps even truly thinks it! But we Ashasai . . . we are connoisseurs of pain. Beautiful Aziza . . . she is a prodigy with the knife, it's really quite impressive.

And if somehow you do prove impossible to break, I'll have you dragged outside the city and my storm-sharded *famdhar* will rip the answers from your mind, leaving you a drooling idiot. Let us find some accord, Heth. There is no reason we must be enemies."

Heth's fingers tightened around the edge of the silken sheets. He felt sick to his stomach, and also appalled that Xend would so casually discuss his torture and death. What could he do? Throw himself at Xend now and try to escape? Looking at Xend's powerful build, Heth had no illusions about how quickly the Unbound King could subdue him, especially in his current weakened state. He swallowed, forcing himself to meet Xend's gaze. Maybe . . . maybe there was another way.

"I have a proposition, Lord an-Azith."

33

DERYN

They slumped on the benches in the Kin guest house, staring in a dazed stupor at the steam rising from the bowls of porridge Mam Nar had set in front of them. Even Alia had not yet touched her spoon, which spoke volumes about what she was feeling right now – Deryn had never seen her fail to immediately attack any meatless dish. She must also be struggling with the revelations that had been thrust upon them in the House of Last Light . . . and perhaps the aftereffects of whatever sorcery Menahla had used to transport them all back to their beds.

For a brief moment after awakening, Deryn had actually believed it was possible that it had all been an incredibly vivid dream. But when he'd clattered down the stairs, he'd found Rhenna and Alia frantically discussing the same experience he remembered so clearly. There had even still been honey biscuit crumbs speckling Alia's shirt. After the initial euphoria had subsided, they'd collapsed on the eating hall benches and had barely spoken since, not even muttering a thanks when Mam Nar had delivered breakfast, each silently wrestling with the implications of all they had learned.

Deryn felt an overwhelming numbness. How was it possible that they had been allowed such knowledge? How many others in the world knew what they now did? He was almost certain the Archivist in the Duskhold's library was ignorant of how their world had formed and the tragedy that had resulted in the creation of the Sharded Few. High Seeker Helash, as well. Did they realize that the shards were the shattered fragments of a god's heart, slivers of divinity lodged in mortal flesh?

"We're done here," Rhenna finally said, her voice empty of emotion.

"Done where?" Deryn asked, dragging his gaze from the steaming porridge.

"Here. Karath. We found our answers, and I know where I must go next."

Deryn swallowed, casting a quick glance at Alia to see if she agreed with Rhenna. "You're talking about the hold of the soul-sharded."

"Yes."

"But Menahla didn't say where it could be found exactly, just that it was somewhere in the Breakers. That's an entire mountain range."

Rhenna picked up her spoon and began stirring her porridge, though she was clearly not interested in eating. "Menahla claimed that to reach the hold one needs to pass through the Tangle. So we at least know which side of the mountains it's on. That's enough for me."

Alia pulled on a lock of her golden hair in agitation. "I heard him say how dangerous it would be, that to succeed it would take many Sharded more powerful than us."

"I have to try," Rhenna said, in a tone that brooked no argument. "My father is in thrall to that witch. If the only way to kill Leantha is to destroy her . . . her . . . what did the Elowyn call it?"

"Phylactery," Deryn said quietly.

"Yes, that. If it must be destroyed, I will destroy it." As if to punctuate this promise and end any debate, Rhenna lifted a spoonful of her porridge and jammed it into her mouth.

Deryn looked away from her, watching the pale morning through the windows. What Rhenna was talking about was suicide . . . but what choice did she have? Her family and her hold were ensnared by Leantha . . . or Aerith, or whatever she was called. She couldn't abandon them.

"Perhaps there's another path," Deryn said slowly, an idea starting to take shape, then cleared his throat as Rhenna and Alia both turned to him. "I only lived in the Duskhold for a few months, so my knowledge of its politics is hazy. But I saw you many times with your brother, Azil, and I simply cannot believe that he was involved with the plot to have you . . . murdered. I would be surprised if he was even aware of your father's plan to wage war against all the other holds."

"Azil," Rhenna said softly, sitting back on the bench. "Of course I have thought about returning to the Duskhold, hoping that Azil and the Balenchas and maybe even Nishi would side with me against my father. But I also know my father would still triumph in any such struggle, and then I would have endangered my brothers and whoever else had come to my aid. But what if they did not try to fight my father directly in his place of greatest strength . . ."

". . . but rather, the one who is pulling his strings," Deryn finished for her. "With Azil beside us, we would have a far greater chance of finding the soul-sharded's hold and destroying Leantha's phylactery."

"We would have to approach him without my father knowing," Rhenna murmured, her brow drawing down as she considered how that might be possible. "It would have to be when Azil is not in the Duskhold – my father will know as soon as we enter the hold. We'd have to draw Azil outside somehow. But what could summon him?"

"Perhaps if another monster attacked us, like on the road?" Alia suggested. "That's when we first met him."

Rhenna shook her head. "No, Azil had always wanted to prove himself against a riftbeast and now he's done that. There's no guarantee that it would be him who answered another incursion." The corners of her lips curved into a rueful smile. "That, and I'm not sure how we would lure such a creature out of the Frayed Lands to begin with."

"Isn't there a way to send messages through the shadows?" Deryn asked, remembering one of Saelus's lessons about the sundry talents of the shadow-sharded.

"Shadow Whispering," Rhenna said, tapping her chin with her finger. "Yes, it might work . . . if we could find someone with that second tier talent. The only places I'm certain have shadow-sharded with that ability are strategically important points in our realm where instant communication with the Duskhold is necessary. Phane will have such a Sharded. Also Gelath, our port on the Glass Sea that watches the horizon for raiders. And our embassy in Ter Drummond."

"We could return there," Deryn suggested. "Though for all we know, the Flame descended and exacted a terrible revenge on the shadow-sharded stationed in the city."

"But if the situation is how we left it," Rhenna said slowly, her voice growing more excited, "then that might be our best choice. It is far closer than the other great cities under the Shadow. I—"

A crash interrupted Rhenna as the door to the eating hall was flung open. They all turned just as Heth strode into the Kin guest-house . . . or tried to stride. He was moving with a clear purpose, but had acquired a limp since Deryn had seen him last. His clothes were different as well, garishly colored and lace-frilled and clearly of very fine make.

"Heth!" Deryn cried as his friend started to climb the stairs to their rooms, having never even glanced in their direction. "Where have you been? Are you all right?"

Heth halted halfway up the steps, turning to look down at them with a vaguely dazed expression. Something had happened, Deryn realized. Something had changed him.

"I need the Sharded dagger," he said, as if this explained his behavior. "And money."

"Why are you dressed like that?" Alia called up to him. "Like a . . . like a . . ."

"Like a fop," Rhenna finished.

Heth glanced down at what he was wearing, as if seeing it for the first time. "Aziza gave it to me," he said, and then continued his ascent. Moments later, he reached the second floor landing and vanished.

Rhenna gave Deryn a confused look. "Who is Aziza? That's an Ashasai name."

"I've heard it before," Alia said, her brow furrowing like she was trying hard to extract something from the depths of her memory. "I think someone said it in the Unfettered manse."

Deryn snorted, shaking his head. "The Unbound King didn't give Heth those clothes. That's ridiculous."

Rhenna was staring speculatively up at where Heth had vanished. "You know, I've been to Ashasai once, and that *might* be the style popular among the wealthy youth . . ."

Heth reappeared and dashed down the stairs, apparently still in a hurry. The Sharded dagger was belted at his waist, along with Rhenna's money pouch. That alarmed Deryn – how would they pay for passage on the river again if something happened to their money?

"Heth," Rhenna said as he passed where they were sitting, headed for the door. "Heth!" she shouted, and this finally pierced whatever had seized his attention. He turned, his lips pursed in annoyance.

"What?"

"We found the House of Last Light," Rhenna said.

That revelation did not have the effect Deryn had anticipated.

"And?" Heth said, looking even more exasperated.

Rhenna folded her arms across her chest. "There was another one of those Elowyn inside. He told us that the soul-sharded are manipulating my father, and that if we want to stop them, we have to find their hold and destroy the objects that give them immortality. It's hidden at the edge of the Tangle."

Heth blinked rapidly, as if trying to process what Rhenna had just said. Then he frowned and shook his head. "Interesting. I have to go out now, but I want to hear more later."

Rhenna's jaw fell open, and it took her a moment to gather herself. "Did you hear me? We know who the enemy is. We're done in this city and will be leaving as soon as possible."

Heth lifted his gaze to the rafters. "No . . . no I can't leave yet. There's something I need to do."

"This isn't a discussion," Rhenna snapped, rising from the bench. "What is wrong with you? What happened?"

"I'll tell you tonight when I return," Heth promised, turning his back on her.

Deryn had never seen Rhenna so utterly lost for words, though she did muster an outraged choking sound when the door slammed shut behind Heth.

34

HETH

Heth drove the Sharded dagger point-first into the table's already scarred wood, and it stuck there quivering even after he'd released the hilt. He'd expected the sleeping Salahi to jerk awake, but Zayin only lifted his head from his arms to regard him with an expression of mild annoyance. The sour smell of strong spirits was nearly enough to make Heth's eyes water.

"*Halatha*," Zayin grumbled, sitting up. "Why do you so rudely disturb my dreams?"

"Zayin," he said, sliding into a chair without asking permission. Around him, he felt the attention of the other tavern patrons – which had sharpened at the sound of metal striking wood – begin to drift away again. Apparently, this was not such an unusual occurrence in the winesinks of the Nethers. "I've been looking for you."

The massive Salahi folded his arms across his chest, frowning. "I told you to stay away, *halatha*. For your own sake."

Heth rested his hand on the dagger's pommel, stroking where the fragment was visible suspended in a circle of amber. He noticed that Zayin's lips had pulled back from his teeth slightly when he realized that the dagger was Sharded, his huge hands clenching and unclenching like he was imagining holding something. "You told me to stay away from the *qenari*, and this is not your *qenari*." Heth swept out his other arm, indicating the dimly lit tavern. Zayin grunted in reply, his attention still fixed on the fragment, and Heth tapped the amber it floated in with his finger. "The other Salahi said you were a dervish, a desert champion. An *araskin*. The *araskin* were Sharded, were they not? Does that mean you were one of the Sharded Few before the Sand was shattered?"

Zayin finally dragged his gaze from the dagger. His mood had clearly darkened at these questions, and a cold little worm of fear squirmed in Heth's belly. He remembered how fast Zayin had moved when he'd disarmed him, and despite his age, the Salahi was perhaps the most powerfully built man he'd ever encountered, larger even than Xend an-Azith.

"I was Sharded," Zayin finally said, grudgingly. "But my shard was taken from me by another. On the field of Gerendal I fought a mighty warrior of Storm. I took his eye, but he cast me down and ripped the shard from my chest." The look on Zayin's face was distant, as if he was lost in a memory. "He said I fought honorably, and so he let me live."

"You never tried to claim another shard?"

Zayin shook his head, the locks of his long gray hair swinging. "I am Salahi, and my people are of the desert. When the Sand was destroyed, it was like our souls were ripped from our bodies. That is why we hide here, in the City of the Dead, slowly dwindling. We are simply waiting for the end."

Heth frowned, then pulled the dagger free from the wood. "Perhaps *you* are waiting, *araskin*. But I saw children in your *qenari*, and other young Salahi still burning with passion. That woman who threatened me, the daughter of the *bhalgras*—"

"Fayraz."

"Yes, Fayraz – she did not seem like she was willing to fade away."

Zayin shifted, laying his hands on the table. They were rough and calloused, Heth noticed, like the hands of a laborer. And yet this man had been a feared warrior, one of the legendary dervishes. Did some of that old spirit remain, hidden behind his tired eyes?

"Fayraz burns, but only with anger and hate. Once her mother passes, I fear she will drag us to ruin. Our shah who called for the Ifashan Jihad – he was not driven by hatred to conquer the world. No, he wanted peace. So long as the world was fractured, conflicts would never end. Sand would slay Stone, Storm would slay Shadow, Blood would slay Flame. Only if the Heart was forged anew could the cycle of war stop. But Fayraz . . . she does not want peace. She wishes to cast this world into an abyss."

Heth held up the dagger, letting the light from the tavern's fire ripple along its curving blade. "Does she want the end of the world, or only an end to the ones who dwell up on that hill? The rich families and their Wardsmen."

Zayin shook his shaggy head again. "She does not discriminate. For her, there is the Salahi and there are *halatha*. Nothing else."

Heth swallowed. This was it, he could feel it. The moment upon which the future hinged. "I want to meet with her."

Zayin blinked, clearly taken aback. "The *bhalgrasi*? Do you forget the last time you saw her? She threatened you with death if you stepped inside the *qenari* again."

"Not in the *qenari*. Elsewhere, but still in the Nethers. I have an offer for her, something I know she wants. A path to save your people."

Zayin studied him carefully. "Whatever you are talking about, Fayraz will never trust you. She will think this is but a ploy to give the Sword a reason to finally rid his city of us."

"A meeting," Heth insisted, slamming the dagger down again on the wood. "That's all I want. And there will be others. The Salahi would not be alone anymore." He slid the dagger across the table to Zayin. "Take this to her to demonstrate how serious I am. It is a gift."

Zayin's brow drew down at this. "A Sharded weapon has great value, even in the City of the Dead."

"It shows that I am serious," Heth continued, pushing his chair back and standing again. "On the Street of Caged Songs there is an eating house."

Zayin nodded slightly. "The Hollow frequent this place. It is owned by Caden Vars."

"You know him, then?"

Zayin's expression was unreadable. "His name is spoken in the *qenari* without rancor."

Well, Heth thought, *that is good to know*. "He will be there. Convince Fayraz to meet with us

tomorrow, just as the sun is setting. Please, *araskin* – this city does not have to be the end of your people. There is another way."

Zayin was quiet for a long time, and so still he could have been carved from stone. Heth tried to hold his gaze calmly, but his heart was beating fast. Finally, Zayin reached out, the hilt of the Sharded dagger disappearing inside his massive hand.

"I will tell her what you have said, *halatha*."

35

DERYN

Deryn sat cross-legged on his bed, the journal of Gehart Othakis closed in his lap and the sliver of the shadowrealm nestled across from him among his rucked blankets. It looked like nothing more than a shard of dusky glass, but he could feel its penumbra of prickling coldness and an answering tingle from the fragment embedded in his chest. A piece of a primordial realm. Deryn remembered the churning darkness that Menahla had summoned to represent the shadowrealm, and he wondered what the Elowyn would have thought if he'd known that hidden back in Deryn's bedroom was an actual chunk of that place. Was the entirety of the realm an enormous expanse of this material? He'd crossed the edges of the shadowrealm before when Shadow Walking, and the ground had been hard and smooth, perhaps unbroken panes of this very substance, and there had also been indistinct shapes in the distance that might have been mountains of this material. Or perhaps this was just what passed for stone in that place, and there would be some otherworldly equivalent for water and soil and trees.

Enough stalling. Deryn reached out and gingerly picked up the sliver, shivering as a pulse of cold traveled up his arm. Shade had been curled beside him, but now he uncoiled and flowed over to rub against the piece's jagged edges. "Does it feel like home?" Deryn asked as a low rumbling issued from the elemental. Shade, as usual, did not answer, but he turned his little head to regard Deryn.

Should he have told Rhenna about what he had taken from the Erudinium? He'd been wrestling with that question for days now, and in truth, he wasn't entirely sure why he hadn't. Maybe it was because the mystery of why Shade had appeared and bonded with him felt personal, disconnected to everything else that had happened. Rhenna was intensely focused on the revelations imparted in the House of Last Light about Leantha and the soul-sharded and the destruction of the Flame. Telling her of what was now in his possession and that he could now decipher the ancient diary would just be one more thing to concern her – it would be better, perhaps, if he approached her only if he pulled some important information from the writings of Gehart Othakis.

Heaving a deep breath, Deryn gently opened the book. The first page was cramped, filled with the incomprehensible markings that he had already spent so many evenings hunched over in a futile attempt to find meaning. As Shade watched, Deryn carefully laid the fragment of the shadowrealm over the diary's opening lines. Through the dusky glass the strange symbols seemed to momentarily squirm like little black insects, and then they settled into an archaic but recognizable script. He began to read, speaking the words aloud.

"Archivist Herethin has bid me to record my experience as the first elementalist in the Duskhold for many generations. But I am a warrior, not a writer, so do not expect overmuch from this diary – in truth, until recently I could barely write my own name. The bond with the entity from the shadowrealm has changed me, and now when I set quill to paper and try to put down what is in my mind what flows forth is this strange writing. It is just one of many mysteries that I grapple with, for I am no longer the man I once was. The elemental infringes upon my very being, coiling around my soul. We are joined, though I do not know when or how that happened.

"Let me start at the beginning. I was meditating on the drum tower after a day of sparring, channeling my *ka* in the pursuit of my elusive seventh shard. Yumi Shen had told me that she felt I may have reached the limit of the number of shards my body could hold, but I knew that I was capable of more, and I had been pushing myself to the very limits to prove her wrong. I was exhausted, both mentally and physically, and so when one of the lengthening shadows around me suddenly spasmed, at first I thought it must be a trick of my tired mind, or perhaps that I had unconsciously beckoned the darkness.

"It was the shape and size of a child, and as it approached me, I knew that this was no simple beckoning. I could feel it reaching out to me, ghostly fingers skittering over my bones, tickling the inside of my skull. I am not ashamed to admit that I was frightened in that moment, thinking one of the Others from the realm of shadows had come. But it did not seize me with grasping limbs – it just settled down to regard me calmly, as if taking my measure. I tried to communicate with words and gestures, but although I suspect it understood me, at least a little, it made no effort to respond in kind. Finally, I went to find the wisest man I knew, Archivist Herethin, and ask him what this creature was. The shadow-child followed, and the Archivist – when he recovered from his surprise – told me that this was almost certainly an elemental, and I had quite unexpectedly become one of the most important Sharded in the world."

Deryn had reached the bottom of the page, and before continuing he sat back, rubbing at his eyes. Reading through the dusky sliver of glass required a focus that was more than a little taxing, and he wondered how long he could continue before he had to set the journal aside. While taking this moment to recover, Deryn reflected on how Gehart's first encounter with an elemental compared to his own. Shade had appeared when he'd been trapped at the bottom of a crevice, not far from the lair of an ancient balewyrm. If the elemental had not gone to seek aid, Deryn would have almost certainly ended up in the belly of that monster. Conversely, Gehart's elemental had approached him when he'd been channeling his *ka* in a place of safety. And he'd described this elemental as being 'child-sized', while Shade had been little more than a hand-span tall when he appeared. Shade was growing larger as Deryn gained more shards – perhaps

Gehart's elemental was larger because he already had a half-dozen shards, while Deryn had borne only a single shard during the Delve.

He sighed, trying to massage away the lingering ache behind his eyes. There must be answers somewhere in this book – when Shade had inhabited his body after he'd been poisoned during the wedding procession, he'd told Heth to take the diary. And it must have been the elemental who placed the piece of the shadowrealm across the pages in the Erudinium, revealing how the strange symbols could be deciphered. Shade knew there was some secret within – but the thought of suffering through so many years of Gehart's entries was making Deryn's head pound. He looked at Shade, who was still watching him with his little black face cocked.

"You know, you could just tell me," Deryn said, not caring how petulant he sounded. "I know you can talk when you need to."

Shade stared at him for a moment longer, then twisted around and proceeded to start licking himself.

"Fine," Deryn grumbled, returning to the diary.

HE READ for as long as he was able. By the time he closed the diary, the light outside had deepened to bronze and the prayer bells in the Broken God's temple had begun to ring, announcing the sun's descent. He had finished perhaps a third of the journal by this time, covering the first few years after Gehart had bonded with his elemental. Much had happened – Gehart had merged four more shards, becoming ten-sharded, when before he had struggled to add his seventh. Gehart believed that the connection with his elemental was the reason for his rapid increase in power, which made Deryn wonder if this was true for him as well. Kaliss had been considered a prodigy, and Deryn had quickly eclipsed her after Shade had appeared. Another interesting occurrence was that the first new talent Gehart had gained had been the Breath of the Mother, Deryn's rare second-tier talent. It seemed unlikely that this was a coincidence ... but what did it mean?

The journal was also an interesting glimpse into how the world had once been different. Gehart did not explain its origins, but there was some animosity between the bloodlords of Ashasai and the Duskhold, and several times the forces of Shadow had marched south to contest with the Blood. Gehart's elemental – which had never been named – had 'stolen' the shadows of several creatures in the Duskhold before finally settling on the form of a great bird. By the time Gehart gained his tenth shard, the elemental was large enough that he could *ride* it into war against the blood-sharded. Would Shade eventually grow to the size of a tiger . . . or even larger? The idea of mounting a cat made of shadows and bounding into battle seemed incredibly far-fetched.

There was also a trend in the diary that he found troubling – as he had read on, the tenor of the writing had changed. It had become more . . . fractured, incoherent, as if Gehart was struggling to remain cogent. Deryn was reminded of a story he had been told in the Duskhold about a fire-sharded elementalist who had slipped into madness and made war against the world. The tale had been beyond belief and had included the taming of balewyrms and a battle that had resulted in a mountain's peak exploding, spewing forth lava and fire, so Deryn wasn't sure how much he should believe, but it made him uncomfortable that he saw traces of madness appearing in Gehart's writing. Accusations of outlandish conspiracies, boasts about deeds that must never have happened – after all, if he had truly caused an eclipse, surely this would have caused a furor across the world? – and records of strange voices whispering to him in his sleep. It felt like he was bearing witness to Gehart's mental deterioration. Would the same happen to him? And if so, how could he escape this fate? Perhaps that was what Shade wanted him to discover within these pages.

This thought was both comforting and disturbing. Trying to put it out of his head, Deryn opened the diary to the page where he had left off and started reading again.

36

HETH

The room was cramped and low-lit, its windowless walls stained dark by mold and decades of pipe-smoke. A circular table filled the space, surrounded by eight chairs of nearly identical design and size, for this was clearly intended to be a meeting place for equals. Heth had been in similar places before – the backrooms of *The Bull* and *The Swan's Song*, Kething's Cross's two largest inns – when accompanying his father while Ferith was negotiating deals with merchants from other towns. The stakes had been very different, though – his father had haggled over the price of ale casks or tree crabs or bales of dyed wool, while Heth needed to convince some very wary folk that they should join him in a rebellion.

Rhenna sat to his left, silent and watchful, her thinned lips speaking volumes. She had been irate when he'd told her his plans, insisting that they instead needed to leave Karath immediately and travel east to enlist Azil against the soul-sharded who had beguiled her father. Only after Heth had made an impassioned plea for her to think of all the suffering they'd seen in this city – and Deryn and Alia had lent him their support – had she grudgingly acquiesced. And despite her obvious annoyance with this delay, she had agreed to be his second at this meeting, for which he was very grateful – Rhenna had grown up in the court of the Duskhold watching meetings between proud and powerful leaders, and she would be far more likely to catch subtleties that he might miss.

Caden Vars sat across from them, next to a man who might have been his brother – just as balding and heavyset, though his beard was anvil-black instead of ginger. Both had pipes clamped between their teeth, and Heth suspected that much of the discoloration on the ceiling and walls was from Caden and his cronies. This was his house, after all, the eating hall where he conducted his business in the Nethers.

"You think they'll really show, lad?" grunted Caden, removing his pipe to tap out the ashes on the table.

"Zayin said he'd pass along my message," Heth replied, shifting uncomfortably in the hard wooden seat. The cuts Daemonel Thiss had given him had been carefully placed so as not to cripple or maim, but they were still painful a few days later, and he'd exhausted the healing salves Aziza had given him.

Caden tamped a pinch of fresh leaf into his pipe's bowl. "The Salahi almost never come out. I've always thought it best to just leave 'em alone. We don't bother them, they don't bother us."

"Which is exactly what the great families want," Rhenna said, speaking for the first time.

Caden's brow crinkled as he turned to her. "Who are you, lass?"

Before she could reply, rapidly approaching footsteps drew the room's attention to the doorway and then moments later Jerik appeared, breathing hard. "Cade!" the boy hissed, his face flushed. "The sandbathers are here! Really! They came!"

Caden held up his hands to calm the boy. "All right, lad. All right. They're guests, so go fetch some drink for them."

Jerik blinked his mis-matched eyes. "What should I get?"

"They're desert folk, so a pitcher of water would be a good start," Caden told him, blowing out a smoke ring.

"Date wine," said the large man beside Caden. "Kaz has a few bottles in the storeroom. Crack one an' bring it with glasses. Knew a

Salahi once, and that was the only thing he drank. Don't have barley
or wheat or grapes in the Salah, but they do have dates. Now go lad,
get. Be quick about it."

Jerik bobbed his head, then dashed away without even glancing
at Heth. His nervousness and excitement spoke volumes about the
enormity of this meeting, even if Caden and his companion were
showing little emotion. It was apparently a very rare thing for the
leaders of the Hollow and the Salahi to meet like this, despite living
nearly cheek-to-jowl in the Nethers.

Heth could feel the tension rising in the meeting room as they
waited in silence for their guests to arrive. Caden was affecting a
relaxed air, but Heth noticed that he was chewing on the stem of his
pipe . . . and when Zayin's massive shadow finally darkened the
entrance a flicker of something passed across the Hollow boss's face,
before quickly being controlled.

"Ho, Salahi," Caden said, sweeping his arm. "Welcome to the
house of the Hollow. Been a long time since we were honored like
this. I was barely a lad when your *balgras* came here to treat with old
Sannuk."

Zayin's gaze slowly drifted around the table until finally stopping
on him. "Caden Vars," he rumbled, "I introduce you now to the *bhalgrasi* of my *qenari*, Fayraz ap-Helas." He moved aside, and a much
smaller cloaked figure stepped into the room. Despite her slight
stature, her presence was anything but dwarfed by the huge Salahi
warrior looming over her, and as she drew back her hood Heth saw
that her dark eyes were piercing and prideful. A raptor's gaze. He
sensed Rhenna stiffen slightly, as if something had alarmed her . . . or
perhaps she simply recognized a kindred spirit.

Fayraz's thin lips twisted contemptuously, though at least this
reaction seemed directed towards the meeting room rather than
those she had come to meet, and then she slipped into one of the
empty chairs. Zayin followed her and found his own seat, his expression unreadable. Heth tried to meet his gaze to see if the old Salahi
would give him any insight about how he expected this gathering to
go, but he seemed to be avoiding looking in Heth's direction.

"This is not a welcoming place for my people," Fayraz finally said, focusing her attention on Caden. "There is no sun and no wind, no fresh air. I would not kennel my dogs here." She wrinkled her nose in disgust.

Caden shifted, casting a quick sidelong glance at the man beside him, then cleared his throat. "Well, what we have to talk about today ain't something that should be done out in the open. This is shadow-talk, real quiet. No safer place in Karath than this room, I promise ye."

"Save the *qenari*," rumbled Zayin, his deep voice like shifting stones. "Would you have preferred we meet there, my *bhalgrasi*?"

Fayraz's gaze slid to the hulking Salahi. She hadn't appreciated that comment, Heth realized. "Shadow-talk," she repeated slowly. "Just what do you think we have come here to discuss, Lord Vars?"

"Ain't no lord," Caden said amiably. "Just someone trying to do right by his people, and I hear tell you're the same. As to the topic under discussion . . ." He nodded towards Heth. "This one can explain more, I think."

"The *halatha*," Fayraz muttered. She reached into the folds of her robes, and Heth saw brief looks of alarm on the faces of the Hollow when she withdrew the Sharded dagger and laid it on the table. "A great gift he sends to me after I threatened his life. How strange."

"It was to show that I am serious," Heth said, feeling Rhenna's disapproving stare. She hadn't known he'd used the Sharded dagger to convince the Salahi to meet.

"Serious about what, lad?" Caden pressed. "I want to hear you give voice to it, get it all out into the open."

Heth licked his lips, letting the tension build. "Rebellion. And revenge for all the wrongs done to your peoples."

Silence followed this pronouncement. He could tell the others around the table were trying to guard their thoughts, but Heth saw interest in Caden's face and in Fayraz's something almost like hunger. Zayin was as inscrutable as one of those white-stone statues of lions that guarded the entrance to First Empire ruins . . . although if he truly had no interest in these matters, he never would have brought Heth's proposal to Fayraz.

Caden cleared his throat again loudly. "Now, I can with some confidence say I speak for the Hollow, or at least a good amount of 'em. You all know my name is one of the first mentioned when something happens that affects the Nethers. My words will bring . . ." his lips moved as he looked to the smoke-stained ceiling, counting something only he could see . . . "I'd say at least a hundred strong lads, most of whom know how to swing a cudgel or ax, and if I would allow 'em, probably another two or three hundred other common folk who want the chance to spill blood for what has been done to their children."

"There are two hundred blades in our qenari, forty of those trained as *araskinal*." The fact that Fayraz had offered up such information so quickly surprised Heth and made him realize that she must have suspected why she had been invited here. And that the possibility of allying with the Hollow to exact vengeance intrigued her.

"There are also a few true *araskin* left," added Zayin. "Survivors of the great war."

"They must be ancient," scoffed the black-bearded man beside Caden, and he looked like he was going to say more but Zayin's flat gaze stilled his tongue.

"They have not forgotten how to fight," Zayin said tersely. "And the *araskinal* we have trained are worthy warriors, even though they have not undergone the desert trials."

"So we would have a good-sized army," Caden said, folding his hands together on the table. "Maybe even a thousand if I allow every Hollow who wants to join to fight . . . but I have to know, *bhalgrasi* . . . do you truly speak for your people? Your mother is still the *balgras*, yes?"

"A woman only leads so long as she proves herself wise," Fayraz said, her hand going again to the hilt of the dagger on the table. "My mother has let fear instead of wisdom guide her for too long."

"But do you have the support of your tribe?" Caden pressed. "Your warriors?"

Fayraz's mouth tightened and her eye flashed, as if she had been insulted by this continued questioning . . . but then her gaze shifted to Zayin.

"We will follow her," the Salahi warrior stated, and from how Fayraz flushed it was not difficult to understand what was truly being said. They would follow him, and he had thrown his support behind Fayraz.

It seemed there was still something of the desert fierceness in the old dervish.

"But we do have reservations," Zayin said, folding his massive arms across his chest. "The council is protected by the Sword and tall stone walls bristling with spears. Even if we draw most of the Wardsmen out into the city and give them battle, we have no way to tear down the fortresses on the hill."

Caden nodded at these words as if recognizing their wisdom, then made an elaborate gesture towards Heth. "Tell him, lad."

"Perhaps we should instead wait for them to arrive," Heth suggested, casting a quick glance at the room's entrance.

"Wait for whom?" Fayraz asked, her eyes narrowing suspiciously.

As if in answer to this question, the faint sound of footsteps could suddenly be heard. They watched the doorway until Jerik appeared, looking even more agitated than before. "They're coming!" he hissed, and then vanished again. As the sound of his frantic retreat faded, something else replaced it. Heavy, measured strides, coming closer.

"You told him only two, right, lad?" Caden asked. "Sounds like an army approaching." The Hollow boss was on edge, Heth realized, even though they were in the safety of his sanctuary. Did that mean that he should be nervous as well?

A woman filled the entranceway, tall and broad despite her steel-gray hair. She was clad in tarnished armor that looked to have seen much use, though she wore no helmet, and the hilt at her side was without ornamentation. She surveyed the room briefly and then stepped inside, nodding slightly in the direction of Caden Vars before letting her gaze linger for a moment on Zayin. A look of recognition mixed with alarm passed across Fayraz's face, but she did not challenge this newcomer. Another woman slipped past the first, but she was very different in appearance – lithe and beautiful, with the copper skin of an Ashasai, her neck and wrists encircled by strings of rough-cut red stones. Aziza. The other woman must be Palimas, the one Alia had claimed was the Unbound King's general. Xend had sent his two top lieutenants to this meeting, demonstrating how seriously he was considering the offer Heth had made. That realization finally sent cracks through the calm he'd been striving to maintain – the events he'd set in motion might actually reach their end. That was more than a little terrifying.

"Welcome. Come sit down, join us," Caden said, indicating the last two empty seats at the table.

"But then, where will I sit?"

All eyes returned to the entrance, which had been filled by a huge, shrouded figure. The dark cloak the man wore trailed to the ground, and his face was hidden by a cowl, but Heth knew that voice and his pulse quickened. He cast a quick, panicked look at Rhenna beside him and saw that her fingers were bloodless from clutching at the table.

He wasn't supposed to be here. He had said he wouldn't come, that it was too dangerous.

Xend an-Azith pulled back his hood as he stepped into the meeting room, smiling broadly. Caden's face was ashen and his subordinate sucked in his breath, while Fayraz loosed an alarmed hiss, her dark eyes widening. Only Zayin looked unperturbed by the unexpected appearance of the Unbound King, tilting his head as he regarded Xend with calm interest.

"Lord an-Azith," Heth managed to choke out as Xend moved over to where Palimas had drawn back one of the chairs. "I thought you said you would not attend this meeting."

Xend shrugged out of his cloak before sitting, draping it over the back of his chair. He was dressed less flamboyantly than when Heth had last met him, in a simple shirt and trousers, though jewels still glittered in his ears and upon his fingers. This must be his attempt at staying inconspicuous, though there weren't many Ashasai in the city with his height and build. Xend sank into the chair with a sigh, folding his hands together on the table.

"So I did. Greetings to my fellow traitors."

"What are you doing here?" asked Fayraz in a strangled voice, and she looked like she was about to leap from her chair and either flee the room or bury the Sharded dagger in Xend's eye.

The Unbound King spread his arms wide. "I am part of the conspiracy."

"*You* serve the families," Fayraz snarled, gesturing at him with the point of the curving blade.

The skin above Xend's right eye crinkled – he would have just cocked an eyebrow, if he had eyebrows. "I provide a service to the Quinumvirate, and in exchange my people are allowed to live in the city. It is an arrangement I believe the Salahi have also made."

"*My people* are taken down into the mines and twisted by that devil-metal," Fayraz spat.

Xend shrugged. "That is what you can offer them. My Unfettered are asked to risk their lives outside the city, contesting with the holds."

"And they give you a manse and wealth and servants," Zayin rumbled, and Xend shifted his attention to the massive Salahi.

"They do," Xend agreed. "But we are still slaves – pampered, valued slaves, but slaves nonetheless. The caged songbird is still a prisoner."

"Why are you here?" Fayraz snarled. "Convince me, *Unbound King*, why I shouldn't leave this room right now, and take my swords back to our *qenari*?

"Because you want blood," Xend replied, his voice suddenly hardening. It sounded like he was reaching the limit of his patience with Fayraz, and Heth wondered if he should try to calm the situation. He had no idea what he could possibly say, though. Rhenna might, but she was staring at Xend with her jaw clenched. Heth had only asked her to come because he'd been assured Xend would not personally appear – now that the Unbound King was here, it felt like events were spiraling out of his control. If Xend realized who she was, he might still attempt to fulfill whatever bargain he had struck with Cael Shen.

"You want blood, Fayraz ap-Helas," Xend repeated, locking gazes with her. "For what they have done to your proud people. To your husband. Your daughter."

"Her question is still a good one, Lord an-Azith, and ye did not answer it," Caden murmured, his tone far less jovial than usual.

"Caden Vars," Xend said, swiveling to face the Hollow boss. "A man I respect. You care for your people and would do anything for them. You are much like me, I think . . . well, except that I am an exiled bloodlord of the Sanguine City and you were born in a stable on the road outside Ter Vhalin to a milk maid and a tanner's son."

"How do ye know that?" Caden whispered, but Xend ignored this question.

"We are all leaders of people who deserve to be free and proud," the Unbound King said, his gaze traveling around the table. "And yet we all wear shackles in this city. It is time to cast them off."

"What about the murders you mentioned before?" Heth interjected, surprising himself. This was something he had been thinking about ever since Selavin had delivered him to Xend, and it was a question he wanted answered before they all committed to this course. "You said the Sword has failed you in this matter. Is that why you've come here today?"

"Murders?" Caden said, his brow drawing down.

Xend smiled, though it did not touch his eyes. "It is true that this has driven a wedge between the city and my people, but I can assure you it is not the reason I am here today."

"What murders?" Caden persisted, running his fingers through his snarled ginger beard. "Someone's killing your Unfettered?"

"Yes, someone is killing my Unfettered," Xend admitted tightly, casting an annoyed glance at Heth. "Seven in the last few weeks. Though we've only discovered two of the bodies. It is the Sword's duty to protect us, and he is failing."

"Perhaps ye should tell them more," murmured the armored

woman standing behind Xend's chair. "There's a chance they know something."

Xend frowned, but then sighed and nodded. "Very well. The bodies we recovered . . . there was something strange. Their shards were . . . dead."

"This is the City of the Dead," said Zayin.

"But our shards are still alive," countered Xend. "Just suppressed. These shards were as dead as . . . ." he looked at the Salahi, "as the Sand."

"And the Flame," added Rhenna sharply.

Xend glanced at her as if seeing her for the first time, and a shiver of fear went through Heth. "Just so. But these were not flame-sharded Unfettered. They were stone and storm, and yet the shards in their chest were gray and lifeless." He leaned back in his chair, spreading his arms wide as if inviting the others around the table to speak. "So. Does anyone here know about this assassin stalking my people?"

Silence followed, and after a moment, Xend nodded. "As I suspected. But now you know of this . . . hunter that has come to Karath, and as a gesture of good faith, if you hear anything, I would entreat you to send word."

"Aye," Caden grunted, taking out his pipe and tapping its bowl on the table. "We'll let you know."

Fayraz shrugged, but Xend seemed to interpret this as agreement, because he flashed her a warm smile.

"Now, enough of this disagreeable subject. Let us return to the matter at hand."

"I have a question for you, Lord an-Azith," Rhenna asked, and Heth just kept himself from wincing. Why was she insisting on drawing attention to herself? At least she had managed to strip the anger from her voice when she spoke.

Xend made a gesture inviting her to continue.

"What happens if we win? Who replaces the Quinumvirate and the Wardsmen?"

Xend's response was immediate. "I will be crowned the king of Karath."

The uproar that ensued did not surprise Heth in the least. Fayraz jumped out of her chair, slamming the dagger down on the wood with a sharp crack, and the Hollow beside Caden pounded the table with his fist. Even Zayin scowled and shook his head, as if disappointed that Xend had tipped his hand so early.

"Why would we trade the Quinumvirate for *you*?" Fayraz asked, her dark eyes flashing.

"Because I will not rule as they do," Xend replied mildly, unperturbed by the chaos he had caused. "There will be no more Tithing. No longer will anyone be confined to the Nethers. Hollow or Salahi who remain in the city afterwards will be treated as any other citizen."

"What do you mean 'remain in the city'," asked Zayin.

A look of surprise crossed Xend's face as he turned towards Heth. "They do not know?"

"I, *ah*, hadn't found a time to tell them yet. The Hollow know . . . or, at least, Caden knows."

"I've told my most trusted," Caden said, packing his pipe's bowl once more. "Thing like this, can't be too careful."

"What are you speaking about?" Fayraz muttered, her sharp gaze flicking between Caden, Xend and Heth.

The Unbound King made an expansive gesture towards Heth, inviting him to speak. "You've been quiet, especially considering how this meeting was your doing. But it's time you placed all your tiles on the table."

"Maybe I should just show you instead," Heth offered, fumbling with the topmost buttons of his tunic.

"So you're Sharded," Fayraz said after he'd revealed the fragment sunk into his chest. "Why does that matter?"

"You don't think the color is strange?" Heth asked, wishing the room wasn't so dimly lit.

"No," Fayraz said with a frown. "Should I? I have only seen a few shards in flesh. There are those among the Salahi who kept their shards even after the Sand was destroyed . . . the rest of us, we never tried to claim one from elsewhere."

"So you are Imbued?" Heth asked, unable to keep the excitement from his voice.

Fayraz nodded. "Many in our *qenari* are. Most, even. We are the descendants of the Sharded Few who fled the northern armies after the war was lost. But it is a rare thing for a Salahi to claim a shard nowadays – they would not be welcome in the *qenari* anymore. We would cast them out for betraying the old ways."

"I've had a few Salahi join my Unfettered," Xend said, drawing an annoyed look from Fayraz.

"Traitors to our people."

Xend shrugged. "Refusing to take a shard is such a terrible waste of potential."

"Why don't you let Salahi who are Sharded stay in your tribe?" Heth asked, trying to forestall the conflict he saw developing.

Fayraz shook her head. "Because the Sand was the Salahi and the Salahi are the Sand. But perhaps more importantly is that we can have no other master. To take the shard of another hold divides one's loyalty. Could a flame-sharded Salahi be trusted, or would they feel compelled to go be with their brethren in the Ember? The holds have a powerful sway over their Sharded . . ." she trailed away, her mouth twisting as she glanced at Xend. "Well, most of them. And the ones that don't end up in thrall to him."

"In thrall, she says," Xend muttered, then guffawed. "In thrall!"

"What if you could found a new hold?" Heth asked. "Around a new shard."

"There is no such thing," Zayin grumbled, but his eyes went once more to the faintly glowing yellow-white shard in Heth's chest.

"Have you seen a shard like this before?" Heth leaned forward to give a better view of his fragment.

"I have never seen an ice shard or a seed shard," Zayin said, shifting almost uneasily.

"Do you think the ice or the seed shed this color of light?" Heth continued, cursing Karath for dampening his shard's glow. "This is from the Light shard, and to my knowledge I am the only light-sharded in the world."

Fayraz subsided into her chair, her lips quirking in amusement. "You jest." Then her brow furrowed when she noticed that Caden Vars and Xend seemed unsurprised by this statement. "You . . . you both believe this claim?"

Caden pulled at his thick beard. "Aye, well, what the lad claims *sounds* like madness, I'll agree with ye, but there's something about the tale that rings true . . ."

"I can assure you that there is no record of a shard like he bears," Xend said confidently. "And I am an expert in these matters."

"I found the Light shard in an ancient ruin, where it has lain undisturbed since the days of the First Empire. I can take you there, and you can claim fragments of your own."

Fayraz's expression was scornful, but Zayin had gone very still.

"I don't want to be the ruler of a hold. But join with me and we can create something new, a haven for those wronged by the Sharded Few." He sensed their skepticism, but pressed on, searching for the right ingress. "You are the people of the Salah, yes? The Salah is sand, and that was your shard, but what else is the desert? The scorching sun. Light, blazing on the dunes, winnowing your people into something hard and sharp and strong. Maybe this is the destiny of the Salahi. Maybe I was meant to bring you into the Light."

"And leave this place," Zayin said slowly.

"Yes!" Heth cried, rising to his feet. "Leave Karath to Lord an-Azith and his Unfettered. You are not meant for the city; I could tell that just from stepping inside your *qenari*. The Salahi are withering here, are they not? Take this chance and return your people to glory!"

Heth could feel Rhenna staring at him in surprise. Where had this impassioned outburst come from? It had just welled up from within him, and he could see the effect of his words. Fayraz was no longer scowling, and there was a spark in Zayin's eyes. Caden was grinning, and even Xend seemed to have been inspired.

Fayraz blinked and shook her head, as if trying to avoid being swept away by what Heth was saying. "What about the other orders of the Sharded Few? Surely they will not allow a new hold to arise."

"We must move fast," Heth told her, trying to sound confident.

"The Light shard is located somewhere difficult to reach but easy to defend . . . and there are great events unfolding in the world that will distract the holds for a while yet. I will lead you to the shard, then we will claim its power before anyone else realizes what is happening . . . " Heth gestured at Zayin. "You were a powerful Sharded. A *famdhar*, yes? I have been told that those who have lost their shards retain the knowledge of how to merge more shards, that their pathways remember how to gentle their *ka* and harness the power of the fragments. The *araskin* who still live could become the most feared warriors in the world once more."

Fayraz looked overwhelmed by what Heth had just proposed. He couldn't blame her. She had come here seeking bloody vengeance for what had been done to her daughter and instead was being offered a chance to change the destiny of her tribe.

If what Heth was saying was true. Which it was, but to take this sort of risk with her people's future would be a tremendous leap of faith.

And this was exactly what she was thinking. "How can I trust you, *halatha*?"

"I believe him," Xend piped up cheerily, and Fayraz turned her attention to him.

"And how can I trust *you*, *halatha*?"

"I think ye know I've been a friend to the *qenari*," Caden interjected, "and for what it's worth, I trust him as well."

Fayraz opened her mouth like she was about to also dismiss the Hollow boss's words, but Zayin spoke first.

"As do I," rumbled the old warrior. "The first time I saw him, he was defending the weak from the Wardsmen. And when I confronted him about his *araskin* blade and told him he must return it to our *qenari*, he did just that. Others would have fled the city or refused. This . . . offer seems incredible. Impossible. But perhaps it is what is meant to be. Perhaps this is the salvation we have been praying for."

Fayraz was quiet in the wake of Zayin's pronouncement, her lips pursed. Then she lifted the Sharded dagger, running her finger along its curving edge. "A wise *bhalgrasi* trusts the advice of her *araskin* in matters of war," she finally said.

Caden clapped his hands together loudly, looking relieved. "That's worthy of a celebration. And look, what do we have here?"

Heth saw that Jerik had appeared again in the doorway, laden down by a dusky stoppered jug and a stack of clay cups. "Sorry!" the boy cried, ducking his head in apology. This movement nearly made him lose his grip on the heavy jug, and the man beside Caden had to rise and help him with his burden. "Took me forever to find the Salahi wine. Your storeroom is terrifying, Cade! You need more light and fewer spiders down there!"

"Salahi wine?" Fayraz murmured in surprise, lifting an eyebrow.

"Date wine," Caden said, taking the jug and wrestling out the ancient cork. He began to pour the amber liquid into the cups and a sweet, almost floral aroma cut through the stale miasma of pipe-smoke and sweat.

Zayin leaned forward in interest. "*Nebith*," he murmured, almost in wonder. "It has been many years, but I know that smell."

"To the rebellion," Xend proclaimed, raising the cup Caden had placed before him and then quickly draining it.

"To the rebellion," Heth murmured under his breath, trying to ignore the coldness that had settled in his stomach.

37

DERYN

The fortress of the Shield had been constructed from pale pink stone, and Deryn had watched its coloration gradually deepen as the morning sun ascended over Karath. He had arrived at the small market square outside its gates well before dawn, when the crenelated towers were still darker shadows etched against the sky and the surrounding city was still and quiet. The market had begun to stir as a rosy blush infused the stone, merchants opening shuttered stalls and haggling with the owners of the carts laden with produce and meat that had trundled up the steep cobbled roads of the Skull. During this time, he had remained recessed in the shadows, waiting and watching.

"The city wakes."

Deryn startled – the voice had come from behind him, but he hadn't heard anyone approaching. He turned to find a small, shrouded woman behind him in the alley, hands thrust into the folds of her robe.

"It readies for a new day," he replied, giving the response Heth had instructed him to say.

The woman's hands appeared, no doubt slipping from the hilts of whatever weapons she was concealing, and reached up to pull back her hood. The Salahi woman might have been beautiful if not for the hardness of her eyes and the grim set of her mouth; she looked him up and down, and Deryn felt like he was being measured.

"You are the *halatha* Deryn, friend of Heth Su Canaav."

"I am," he admitted, peering into the shadows behind her. He couldn't see anyone else, but this woman most definitely had not come alone. If she had, something had already gone spectacularly wrong.

"I am Fayraz, *bhalgrasi* of this city's *qenari*. You have been watching all night?"

"Yes," Deryn replied, nodding. Was he supposed to bow to her? Heth had said the *bhalgrasi* was a kind of Salahi noblewoman.

"And there was nothing strange?"

"Before dawn a large group of Wardsmen entered the fortress accompanying a windowless carriage banded with iron. I'm not sure who was inside – maybe the Sword? Later more carriages arrived, but these were ornate and pulled by teams of beautiful horses. Even in the dimness I could tell their quality, and their hooves rang light on the cobbles."

"How many?"

"Five, each with a sizeable retinue."

Fayraz smiled, but there was no warmth to it. "Then they are all inside. This is good. The Quinumvirate has answered Xend's request to treat with him."

Deryn hoped Fayraz was correct. Their entire plan hinged on the heads of the five great families all being inside the fortress, along with the Sword and the Shield. Late last night, Xend had dispatched messengers to each of their estates, claiming that the continuing murders of his followers threatened to abrogate the old treaties between his Unfettered and the city. He had demanded a meeting with the council this morning in the fortress of the Shield to discuss these matters further, and apparently the tone had been enough to compel the family heads to rise before the sun and gather here to discuss what could be done to mollify the Unbound King.

"Did you come alone?" Deryn asked, once more searching the shadow-shrouded alleyway she had emerged from. He had almost forgotten what it was like to have darkvision – when they finally left this city, it would be like that first morning when he had awoken with a shard.

Fayraz's answer was to put two fingers in her mouth and give a low whistle. The darkness trembled, and then a pair of figures flowed from where they had been pressed up against a wall.

"*Bhalgrasi,*" one of the veiled warrior murmured, his hand on the pommel of the curving sword at his side.

"*Araskinal,*" Fayraz responded, followed by a rapid stream of incomprehensible Salahi. Both warriors bobbed their heads, then melted back into the shadows.

"Not alone," Fayraz said to Deryn. "But we are not all here yet. A hundred armed Salahi marching towards the Skull would be noticed. My people are trickling their way through the city, avoiding the most watched approaches. But we will be ready when Xend gives the signal, do not fear."

"Good," Deryn said, still surprised by the silence and grace with which the Salahi warriors had moved. A hundred warriors. And Caden had said he would be able to muster at least as many of the best brawlers among his people. The Hollow didn't have an army, of course – likely almost none of them had ever even swung a sword or ax in real anger – but the Nethers was a rough district, and many had learned how to defend themselves. Two hundred fighters. That would be enough, surely, for Xend's plan to work. It had to be.

So far, things had unfolded as the Unbound King had predicted. The leaders of Karath had gathered in the fortress of the Shield, waiting for him to arrive. Any moment now Xend would do just that, accompanied by an honor guard a dozen strong befitting his station in the city. Hidden among those Unfettered would be Heth and the dervish Zayin. After they had all been admitted to the fortress, this force would overpower the Wardsmen guards and open the gate, allowing the Hollow and Salahi waiting outside to enter. This should be an overwhelming number of attackers – Xend had doubted there would be more than a few dozen Wardsmen within the walls – although each family head would have also brought their own elite bodyguards, some of whom were so famous that even Deryn had heard their names. Old lord Bharach was always accompanied by the feared Kez'Athon, a former champion of the Ashasai bloodpits, who it was said filed his teeth down to points so that he could tear out the throats of his defeated enemies. The Chaim matriarch had enlisted a trio of sword-sisters hailing from a legendary island far out in the Sea of Salvation, a place where only women were allowed to learn the fighting arts, and the Valari had raised a pair of rare red-scaled zemani ever since their hatching, training them to be the equal of any human bladesman.

Still, despite these fearsome defenders, Deryn couldn't imagine they could stand for very long against the tide of warriors ready to wash over the fortress.

"You are to remain outside," Fayraz suddenly said, as if she could read his mind.

Deryn blinked in surprise, turning to her. "Did Heth tell you that?" He had made Deryn promise the same, but asking Fayraz to ensure he remained safe was more than a little belittling. They had fought together in more dangerous battles than this, after all.

"Yes," she cocked her head to one side, looking down at the tarnished gray-metal hilt of his wind-sharded sword. "Did he do this because you cannot fight?"

"I can fight," Deryn replied, more than a little indignant.

"Then he merely wishes to protect you. And I have given my word, so you will not join the coming battle."

Deryn frowned, turning away from Fayraz in annoyance. He wasn't a child. Just because he was lacking his Sharded strength did not mean he was helpless. But Deryn could sense there was no point arguing with her – she had spoken with the casual finality of someone who expected obedience.

Heth had also asked Rhenna and Alia to stay far away. This was not their fight, he had argued, and they had a far greater purpose that could not be endangered. Rhenna had grumbled, but in the end acquiesced, and Deryn had seen a newfound respect in her eyes. Heth seemed to be a different man these days – no longer the humble Hollow servant, but a commander of men.

"Something is happening," Fayraz murmured, drawing Deryn from his sulk. She was right – a tremor had gone through the awakening market, heads turning, and voices were swelling as conversations started about who could be approaching. Deryn saw that a large group had just entered the market, and as others realized who was swaggering at its head there came a scattering of gasps.

Xend an-Azith did not look like he had come to start a rebellion – he was dressed only in a silver vest and black trousers cinched by a thick crimson sash, although jewelry he had adorned himself with glittered in the morning light. The dozen or so accompanying him looked less like a well-trained honor guard and more a mob of revelers returning home after a night of celebration. Some wore armor, while others were garbed similarly to Xend. Deryn did see that most were armed, at least. He looked for Heth and found him quickly – or, at least, he thought it must be him, a cloaked man with his hood drawn up in the middle of the disorganized mob. A good place for him, given the scars that made him easily identifiable, in the slim chance that Daemonel Thiss or another of the Wardsmen who had encountered him before were at the gates. Beside him was a huge Salahi, broad and imposing despite his gray hair. That must be Zayin. Heth had told him how quickly the old dervish could still move, though given his age and massive size, Deryn didn't know how that was possible.

The arrival of the Unbound King had roiled the market. Xend must be a popular figure, because more than a few were cheering, and he waved jauntily in return as he strode towards the closed gates. The Wardsmen stationed on the walls seemed less thrilled to see him, hands remaining firmly clenched on the hafts of their halberds. Still, as he neared the fortress a grinding sounded as somewhere a massive winch was turned and the gate slowly began to open.

"They are early – we are not all here yet," Fayraz muttered beside him, gesturing sharply towards where her Salahi warriors had vanished into the darkness. One of them stepped forward, and Deryn saw that he had undone the veil previously hiding his young face. In his hand was an ancient curving war horn banded with tiny black writing.

"*Araskinal*, be ready," Fayraz commanded. "It is almost time."

38

HETH

The procession had departed from the gates of the Unbound King's manse when night's blanket had still been spread over the city. Heth hadn't slept except for a brief nap on a divan that had been placed on the edge of the lush gardens, nodding off to the sound of Xend and his lieutenants drinking wine and discussing strategy for the next day. He had returned to himself groggy and disoriented, shaken awake by Xend himself, who looked as if he had just sprung from his bed after a full night's sleep. The man seemed almost inhuman in his ability to consume wine and remain unaffected, as if the passive beckoning of the blood-sharded somehow did still extend to him, even within the walls of Karath.

Zayin had joined them soon after they had begun the climb to where the Skull and the fortresses crowning its pate reared above the city. The Salahi had consulted briefly with Xend, no doubt informing him about the movements of his kin, and then fallen in step beside Heth. It was comforting having the giant warrior next to him, his stolid presence a rock from which to draw strength.

The streets and houses grew progressively nicer as they made their way through the city: white stucco walls veined with flowering vines, red-tiled roofs adorned with waterspouts carved into the shape of fish, pillared porticos decorated by elaborate stonework. There was not a broken window or collapsing doorway or dead cat to be seen anywhere. Heth wondered what Caden Vars's Hollow and the Salahi thought as they entered these carefully swept and cared for districts – did they feel a hot rush of indignant anger, knowing that the Tithing that stole away their children was responsible for much of this wealth? He hoped so. He wanted what happened today to be seen as an act of righteous fury by long-oppressed peoples, not simply naked ambition.

His pulse quickened when they started to ascend the Skull, his palms growing clammy. Xend seemed entirely unaffected by the knowledge of what awaited them at the top of the hill, whistling as he strolled through the streets and making flamboyant gestures in the direction of those gaping down at his Unfettered from open windows and balconies. The Hollow and Salahi fighters should be keeping pace with them, and Heth peered down side-streets and alleyways trying to catch a glimpse of the other rebels, but saw nothing.

And then they arrived. The steep road they'd been climbing crested, spilling into a small market square outside the Shield's fortress of pale pink stone. The walls were not as formidable as what had girdled the ruined forts they'd seen in the wilderness beyond the Frayed Lands, but they still soared twice as tall as a man, and the closed gate was made of thick iron bars that might have even kept out weaker Sharded. There was a scattering of merchants and shoppers at the stalls in the square, and a ripple of excitement went through them when Xend and his entourage appeared. Heth again tried to catch sight of their allies, if only to reassure himself that they would not find themselves alone after seizing the gate, but they must have hidden themselves well. Deryn was almost certainly here some-where, since Heth had agreed to let him act as a lookout to ensure that there was no unexpected activity during the night which might suggest the Sword had somehow been alerted to their plans.

As they approached the gate, one of the Wardsmen manning the walls called down to someone below, and a heartbeat later a harsh grinding sounded. Xend did not hesitate or break his stride as the gate opened, leading them into the shadowed interior of the small barbican as if he was the lord of this fortress returning home. Heth tensed, expecting any moment for the Unbound King's command to attack to ring out.

On the other side of the gate was a small, sun-splashed courtyard, and it was here that Xend finally came to a halt. The main building in front of them was a tiered tower that looked more like a queen's palace than a keep, with windows of colored glass and beautifully wrought balconies of pink stone instead of murder holes and fortifications. Heth couldn't stop himself from reflexively ducking his head when he saw who was standing on the broadest balcony overlooking the courtyard, staring down at them with his hands resting on the balustrade.

Selavin Thiss. The Sword of Karath was dressed in what looked to be the exact same garb that Heth remembered from before – gray armor of leather and chain, his dark cloak secured by a white brooch containing the silhouette of a black hand. He looked a corpse in the morning light, pale and gaunt, with hollow cheeks and thinning hair. Heth had been told once that Selavin had been a Blade before coming to the City of the Dead, but it was hard to imagine this man dueling with the champions of Flail.

A niggling sense of wrongness had been growing in Heth ever since they had entered the fortress proper, and suddenly he realized why. They were alone in the courtyard. No one had been waiting to greet them, nor had servants emerged from the tiered building to usher them inside or offer refreshment. Selavin hadn't even called out a greeting, and the Wardsmen ringing the walls looking down on them were silent and motionless, as if waiting for something.

Xend must have felt the tension as well, but his actions said otherwise as he stepped forward, throwing his arms wide as he approached where Selavin loomed over them.

"Sword of Karath! No need to look so grim! It's a beautiful morning, let the sunlight brighten your mood!"

"Xend an-Azith," Selavin called down. "Greetings to the Unbound King."

The Unfettered around Heth began to mutter and shift, as if just realizing that something was wrong.

Xend barked a brief laugh. "So we're not standing on ceremony today, Selavin?"

The Sword's thin lips quirked into a humorless smile. "You were a lord of this city, Xend, and given everything you could desire. And yet you betray us."

Cold fear washed through Heth, and he glanced back at the gate as it finished closing behind them. On the walls, the Wardsmen were unlimbering crossbows from their backs.

"I'm not certain what you are speaking about," Xend shouted up. "I have always been loyal to the city."

Selavin shook his head, almost sadly, then turned and made a beckoning gesture to someone standing nearby. A huge Wardsman that Heth hadn't been able to see stepped forward, coming to stand next to the Sword and holding upright a limp man whose face was hidden by a tangle of hair. Selavin's hand lifted from the balustrade and grabbed a fistful of the black curls, then yanked the man's head up so that his bruised face could be seen.

"Jerik," Heth whispered. The boy's face had been beaten badly, but Heth knew it was him.

"This one had an interesting tale to tell," Selavin said, his words echoing in the suddenly silent courtyard. "Sedition and betrayal by those who had been given refuge in their hour of greatest need."

Xend began to walk towards the balcony where the Sword stood, but not before making a sharp gesture to keep the Unfettered from following him. Heth marveled at his bravery – he looked so alone in this great expanse of pink stone, two dozen crossbows following him across the courtyard. He stopped almost directly below Selavin, shielding his eyes from the sun as he looked up at the Sword.

"How can you trust any story drawn out through torture?" he asked loudly, again spreading his arms wide. "But even if you believe this boy, you know how important my Unfettered are to Karath. The families need us. The Shield needs us. You need us, or it will be impossible to oppose the holds beyond the walls of this city. Let us turn and leave now and we can all forget this morning ever happened."

Selavin cocked his head to one side, as if seriously considering what Xend has just suggested. "Forgive and forget. Today, you made your play for the city, and now you know that we are not fools. Your arrogance has always been your great weakness, Ashasai."

"This is a lesson in humility I will not forget," Xend promised, bowing his head in contrition.

"No," Selavin replied, pulling Jerik from the grasp of the hulking Wardsmen and dragging him to the edge of the balcony. "You will not."

Heth cried out as the Sword shoved Jerik over the balustrade – the boy tried to resist, but he was too weak, his scrabbling fingers leaving bloody streaks on Selavin's armor as he toppled forward. His arms flailed, and the raspy scream that bubbled forth had barely begun before he struck the stone of the courtyard with a horrible wet thud that staggered Heth like a blow to his chest.

Xend had not flinched, even though the boy had landed almost on top of him. He seemed intensely interested in the redness that was reaching towards his boots.

Selavin smiled at what he had wrought, then raised his arm and brought it down sharply.

Over the roaring in his ears, Heth heard the thrum of several dozen crossbow bolts being loosed.

39

DERYN

The gate shut with a heavy clang, Xend and his Unfettered vanishing from sight. Deryn stared at the formidable-looking barrier, trying to calm his racing heart. The moment of truth was fast approaching. Either the Unbound King would overcome the Wardsmen guarding whatever mechanism lifted the gate and open the way for the Salahi to stream inside, or they would fail, and the rebellion would end before it ever truly started. Deryn watched the guards up on the walls, searching for some clue about what was happening. They had turned around to watch the Unfettered march into the fortress, and Deryn suddenly noticed the crossbows slung across their backs . . . those would be a problem, as they could fire down on Xend's followers without fear of reprisal, since the Unfettered had no ranged weapons. He felt a stab of fear for Heth, but tried to push it aside. There was no use worrying – nothing could be done from out here. He just had to hope that Xend had accounted for crossbows and had some plan to deal with the Wardsmen on the walls.

"Are you worried?" Fayraz asked, and Deryn saw that she now held a long, curving dagger. She apparently intended to charge the gate once it started to rise again, and he found this rather surprising.

He couldn't imagine the noblewomen and rich wives of Kething's Cross being so excited about the possibility of stabbing their enemies.

"No," he lied, and from her mocking smile, she knew he was not being honest.

"What will happen, will happen," she said, running a finger down the length of her blade. "All that matters is that you show your worth. If you die, let it be a glorious death, and laugh in the face of the Dark Lady when she comes to fold you in her wings."

Deryn swallowed. "I'll try to remember to . . ." His voice trailed away as he caught sight of something unexpected. A man in the coarse homespun common to the Nethers had run out from one of the side streets and into the middle of the market square, and now was looking around frantically as if searching for something.

Searching for them.

"Hey!" Deryn cried out, eliciting a hiss of surprise from Fayraz. The man turned at the sound, squinting into the darkness of the alley where they were recessed, and Deryn stepped out into the light. A few other heads swiveled in their direction, but most of the people in the square ignored the disturbance, still discussing the unexpected appearance of the Unbound King and his entourage.

The man rushed over to Deryn, a look of relief crossing his face when he spied Fayraz lurking in the shadows. He was clearly exhausted, struggling to breathe as he tried to collect himself.

"What is it?" Fayraz asked, motioning for the desert warriors to join them at the alley's mouth. "What's happened?"

"It's . . ." the man gasped, then swallowed hard. "It's the Wardsmen. They're . . . they're here."

"Of course they're here," snapped Fayraz, pointing with her dagger at the fortress of the Shield.

"No . . . no," the man said, finally managing to straighten. "They've encircled the Skull and are marching up the hill. We're fighting, us Hollow I mean, but they're better armed and wearing armor. We've just got knives and clubs and such. We can't stand before 'em, have to fall back."

Deryn shared a glance with Fayraz and saw the concern in her eyes. "How many are there?" he asked, and the man shook his head.

"I dunno. But Caden said hundreds. They must have nearly emptied the garrison at the mines,

brought every sword into the city. We need help, any fighters you can spare, or they're gonna roll right up the hill and crush us against the walls of this fortress."

Fayraz snarled in frustration. "*Araskinal* Naseer," she said, and one of the veiled Salahi bent his head towards her. "Run quickly and tell all you can find that the Wardsmen know and that they're coming to kill us all. We must fight like we should have done that day in Derambinal – to the death. Do you understand?"

The Salahi nodded sharply.

"Then go," Fayraz commanded, and he plunged into the alley's darkness.

They know, Deryn thought, and a sickness roiled his stomach. Heth had just walked into a trap. He looked to the walls, but the Wardsmen with their crossbows had vanished. Perhaps they had descended to apprehend the rebels instead of killing them from afar. He had to hope.

"What do we do?" Deryn asked.

"We fight and we die and we take as many of the *halatha* with us as we can," Fayraz replied. Deryn did not hear any fear in her voice, and he wished he could be like her right now.

Their attention was drawn to the gate as the grinding of its chains sounded once again. Deryn's hand went to the hilt of his wind-sharded sword – this must be the Wardsmen within, sortieing out to attack them while they were distracted by the soldiers ascending the hill.

Fayraz was muttering some chant in Salahi, pressing the point of her dagger just below her eye until redness trickled down her cheek like a bloody tear. Deryn pulled his sword free, and he felt Shade practically dancing in his shadow, as if the elemental was excited about what was coming.

The gate was by now fully raised, but the horde of Wardsmen

Deryn had been expecting failed to appear. His grip tightened on his blade, and he took a deep breath, trying his best to master himself.

Fayraz broke off her chanting. "Who is *that*?" she whispered, for the first time sounding unnerved.

A lone figure had emerged from the shadow of the barbican, broad-shouldered and powerfully built. Whatever shirt he had once been wearing had been torn away, and his naked upper body was absolutely sheathed with blood. It drenched his hairless head and ran in heavier streaks of gore down his chest to drip onto his once-flamboyant pantaloons, which were now nothing but tattered rags. Xend. Deryn moaned, searching for the wounds that could cause such bleeding. The top of his head must have been split open, and beneath those darker rivulets of blood his flesh looked to have been sliced to ribbons.

Yet he did not collapse or even stumble as he walked out into the center of the market square. Others had seen him by now, screaming as they fled from this horrific apparition. How was he standing, Deryn wondered? Any lesser man would certainly already be dead.

And he was not only on his feet, but striding towards them.

"Silver Shrike," Deryn whispered hoarsely when Xend drew near enough that a gleaming white smile was visible in his blood-spattered visage.

Shade was thrashing now, but Deryn barely noticed the elemental's agitation.

"*Bhalgrasi!*" Xend shouted, giving his head a quick shake and sending droplets of blood flying. "Why are you just standing here? The gates are open and your fighters are needed inside."

"Lord an-Azith," Fayraz said slowly, sounding unsure if this really was Xend or some demon impersonating the Unbound King. "We . . . we just received word that a huge force of Wardsmen are coming up the Skull. If we do not turn and fight, they will take us from behind."

Xend frowned, peering down the street that emptied into the market square, as if expecting to see an army suddenly appear. "Ah. I see. I suppose that makes sense – Selavin was always such a careful little fellow." He laced his bloody fingers together and stretched his arms out, as if trying to crack his knuckles before a hard bit of work. Surprise washed through Deryn when he noticed that the one piece of clothing Xend was wearing that had survived entirely in one piece – a thick crimson sash tied about his waist – was rippling like it was caught in a great gust of wind.

But the air was absolutely still.

Shade was frantic, battering himself against the edges of Deryn's shadow, although apparently unwilling to emerge fully into the light.

Xend turned to Deryn, putting a bloody hand on his shoulder. "You're Deryn, yes? Heth said to find you, if you were still out here. He wants you to go to him."

"Is he . . . is he all right?" Deryn murmured, unable to tear his gaze from the undulating strip of cloth encircling Xend.

"*Hm*? Oh, yes, he's fine. Or he was when I left. It's dangerous in there, though. He needs your help."

"I'll . . . I'll do that," Deryn replied numbly, finally managing to wrest his attention from the sash. Could it be?

"Good!" Xend said brightly, clapping him so hard on the shoulder that Deryn staggered slightly. "I'll lend my aid to the fight out here, keep these bastards off your backs. Now, be a good lad and go conquer the city for me."

MANY MONTHS AGO, when Alia had fled the shadow-sharded, Heth had led him down into the bowels of the Duskhold to where she'd been forced to work as a butcher. He could still remember the smell rising from the chunks of fly-swarmed viscera strewn on scarred tables, a mix of stale blood and rotten meat. There had been all manner of beast hacked apart, dismembered limbs hanging from hooks over black-stained drains or simply scattered about on the floor.

As he emerged from the barbican into the courtyard, what he found reminded him of that terrible place.

An abattoir.

There were corpses everywhere – a few were the sprawled bodies of Xend's Unfettered, staring sightlessly past the quarrel protruding from their brows or curled protectively around something buried in their gut. But they were in the great minority. Most of the dead had once been Wardsmen, or at least that was what Deryn thought. It was hard to tell. They had been . . . ripped apart. Arms and legs had been torn away and tossed about like a child playing with toys. Heads had completely vanished, leaving only bloody stumps and the ragged ends of spines. Some looked like they had been savaged by an enormous beast, their ribs splintered, leaving only a gaping chasm where their hearts and lungs should have been.

"*Malasha*," came a voice behind Deryn, and he turned to see that one of the veiled Salahi had followed him inside. The warrior met his gaze with wide, terrified eyes. "A demon did this," he murmured, then sketched a quick symbol in the air, three quick slashes bounded by a circle.

"Something very similar," Deryn replied in little more than a whisper, searching the carnage for any sign of Heth. Most of the Unfettered who had survived whatever had happened here had congregated near the huge double-doors leading into the main building, apparently trying to decide what they should do next. Or perhaps they were spending a moment to recover before going inside – they looked dazed, like they had just witnessed something that they still couldn't fully comprehend.

"There," Deryn breathed in relief when he finally caught sight of his friend. Heth was crouching beside something almost in the shadow of the tiered keep, a much larger Salahi man beside him. Deryn hurried across the courtyard, trying to avoid stepping in the guts and gobbets of flesh that had been haphazardly spread across the pink-stone flagstones. The Salahi warrior followed him, muttering hoarsely in his desert tongue.

As Deryn drew closer he saw the Heth was hunched over the splayed corpse of a boy, his head cradled in his lap – no, not a corpse, as the boy's chest was still rising and falling slightly, and Deryn could hear ragged breathing through his bloodstained lips.

"Heth," he said, and his friend turned away from the boy's battered face. Tears streaked his cheeks, and the pain in his eyes made Deryn flinch.

"He's hurt," Heth whispered. "Selavin . . . he threw him from up there."

Deryn swallowed, glancing at the balcony above. It was a long fall. "What happened?"

Heth looked out over the courtyard. "I . . . I don't know."

"*Araskin* Zayin," the veiled Salahi said, staring at the dying boy. "Are you unharmed?"

"I am, *araskinal* Azavel," rumbled the massive, gray-haired warrior. "The Unbound King did this."

"But how?" murmured the younger Salahi. "How can he use his blood shard here? It is impossible."

"It was not a blood-sharded talent," Deryn said softly.

Zayin shook his head. "It was. I saw it. A creature made of blood, twisting through the air, tearing men apart."

"A creature," Heth said slowly, as if in dawning realization. "Deryn, is it possible?"

"It must be," he replied, feeling dizzied. "Xend an-Azith has an elemental."

"An elemental?" Zayin said, his face crinkling in confusion. "I thought there were no more of such things in this world."

"There is," Deryn said, and as if summoned, Shade emerged from his shadow to pad closer to the dying boy.

The veiled Salahi gasped, clutching at the hilt at his side, but Zayin held up his hand to keep him from drawing his blade. The old desert champion was staring at the shadow elemental in something like wonder.

When Shade reached the boy, he brought his little face close to the boy's mouth, as if listening to his labored breathing. Then his head made a quick motion, and Deryn thought he might have licked the blood from his cheek.

The boy coughed, spattering Heth with red droplets.

"Jerik!" Heth cried as the boy's eyes opened and found him. "Be still. Be still."

"Heth . . ." he rasped. "I'm sorry, I'm so sorry."

"It's nothing," Heth assured him, gently brushing his fingers through the boy's matted hair. "We're fine. Selavin is dead. His heart is over there, but the rest of him is still up on the balcony."

"That . . . bastard. Good. He . . . he took me. Hurt me. I wouldn't . . . I wouldn't have said anything, but . . . but . . . he has Ferra. I couldn't let him hurt her, had to talk . . ." He squeezed his eyes shut, his lips twisting into a wrenching sob. "I'm sorry."

"It's all right," Heth murmured, stroking his head.

The boy's eyes flew open again, and he clutched at Heth's arm with surprising strength. "It's not! She's still in there! Please, you have to save her . . . and . . . and she's not alone. Two others were brought this morning. They know you!"

"Who?" Deryn asked, his heart rising up into his throat. "What are their names?"

"Don't know," Jerik said, shaking his head weakly. "A girl with green eyes, and a woman . . . she spat in Selavin's face. He was so angry . . ."

"Rhenna and Alia," Deryn said, a sickness in his stomach. "It must be. There was a carriage that arrived before the dawn, no windows . . ."

"We have to save them," Heth said, then looked down at the boy in his lap. "We will save them all."

"It hurts . . ." Jerik hissed and then grimaced as his body was wracked by a spasm. The fingers curled around Heth's arm tightened, then relaxed as a rattling started deep in his throat.

Jerik's arm fell away, his mismatched eyes staring at the sky.

Heth bowed his head.

"I'm sorry," Deryn murmured. "I know he . . ." His words trailed off when he saw what was happening with Shade. The elemental was convulsing, dark ripples traveling across the shadowy substance of his form as a sound like nails being dragged across slate shivered the air. He was changing, Deryn realized. Growing larger, though keeping his feline form. They watched in astonishment as Shade swelled from the size of a house cat to something that at its shoulder reached Deryn's waist. From a distance, the elemental would have looked like one of the fell cats that had prowled the skyspear forests, animals large enough to kill a man and drag his body up a tree. The Salahi had both taken stumbling steps backwards, and now Zayin also had his blade in his hand, staring apprehensively at the still-trembling elemental. Shade was making a strange crooning sound now . . . and through the bond they shared Deryn could sense that this transformation had *hurt* the elemental. But Shade also thought it was necessary . . . because . . . because . . .

"Rhenna and Alia," Deryn breathed, stepping closer to the creature from the shadowrealm and laying his hand on its glistening back. It felt like flesh covered with cool, slick fur. Shade knew their friends were in danger.

Heth was also staring at the elemental, though he did not look as shaken as Deryn would have expected.

"You don't look surprised," Deryn said, swallowing back the dryness in his throat.

Heth turned to him, his gaze empty. "I just saw a sash tear a man's heart from his chest and then eat his head." He gave himself a small shake, as if to make sure he wasn't dreaming, and gently shifted Jerik's head from his lap. He rose, staring down at the boy's broken body. Deryn felt a pang of sorrow for Heth – he hadn't met the Hollow boy, but Heth had spoken about him several times. Jerik had been his friend, maybe the first true friend he'd made since they'd fled the Frayed Lands.

"Come on," Heth said, turning away and starting towards where the others had gathered. Deryn followed, Shade padding alongside him, and after sharing a long look the two Salahi joined them as well, making sure to keep their distance from the elemental.

Only three of the Unfettered had perished in the courtyard, though a few of those who remained had strips of blood-stained cloth wrapping limbs where they had been wounded. The one who seemed to have assumed leadership in Xend's absence – an older woman with steel-gray hair in battered but finely made plate – must have had a quarrel graze her brow, as she kept having to wipe away blood dripping from a shallow wound. There were also three wind-sharded warriors, though Deryn could not recognize their tribe from the tattoos twisting across their skin, and a massive bear of a man with a bristly beard who was arguing furiously with the armored woman. Whatever debate they were having died as they caught sight of the massive black shadowcat approaching. A few looks were exchanged with lips pursed, but to Deryn's surprise none of them brandished a weapon or cried out – they had evidently seen things in the service of the Unbound King. Including very recently.

"Does that creature serve you?" asked the gray-haired woman, arms folded across her scarred cuirass.

"It does," Deryn replied simply, and this seemed to immediately satisfy the woman as she shifted her attention away from Shade.

"All right, then. We're discussing the best course. Bhevash here wants to wait for Xend to return before we enter. I say we go in now before anyone can find their way to whatever secret passages lead from here."

"Xend won't be coming back quickly," Deryn said with a shake of his head. "There's an army of Wardsmen coming up the Skull. He said he was going to stay outside and help the Hollow and the Salahi fight them. And we can't wait – there are prisoners in there. Our friends. We're going in."

The woman grimaced, as if this news pained her. "Then that's that. We attack, cut the heads off the snakes."

The bearded man opened his mouth as if he wanted to argue more, but then seemed to think better of it. "Aye," he finally said in resignation, adjusting his grip on the haft of the great ax he held. "We go in."

40

HETH

They were in danger, maybe even dead already. Heth shook his head to banish that thought. No, no – Rhenna and Alia were alive, they must be. Selavin Thiss had been a cold bastard, but also a pragmatist. He wouldn't have killed them if they might be of some value later on. Daemonel on the other hand . . .

Heth hissed under his breath, his steps quickening. The corridor they were traversing was wide and high-ceilinged, with statues lining its length, and at its end was a huge set of silverwood doors incised with intricate carvings. There were no guards – likely whoever had once stood here was now in a red puddle back in the courtyard – but from the grandeur of this entrance, what lay beyond must be the meeting chamber of the Quinumvirate.

"Heth, slow down," Deryn said from behind him, panting as he struggled to keep pace. "You can't just rush in there. We have to make a plan—"

"No time," Heth said brusquely, though he did slow as he approached the massive doors. The carvings were of five shrouded figures set like they were points in a star, a sword and shield floating in the space between them. He laid his palm against the wood and pushed, and to his surprise, the door gave slightly.

Deryn grabbed his arm. "Heth. Stop."

Heth turned. The Salahi and the Unbound King's Unfettered had gathered behind him, having followed him on his reckless dash down the corridor. And reckless it had been, he suddenly realized – if there had been murder holes hidden the walls, they all could have been feathered by quarrels before reaching this door. "The longer we wait, the more likely those within will realize something is wrong."

"There might be a dozen crossbowmen just on the other side—"

"The boy is right," the woman in the battered plate said, interrupting Deryn. "The council is waiting for Selavin's return and news of Lord an-Azith's death. We should rush inside and subdue them before they realize things have not gone to plan."

"We must save our friends. That's all I care about right now."

Palimas ducked her head slightly. "Do what you will, though we might need all the swords we can muster." She placed both hands flat on the great door. "Now, show no mercy," she said, pushing forward. Heth flinched as the doors swung wide, expecting a volley of crossbow bolts, but it seemed that word of what had happened outside in the courtyard had not yet made its way this deep into the fortress.

The meeting chamber was vast, with a high ceiling covered with colorful frescoes and a huge window of many-colored glass taking up much of the far wall. The stained light pouring through drenched a table of glistening black stone set up on a dais, and the finely dressed men and women who had been seated around it leaped to their feet as they entered. A tall, gray-haired man was the first to react, gesturing wildly at them.

"Guards!" he cried. "Kill them!"

Figures surged from where they had been waiting in the chamber's recesses. Heth glimpsed the sigil of the Sword emblazoned on the white surcoats of Wardsmen, but many of the warriors rushing forth were as varied as the Unbound King's entourage – at their vanguard was a massive Ashasai wearing only a black loincloth and brandishing a pair of what looked like the same sort of hand-sickles used to cut wheat, his bulging copper belly laced with old scars.

Behind him were several slim women with unbound, green-dyed hair and armor of gleaming bronze scales. They were making shrill ululations, the unnatural sound unlike anything Heth had heard before. There were also crimson-scaled zemani, and a dwarf in motley carrying a warhammer nearly as big as he was.

All this Heth saw in an instant, and then the People of the Wind screamed their own war cries as they leaped forward to meet the council's guardians. The Salahi followed, curving swords flashing, and to Heth's surprise Deryn and his white blade were right behind them. The sight of his friend throwing himself into the fray even without his Sharded strength snapped Heth from his paralysis, and he pulled his own sword from its sheath as he charged ahead.

The two sides came together with a rending clash. One of the wind-sharded thrust his spear of pale wood through the neck of a Wardsmen, then twisted away to avoid being slashed by the blade of a green-haired swordswoman. The large bearded man who seemed to have some authority among the followers of the Unbound King was unfortunate enough to be in the path of the enormous Ashasai, who easily knocked aside his ax before separating his head from his shoulders with a vicious blow from a hand sickle. That was all Heth could glimpse from the larger battle before he found himself face to face with one of the red-scaled zemani – for a moment fear gripped him as he remembered the feeling of claws tearing his flesh, but then this vanished beneath a hot swell of rage. The lizard man croaked a challenge and swung its scimitar, neck frills that Heth had never seen before on one of these creatures flaring. Steel rang as he parried this first attack, then the next and the next, the strength behind each blow sending a painful jolt up his arm. He'd forgotten what it was like to fight without his Sharded strength and speed, and unless he summoned some of the old skill he'd once shown in the sword halls this lizard man was going to soon carve him to pieces. The zemani's head spines shivered in excitement as it pressed its advantage, and Heth was just about to lunge forward in a desperate counter attack when a whirling blur in the robes of a desert warrior appeared. The lizard man reeled back, clutching at a deep cut in its shoulder, and the veiled Salahi flowed after it, curved sword flickering. Another gaping wound opened in the zemani's throat before it collapsed, dark blood speckling Heth's face.

Then the Salahi was gone, spinning away to find another enemy. Heth stared after him in dazed surprise before shaking himself and taking stock of what had happened in the first few heartbeats of the battle. Their side seemed to have the upper hand, as the Salahi and the People of the Wind were tearing through the council's guardians, but there were a few pockets of stiff resistance – the three green-haired women were fighting back to back to back in a style so coordinated it almost looked like a dance, and elsewhere a space had been cleared for the huge Ashasai and Zayin, who were circling as if taking the measure of each other. Deryn was one of a half-dozen Unfettered around the swordswomen trying to find a gap in the defense their whirling swords were weaving.

Alia and Rhenna. For all he knew, they would be executed as soon as whoever was guarding them realized the fortress was under attack. He had to find them. Heth glanced from the raging battle to the council members gaping at the chaos from atop the dais to where a handful of servants cowered against the wall. They would have answers. There was an old man and a few young girls, all of them hunkered beside a long side-table covered with decanters and platters of food. They looked to have been trapped between the council's dais and the rebels and now were trying to avoid drawing any sort of attention. Heth took one last look at the swirling chaos to make sure that his sword was not desperately needed and then dashed across the chamber.

The girls shrieked and covered their faces when he arrived bloody and panting, and the old man gaped in fear up at him like he was the spirit of death incarnate. Heth reached down and grabbed the collar of the servant's tunic – perhaps he could use the man's terror to his advantage.

"Three women!" Heth cried, trying to look menacing. "Prisoners. They were brought here today. Where are they?"

The old man's watery eyes blinked rapidly, his mouth opening and closing soundlessly.

Perhaps he was a bit too frightening, Heth thought, now hoping that the servant wouldn't pass out. He let go of the man and turned instead to the other servants. Only one of them dared to meet his eyes, a girl that couldn't have seen more than ten summers.

"Three women," Heth repeated, trying to sound less terrifying, though this attempt was undermined somewhat when someone behind him in the hall loosed a blood-curdling shriek. "One has golden hair. Another black as night."

To Heth's relief, his words seemed to penetrate her shock. She raised a trembling hand, pointing at a small door on the far side of the room. She said something that was lost to the clash of metal and the screams of the dying, but Heth thought it might have been 'cells'.

Cells. A wave of relief washed over him – they hadn't executed Alia and Rhenna yet.

Heth turned from the servants and made for the far door, skirting the edges of the battle. The rebels most certainly were winning now – only a handful of the bodyguards were still alive, including one of the green-haired swordswomen standing over the body of her sisters, milk-white tears streaming down her cheeks as she kept the flickering spears of the wind-sharded at bay with a breathtaking display of skill. The outcome of that fight was inevitable, Heth knew, but less certain was the other duel that seemed to have drawn the attention of most everyone else. The monstrous Ashasai, his glistening copper flesh laced with fresh cuts, was trading blows with Zayin in an exchange that was almost too fast to follow. The old Salahi's sword was a blur as he fended off the flashing hand-sickles, each clash so loud that Heth was surprised one of the weapons had not yet shattered. A few of the Unfettered were poised to leap into the fray, waiting for their chance to intervene, though they seemed almost mesmerized by the duel. Then Zayin was a heartbeat late on a counter and one of the curving sickles scored his shoulder, opening up a red gash. He stepped backwards, putting some distance between himself and the Ashasai, and the waiting Unfettered began to surge forward . . . only to halt as

Zayin held up his hand angrily and shouted at them to stop. The Ashasai saw this and grinned, baring pointed teeth like a beast, then slammed his sickles together again and laughed.

No time. Heth dragged his attention from the fight and pulled open the wooden door. A flight of stairs spiraled downwards into darkness, and Heth started on the steps before he could allow himself to consider staying.

Down and down he went, the sounds behind him fading until all he could hear was the scuffing of his boots on stone. Smoldering torches lit the way, but many had gone out and at times he descended in darkness. Heth strained to catch any noises rising up from below, but the silence was so seamless he might as well have been back deep beneath the ruins of the Winter Palace.

The stairs finally ended at another unassuming door. Heth grasped the iron ring dangling from its wood, then took a deep breath and pulled. The chamber on the other side was better lit, a crude chandelier hanging from the high ceiling illuminating a round table where two Wardsmen sat, rows of round white stones placed between them. So intent were they on whatever game they were playing that they only looked up when Heth stalked closer – and then their hands scrabbled for the hilts at their sides as they lurched to their feet, pieces scattering. Heth cut them down before they could scream a warning, his blade taking one in the face and the other in the gap where his gorget joined his cuirass. It felt like something else was guiding his hand, and he was shocked by how easily he had just slain two men.

Another door. Heth wrenched it open and found a larger chamber, its recesses lost to darkness. Rusted cages lined the wall to his left, and he glimpsed movement within these as the door banged against stone. He thought he might have caught a flash of golden hair, but he didn't stop to see if it was indeed Alia, because his attention was fixed on what was in the middle of the room. Rhenna slumped in a chair, hands bound, her head hanging so that her dark hair veiled her face. For a moment Heth thought she was dead, but then she stirred slightly, lifting her arms and making a weak attempt to free herself from the leather straps binding her wrists. Behind her was Daemonel Thiss, his hands resting on two of the many sharp implements arrayed on a high bench, his mouth open and eyes wide.

Heth rushed towards him, but skidded to a halt after only a few steps when the fat man pulled Rhenna's head back and placed the serrated edge of a wicked-looking knife to her neck. Blood smeared her face, and her eyes fluttered as she fought for consciousness.

"You!" gasped Daemonel, piggish eyes flicking to the open doorway and the sprawled corpses of the Wardsmen visible in the room beyond.

"Heth!" cried a familiar voice, and Heth glanced at the cages and saw that Alia had pressed herself against the bars. Jerik's sister was in the cell beside her, and although her face was darkened by bruises she had not been cowed, as her mouth was twisted into a hateful snarl.

"Do not harm her, Thiss," Heth said adjusting his grip on his sword's hilt, "and I'll let you leave this room alive."

"How did you get in here?" Daemonel shot back, positioning himself so that Rhenna was between them.

"I walked in the front door," Heth replied, taking a small step forward. "After stepping over Wardsmen corpses and the heart of your uncle."

Daemonel hissed, and Heth stopped again as a trickle of blood slid down Rhenna's neck.

"They're dead," Heth continued, watching that single droplet until it disappeared beneath the collar of Rhenna's tunic. "They're all dead. Give yourself up now and you can beg the Unbound King for mercy. Otherwise, this ends with my sword in your gut."

Daemonel grimaced, and for a moment Heth feared he was going to draw his blade across Rhenna's throat. "Mercy?" he cried. "Mercy from *that one*? No, I'm leaving. *We're* leaving. There's a passage here out into the city. You're going to go first, Sharded scum, and if you so much as turn around and look at me, I'll cut this wench's head clean off. Do you understand?"

"Kill this bastard," Rhenna murmured through bloody lips, and Daemonel cuffed her in the back of her head.

"Silence!" he screamed, then gathered a fistful of her hair and yanked her upright again.

Heth tensed, readying himself to lunge at Daemonel, but a shiver in the shadows made him hesitate, cold fear pooling in his stomach. Oh, Broken God, it was here, that thing from the torture chamber, that dog-monster, it had followed him . . .

Huge black claws materialized on Daemonel's arm. The knife dropped from his fingers as blood poured forth, and the fat man turned to gape at the curving shards of darkness disappearing into his flesh. Then over his other shoulder a monstrous black head swelled, and jaws clamped down with enough force that Heth heard the crunch of shattering bones.

"*Ahhgh!*" Daemonel shrieked as he was dragged backwards into the darkness. His cry ended abruptly, replaced by wet tearing and snapping sounds. Fear was thrumming in Heth, but he had to be ready when whatever that thing was finished with Daemonel – he stepped forward with his sword raised, prepared to fling himself forward to protect Rhenna . . .

. . . then gasped in relief as Shade padded from the darkness with Daemonel's head dangling from its mouth. The elemental dropped it on the stone, then gave the head a strong whack with a paw that sent it tumbling away before settling back on his haunches in front of Rhenna.

"Shade," Heth said, warily approaching the shadow cat.

"Is this . . ?" slurred Rhenna as Shade laid his huge head in her lap, staring up at her.

"It's the elemental," Heth said, coming closer to cut her bonds. "It changed."

Rhenna placed her trembling hand between the shadow cat's black ears. "Good kitty," she murmured exhaustedly as a rumbling emanated from Shade's rippling depths.

Mostly convinced that this new version of the elemental wasn't about to savage Rhenna as well, Heth turned towards the cages holding Alia and Ferra. They were both wearing expressions of dazed shock, staring at the elemental. He hurried over to Alia and she reached through the bars to clutch at his arm as he examined the lock on the cage door.

"The guards outside had keys!" she exclaimed, still looking past Heth to Rhenna and the elemental. "Is that Shade? What happened? Is Deryn here? Where's the man in gray, is he dead?"

Heth opened his mouth to explain how he had ended up down here, but then turned to Ferra when he noticed that she was gesticulating frantically, trying to get his attention. Sweat glistened on her face as she struggled to pull forth words.

Heth flinched; he knew what she was trying to ask.

"Br ... broth ... broth ..."

Heth swallowed, giving his head a small shake. "I'm sorry," he whispered, and Ferra collapsed, the sound rising up from deep inside her unlike anything he had heard before.

THE FIGHTING HAD FINISHED by the time they returned to the council chamber. The corpses of the bodyguards had been heaped at the bottom of the steps leading up to the dais where the heads of the five families sat stiffly. Only the tall, gray-haired man was staring down at the rebels in something other than fear, his thin lips curled in contempt. The Unbound captain in tarnished armor must have just finished saying something as they emerged from the stairs leading to the cells, because she was looking up at the man expectantly with her arms crossed, and after a moment he slowly rose to offer a response.

Before he could begin, Heth quickly glanced about looking for Deryn. He breathed a sigh of relief when he saw him standing beside Zayin, apparently unscathed – the Salahi warrior, on the other hand, had not escaped entirely unhurt, as he was holding a blood-darkened piece of cloth to a wound on his shoulder. Heth hoped that the Ashasai had not poisoned his blades, as he'd heard that this was a common practice in the bloodpits. There would be no asking the

Ashasai if he had, because the pit fighter's massive corpse was splayed out on the floor, his head cleanly separated from his shoulders.

"Palimas Jorel," the gray-haired man said, his voice deep and commanding. "You would be wise to throw down your arms and beg forgiveness. Your audacious little raid here may have succeeded, but the war is unwinnable. Any moment now, our Wardsmen will finish crushing your ragtag little rebellion and reach this fortress. When they do, it would be best for you if we are unharmed – a quick, clean death could be yours, rather than a messy, drawn-out affair. I know your father, woman. He would not want to see you degraded in death."

A sharp hiss came from beside Heth, and he turned to see that Ferra had emerged from the stairwell leaning heavily on Alia, her withered leg trembling from the stress of climbing the steps. Heth had gone ahead to make sure it was safe, though he knew all three of the girls would have charged out into the chamber if the battle had still been raging. Even Alia – sweet, peaceful Alia – looked like she was ready to inflict violence.

"We will wait for Xend, Lord Bharach," Palimas replied in a matter-of-fact tone.

The gray-haired man – who Heth now realized was the Shield of Karath and the head of the powerful Bharach clan – scowled, his sharp blue eyes narrowing in disgust. "I thought I might show you mercy, since we share the same noble blood, but now I see you are as much a mongrel as—"

"Callister! We missed you at the mid-autumn fete this year!" A jovial voice rebounded in the great space, and all eyes turned to the chamber's entrance where a man had just strolled inside with his thumbs hooked into the crimson sash wrapped around his waist. If it wasn't for that piece of clothing – or whatever it was – Heth might not have realized that this was Xend an-Azith, as the Unbound King was so coated in gore that he looked unrecognizable.

"Xend," Callister Bharach managed through clenched teeth,

leaning forward with his knuckles pressed against the black-stone table. "You traitor."

"I prefer 'liberator'," Xend said, almost swaggering as he crossed the room and started to ascend the steps of the dais.

"You've done well," Callister said after taking a moment to master himself once more. "It's impressive that you've come this far. But we have thousands of swords and the outcome is inevitable."

When he reached the top, Xend motioned for a pale, scared-looking boy dressed in a ridiculously ostentatious outfit of fur and feathers to vacate his chair. Almost immediately the boy flung himself to his feet and swept out his arm, inviting Xend to sit. Which he did with a satisfied grunt, leaning back as he laced his hands across his stomach and placed his feet up on the table. His boots were just as filthy as the rest of him, as if he had just waded across a river of blood.

Which he might have. Heth had seen what had happened in the courtyard.

And Lord Bharach clearly had not.

"Callister, Callister, Callister . . ." Xend began, shaking his head in something like exasperation. "You know, I've always appreciated the way you comport yourself. So stern! So unyielding! It's truly quite admirable. But now, in this moment, is when you must bend. Bend your principles, along with your knee, and name me the king of Karath."

Lord Bharach's face twisted in fury. "We'll never be ruled over by one such as you, Ashasai! I would rather my dog—"

A flash of crimson, and suddenly Xend's red sash was wrapped around the old man's head. Lord Bharach jerked backwards in surprise, his hands reaching up to tear away what had blinded him, but before his fingers could even brush the cloth there was a sound like a great egg cracking and the sash seemed to collapse inwards upon itself. Then with the languid movements of a sated predator it uncoiled from the nub of flesh where Lord Bharach's head had once been and slowly undulated through the air back to Xend. Still smiling broadly, the lord of the Unfettered laid his hand on the end of the rippling cloth and stroked it like it was a beloved pet. For a heart-beat the body of the Shield of Karath stayed standing, swaying, then it toppled forward to sprawl across the table, blood spurting from the stump of its neck to slide across the black stone.

For a moment, no one moved or spoke.

Then an old woman in a shimmering green shawl leaped with surprising spryness to her feet and bowed her head in the direction of Xend.

"All hail Lord an-Azith, the first king of Karath!"

The crimson sash, still dripping with blood, slithered its way back around Xend's midsection as this cry was picked up and echoed throughout the hall.

41

DERYN

They wasted no time with the coronation. The sky outside the great stained windows had barely begun to darken when a silver circlet was placed on Xend's brow by the old woman who had first proclaimed him king. Lady Wertha, Deryn had discovered, was the head of the powerful Chaim family. She was known in the lower city to be wily and pragmatic, and those traits had been on full display during this long and exhausting day. She had thrown her support behind Xend with startling enthusiasm, as if she had read the messages in the oracular bones and realized that this would be an opportunity for her clan to rise above their rivals. A veritable army of Chaim retainers had been summoned from the family's nearby estates and set to work assisting those servants who had not been traumatized by the day's events with disposing of the corpses, scrubbing blood from stone, and bedecking the fortress with decorations worthy of Karath's first king in centuries.

Deryn felt a surreal sense of displacement standing in the fortress's great hall after Xend had been crowned, surrounded by nobles from the Skull, Hollow from the Nethers, and the Unfettered. Servants threaded between each faction, offering glasses of blue and red wine and a variety of sliced meats and snails on silver trays. There was not much mingling, but also far less friction than Deryn had expected – Caden and his Hollow brethren seemed to be in a dazed stupor, as if they couldn't believe where they had come to find themselves in the span of a day, and the nobles from the families seemed equally perplexed about this sudden turn of events. Fayraz and her Salahi had declined Xend's invitation to attend the ceremony, claiming that they needed to return to the *qenari* and inform the rest of their people about what had transpired. Some would choose to stay in Karath, Zayin had predicted before leaving earlier, but only a few.

"Do you think he'll be a good king?" Deryn asked, his gaze on the knot of important people surrounding Xend. Heth was among them, as was Caden Vars – the Hollow boss was speaking with so much passion that he was punctuating his words with sharp gestures, and the frowns on the faces of the flamboyantly dressed nobles listening to him aptly demonstrated their opinion about what he was saying. Xend had his hand on the shoulder of the Hollow boss, and Deryn hoped that Caden's concerns were being appreciated by the one ear that truly mattered.

"The Unfettered love and fear him," Alia said, then blanched and visibly recoiled as a passing servant proffered a tray of glistening snails. There was a slight purpling on her arm where she had been handled roughly, but otherwise she seemed to have escaped the day unscathed. Rhenna had resisted their abduction more forcefully and suffered significantly more, but she had still insisted on staying in the fortress to witness Xend's coronation. Deryn had to restrain himself from flinching every time he glanced at her bruised face, but if she was in pain, she was hiding it well.

"Saelus told us that love and fear were the keystones every successful reign was built upon . . . although my father disagreed. He believed love could be replaced with respect."

"Everyone respects your father now," Deryn said. "They have to."

"Yes," Rhenna said softly. "They do."

The Nether's Rebellion, as it was already being called, and the Unbound King's ascension had stunned the city, but something had happened in the wider world of such immense magnitude that half the conversations at this moment in the hall were discussing the news.

The Shadow had turned on the armies of the Storm after the Flame had been extinguished. Cael Shen had slaughtered the storm-sharded in the Ember and then led his army to lay siege to the Wind-wrack. Baelin Khaliva was dead, along with most of his Wardens. The fall of the Storm holdfast seemed inevitable . . . along with the estab-lishment of an empire the likes of which had not been seen since the days of the Radiant Emperor. The web of the White Spider now covered the entirety of the north.

Deryn did not doubt that it was only a matter of time before it spread further. The memory of their time in the House of Light retained the hazy unreality of a half-remembered dream, but the revelations shared by the Elowyn Menahla remained undimmed – Leantha desired nothing less than to make herself the ruler of every-thing, as her father had been before her. Cael Shen had to be turned from the dark path she had led him down before he plunged the world into fire and blood. They needed the one shadow-sharded with the strength to oppose the lord of the Duskhold, the only one held in high enough regard to muster real opposition . . . or perhaps even sway his father's heart.

They needed Azil Shen. And he was closer than they had believed. The Duskhold was far away, a month of travel at least even on the swiftest of horses, but the Windwrack was only ten days' journey north, and perhaps could even be reached in less time if Heth was successful in convincing the Unbound King to lend them aid.

"Oh, they're coming this way," Alia said, and Deryn saw that Xend had disengaged from the sycophants clamoring for his attention and begun to make his way towards them, the crowd parting like he was a flame pressed to paper. A fitting reaction to a newly crowned king, but Deryn wondered if the speed with which they drew back was mostly due to the crimson sash wrapped around his waist – by now, everyone knew what sort of creature protected Xend. Heth followed a pace behind, and Deryn couldn't tell from his expression whether he'd been granted the favor they had requested.

"King Xend," Deryn said, dropping to one knee and bowing his head. Rhenna and Alia mirrored him, though he noticed that the Wild girl did not lower her eyes to the stone, instead staring brazenly at the towering Ashasai.

"Stand, stand," Xend commanded, laying his hand on Deryn's shoulder and pulling him up. "No need to bow and scrape. I've never liked being called a king before, and I won't start now."

"And yet you asked for the crown," Rhenna said, and Deryn winced. Alia respected authority only grudgingly, but for the daughter of Cael Shen, the problem was different: she was used to speaking whatever was on her mind and was not intimidated by anyone.

Still, Xend did not seem to care about her impertinence, and he even chuckled, shaking his head as they rose. "The crown is a burden I must bear, because there is no one else in the city strong enough to keep order. What if Caden Vars had tried to make himself ruler? The families would never accept this. And what about another council, no longer a Quinumvirate but one where a Hollow and Salahi and Unfettered sat beside Wertha Chaim? There would be blood on the table before the first meeting was finished. No, Karath needs me." He smiled and then sighed deeply. "Unfortunately."

Heth cleared his throat, and Xend blinked as if remembering why he had just crossed the chamber. "Ah. Yes. Heth here tells me that the news of the Windwrack's siege has upset you all greatly because you have family there that you're worrying about. I warn you, with the Shadow occupying Flail, it will be very dangerous to enter the city. But he insists you must go."

Deryn nodded. "Yes. We want to leave as soon as possible."

"And you want to arrive quickly," Xend said. "So I've agreed to lend you one of my most trusted lieutenants, Green River Flowing. He is wind-sharded, and has the Wind Dragon talent. He could have you on the outskirts of Flail within two days. Not too close to the city, because I don't want to lose him to the Shadow."

Deryn swallowed, trying to keep his excitement from showing in his face. Heth had managed to secure exactly what they had wanted. Hopefully the siege would last at least a few more days, so that Azil would still be in the city when they arrived.

"We thank you, King," said Rhenna, sounding as grateful as Deryn had ever heard her. "If Fortune favors us, we can return quickly from Flail – I know Heth has obligations here that he must keep."

Xend brow creased in surprise, and he turned slightly to Heth. "You're going to Flail?"

"Of course he's going," Rhenna said, apparently not caring that she was not the one being addressed. "Heth has family in the north as well."

Now it was Deryn's turn to feel a frisson of surprise. Heth's expression had become pained, but not at Xend's question . . . rather, he was looking at Rhenna in something like apology.

"I'm not," he finally said, and then after a small pause hurriedly continued. "I made promises here to the Hollow and the Salahi . . ." he flashed a quick glance at Xend ". . . and to the Unfettered. To lead them to where I found the Light shard."

"That can wait," Rhenna said, her voice rising in frustration. "Surely it will take weeks for everyone to ready themselves for the journey. You told them that the shard resides in a distant land, yes?"

Heth nodded. "They know the way will be long and dangerous, since we will be passing through lands claimed by the northern holds. But as Caden Vars said, this moment, right now, would be the best time to go. The army of the Duskhold is encamped in Flail besieging the Windwrack. We should take advantage of this distraction while it persists, for if the rumors are true . . . it won't be overlong."

Rhenna folded her arms tightly across her chest, glowering at Heth. She had always thought this rebellion he'd fomented had been just a promise made recklessly to escape from the Unfettered after the Sword had brought him to Xend, but Deryn had suspected that Heth was far more invested in overthrowing the city. It was obvious that during his time in the Nethers Heth had come to care deeply about the plight of many of its inhabitants.

"Have you thought this through?" Rhenna asked, clearly exasperated. "This isn't a caravan crossing the Middle Lands. It's a *migration*. Thousands of people, including many families with young children. It will be slow and vulnerable. How will you protect them all? A scouting party of shadow-sharded or a few Unbound raiders could slaughter the lot of you."

Xend held up jewel-encrusted hands, as if trying to placate Rhenna. "I owe our allies a great deal, and I also wish to know more about this Light shard. I am sending two dozen Unfettered with Heth, including Aziza, my most trusted advisor. They will ensure this . . . *migration* reaches its destination."

"The greatest danger would be encountering a large force of shadow-sharded," Heth explained. "Which is why we must leave soon, while the army of the Duskhold is in the north."

Rhenna scowled, but Deryn could tell that she was finally starting to accept his reasoning. Then she blinked, as if something else had just occurred to her, and she shot Heth a triumphant look. "Food. You might be able to take enough supplies with you for the journey, but I also know where the Light is hidden. It's barren and inhospitable. The land there cannot sustain thousands of folk – you'll starve if you try to stay any length of time."

Heth winced, and at first Deryn thought this reaction was because he hadn't considered what Rhenna had just pointed out. Then he realized the real reason as Alia stepped forward.

"That's why I'm going with him," Alia said softly, looking up apologetically at Rhenna through lowered lashes.

"You're *what*?" exclaimed Rhenna, her hands balled into fists.

A trickle of worry wormed its way through Deryn – surely it must be obvious by now that Rhenna was someone of significance, as very few would dare show such emotion in front of a recently crowned king, but Xend looked more amused than anything else watching this little drama unfold.

"I'm going with Heth," Alia repeated, stepping forward and

raising her head to look Rhenna directly in the eye. "He needs me; all those people need me. I can make crops grow quickly in the thinnest soil, I know this. No one will go hungry if I'm with them."

"But what about . . ." Rhenna began, then swallowed back whatever she had been on the verge of saying. ". . . Flail?"

Alia reached out to touch Rhenna's arm lightly. "Come to us when you're finished there. You should be able to catch us before we reach where we're going."

Rhenna frowned, but Deryn could tell her anger was fading as quickly as it had appeared. She looked more miserable than anything else. "We have such important things to do . . ."

"I know," Alia said, giving her arm a squeeze. "But this is important, too."

"Truly, what could be more important than this?" Xend interjected, grinning broadly. "The establishment of a new hold! The Salahi returning to the ranks of the Sharded Few! The Hollow claiming shards! If that happens, every Hollow in the world will try to slip their chains and make for your new hold." He shook his head, clearly awed by the implications of this. "The world will never be the same!"

"No," Rhenna murmured, almost sadly. "It most certainly won't."

42

KALISS

I t was smaller than she had expected.

When the armies of Shadow had first entered Flail and begun to ascend its tiers, the Windwrack had been a mysterious, brooding presence far above, wreathed by flickering storm clouds that allowed only partial glimpses of the fortress. Constant grumbles of thunder had rolled down the mountain's slope, as if the hold were a massive beast trying to warn away an intruder that had invaded its domain. For eight days ancient defenses had held the Shadow at bay – assaults led by Azil and Joras Shen had been repulsed, great blasts of lightning consuming the weaker shadow-sharded who had lifted from Flail's highest tier on their Black Discs and forcing the strongest to retreat. The last of the legendary Wardens, Deveris Moonfire – who had stayed behind when the army of the Storm had marched to war with the Ember – had even emerged to taunt the shadow-sharded after Joras had fled the field, his pearlescent armor glimmering as he floated out from within the billowing dark clouds. Cael Shen had lifted on his own Disc to formally offer the chance to surrender and spare the lives of those within, but the Warden had only laughed. Cael had then suggested a duel, his amplified voice echoing over the city, with the promise that his army would withdraw if he fell. In reply, Deveris had spat at the lord of the Duskhold hovering below, naming him faithless, and then withdrawn again into the churning black.

Two days later, not long after the last shreds of twilight had vanished from the sky, Cael Shen and his *famdhar* had risen again from the city and plunged into the clouds. Flashes had illuminated Flail, blinding some who had been unfortunate enough to be looking up, and the sounds that issued forth from within the storm had made it seem like the mountain itself was being torn asunder.

Then, nothing. No rending crashes, no stuttering brilliance. When the dawn finally broke, it revealed a white-stone fortress perched on a ledge much smaller than Flail's other tiers. Of the storm that had perpetually swaddled the hold, there was no sign. All had been still and silent, as if the fortress was abandoned – the only evidence that it had recently been inhabited was a web of shadows spread across the outer wall of the inner keep, in the center of which hung the body of a man clad in shining armor.

All this Kaliss had witnessed from her balcony. Like the vast majority of the shadow-sharded, she had been given quarters in the Aureate Tier, the highest level of Flail proper and only a few hundred span below where the Windwrack's storms had endlessly surged. Noble villas and luxurious inns had been requisitioned for the army of Shadow, and while the amenities were excellent, far nicer than anything in the Duskhold, every Sharded in the city had wished they could have been part of that final assault on the Windwrack. Some – mostly *kenang* – had been allowed to enter the holdfast after it had fallen, tasked with searching for hidden treasures and helping round up the surviving wind-sharded. Kaliss had begged to be one of these lucky ones, but she'd been rebuffed by the *famdhar* who had been given command over her after she had been dismissed from Leantha's service.

It was so unfair. There were shards to be gained in the Windwrack, and Sharded artifacts of great power. She had been instrumental in the fall of the Ember, had witnessed the death of Lord Char and Bailen Khaliva, and yet now it seemed like she had been entirely forgotten, just another low-ranked Sharded left to struggle over whatever scraps the powerful decided weren't worth claiming.

Kaliss scowled up at the Windwrack, then pushed herself away from the wrought-iron balustrade and strode back into her quarters. She flung herself down on the great canopied bed, staring up at the layers of lacy gauze hanging above her. This place reminded her of the lavish bedrooms she'd slipped into while in the service of Mazim Chain. Bedroom balconies had often been the easiest way to enter those manses, as they were most likely to have been left unlocked.

Which was why Kaliss had made sure hers was always secured at night. It wasn't the common folk of Flail she feared, or some vengeance-seeking storm-sharded who had escaped the Windwrack's fall . . . no, she'd been having a recurring nightmare in which she woke to find Leantha looming over her, poised to plunge the haunted dagger into her chest. Foolishness, of course, to think Leantha would decide to murder her . . . or that locking the balcony door would prove any barrier if she did.

But it still made her feel better.

Sighing, Kaliss turned inward, working on gentling her *ka*. She suspected she was close to being able to merge another shard, but her troubled mind was making it difficult to find the concentration necessary to fully smooth her pathways. She closed her eyes, searching for that elusive calm, kneading the knots from the lines stretching throughout her body . . .

A knock sounded.

"Frozen hells," Kaliss snarled under her breath as her *ka* squirmed free. "Go away!" she shouted, her black mood darkening further.

Another knock.

Idiot servant, Kaliss thought, extricating herself from the bed's overly-soft clutches and stomping across the room. "Just leave the food outside!" she said, ripping the door open with such force that she nearly tore it from its hinges.

"Lord Shen," she gasped, hurriedly bowing her head in the

desperate hope that this would hide the flush she felt rising in her cheeks.

"Kaliss," Azil said mildly, as if he hadn't even noticed her outburst. "May I come in?"

"Of . . . of course," she stammered, sweeping out her arm to welcome him. "Apologies, my lord, I didn't know it was you."

"How could you?" the Black Sword of the Duskhold responded, gliding into the room. He always moved with such exquisite grace, Kaliss thought numbly. Like water flowing.

"The accommodations are sufficient?" he asked, slowly turning as his gaze swept her bedroom. Kaliss's face burned hotter, and she silently cursed herself for not cleaning up the remnants of her midday meal on the table or the clothes she'd left scattered about.

"They are, my lord," she replied, then decided to risk saying what had really leaped into her mind at this question. "The bed is too soft, though."

Azil chuckled. "I agree. We of the Duskhold are not used to being pampered. You should see inside the Windwrack – everything is draped with the finest fabrics and even the most common of items are gilded and encrusted with jewels. Can you imagine a golden bedpan? The shadow-sharded who found that thought someone had requested a midnight snack and then slipped the plate under their bed. It was Saelus who told him what it truly was, but only after he'd used it to deliver lunch to my uncle Joras."

Kaliss laughed at this, then clapped her hand over her mouth in embarrassment. Azil didn't seem to mind her impropriety, smiling slightly as he drifted across the room to gaze through the balcony's open doors at the Windwrack looming high above them.

Clearing her throat, Kaliss spent a moment composing herself before broaching the question that had been buzzing among the shadow-sharded ever since the holdfast had fallen. "And the Storm shard? Has it been brought down from the fortress yet?" The sensation when the Flame shard had been fed to the Shadow under the Duskhold had been the most intense in Kaliss's life, like a dam had suddenly broken inside her, the *ka* flowing from her shard strengthening even as it grew tumultuous and wild. Every shadow-sharded in the world had grown more powerful in that moment, and the same would happen again when the Storm shard arrived at the Duskhold.

Azil did not turn away from the soaring fortress. "The Storm shard is missing," he said, and from his tone he sounded less upset about this than Kaliss would have expected.

"How?" Kaliss asked in bewilderment. The army of the Duskhold had immediately marched to besiege the Windwrack after the fall of the Ember, only sending a small contingent led by Leantha back east to merge the Flame with the Shadow. The hope had been to trap all the remaining powerful storm-sharded before they could even think of fleeing, and it had seemed to work – the last Warden had chosen to die defending the hold in the exact kind of doomed, romantic gesture Cael Shen had predicted he would make.

"The Mother of Storms and her grandson," Azil said simply, finally turning away from the open balcony. "Somehow after evading us in the Ember they managed to arrive at the Windwrack first and flee with the Storm shard. The defense of the hold afterward was merely an attempt to buy them more time to escape."

Kaliss sat down on the edge of the bed, stunned. Everyone thought the Storm was on the brink of destruction, but in truth the war was not over. She wondered how many other storm-sharded had fled with them.

"We have hunters on their trail, but I doubt they'll catch her. Lady Khaliva is as canny as an old fox."

"Then . . . what will we do now?"

"My father plans to stay here and consolidate his power. Flail is the greatest city in the north, and it will be challenging bringing it under the Shadow, especially since the Duskhold is so far away. Eventually, I believe my uncle will remain here as lord, but it could also go to the Balenchases. They feel they are owed much after the death of their scion . . . though I also doubt my father would want to give his greatest rivals such a stronghold."

Kaliss shifted uncomfortably. Why was the Black Sword telling her all this? Surely the inner politics of the Duskhold were not for her ears.

"My lord," she ventured, rising from the bed. "If I may be so bold . . . why are you here? Why did you come to see me today?"

Azil finally turned to face her, the force of his attention making her swallow. "Because I wish to offer you a position in my house. I know that Leantha relinquished her role as your patron – otherwise you would have returned with her to the Duskhold – and I saw your worth on the day the Ember fell. It would please me if you entered my service."

Kaliss's jaw dropped. Had she fallen asleep earlier? Was this a dream?

"I . . . of course I accept, Lord Shen."

Azil smiled warmly, and Kaliss felt her heart flutter. "Excellent. Then you are now my retainer. I promise to protect and guide you, and in return, I expect your obedience in all matters."

"Of . . . of course," Kaliss stammered, her head still spinning.

"And it is customary that a patron offers a gift to seal such arrangements. Also, I owe you a very large debt for your deeds inside the Ember, for I am not sure that I would still be drawing breath if you had not hurled your Spear at the fire-sharded *famdhar*, even though it almost certainly should have meant your death."

"My lord," was all Kaliss could whisper in reply, her throat suddenly dry.

Azil reached into the folds of his robe and drew out a sword sheathed in a golden scabbard. "Unfortunately, its twin was lost in a river of flame beneath the Ember."

Kaliss felt numb. She had seen this sword at the side of the Falcon of the Fangs, and such a legendary warrior would only wield a Sharded artifact of great power. Azil drew forth the sword, and it slid from its sheath silently. She'd thought before that the blood-red substance of the blade was metal of some kind, but now she could see that it was moving slightly, sluggishly, roiling like . . . like . . .

Like blood.

"I do not know your relationship with your Ashasai heritage,"

Azil said, reversing the sword so that the gilded, ruby-encrusted hilt was extended towards her. "And I hope I have not insulted you by offering a blood-sharded weapon."

"Not at all," Kaliss murmured, hesitating only briefly before reaching out to take the sword. A tingling surged up her arm as she grasped the hilt, making her gasp. "Thank you, my lord."

43

DERYN

They soared over endless swells of red and gold leaves, a vast forest sea stretching to the horizon. The Wind Dragon undulated through the darkening sky like a puppy enjoying its freedom after being trapped inside for too long, swooping down to nearly brush the fiery canopy before ascending higher once more. Despite the Dragon's exuberance, Deryn was finding the experience far less terrifying than the last time he'd ridden such a creation of the wind-sharded. While the previous Wind Dragon had been virtually invisible and soft enough that he had felt at times like he was sinking into nothing, this one had an oily, iridescent sheen and its conjured substance was as solid as a creature of flesh-and-blood. If he closed his eyes and ignored the strength of the wind rushing over him, he could almost imagine that he was riding a horse bareback as it galloped across the Frayed Lands.

Deryn suspected that the Wind Dragon's behavior was a representation of what Green River Flowing was feeling, because he felt much the same. To have his Sharded strength flow back into his limbs and his senses sharpen once more after living for so long in Karath was exhilarating. He could tell that Shade's mood had improved also, although the now much-larger elemental had been forced to squeeze into Deryn's shadow for this journey. Rhenna . . . well, Rhenna was always difficult to read. She sat straight-backed halfway between Deryn and the wind-sharded along the Dragon's serpentine length, her attention intensely focused on the distant Fangs gnawing at the sky. Perhaps she was trying to think of how they could enter Flail and make contact with Azil without her father or any of the other shadow-sharded noticing.

That was what Deryn had been worrying about, although right now he was just trying to enjoy being beyond the influence of the City of the Dead. Were Alia and Heth also reveling in the return of their Sharded nature? They had borne their shards for less than a month before entering Karath, so for them losing their power hadn't been so jarring. Deryn suspected that they were quite distracted, particularly Heth. So many strong and proud leaders were part of their expedition heading east – Fayraz, Caden Vars, the enigmatic Ashasai Unfettered, Aziza – and none were willing to grant the others authority over their people, so Heth had been forced to assume leadership.

Perhaps surprisingly, Deryn felt confident that Heth could manage this fractious situation. He seemed so much stronger and more assured than when he had been one of the Duskhold's Hollow, or even before that, as a slaver's son. It was still hard to believe that he had somehow orchestrated the overthrow of a city.

"We will rest soon."

Deryn jumped in surprise, for it was as if Green River Flowing had spoken directly into his ear, even though the wind-sharded still straddled the Wind Dragon up near its head, his back to them. Rhenna twisted her head slightly, looking for something that wasn't there, and he knew she had also received the same message. Her lips moved, although what she spoke was taken by the wind.

Green River Flowing must have heard, though, as his response was immediate. "No. We have been flying all day, and it is tiring to maintain a Dragon for so long. I want my strength and my wits about me when we make our final approach to Flail."

Rhenna grimaced, but she did not try to argue. She knew the

dangers that awaited them better than anyone. If they did not exercise the utmost caution, they would end up in the hands of her father . . . or worse, Leantha. Though Deryn had to admit he was curious about what would happen if Rhenna returned to the shadow-sharded and revealed that the war with the Ember had been planned long ago by the White Spider. Would the shadow-sharded fracture from this revelation . . . or rally behind the warlord who had brought them to preeminence in the north? Deryn had a sinking suspicion that most of the shadow-sharded would grudgingly congratulate Cael Shen for the success of his masterstroke.

Not Azil, though. Azil would never forgive anyone – even his father – for sacrificing Rhenna on the altar of his ambitions.

"There. Something in the forest." Green River Flowing's clipped words materialized again in Deryn's ear. He squinted into the distance and spotted what the wind-sharded had already seen – an ancient white-stone ruin hunkered among the trees, and from the shattered remnants of the dome rising above the canopy, it looked like this had once been a temple to the Broken God from the days of the First Empire, though the forest had long since swallowed it. Better than sleeping on roots, Deryn supposed, although their time in the Winter Palace had demonstrated that remnants of the past sometimes lurked in the ruins of the old world. Still, Rhenna and Green River Flowing were both powerful Sharded, and lest he forget, he was *kenang* with a shadow fell cat companion. There was very little that could threaten them.

SPEARS OF DUSKY light pierced the canopy, illuminating a mossy forest floor and a few scattered chunks of white stone veined by vines and brambles. Something large and hunched hooted among the branches above them, but then quickly receded with a rustling of leaves. With his darkvision, Deryn could discern something ape-like hidden in the shadows, staring down at them in fearful stillness. Green River

Flowing did not even bother glancing up at the creature as he picked his way over roots towards the crumbling temple.

"It will rain tonight," the wind-shared said brusquely, not bothering to see if they were following. "I can taste it."

Deryn glanced up skeptically at the temple's shattered roof, wondering how much more protection they would find inside, but Rhenna was already striding after the wind-sharded, so he set aside his misgivings and followed. The ruins here had suffered far more depredations than the Winter Palace – its barren mesa had been battered by wind, but here the forest seemed to be devouring the temple. Its entrance was still intact, though listing slightly to one side, and cracks threaded its great white slabs of stone.

"If only the common folk knew the truth," Rhenna murmured.

"About the Broken God?"

Rhenna's lip curled, and she pointed to where the eroded carving of a sunburst was visible above the entrance. "We know his name now: Algeroth. He murdered the old world, along with his siblings." She shook her head. "Those fools mumbling their prayers and lighting candles in his temples all across these lands know nothing."

Deryn bit his lip. His mother had been one of those fools. He had never truly believed, but he had appreciated how much comfort she had derived from her faith.

"Well, once we stop Leantha, we can share what we've learned," Deryn said, taking the temple's crumbling steps two at a time. "Although it might be hard to convince anyone. The scholars at the Erudinium would dismiss us immediately, I'm sure, unless we bring evidence."

Rhenna said nothing else as they passed into the temple proper. Much of the interior was draped in shadows, the light trickling down through the remnants of the dome above puddling in the center of the large space. A few stunted, gnarled trees had broken through the floor, and dark water had collected in what might have once been bathing pools. Otherwise the temple was empty, although thick, mostly intact pillars formed a ring in its middle. Enough leaves and dirt had drifted into the ruin that Deryn thought they could make themselves somewhat comfortable, and they'd certainly be able to stay dry if it did rain.

"I suppose this will—"

A sharp gasp from Rhenna made him whirl. She had fallen to her knees with her head bowed, her entire body trembling like she was straining to stand but could not.

"What is it?" Deryn cried, reaching for his *ka* as he stepped towards her. She managed to turn her head slightly towards him, though her face was flushed from the effort.

He reached out to her, and then he felt it – a finely woven braid of hardened wind was coursing through the air, and he suddenly realized that several such bindings were striking her from different directions. This was the same talent that had been used against Yvrin in the Frayed Lands. Ripping his sword from his sheath, Deryn summoned his Ghost Chitin as he looked around wildly for the wind-sharded who had just forged a Cage around Rhenna.

A man moved out from behind one of the central pillars, a long spear in one hand and the other outstretched towards Rhenna. Deryn thought about charging at him, but he knew this wind-sharded was not alone – Yvrin has said the Wind Cage was a talent meant to be created in conjunction with others. A shiver of movement came from the shadows, and another wind-sharded stepped forward, his hand also extended towards where Rhenna had been immobilized.

Green River Flowing.

"What is going on?" Deryn shouted. "Why are you doing this?"

"Because you haven't been entirely honest, have you?"

That voice. Deep but honey-smooth, still friendly despite the circumstances. With some effort, Deryn turned away from where Rhenna was struggling against the invisible bonds.

Xend an-Azith stood in the circle of dusky light bounded by the broken pillars. He was not alone. The gray-haired woman in battered plate was beside him, her expression grim. And also . . . Deryn sucked in his breath. High Seeker Helash had traded the umber robes of the Erudinium for a bulky coat of silver fur, and in his hands he held what appeared to be an empty glass sphere. He was looking at Deryn with the same slightly distracted smile he'd often worn when fiddling with the contraptions in his workroom.

Rhenna. They must have realized who Rhenna was. Deryn's fear twisted into helpless despair – they were doomed, the power wielded by Xend alone would have made escape impossible, and the Unbound King had left nothing to chance. But why was the High Seeker here?

"Lord an-Azith," Deryn said, trying his best to keep his voice steady. Behind him, a strangled moan escaped from Rhenna, and the pain he heard made his heart clench. "I promise there's been some sort of misunderstanding."

Xend sighed as if disappointed, shaking his head. The crimson sash he wore rippled as it began to slither around his midsection. "Deryn, Deryn, Deryn. What were you looking for in the Erudinium? What interest have the Dukes taken in the affairs of our little world?"

"I . . ." Deryn began, unable to tear his eyes from the almost hypnotic undulations of the blood elemental as it twined itself around Xend. "I don't know what you're talking about. I was sent to discover what I could about the House of Last Light."

Xend waved his hand dismissively. "Oh, spare me your lies. You've already broken the heart of the poor High Seeker here."

"You don't understand. I had to know . . ." His voice trailed away as the serpent of blood lifted from Xend, writhing in the air. Deryn could feel the malice radiating from the elemental, a palpable sense of danger. He remembered the sound of Lord Barach's skull crumpling under its coils.

And he was not the only one who could sense the elemental's hostility. Shade was thrashing in his shadow, desperately trying to emerge, but for the first time ever Deryn tried his best to restrain him. This blood elemental was far too strong, but holding back Shade was like trying to keep a maddened dog from slipping its leash – slowly Shade squirmed from his grasp, breaching the edges of his shadow . . . and then the glistening black fell cat broke free, leaping towards Xend and his blood elemental.

"No!" Deryn cried, but in his heart, hope flared. Shade flowed through the air, massive claws unsheathed, jaws spread wide. Maybe . . .

Shade froze, and Deryn blinked in shock. The elemental was still in the act of jumping, long feline form arched, but he had suddenly become absolutely immobile. Through the bond they shared, Deryn could sense churning confusion – even the cat's tail had halted mid-lash.

Motes of darkness began to detach from Shade's body and drift away as if carried by an invisible wind. Deryn rushed forward, putting his hand on the elemental's flank – it was cool and yielded to his touch, his fingers sinking into the blackness. "Shade!" Deryn cried, feeling the elemental's bewilderment turn to panic.

The specks of darkness rising from the cat strengthened into a flurry, and before his horrified gaze Shade began to dwindle. A river of blackness formed, coursing from the elemental and twisting through the air to enter the glass sphere held by the High Seeker, which had darkened as more and more of the elemental was drawn inside.

"Stop!" Deryn snarled, lunging at the scholar with his sword upraised, poised to unleash its cutting wind . . . but then an invisible hand closed around him and he was smashed against the floor with such force that the hilt flew from his numb fingers. He lay there, dazed, unable to rise as an unseen force ground him into the ruin's broken stones, and he could only watch in stunned horror as the last of Shade was pulled into the now pitch-black sphere. Deryn tried to speak, but nothing emerged except a hoarse croaking. He couldn't even turn his head, forced to watch the High Seeker as the scholar stared in fascination into the shadowy depths of the globe until finally someone moved in front of Deryn, blocking his vision.

"So you were telling the truth," Xend said, and he realized that it was the Unbound King standing over him.

"Of course," replied the High Seeker.

"*Hm.* I'm not sure how I feel about the existence of such a device."

"It will never be used on your companion, that I promise you, and this is the only one known to have survived the fall of Gendurdrang."

Xend grunted something unintelligible, then crouched beside Deryn. He stared for a moment into Deryn's frightened eyes, and then there was the sound of leather ripping as Xend tore open his travel bag.

"Ah, here we go," murmured the king of Karath, dragging something out and holding it up to the last vestiges of daylight. The dusky piece of glass seemed to absorb the twilight, darkening the temple's interior.

"Perhaps a bit better security is needed," Xend suggested, straightening as he handed the fragment of the shadowrealm to one of his wind-sharded warriors. His blood elemental had risen higher, nearly vanishing through the hole in the roof, trembling as if agitated.

"I've already set a few of the zemani to guard the storeroom," High Seeker Helash said with a sniff, turning his hurt gaze to Deryn. "Such a shame, my boy. I liked you, I truly did. But I suppose this was the inevitable outcome once I knew *you* were the elementalist you had spoken about." He must have seen the surprise spark in Deryn's eyes. "Oh, come – did you truly think you could hide the existence of an elemental right under my nose? *Me*? I have made it my life's work to study the denizens of the primordial realms." He shook his head, making a clucking sound with his tongue. "You know, if you'd been honest—"

"If you'd been honest, this would have happened anyway," finished Xend as his blood elemental finally returned to coil about his waist. "Because you would have told me."

"Yes, yes, of course," mumbled the High Seeker, clearly chastened.

"Now," Xend said brightly, running his hand affectionately along his rippling elemental. "The charm of this rustic excursion has worn off for me. Let us return to my city."

Deryn felt the force immobilizing him adjust its grip, and then suddenly he was being dragged across the stone. His perspective changed, moving from Xend and the High Seeker to another section of the temple, the one with the pools of still dark water. Rhenna was also forcibly being pulled by invisible forces; she was struggling weakly, and he could just hear her piteous little mewls. Where was she ...

Oh. Deryn clenched his jaw so hard it felt like his teeth might break. No. Please no.

Rhenna had also realized where she was being pulled, but there was nothing she could do as the Wind Cage forced her into the water. She slid in with hardly a ripple, vanishing from sight.

He didn't want to drown. Not that. Anything but that.

He managed to somehow work a finger free from the bonds holding him tight, digging it into the floor so hard that the stone crumbled, but this didn't slow his approach towards the pool in the slightest. *No. No. No.* He remembered standing on the side of the pond where his mother had drowned herself, the waterfall roaring as it tumbled down the side of the mountain, imagining what she must have felt as her throat and lungs filled and she began to sink ...

Deryn pressed his lips together tightly as he was dragged head-first into the pool. The water reached up to envelop him ... but to his surprise it wasn't water but something else, something thicker and surprisingly warm and the taste that slipped past the seal he'd made of his mouth was sharp and coppery ... and familiar.

Screaming soundlessly, Deryn sank into a pool of blood.

44

HETH

The last red rays of the day trembled, as if imbued with a strange solidity. Heth almost felt like he could reach up to grasp the light and pull it from the sky, examine its contours, its odd angles and sharp crevices. Even though he had spent months in Karath with his connection to his shard severed, it seemed like his awareness had continued to deepen. These days he often found himself drawn into the wash of colors filling the sky, losing all track of time and purpose.

Just like now.

"Lord Su Canaav! My lord?"

The voice was distant, somewhere far below. Heth frowned, wanting to remain where he was, up here, reveling in the rich scarlet light flowing from the sinking sun.

But unfortunately, he knew he couldn't.

Heth blinked and shook his head, returning to himself. A scrawny man with a patchy beard was in front of him, his forehead creased in uncertainty. How long had this Hollow been trying to get his attention?

"Lord, sorry to bother ye, but I was hoping ye could come settle something for us."

Heth sighed, looking around. They stood in the center of camp, in the empty area that always appeared between the three factions. To his left, the beautifully embroidered tents of the Salahi stretched away across the grass in a profusion of small circles, each surrounding a shared fire, while on his right sprawled the far more chaotic Hollow camp, a jumble of crude shelters and hastily stitched sack-cloth tents. The far smaller contingent of Unfettered clustered around the trio of covered wagons the new king of Karath had given to his followers for the journey. No walking for the Sharded Few, even though they could walk from dawn to dusk without tiring.

"What is it?" Heth asked, trying to infuse this question with all the annoyance that had been slowly building during the day.

The Hollow didn't appear to notice. Of course.

"Well, see, Old Boona, she has this chicken."—*Oh, gods*—"She found it today, just clucking away in the grass when we was walking." —*gods save me*—"Grabbed it, of course, and now tonight she wrings its neck and is jus' about to throw it in the pot when this tall sand-bather walks up bold as can be and claims it's his,"—*gods, why*— "even that she had to pay, uh, what was that word he used . . . *recompense*."

The Hollow paused, looking at Heth like he should also find this outrageous. "And?" Heth finally asked as the silence stretched on.

The pronounced apple in the man's throat bobbed up and down. "Things are getting' a bit testy, you see. We was hoping you could tell the sandbathers that the chicken ain't theirs. Old Boona caught it fair and square."

Heth closed his eyes, searching for solace from the stupidity of the world. "Yerl," he finally said, suddenly remembering the Hollow's name. "How many chickens have we seen out here on the plains?"

Yerl's brow furrowed. "Just this one, my lord."

"Hm. Now, do you think it more likely that Old Boona caught a wild chicken native to these lands, or that she picked up a chicken that had indeed wandered away from its rightful Salahi owner?"

Yerl's jaw worked as he mulled this over, and to Heth he looked like a cow chewing its cud. Please, Silver Shrike, save him from all of this.

"So you're saying the chicken really was the Salahi's?"

Heth closed his eyes in frustration. "Yes, Yerl. And I do think something is owed to its owner. Tell Old Boona to find another chicken to replace the one she took."

Yerl frowned. "Old Boona ain't going to be happy."

Heth fought back the urge to scream. "Why didn't you go to Caden Vars with this problem first?"

"I did," Yerl said, wiping at his leaking nose. "He said to go see you."

Of course. Any disagreement between the factions inevitably seemed to get passed up to him, no matter how minor. Caden and Fayraz and Aziza always wanted to avoid being seen in direct conflict with each other.

Unfortunately.

It pained him to think it, but he wished he had someone like his father's old overseer Jogans to dispense justice and serve as a shield between him and everyone else.

Heth drew in a deep breath, arranged his face into a solemn expression, and placed his hand on the Hollow's bony shoulder. "Yerl. It's up to you to make this right. I will go talk with the Salahi *bhalgrasi* – you know her?"

A slow nod. "Aye. She puts the shivers in me."

"You do know her. Well, *I* happen to know that Salahi take matters of personal honor very seriously. Unless you want to put forth a champion to duel to the death so you don't have to compensate the Salahi for a chicken, I suggest you get Old Boona to pay up."

This time, the nod came much more quickly. "Aye, I'll do that."

"Good man," Heth said, giving Yerl a final clap on the shoulder before abruptly striding away. He was mentally preparing himself to hear the Hollow pipe up again with another ridiculous question, but apparently he needed to mull over what Heth had just said. Thank the Broken God.

Heth kept his eyes straight ahead as he moved purposefully

through the camp, afraid that someone else would attempt to waylay him if he caught their gaze. It wasn't until he ducked through the flap of his tent that he let himself sag in relief. Freedom. He was finally free . . . at least until tomorrow. He'd have to send someone to bring him back some supper, but there were always young Hollow dashing between the tents in the evening, and they all knew he was someone to be obeyed.

Heth threw himself down on the pile of blankets and furs he used as a bed and closed his eyes. The idea of falling asleep right now was appealing, though Alia would likely come by later to visit. She'd spent the day with the Unfettered in their little wagon train, as she had for most of the journey since they'd left Karath, in the company of a few Unbound she had become friends with back in the city who had surprisingly decided to leave Xend's service. There were only a few of them, as most of the honor guard that the Unbound King had sent with them would return to Karath after seeing them safely to their destination, but their mere existence surprised Heth. It seemed like the bond they'd made with Alia was an important reason for their defection. Under other circumstances Heth might have been a little jealous, but these days he had been honestly too busy to care, and Alia still made sure to stop by most evenings after dark to chat.

A light scratching on the fabric of his tent made him open his eyes. Alia was early today.

"Come in," he called out, pushing himself up onto his elbows.

And then he stiffened as someone unexpected slipped into his tent.

"Aziza," he said, suddenly very aware of the mess. The beautiful Ashasai ignored his discomfort, offering him a crooked smile.

"Heth Su Canaav," she said, raising the long-necked bottle she carried. "May I sit down? I've brought libations."

"Of course," Heth replied quickly, motioning towards the little cushion that Alia usually sat on when she visited.

"Thank you," Aziza murmured, gracefully settling herself cross-legged.

Heth had to fight the urge to stare. There was something almost hypnotic in the way she moved, like a cat or a snake. Even her smallest actions seemed to flow seamlessly together, without the slightest of hesitations, as if she knew exactly what she would do well before it happened.

"I assume you'll have a drink with me?" she said, waggling the dark-red bottle in his direction. It wasn't really a question, he realized, but he nodded anyway.

Heth found her attractive and intimidating in almost equal parts. She was beautiful, long and lithe, with unblemished copper skin and staggeringly high cheekbones. Her large dark eyes always appeared to hold a hint of wry mirth, as if she knew exactly what others were thinking when they looked at her, and she wore her confidence like a cloak. Heth found himself tripping over his words in her presence. And it wasn't just him – he'd seen Caden Vars stammer and blush when trying to explain something to her, tugging on his beard so hard Heth had been surprised he hadn't ended up holding a clump of hair.

She was wearing the same traveler's garb as when he'd glimpsed her earlier from afar, a pleated skirt and gauzy red blouse, but her outfit looked to have somehow escaped the stains and dust of the day. Heth felt self-conscious, aware that he badly needed a bath. And how could her clothing be so billowy, yet so clingy at the same time?

"A long day," Aziza said, and Heth snapped his attention back to those well-deep eyes as she pulled the cork out of the bottle smoothly, as if she was plucking a piece of grass. Outside of her beauty, that was also what made her daunting – she was easily the strongest Sharded in their motley assembly, very likely a *famdhar*. He felt nothing flowing from her, none of that warm prickling that had accompanied the other Sharded he'd been around, and Rhenna had told him once that only the very strongest could completely mask their power.

"Yes, a very long day," Heth replied, suddenly aware of how dry his throat was. He badly needed a drink.

Aziza must have read his mind, because she handed him the first glass she poured.

"The scepter of the First is not easy to lift," she said, deftly filling the other cup almost to the brim. "Of course, in the Sanguine City, every bloodlord dreams of wearing the First's red robes. At least you do not have to be concerned about a knife in the back . . . though that Salahi Fayraz does seem overly fond of stabbing things."

"I'm not worried about her," Heth replied, lifting his glass as Aziza raised her own. "She doesn't want to command anyone other than her own people."

"For now," Aziza said mildly, sipping her drink. "The last time the Salahi were Sharded, they tried to conquer the world. I wonder if it is wise to return them to the ranks of the Few."

Heth hid his surprise with a hurried gulp of wine. He hadn't considered that some Sharded accompanying them might have such reservations – did Xend share these concerns?

"These are not the same Salahi. They've changed."

"They've been humbled," Aziza agreed, setting down her cup. "And perhaps that is enough to dissuade them of their old ambitions. Still, if the Shadow catches wind that their enemies have returned, I imagine they will move fast to destroy them."

"So you think their presence endangers us?"

Aziza offered another lopsided smile. "No more so than filling the heads of three hundred Hollow with the dream of becoming Sharded. All the holds rely on the Hollow to cook their food and clean their chamber pots – you are offering freedom, if what you've claimed is true. Once word escapes, every Sharded faction will unite against you."

Heth coughed, then hurriedly wiped his mouth. "That sounds rather bleak."

Aziza shrugged. "You should know what lies ahead."

"Then aren't you worried about accompanying us?"

The Ashasai swirled her half-empty glass. "I have been charged with making sure you arrive safely where you are going. After that, your survival is your own responsibility. If you want my advice, I would consider moving your new hold to somewhere beyond the easy reach of others, perhaps across the sea or into the depths of the

Wild." Her dark eyes glittered mischievously. "Or perhaps you might consider returning with us to Karath. I'm sure Xend would give you and your Light shard sanctuary."

"I doubt the others would want to return," Heth said, though he did see the wisdom in her suggestion. Where else could they find safety without venturing past the edge of the known world?

"Give my words some thought," Aziza said, then tossed back the last of her wine. "Though I should admit I did not come here tonight to give you counsel about the future."

"Oh?" Heth said, trying to sound nonchalant despite the sudden quickening of his pulse.

Aziza slid closer. "There was something I offered you. Do you remember?"

Heth's hand drifted to his face. "You mean . . ."

"Yes," Aziza said, reaching out to run her finger along his scar. He flinched at her touch, but she did not pull away. "The wound was made too long ago to heal completely, as the memory of what you were like before has faded from your flesh. But I could do what I can, if you wish."

She hadn't yet used her Sharded powers, but already a tingling seemed to be spreading from where her fingertips brushed the knotted ridges of his scar. "Please," Heth said softly.

Aziza nodded, drawing herself so near that he could feel a warmth flowing from her. Was that because she was Sharded? Or Ashasai? And the smell of flowers clung to her so strongly that for a moment he was taken back to the gardens of the Unbound King. Had she dabbed herself with perfume before coming here? Surely that was not her natural scent . . .

Heth gasped as heat flowed through him, originating where she touched his scar but quickly traveling through his body, tracing the same pathways used by his *ka*. "Silver Shrike," he whispered hoarsely, the blood pounding in his veins rising to fill his ears and blot out all other sounds. Aziza held his gaze, her eyes dark and knowing. The desire he felt *must* be a product of her blood-sharded power coursing through him, and he had to fight back the urge to lean forward and reach for her.

"There," Aziza said with some satisfaction, her breath hot on his cheek. "Much better."

Heth's hand again went to his face, tracing what remained of his scar. It was still there, a slight rippling in his skin, but it was far less pronounced than it had been a moment ago.

"Thank you," he breathed. The heat of her healing was slowly dissipating . . . but if anything, the intense, overpowering yearning he felt for her was growing stronger.

"You are welcome," Aziza said. She had not pulled away, despite having withdrawn her power. She moved her head closer, her lips brushing his.

A jolt shivered through him. All he could think about as the kiss deepened was the softness of her mouth, her arms going around him, her fingers tangling in his hair. And then her body was suddenly pressed against his as she pushed him backwards onto the blankets.

"Let's see your shard again," she murmured huskily, and he could hear the want in her voice. Aziza's hands clutched at his tunic, and then she tore the cloth away effortlessly.

The light of his fragment spilled into the tent.

TEARS BLURRED Alia's vision as she stumbled through the camp. Someone shouted as her foot knocked over a pot filled with peeled potatoes, but she did not stop to help or apologize – all she could think about was what she'd glimpsed in the moment before she'd let the flap swing closed again, the shapes moving together in the dimness. And the *sounds*. A woman's voice, moaning with pleasure. She'd heard Heth, gasping something she couldn't understand, but it had been him, she was certain.

Alia slowed her headlong flight between the tents and campfires, rubbing angrily at her eyes. Why do this *now*? He'd known she was going to visit tonight. Had this been a message for her . . . had he wanted her to see *that*?

By the First Seed, what had he been *thinking*?

Trying to stop herself from shaking, Alia squatted down and wrapped her arms around her knees. Maybe he didn't care if she saw. Somehow that was even more painful, and her stomach twisted at the thought. She wanted to scream, but a grubby boy who had emerged from one of the tents was staring at her with wide eyes, and she knew if she let loose what was building inside her she'd terrify him.

Alia sucked in a deep breath, trying to master herself. He was a man, and they were not trothed. They'd never even kissed . . . she had no claim to him.

Then why did it hurt so much?

"Alia!"

She looked around. That had sounded like Sharl, but there was a rawness to her voice, almost like she was on the verge of panicking. Alia quickly found the Whispering Island girl wending her way through the maze of tents towards her.

"What is it?" she asked, trying to pretend like she hadn't been on the verge of tears a moment ago. She thought Sharl would still notice how upset she was, but then she realized her friend was just as distressed, if not more so.

"It's Markis," Sharl said breathlessly when she reached Alia. "Have ye seen him?"

Alia thought back to earlier in the day. Markis had been in the same wagon with her, along with Sharl and the other younger Unfettered.

"Not since we stopped. He's missing?"

Sharl glanced around, as if the Flail boy might be hiding in one of the tents. She was truly worried, Alia realized uneasily. "Aye. He's vanished. Never does dat boy miss a meal, but he dinna turn up for supper an' no one knows where he is."

"I'm sure he's fine," Alia told her soothingly. "Maybe he went for a swim in the river and lost track of time. Or he's trying to catch one of those animals that live in the mounds we keep seeing. He's Sharded –

there's nothing out here that can hurt him." *Or maybe he's in another woman's tent.*

Alia shoved that thought aside with a mental grimace. Markis and Sharl had grown so close that Alia wouldn't have been surprised if they had exchanged troth vows in secret, and she couldn't imagine him betraying Sharl in that way.

"Will ye help me look for him?" Sharl asked, and Alia reached out to twine her fingers with her friend, giving her hand a comforting squeeze.

"Of course."

45

DERYN

He woke in a sea of silk.

The cosseting sheets were cool and smooth, the mattress so soft he felt like he was sinking into a cloud. A light breeze stirred the drapes hanging from his bed's canopy, and somewhere beyond the room a bird was greeting the morning with a sweet silvery trilling. Deryn's head was musty, as if packed with straw, although the sensation was not unpleasant – he felt like he had slept for a very long time and all the weariness that had sunk deep down into his bones had finally seeped from his body, leaving him drained but also invigorated. For a few long moments he drowsed in the bed, wondering how he had come to be here, where *here* even was, until suddenly the memory of what had happened to him returned like a lightning strike.

Rhenna's arm, slipping into a dark pool. Shade dissolving into mist. Warm, coppery blood flooding his nose and mouth, choking him as he drowned ...

Deryn sat bolt upright and looked about wildly, his heart hammering. The room was richly appointed, with furniture of elegantly carved black wood and thick carpets patterned with interlocking circles. Sunlight was pouring in through an open balcony, and the sky outside was a seamless blue that seemed a different shade than he had ever seen before. Vases of colorful flowers in bloom were scattered about, and on a side table next to his bed was a bowl of mixed fruit and a glass pitcher filled with water. On a divan pressed up against the far wall his belongings had been carefully piled – his travel pack, the clothes he had been wearing, his boots, and his Sharded sword.

Had the Unbound King brought him to his manse in Karath? No, Deryn could feel the power of his shard thrumming in his veins. And the presence of his sword confused him – how could they possibly allow him such a weapon, given what they had done?

Deryn slipped from the bed and padded across the carpet, then quickly dressed and buckled on his blade. His clothes had been neatly folded and freshly laundered and then afterwards rubbed with some fragrance. Deryn's stomach rumbled, but he only eyed the fruit that had been left out suspiciously – until he knew what was going on, he should avoid drinking or eating anything.

Although if whoever had brought him here meant him harm, it was certainly odd how much attention had been given to ensuring his comfort.

Deryn glanced at the door, then went over to the open balcony to find out where he was, squinting into the day's brilliance.

And sucked in his breath. Below him a vast city unfurled in every direction, a rumpled sprawl of reddish buildings that reminded him of the insect nests he'd occasionally come across in the forests of the Fangs, warrens of red clay shaped into uneven towers linked by tunnel-laced piles. The city's monotony was broken here and there by massive black ziggurats – some of these stepped pyramids were ancient and crumbling and looked long-abandoned, while others gleamed as if sheathed in obsidian, or had such riotous growths covering their tiers that it seemed like a jungle was bursting forth from within. Each was larger than any structure Deryn had ever seen, save the Duskhold taken in its entirety, and there were at least a dozen in his sight right now, like plague pustules bubbling upon the skin of the world. Looking down, Deryn realized that the building he was inside also had tiers of black stone cascading down to the distant streets below – he was in one of these pyramids, somewhere up near its summit.

"Ashasai," he whispered, awed. The wealthiest and largest and most dangerous city in all the world, ruled over by bloodlords whose champions soaked the sands of the fighting pits as the crowds roared.

Far in the distance, Deryn glimpsed the bronze shimmer of what must be Lake Gavras, wide enough to be considered a land-locked sea. He turned away from the overwhelming view, taking a few dazed steps back into the bedroom, his thoughts whirling. What was he doing here? Xend an-Azith was the most famous exile from the Sanguine City – surely he would not have brought Deryn to the place he had been banished from. And Ashasai was weeks if not months of hard travel from where he and Rhenna had been ambushed, unless some Sharded talent had transported them here faster.

Rhenna. Deryn swallowed, a cold sweat prickling his skin. Was she waking up even now in a room just like this? Or had Xend fulfilled whatever bargain he had struck with Cael Shen? Had he even realized who she truly was, or had this betrayal been entirely motivated by his theft of the shadowrealm fragment from the Erudinium?

So many questions. Taking a deep breath, Deryn took two purposeful strides towards the door . . . and then stopped short as it was swung open by a child.

At least, Deryn thought it was a child. The boy's skin was as white and smooth as porcelain, his hair and garments a faded gray. It was like he had been drained of all color, save for his eyes, which were a striking shade of amber that would not have looked out of place on a cat. The child stared at him without expression, then abruptly turned and left the room, leaving the door open. Deryn had the strong sense that he was meant to follow.

What choice did he have? Gritting his teeth, Deryn hurried after the boy and found himself in a long corridor of black stone, lit by the ruddy glow of pinkish crystals set into the floor. The boy was walking at an untroubled pace towards a distant doorway that was framed by the wan light leaking around its edges.

"Where am I?" Deryn asked when he'd caught up with the boy. "What's beyond that door?"

The servant did not answer or even turn to acknowledge his presence. This close, Deryn could see that his striking eyes were wide and glassy.

Unsettled, Deryn began gathering his *ka*. If there was something dangerous ahead, he would see how it liked having a portal to the shadowrealm opened and the Breath of the Mother fill the insides of this pyramid.

The boy reached the door and pulled it wide, then made a slight motion for Deryn to enter. After devoting a small portion of his *ka* to forming his Ghost Chitin, Deryn stepped forward.

The chamber he found himself in was vast and circular, with a high arched ceiling. Its center was sunken, with several sets of stairs leading down to where a few ornate couches of dark wood surrounded a table of murky red stone. A man in richly embroidered robes was sprawled on one of these settees, and he raised his hand in greeting when he saw Deryn, then returned his attention to the book he had been reading. A glass sphere filled with what looked to be roiling black mist had been placed at the center of the table in a metallic cradle.

Shade.

Deryn stretched out his perceptions, trying to re-establish the link he had once shared with the elemental, but he felt nothing. His fingertips brushed the hilt at his side – could Shade's prison survive a blow from Sharded palesteel? Maybe he should find out.

The man seated below lifted his hand again, this time without looking up from his book, and made a rather impatient beckoning gesture. Not taking his hand from his sword, Deryn began to make his way towards the closest set of steps leading down. He'd entered the vast chamber onto what almost seemed like a gallery where others could observe what was happening below – potentially many people, as the walkway was wide enough to accommodate a crowd standing six-abreast. A few other doorways like the one he'd passed through were scattered along the gallery's length, along with the rounded mouth of an enormous entrance. What could possibly justify having such a huge, open doorway? Did riders on horses sometimes prance in circles up here in the gallery while the blood-lords of Ashasai conferred below?

Trying his best to tamp down his rising trepidation, Deryn descended into the pit. When he reached the bottom, the man held up a finger, as if asking Deryn to wait until he finished what he was reading. Deryn took this moment to study him – he was different from the other Ashasai Deryn had met before, who all had been hair-less and with skin of varying shades of copper. This man also had no hair, but his complexion was a sickly gray, almost like that of the Kin river traders. This drabness was offset by the colorful, sumptuous robes he was wearing, a swirling collection of deep blues and crimson and black.

The thin-faced man finally snapped the book shut and laid it down on the red-rock table, then leaned back to regard Deryn.

"Please, sit," he said softly, gesturing at the divan across from him.

Deryn warily unbuckled his sword and leaned it against the armrest – making sure to keep it within easy reach – and then sank onto the overstuffed cushions. The mist inside the crystal sphere between them seemed to roil and eddy in agitation, as if Shade could sense his presence. But that might have been his imagination, because he still could not feel the elemental through the bond they'd once shared.

"Who are you?" Deryn asked. He knew he should speak to this man – clearly a bloodlord – with more respect, but his patience had been eroded down to almost nothing.

"Anaska an-Deviz. And you are?"

"Didn't Xend tell you who I am?" Deryn asked, trying to establish whether the Unbound King and this man were indeed allies.

The hint of a smile curved Anaska's thin lips. "It is considered good manners to let a guest introduce himself."

ALEC HUTSON

"A guest? Most people who have been kidnapped think of themselves as prisoners."

Anaska blinked his garnet eyes slowly, as if in mild surprise. "Have you been mistreated? I will discipline my servants if anything about your accommodations was inadequate."

"Being dragged into a pool of blood and then transported against my will across the world is mistreatment. Where is . . ." Deryn just stopped himself from saying Rhenna's name. He had to hope that they still did not know her true identity. "My companion."

"She is unharmed," Anaska said, leaning forward to lightly tap the smoke-filled sphere. "As is your other friend." His hand moved to rest on the table, fingers spread wide so each aligned with another splayed hand pressing against the underside of the transparent stone, a hand frozen in the act of rising up from the red depths.

Deryn leaped to his feet. "What have you done to her?" he demanded in horror, poised to unleash the Breath of the Mother. The bloodlord regarded him calmly, clearly unconcerned about anything Deryn might attempt.

"The same that was done to you," Anaska replied. "And here you are, perfectly fine, despite your imprisonment."

"Free her."

Anaska chuckled. "In good time, if you give me what I want."

"And what is that?"

"Answers." The bloodlord indicated the misty sphere with a slight tilt of his head. "About your companion here."

Deryn sank back down onto the divan, though he did not let go of his *ka*. "What do you want to know?" he asked tightly.

"Why is it here? Why did it choose you?"

"I don't know. He just appeared."

The man pursed his lips, studying Deryn for a long moment. Then he nodded. "I believe you."

The confidence with which Anaska said this surprised Deryn, and the Ashasai's mouth lifted in amusement.

"I can read your pulse like this book. It is a power many bloodsharded *famdhar* possess, and it tells me that you speak the truth."

Deryn clenched sweat-slicked fists. "So now you realize I know nothing. Will you let us go?"

Anaska sighed. "Even though you do not apprehend the purpose for your elemental's presence, I can assure you that it has one."

"How?"

Anaska turned his attention once more to the roiling sphere. "Because they are not mindless creatures that accidentally find their way into our world. They are . . . messengers. Envoys. A power from another realm has taken an interest in you and so Xend is indeed right, at least about this – it behooves us to know why it has come."

Deryn sensed something then, a slight trembling. He glanced up nervously at the high ceiling, imagining the vast amounts of stone hanging over their heads. Was Ashasai ever wracked by earthquakes? He didn't want to be inside a giant pile of stone if one struck. Deryn's alarm grew as the shaking strengthened, until Shade's prison was visibly shifting in its cradle, and he glanced at the bloodlord in confusion.

Anaska returned this look with a knowing smile.

Movement erupted in the gallery above. Through the large, rounded entrance something huge surged, long and red and glistening. It filled the wide walkway with its massive bulk, slithering at a frightening speed until its length spanned the entirety of the galley, and yet still more was emerging, coil after rippling coil. Panic gripped Deryn as an enormous head lifted to regard the two men in the pit below – its features were vague and shifting, but it was obviously supposed to represent the great head of a serpent, and as its great jaws opened wide long filaments of blood stretched thin before eventually snapping. An abyssal gullet yawned, dark and churning.

Deryn felt like he was again in the presence of the balewyrm, but this time there were no rocks to cower beneath, no shadows to hide in. No escape. Once more he was a mouse, frozen under the gaze of a great predator.

"And so now you understand our interest," Anaska said as the blood elemental's head descended into the pit.

Deryn shrank away, but the great serpent's attention was only for bloodlord. Anaska laid his hand affectionately on a snout formed from sluggishly flowing blood.

"You do not know why the shadow-thing was sent to you," the bloodlord said, trailing his fingers through the elemental's viscous flesh. "And I cannot make the creature tell me . . . it may not even yet know its purpose here. Perhaps I should simply destroy you both."

Fear was pulsing in Deryn so fiercely that he felt light-headed. It would take only a word from the bloodlord and this monster could swallow him whole.

"That would be the safest choice," Anaska admitted, withdrawing his touch from the serpent and folding red-stained hands on the table. Deryn watched in horrified fascination as shivering droplets of blood peeled from the Ashasai's skin and drifted back to rejoin the enormous serpentine head hovering beside him.

"But I have not attained my present position by always walking the safest path." The bloodlord leaned back on the divan, studying Deryn with a slight smile. "No, I have another, far more interesting use for you."

EPILOGUE

D rip. Drip. Drip.

Markis's eyes opened to a darkness so absolute that for a moment he feared he had been blinded. His cheek was pressed against damp, rough stone, the air stale and musty, and even though he couldn't see anything, he sensed a great heaviness suspended above him.

A cave. He was underground, somewhere far below the surface.

He pushed himself into a sitting position. How had he come to be here? The last thing he remembered was leaving the campsite they'd just finished setting up and starting on a small animal path up a grassy knoll, hoping to get a view of the lands they would travel through tomorrow. After that, nothing. Had he tripped and hit his head, slipped into some hidden crevice? Silver Shrike, why did he feel so *tired*?

Drip. Drip. Drip.

Water. Somewhere nearby water was trickling into this cave. Maybe if he followed it back to its source, he could find a way out of here. Sharl and Alia must be worried, especially if he'd already missed the evening meal . . .

With a grunt of effort, Markis rose to his feet with an arm lifted so he wouldn't bash his head if the ceiling was lower than he expected. He felt so sore, so exhausted, that it was almost like he was back in Karath.

As if he was no longer Sharded. In a rising panic, his fingers sought his fragment, and relief flooded him when he felt the hardness embedded in his flesh. But where was the light of his shard? He fumbled with the buttons of his shirt and found that only the faintest of sparks could be seen, deep within his shard, not even strong enough to penetrate the thin cloth. Could a seam of karathinite be running through the walls here, even though they were weeks of travel away from the City of the Dead?

That would be just his luck.

Markis froze as he heard the rasp of something scraping against stone.

"Hello?" he called into the echoing stillness. "Is there someone here?" He held his breath during the silence that followed, listening hard.

Drip. Drip. Drip.

Nothing. It must just have been stone shifting, perhaps caused by his movements.

"Do not be afraid."

Markis gasped, putting his back to the rock behind him and raising his arms to ward away whatever had spoken. It had sounded close, and the only thing that kept him from dashing blindly into the dark was that he had heard no malice in that voice, no threat. He couldn't tell if it was a man or a woman – or perhaps even a child, since it had sounded so sweet and lilting.

"Who are you?" he asked. "What do you want?"

He thought he sensed something large moving in the darkness, and then warm air caressed his cheek. He tried to grab whatever it was, but it was already gone.

"We are travelers," another voice came, just as melodic but differently pitched, *"and we seek the light."*

Broken God, there were two of them. Or more. Markis moaned,

clutching at the rock he leaned against, trying to gather the courage to flee.

"The light? What do you mean?"

"*Tell us about the one who bears it.*"

"I don't . . . I . . . I . . ." Something soft and wet brushed Markis's shard, and it suddenly felt like he was being emptied, like a hole had been cut into him and his essence was draining away. The strength fled his limbs, his consciousness slowly spiraling around a beckoning abyss.

"*Tell us.*"

ABOUT THE AUTHOR

Alec Hutson grew up in a geodesic dome and a bookstore and he currently lives in Shanghai. If you would like to keep current with his writing, please sign up for his newsletter at www.authoralechut son.com.

ALSO BY ALEC HUTSON

www.ingramcontent.com/pod-product-compliance
Lightning Source LLC
Chambersburg PA
CBHW031137020726
PP18521300001B/2